“No description of plot or
lessly entertaining this story really is. But if you smile at the thought of a queen who curses her husband with phrases like ‘May bats nest in your ears for the winter,’ this is a tale you’ll enjoy.”

—*Cleveland Plain Dealer*

“If you think you would love the result of a collaboration between J. R. R. Tolkien and P. G. Wodehouse, you’ll love this one!”

—*Analog*

“A wild, weird, and altogether silly adventure . . . There’s an ample supply of the inspired, over-the-top comedy that’s a Friesner hallmark, and Watt-Evans fans will recognize his ability to create amusing yet logical plot complications from thin air. The results are seamless and screamingly funny.”

—*Dragon Magazine*

Other Tor books by Lawrence Watt-Evans
The Rebirth of Wonder

Other Tor books by Esther M. Friesner
Yesterday We Saw Mermaids

LAWRENCE WATT-EVANS
ESTHER M. FRIESNER

A TOM DOHERTY ASSOCIATES BOOK
NEW YORK

SPLIT HEIRS

Cover art by Walter Velez

A Tor Book
Published by Tom Doherty Associates, Inc.
175 Fifth Avenue
New York, N.Y. 10010

ISBN: 0-812-52029-7
Library of Congress Catalog Card Number: 93-1328

First edition: July 1993
First mass market edition: June 1994

Printed in the United States of America

0 9 8 7 6 5 4 3 2 1

Dedicated to our own heirs:
Mike, Annie, Amanda, and Julian

SPLIT HEIRS

Chapter One

"Three?"

The scream from the north tower of the Palace of Divinely Tranquil Thoughts was loud and shrill enough to shatter seven stained-glass windows in the banqueting hall below—six of them among the handful of remaining works by the master artisan Oratio, dating from some fourteen centuries back, and the last a cheap imitation installed during the reign of Corulimus the Decadent, a mere millennium ago.

As shards of glass rattled across the table King Gudge, Lord of Hydrangea, looked up from his wine at the sudden influx of daylight and growled, "What in the name of the five ways to gut an ox was *that*?"

Trembling at his royal master's elbow, Lord Polemonium replied, "I think—I *think*, Your Omnipotent and Implacable Majesty, that it is the ebullient and convivial exultation of Her Most Complacent Highness, Queen Artemisia, your connubial helpmeet, as she experiences the transitory distress of parturition, preparatory to the imminent joy attending the nativity of your supremely longed-for progeny."

King Gudge plucked a sliver of blue glass from his goblet and munched it thoughtfully as he considered this reply. Then, moving with the remarkable speed for which he was known, he drew his sword Obliterator and lopped off Lord Polemonium's head, adding to the mess on the table.

"Now, let's give that another go-around, all right?" the king said, wiping the gory blade clean on the lace tablecloth as he gazed at his remaining ministers. "I'll ask one more time: What was *that*?"

"The queen's having the baby," said Lord Filaree, with all dispatch, watching Lord Polemonium's head. It was still bouncing.

"Oh." King Gudge thrust Obliterator back into its scabbard and picked up his wine. "About time." He swilled down the measure, getting most of it in the black tangle of his beard.

Farther down the table, out of earshot and swordreach, Lord Croton nudged Lord Filaree in the ribs. "Is it just me, or did our royal lady holler 'Three'?"

Lord Filaree shrugged, not really paying any attention to the question. Every time he was "invited" to one of King Gudge's council meetings/drinking parties, he only had eyes and ears for His Majesty. It might have been the same sort of morbid fascination that made commoners stop and stare at a particularly gruesome cartwreck, or perhaps just the fact that any minister caught *not* having eyes and ears for King Gudge alone wound up not having eyes and ears.

"I said," Lord Croton repeated testily, "why would she scream 'three'?"

"Maybe she and her handmaid are playing a round of gorf," Lord Filaree hazarded without turning.

Lord Croton snorted quietly. "Filaree, the correct gorfing cry is 'five on the loo'ard side and mind the pelicans!' Any fool knows that. Besides, pregnant women never play gorf."

"My dear Croton, you know how these women are when they're giving birth. They say all sorts of nonsense. Didn't your own wife . . . ?" He let the question hang unfinished.

"Well, yes," Lord Croton confessed. "While she was in travail, my darling Ione called me a bubble-headed, lust-crazed, self-indulgent, slavering babboon. And she swore I'd never lay a hand on her again as long as I lived. Which was not going to be too much longer because she was going to kill me as soon as she got her strength back. All very well, Filaree, but she did not yell 'three.' "

"Well, perhaps Her Majesty has decided that our new sovereign-by-right-of-conquest already knows that he is a bubble-headed, lust-crazed, self-indulgent, slavering baboon," Lord Filaree suggested.

"*Knows* it! He'd take it as a bloody compliment."

Filaree nodded. "Indeed. Therefore, let us assume that Her Majesty is not exclaiming 'three' but 'whee!' "

" 'Whee'?" Lord Croton echoed doubtfully.

"A cry of joy," Filaree explained, "denoting that her labor has been successfully accomplished and that she no longer needs to remain in isolation in the north tower, according to ancient Hydrangean tradition governing pregnant queens."

Lord Croton shook his head. "I don't know, Filaree. Now that the baby's here and she can come out of the north tower, it also means that she'll have to go back to sleeping with King Gudge. That's not the sort of thing I can picture any sane woman celebrating."

"Well, it makes a heap of a lot more sense than caterwauling *numbers*!" Lord Filaree countered. "Anyhow, why on earth would Queen Artemisia shout 'three,' tell me that!"

Lord Croton thought about it. "Right," he concluded. "No reason for it at all. 'Whee' it is. Was. Should be." He doodled on the council table a bit with his penknife for awhile, then said, "You know, it's funny, Filaree; this ancient Hydrangean tradition about isolating pregnant queens . . ."

"Um?"

"I never heard of it before Artemisia brought it up."

"*Three?*" shrieked Queen Artemisia from the bed. "O merciful stars, don't tell me there's *three* of them!"

Old Ludmilla stood by the royal receiving cradle and looked helpless. "Oh, my darling lambikins, you know I'd never tell you the eentsiest thing as might trouble your dear thoughts at a time like this." The green silk-wrapped bundle in the crook of her arm began to wail. "Certainly not, not when my precious Missy-mussy has just been through such a strain, bearing up like the adorable little brave trouper that she is when other girlies would be a-weeping and a-wailing and a-carrying on something disgraceful to . . ."

"Three!" howled the queen. "Three, three, *three,* the pox take all Gorgorians and the horses they rode in on! There is—there is most definitely—there is going to be—"

All aflutter, old Ludmilla laid the swaddled newborn in the huge ceremonial cradle with its scarlet hangings and gold-leafed dragon headboard and hastened to her lady's bedside. "Lawks and welladay, sweet Missy-mussy, whyever are you panting so? And your face! I do declare, it's gone the most unbecoming shade of lavender, it has. Oh, wurra-wurra and—"

"—there is going to be a third one," Queen Artemisia said with jaw taut and sweat drenching every inch of her body. *"And here it comes now!"*

Some time later, old Ludmilla lifted a beautifully formed little boy from the Basin of Harmonious Immersion—one of the oldest pieces of the Old Hydrangean royal house's childbirth accessory set—and whipped a green satin swaddling cloth around his trembling limbs before showing him to his mother.

"There, now, Missy-mussy," she said, as pleased as if she'd handled the business end of the birth herself. "All washed and neat and tidy. Isn't he a lamb?" She bore the babe to the receiving cradle in triumph, but before she laid him down in it she paused and turned to her mistress. "Ah . . . not any more coming, are there, love?"

"No," said the queen, lying pale and limp against an avalanche of overstuffed pink brocade pillows. She sounded near the brink of total exhaustion. She also sounded more than a little cranky.

Old Ludmilla cocked her head, the better to turn her

one functioning ear in Queen Artemisia's direction. "Quite sure, are we?"

"We are positive," the queen returned.

"You were wrong before, you know. Of course, arithmetic never was one of your strengths. I remember saying to your dear, departed, decapitated da, King Fumitory the Twenty-Second, I said to him, 'Our Missy-mussy has her charm, but she couldn't add a wolf to a sheepfold and get lambchops.' That's what *I* said."

"And *I* say—" Queen Artemisia's clear blue eyes narrowed, "—*I* say that if you call me 'Missy-mussy' one more time, I shall ask my husband—may his skull crack like an acorn under a millstone—to give me your liver roasted with garlic as a childbirth gift. What do you say to *that*?"

Ludmilla gave an indignant sniff. "I say there's some people who've grown a shade too big for their breeches, that's what. My liver roasted with garlic indeed! When you know as well as I that garlic gives nursing mothers the wind something scandalous."

She placed the satin-swathed infant in the cradle and then turned on her mistress in a fury. "But that's just *my* opinion, isn't it? And who am I to you, eh? Just the woman who raised you from a nasty little snippet of a royal Hydrangean princess, is all! Only the one who stood by your side on the royal city ramparts while your dear, departed, decapitated da, King Fumitory the Twenty-Second, was doing his best to fight off the invasion of those loathsome Gorgorian barbarian hordes! Merely the loyal soul who helped you hide in the royal turnip cellar after that thoroughly rude *Gudge* person did for your daddy right there in the Audience Chamber of the Sun's Hidden Face and got all that blood worked into the carpets so bad that *three* royal housekeepers have quit in disgust! Simply . . ."

"Three," groaned Queen Artemisia, and yanked a pillow out from under her head to slam over her face. Still from beneath the downy bolster came the pitiful, half-smothered whimper, "*Three.*"

"Well . . . yes." Ludmilla pulled her tirade up on a short

rein, taken aback by Queen Artemisia's obvious despair. The crone cast a myopic eye over the contents of the ceremonial cradle. "And the steadfast handmaid who saw her own darling Missy-mussy give birth to three beautiful, cuddly, perfect . . ."

"Death sentences," said the queen, and threw the pillow at Ludmilla.

The ancient waitingwoman sighed. "I'll make the tea."

Later, as the two ladies shared a pot of well-steeped wenwort tea, Queen Artemisia recovered some of her self-possession. "They are beautiful," she admitted, gazing into the cradle at the three drowsy bundles. Ludmilla had most thoughtfully lugged the heavy piece of ceremonial furniture near Artemisia's bed so that the new mother could look at her babes in comfort. Instead of the dreamy maternal smile Ludmilla expected, the queen's expression grew stern. "Too beautiful for Gudge to sacrifice in the name of his beastly Gorgorian superstitions!"

"Ah, well, you know how these men are, dearie." Ludmilla poured more tea. "They do have their little ways. If it's not leaving all their clothes in the middle of the floor then it's believing that more than one babe at a birth means more than one father at a begetting."

"It was bad enough when I thought I was only carrying twins," Queen Artemisia said, nibbling a fortifying bit of seedcake. "It was during that savage Gorgorian holiday, the Feast of the Rutting Goat, when I started getting my insides kicked out by *two* sets of feet and hands. Three." Never again would she be able to pronounce that number without twisting her finely-featured face into the most grotesque grimace.

"I never did understand the point of the celebration," Ludmilla admitted. "Aside from giving all the apprentices a day to run around and cudgel the brains out of innocent chickens. All those ladies rushing through the streets with their biddies hanging out, waving bundles of dried ferns and cucumbers . . ."

"Women's magic." Queen Artemisia's full lip curled

disdainfully. "Gorgorian women. Limited, so I have learned, to minor fortune-telling skills and the occasional attempt at influencing matters of love, sex, and fertility—or at least, so they all insist. The male Gorgorians have absolutely no use for it, Gudge told me, but as long as it keeps their females busy and out of mischief, they *graciously* permit it."

Ludmilla sighed so deeply that the several layers of phoenix-point gold lace fluffing out the flat bosom of her gown fluttered like autumn leaves. "Oh, I do so miss them," she said.

"Miss who?"

"*Our* magic. Our wizards, I mean."

Queen Artemisia did not spare her handmaid any sympathy. "They were of no use whatsoever and you know it," she said.

"Oh! My lady!" Ludmilla clapped one scrawny hand to her mouth and made a slightly complex and very silly warding sign with the other. "Such disrespect for the great, the powerful, the masters of all arcane knowledge, the gentlemen whose mystic studies have made them privy to the secrets of . . ."

"Privy is the word," the queen snapped. "And *to* the royal privy with them and all their useless spells and cantrips! Their magic was like a gold-dipped pig's bladder: all flash and glitter, all wind, all worthless. What good did their so-called arcane knowledge do my poor father when the Gorgorians attacked? Where were our wizards and their sorcerous weapons then?"

"Hmph!" Ludmilla's paper-thin nostrils flared indignantly. "*Some* of us know that worthwhile magic is not something you can just whistle up to do your bidding, like a sheepdog. *Some* of us know that preparations for a thaumaturgical assault of any real strategic value requires careful, one might even say *meticulous*, preparation. Why, a single wrong word, an improperly pronounced syllable, a pass of the wand from left to right, pinky extended, rather than right to left, pinky down, could mean all the difference between winning the battle and having your guts ripped out by the demons of the abyss. Throtteliar the Magnificent told me so his very own self, not twenty minutes before fleeing the palace—or trying to flee, at any rate."

Queen Artemisia made a noise that in a person of lesser status might have been called a snort. "So instead of anything useful," she said, "our wondrous wizards pottered around with a bunch of overrefined spells that are too complex and too damned *long* to be practical, and while they were still just warming up their preliminary incantations they wound up having their heads lopped off by my royal husband, may bats nest in his ears for the winter."

Ludmilla nodded, sighing. "Since the wizards never did the man a lick of harm, I do wonder sometimes, why *did* he insist on executing them all?"

Queen Artemisia handed the empty teacup to her handmaid. "You know Gudge. So do I, more's the pity. Ordinarily you'd imagine that if a thought ever managed to crawl into his skull it would die of loneliness and despair, yet at the same time there is a certain primitive cunning to the creature. Just because our wizards weren't able to get their wands up in time to prevent his conquest of our kingdom, he still saw their powers as a possible threat for the future. My louse-ridden lord is a simple, direct, and practical man: He decided that the best way to safeguard his future was to eliminate theirs."

"Oh my, so sad, so sad." Ludmilla took a purple handkerchief from her sleeve and dabbed her eyes. "I know I shouldn't weep—the public beheadings were almost a year ago, and it does so weaken my sight—but I can't help it. It was such a moving ceremony."

"Moving indeed," Queen Artemisia observed drily. "The way some of those wizards kept moving even after their heads were cut off was quite impressive, which was doubtless why Gudge ordered his men to round up the truant parts and burn them all. I heard that they had to chase Master Urien's head all the way to the Street of the Mushroom Vendors before they caught it and brought it back to the bonfire."

Old Ludmilla grew more and more nostalgic and misty-eyed over the past. "Do you remember, precious lambikins, how beautifully Master Urien's head prophesied just before King Gudge drop-kicked it into the flames? 'Thine own downfall, O thou crawling blight of Gorgorian honeysuckle which doth strangle the fair and noble oak of the Hydrangean kingdom, shall spring from thine own—' " She stopped and wept afresh. "That was when your hubbikins punted the poor thing into the fire. I think it was very rude of the king not to allow Master Urien's head to finish what it had to say."

"Then it shouldn't have called Gudge a honeysuckle," Queen Artemisia concluded. "All I remember of the whole disgusting business is that the smoke from the burning wizard-parts made me throw up. That was when I first suspected I might be pregnant." She closed her eyes and sank deeper into the pillows. "Well, what's done is done. At least I was able to keep Gudge from finding out I was *that* pregnant by making up the whole ancient Hydrangean custom of secluding the royal mother-to-be. Not that he cared." She made that same unladylike noise again. "For Gudge, women are either beddable or invisible."

"My lady," Ludmilla said softly, "shall I go ahead with the plan?"

"Yes, yes, do." Queen Artemisia's voice sounded weaker and weaker. "Only you'll have to travel with two babies instead of just one. Are you up to it? You're not as young as you used to be."

"And who is, I'd like to know?" Old Ludmilla's face was already a web of crepey wrinkles, but she carved out two more frown lines right between the eyes as she glowered at the queen. It was wasted on Artemisia, whose eyes remained shut. "Don't you worry about me, I'm sure. I know my duty, even if *some* people don't know the first thing about courtesy to their good and loyal servants. I'll take the babies straightaway to your royal brother, Prince Mimulus, and . . ."

"Weasel," came the faint comment.

"Eh?" Ludmilla cupped her good ear.

Queen Artemisia sighed faintly. "You'll never find him if you blunder around in the eastern mountains asking for Prince Mimulus. Gudge's soldiers did that for ages and came up empty-handed. The whole point of going undercover to lead the secret Old Hydrangean resistance movement is to keep everything about it a secret. You don't want Prince Mimulus of Hydrangea . . ."

"Don't I, then?" Ludmilla blinked in puzzlement.

"You want the Black Weasel, brave and dashing heroic leader of the Bold Bush-dwellers."

"Right, then, my poppet." Ludmilla nodded. "I go to the eastern mountains with the babies, then, and I ask around for the Black Weasel."

"The Black Weasel, *brave and dashing heroic leader of the Bold Bush-dwellers,*" Artemisia corrected her. "It's no use asking for him any other way, he's given strict instructions to his followers that they are not to say one word about him to anyone who doesn't use his full title. Do you remember the first message I sent him when I suspected I was carrying twins?"

"Yes indeed, my cherub." Ludmilla smiled at the memory—not so much because it was a particularly pleasant one, but merely because it was there at all; many of her memories weren't, these days. "We had young Pringus Cattlecart run up to the mountains with it. Such a pretty laddie, Pringus!"

"Looks aren't everything," Artemisia muttered. "He forgot to ask for the Black Weasel properly, and he was still wandering from one mountain village to another when Gudge's patrol caught him. Luckily for me, the message was unsigned and in code. Unluckily for Pringus, Gudge got so annoyed when no one could translate the note that he gave the poor boy over to his Gorgorian bodyguards as their regimental . . . mascot."

"Oh." Ludmilla blanched. "Now that you mention it, the last time I saw the young man he didn't look half so cheerful as he used to. Well, never you mind, my waddle-duckums, your Ludmilla will do everything right."

"Ummmm," Artemisia murmured drowsily.

"Now first off, let's see . . ." Ludmilla began to gather herself together. "Where *are* those portraits? Whoop-sadaisy, here they be, right where I left them. Dearie, rouse yourself a bit, there's a good girl. You've got to name these sweet dollykits before I go, you know. Now here's the miniature of Prince Helenium the Wise. Which one will you name for him?"

"My firstborn son," the queen replied, her voice muzzy.

"Well, and which one's that?"

"Oh, Ludmilla, the one that's not a *girl*!"

"Hmph! There's *two* of 'em as aren't girls, and as like as two straws in a haystack they are. Or haven't you been paying attention?"

Artemisia opened one cold, blue eye. "I shall pay the closest attention to your execution if you don't stop dithering. Didn't you tie the sacred red cord around the wrist of my firstborn?"

"Lawks! Well, I never—I am *such* a goose; of course I did. Let me just unwrap the babes a wee bit and . . . ah, there it is, red as red can be. So! I'll just untie it a moment so's I can thread this charm on the cord and we're all—oh, it *is* a striking resemblance to Prince Helenium, isn't it?"

Prince Helenium had died two centuries ago, but considering how old Ludmilla looked, it was entirely possible that they had been acquainted. She babbled on about the many virtues of the Old Hydrangean prince until her royal mistress rather peevishly instructed her to get on with it. "We'll never get these babies officially named and off to safety at the rate you're going."

"Oh! Now see what you've made me do, you willful girl! I've gone and dropped the naming tokens in the cradle. All righty, my little dovey-byes, let's just get you all named spang-spang-spang, jig time, like you was no better than a litter of puppies."

Ludmilla was in a full-blown snit. Artemisia fought to open both eyes in time to watch her handmaid fussing about in the ceremonial cradle, muttering darkly as she worked. "*You* are Prince Helenium, and *you* can just be called after Lord Helianthus the Lawgiver, and never you mind about the proper naming rituals! No, we're in a *hurry*, we are! Now where did I put the cord for tying your token 'round your little wristy—? Ah, here it is. I'll be forgetting where I put my own head next, we're so desperate *quick* about things! And *you*, you can be named for Queen Avena the Well-Beloved—oh, bother these slipknots, I never could tie a decent . . . *there*! Fine. Done. All tagged with their proper tokens and with no more observance of the decencies than was they three sacks full of grain for the market. Will there be anything else, Your Majesty?"

Icicles hung from Ludmilla's last words, but Artemisia was too tired to mind. "Just change into your disguise and take Avena and Helianthus to my brother. And then let me get some rest before I strangle you," said the queen as she drifted off into a well-deserved sleep.

Chapter Two

Queen Artemisia could not recall when she last had enjoyed such a refreshing rest. It was the first decent sleep she'd had since the Gorgorian invasion. (It stood to reason that you didn't catch too many catnaps while hiding down in the palace cellars from the barbarian hordes, she reflected, and witnessing your noble father's beheading gave you such upsetting dreams for months afterward that you didn't really *want* to sleep all that much.)

And then she had married Gudge.

The Gorgorian chief kept her up until all hours of the night, insisting that his new wife join him for all royal council sessions. He said it was to show the Old Hydrangeans that there were no hard feelings and that they would still have a voice in the government. That would have been a flattering command, coming from a sane man—but this was Gudge.

Artemisia soon learned that the real business of running the kingdom was transacted during the day. For the Gorgorian, nighttime council sessions meant long, sloppy drinking bouts with his cronies and any of the Old Hydrangean nobility stupid or unlucky enough to attend. Few of the native aristocracy managed to survive some of Gudge's more imaginative "Fun With Beer" games, especially the ones involving reptiles, squash, and holding your breath.

After the invasion was finalized, the late King Fumitory's former prime minister, Lord Desmodium, had tried to make the best of a bad deal. He had suggested that there might be *something* valid or interesting about Gorgorian culture; it only wanted to be studied. He had then spent several months visiting the tents of those Gorgorians who had flatly refused to live within city walls, asking them to tell him all the old legends.

There wasn't one of those tales that didn't include the gods getting disgustingly drunk just before perpetrating some unspeakably obscene and revolting "miracle" upon helpless humanity. About the time the seventy-third Gorgorian crone began the nasal chant, "The world came to be when Skufa, the Great Mother, needed a new place to void her blessed bowels and sacred stomach and holy bladder after drinking with her husband-son, Pog, Lord of Fermented Grain Products . . . ," Lord Desmodium got the idea, and quietly retired to his country villa to raise goldfinches.

So it appeared that Gudge was a man true to his gods.

To do him justice, he was quite willing to accept new gods, and add them to the old. The Old Hydrangeans had long ago perfected the fine art of brewery, and Gudge's first pious act had been to commission one of the court poets to write an epic in which the Gorgorian god Pog, Lord of Fermented Grain Products, fell madly in love when he first beheld the beautiful Hydrangean virgin goddess Prunella, Lady of the Five Hundred Local Beers. Then he raped her.

Gudge showed his religious nature by refusing to do anything at the nighttime council meetings until he had paid proper homage to Prunella. This he did by attempting to sample all five hundred of the Lady's sacrosanct local brews. He made his council members do the same, and it wasn't long before the moment of unparalleled horror came when the goddess's influence convinced Gudge he had the best singing voice in all Hydrangea and yes he *could so too* sing the entire "Epic of Pog and Prunella" with a pitcher of beer balanced on his head.

Artemisia begged off the nocturnal council sessions as

soon as possible, but still she was cheated of sleep when her lord returned to the royal bedchamber and . . .

Well, if it wasn't Pog and Prunella all over again, it was a close blood relative.

It didn't bear thinking about. She had greeted her pregnancy as a rescue from Gudge's rough affection, but pregnancy turned out to be just as big a sleep-cheat as Gudge, especially after the first three months.

How wonderful it is to be able to lie on my stomach again! Artemisia mused between dreams. They were very pleasant dreams, mostly centering on the several futures of her children.

First her imagination painted an idyllic picture of her tiny daughter Avena, being raised in the merry greenwood. The Black Weasel would of course have a Hydrangean court-in-exile, with all the old rites and refinements that poor, dear, decapitated da had enjoyed. The only difference would be that the Black Weasel's living palace of stately forest giants would have a leakier roof, a lot more fresh air, and a woodpecker problem. Surely there would be at least one lady of gentle birth among the resistance fighters, a proud, high-spirited woman who defied the invaders of her homeland, unafraid to face the hardships of exile. Yet this same woman would still be a model of Hydrangean culture and femininity, and to her tender care would the Black Weasel commend his infant niece.

Artemisia sighed with contentment as she dreamed of sweet Avena, wild roses in her hair, weaving daisy chains for the little bunny rabbits and reciting the immortal "Ode to a Nightingale's Kiss" to kindly old Mister Bear. Then the child would dance off, singing, to finish embroidering collars for all the pretty wolfies. Dwarfs might also be involved.

And standing guard over his sister's embroidery, tall and strong, would be young Helianthus. Browned by the sun, hardened by good, plain food and wholesome exercise, a dead shot with the bow, a hunter of keenest eye and sagest cunning, he would become a legend among the Bold Bush-dwellers. While he was still a mere stripling, the Black Weasel himself would recognize the lad's qualities and voluntarily resign the leadership of the resistance to him. There would be a short, moving ceremony, then Helianthus would leap gracefully atop a tree stump to deliver his first speech to the troops. Inflamed by the boy's spirit, the Bold Bush-dwellers would march down out of the mountains, gathering support wherever they went. At last a vast army—an Old Hydrangean army!—would stand arrayed before the gates of the city, eager to destroy the Gorgorians and place the true king on the throne!

But they would be just a bit too late.

Artemisia squirmed deeper under the sheets and purred, dreaming of the fate of her other dear son, Prince Helenium. As firstborn, he was the only one of the three left to her. She would raise him well, as a true Hydrangean royal prince. No expense would be spared, especially not when it came to his military training. Wise in statecraft, Prince Helenium must also be powerful at arms. And then, when the time was ripe, his adored and adoring mama would tell him the whole nasty truth about Dad. Artemisia's dream of her children's reunion ended when Helianthus and his army of Bold Bush-dwellers arrived at the gates just in time to see his twin brother Prince Helenium chucking Gudge's head over the parapet, to the cheers of the crowd.

And then the twin princes embraced joyfully and got down to the serious business of finding a husband for Avena.

Artemisia's perfectly planned future was shattered into jagged fragments by the strident sound of a hungry infant's cry. Smiling like a henhouse dog, she got out of bed and reached into the cradle.

While she was back in bed nursing the baby, a thunderous pounding shook the door.

It couldn't possibly be Ludmilla. The journey to the eastern mountains took days. "Probably one of Gudge's trained apes, come to see if I died or not," Artemisia muttered to the infant snuffling at her breast. She tossed her silky blond hair back as well as she could, sat up straighter against the pillows, and commanded, "Enter at Our pleasure!"

The door opened to a Gorgorian guardsman. Gudge had insisted on integrating the palace guard as a gesture of goodwill to his newly conquered people. The qualifications for an Old Hydrangean entering that service were that he bear no other arms but an ornamental lance tipped with a limp silk peony and that he be handsome. For a Gorgorian looking to be a guard, the man must be able to carry forty pounds of steely death in assorted shapes and sizes and agree to shave his back.

The guard dipped his head to the queen and said, "King Gudge's compliments, and how are you feeling?"

"Why doesn't my lord come and see for himself if he wants to know?" Artemisia teased. She enjoyed baiting the Gorgorians; they *never* caught on. Their idea of subtle wit always involved large quantities of well-ripened pig droppings.

"His Majesty's gone huntin'. Sorry," the guardsman added as an afterthought.

"Isn't that kind of him? No doubt he was afraid that if he had to listen to my cries of pain any longer, he might be so overcome with remorse, knowing that his love was the author of my woe, that he might heedlessly throw himself from the ramparts. This would of course result in a bloody war of succession, and being the wise monarch he is, King Gudge decided it would be best to get as far from the sounds of childbirth as a good horse could carry him."

"Oh," said the guard. "Yeh. Tha's it in a nutshell. What he said. His 'zact words. So . . ." He looked around the tower room. "You all right?"

"Never better."

"And, uh . . ." He nodded toward the suckling child.

"Go down the stairs," Queen Artemisia directed, pronouncing each word with elaborate care. "Go fast. Try to slip and break your neck on the way down. If you can't manage that, go to the stables, get a horse, and ride after His Majesty. See if you can fall off it in a painful, preferably fatal way before you find him. If you botch that, then do find him and tell him that he is the father of a prince."

"A prince?" the guard echoed. "It's a boy, then?"

"Princes generally are."

"Right. Right, thanks, I'll just be on my way, in that case. Uh—you want anything before I go, Y'r Highness?"

"No, no, seeing the back of you is all I'll ever ask of life."

The guard gave her another one of those shallow, meaningless bows. "Anything t' 'blige." Then he was gone. Shortly afterward, the sound of galloping hooves wafted up to the tower room, fading away in the direction of the royal hunting preserve.

After nursing the baby, Artemisia was about to put it back in the huge, gilded cradle when an unmistakable odor hit her straight up the nostrils.

"My," she remarked, shifting the swaddled bundle to her left arm and studying her damp right hand. "This is definitely not what my seven governesses trained me to do, but I suppose I can learn on the spot." She carried the baby over to the big black walnut chest by the window, where Ludmilla had thoughtfully laid out all the infant-care supplies that might be useful. There was even a soft blanket covering half the chest.

Artemisia placed the baby on the blanket and removed the green satin swaddlings. The child made an ugly face at her, all its limbs trembling. "There, there, I'll do this as quickly as I can," the queen soothed. "Soon we'll have you out of that wet napkin and into a—goodness, these pins are hard to undo—into a dry and wrapped up snug and—this other pin is *not* coming out!—warm and—ah! There it comes—and . . . and . . . and . . . *Aaaaiiiiieeeee*!"

This time the queen's scream did for the other seven stained-glass windows in the banqueting hall.

"No," said Artemisia, staring down at what the unfastened diaper revealed. "There must be a mistake. A horrible mistake." The infant seemed to agree, for it set up a piercing wail. The queen gently seized the baby's wrist and gazed intently at the miniature portrait hanging there from its red cord. "But this is Prince Helenium's face! You have to be Prince Helenium; you're wearing his naming token," she told the baby.

The baby told her in the only way it knew how that it didn't *have* to be anything but warm, fed, and dry, and being only one out of three was grounds for screaming the roof down.

Queen Artemisia hastily tugged the soiled diaper from under the tiny banshee and wrapped her child up in the blanket. Appeased, the infant made comfortable I'll - just - go - to - sleep - now - see - that - I'm - not - disturbed - thanks - awfully sounds into the queen's shoulder. It remained blissfully unaware of its mother's rising agitation.

"How could this have happened?" Artemisia demanded of the air. "How? Oh, that incompetent fool Ludmilla! So busy with her own petty tantrums, and half-blind into the bargain, it's a wonder she didn't tie one of the tokens around *my* wrist! She dropped all three of them into the cradle and then attached them just any old way. I'm surprised she didn't tie two on one baby. But you'd think she'd at least have had the foresight to fetch different colored cords! Red, the tokens were tied on with red, every one, and the sacred red cord is supposed to be reserved for the firstborn. What am I going to do?"

She paced the tower room like a caged panther. All the weakness of a long and arduous childbirth had fallen away from her in the adrenal surge brought on by the discovery that either Ludmilla had screwed up beyond anyone's wildest expectations and taken *both* the twin princes to the Black Weasel's mountain stronghold, leaving their sister behind, or else there was a very *odd* sort of invisible thief on the premises.

"Oh dear, oh dear," she muttered. "The messenger's already gone to tell Gudge he has a son. If he comes back and finds he's got a daughter, heads will roll! And not just heads. He's a moron, but he's no fool; if I said it's a boy and I show him a girl, he'll know that there must be a boy baby around somewhere. And *that* means there is more than one baby. And *that* means that I was the mother of twins, at least. And *that,* O ye gods, according to his benighted Gorgorian superstitions, means that I must have been with more than one man."

She did not need to say what *that* meant. Adultery had always been a serious crime in Hydrangea, even before the Gorgorian invasion. A *queen's* adultery was High Treason, with a suitably creative punishment to fit the crime. Badgers played a significant role. It was one of the few Old Hydrangean customs that Gudge had kept on entire and unaltered, for entertainment value.

Artemisia paced faster, growing more frantic. Every so often the queen would lay the baby down and unwrap it, just to check on whether anything missing had been replaced. She even said a prayer to Uttocari, Goddess of Objects Lost, Purloined, or "Borrowed" by the Neighbors. Nothing worked. The baby in her arms remained as was.

At last Artemisia sat down heavily on a delicately carved chair, the armrests shaped like mermaids with inset sapphire eyes and white enameled breasts, coral tipped. On one arm she cradled her daughter, the fingers of the other hand gouging deep, thoughtful holes in one mermaid's head.

"Think, Artemisia," the queen directed herself. "Don't panic; *think!* Ludmilla bollixed things, but it's nothing that can't be undone. Gudge has been told that he is the father of a boy. This is obviously not a boy." She looked at her daughter's peacefully sleeping face and murmured an automatic "kitchie-koo" for no sensible reason.

"Very well, then," she went on. "Ludmilla is careless, but not stupid. She will have to feed and change the babies soon enough, and then she'll discover her mistake. She'll turn right around and come back here to swap one of the princes for Princess Avena before long and everything will be the way we originally planned it. Good. Fine. So if Gudge comes bulling his way up here before Ludmilla can return, all I've got to do is present the princess to him as the prince! All babies look alike above the belly-band, and unless Gudge offers to change the infant's diapers there is no way he'll ever know that his son is really his daughter."

Queen Artemisia smiled. There was more chance of the sun rising in the west, plaid, with purple fringe trim and shaped like a bullfrog, than of Gudge ever getting near a dirty diaper. Or a clean one, for that matter.

"There, that's all taken care of," she told the sleeping infant. "It wasn't as bad as I thought. Everything will be fine, Aven—I mean *Arbol*. Yes, that's a good name for a prince, Arbol is." The baby whimpered in its sleep. "Oh, don't fuss, my love, you won't have to put up with the name for long. Just until your Nana Ludmilla gets back. We can wait, can't we? Yes, we can. We can wait . . ."

Fortunately for Artemisia's current peace of mind, she had no idea just how long they would have to wait.

Chapter Three

Ludmilla sat by the side of the road, resting her weary legs, and looked back the way she'd come. The pearly pink towers of the Palace of Tranquil Thoughts, rising above the city walls, were gloriously backlit by the declining sun. Doves swooped and soared among the battlements. Golden pennons fluttered and snapped from the topmost pinnacles. These banners were all freshly embroidered with the new badge of the kingdom: On a field of gold, the *sallet* (an Old Hydrangean heraldic beast one-third deer, one-fourth dormouse, one-eighth capon, and anything left over equally split between rabbit and poodle) was being used in a most painful and humiliating fashion by the Great Sacred Ox of the Gorgorians. Taken all in all, it was a heartlifting spectacle.

"Hmph!" said Ludmilla to the royal babies. "We're not clear of *that* hogwallow a moment too soon, my precious pixikins, and no mistake! Oh, I can't help but pity your poor brother, stuck back there to be raised amid the nasty temptations of palace life while the pair of you will have all the advantages of a fine upcountry education. Why, I came from the Fraxinella Mountains myself when I was a mere slip of a girl just—ah—neveryoumind how long ago."

She reached into the huge basket resting on the grass beside her and lavished a fond smile on the two sleeping infants within as she adjusted their blankets.

A cold, black shadow fell across the babies. Ludmilla

raised her head and looked up into a haphazard arrangement of yellow-brown eyes, greenish snaggle teeth, matted black hair, and a nose like a dumpling that had been dropped on the outhouse floor. A charitable person might call it a face.

"Here, now, what've you got in there, Granny, eh?" demanded the Gorgorian man-at-arms. Squat and bandy-legged from a lifetime in the saddle, he had obviously been demoted to footsoldiering as part of King Gudge's mountain patrols, and just as obviously he wasn't at all happy about it. Gorgorians were very good about sharing things with their newly conquered fellow countrymen, the Old Hydrangeans—things like vermin, infections, bruises, and bad moods. This squint-eyed chap looked like no exception, and he was backed up by four more equally unhorsed and unhappy comrades. They gathered around old Ludmilla and the babies like sharks around a hunk of bloody beef.

Ludmilla straightened her shoulders. "And who is it wants to know, you rude creature?" she demanded. Although she had abandoned her gorgeous court dress of dragon-scale silk and phoenix-point lace for the simple brown homespun tunic and apron of a Hydrangean countrywoman, she refused to put aside her spirit.

Backbone and backtalk usually had no place among a real peasant's possessions—they didn't help the crops a lick and they tended to cause unforeseen things like sudden death when exercised in the presence of the upper classes. Since absolutely everyone alive—and quite a few dead—outranked the typical Old Hydrangean peasant, Ludmilla's show of courage startled the Gorgorian badly.

"Hoi! Never mind who wants to know," he replied, getting a little red above the gills. Then, grabbing hold of his aplomb with both hands, he blustered on, "It's *me* as wants to know, Granny, and that'll have to do you. Else *we'll* do you, eh, me hearties?" He winked companionably at his men, although given the number of old scars and new swordcuts hashing his face, it looked more like he was suffering some sort of spasm.

"Uhhrr . . . orright, chief."

"If you says so."

"I 'sposes."

"We'll do her what?"

The patrol leader scowled, which looked measurably worse than his smile. He drew a short-handled cat-o'-nine-tails from his belt and laid about his unenthusiastic followers with the butt end. "Look, when I say we'll do her, the least you blunderation of misborn nanny goats can do is back me up! What's wrong with you lot these days? Back when we was roving the plains or riding the wild wastes of the Litchi Plateau and I said 'There's a helpless villager; let's do him good and proper for the honor of all Gorgorians,' did you stand about with your thumbs up your arses asking 'Do him what?' and acting like you never seen a length of your enemy's guts steaming at the end of your lances on a bright, fresh, frosty morning?"

The patrol, to a man, looked at the ground and made stupid noises in their throats. This enraged their leader even more, a bad idea.

"You did *not!*" he roared. "You sailed right in and you *did* the bugger, that's all! Whatever happened to that old team spirit, hey?"

"S'norses," said the youngest of the men.

His leader's bristly hand darted out, closed around the young Gorgorian's windpipe, and reeled him in. "*What?*"

"I said, sir—" his hapless captive gasped as a fine bluish patina crept over his stubbled cheeks, "—I said that it's not the same without the horses."

"Think I don't know that?" the leader bellowed in his face, then batted him into one of his comrades with the whip handle. " *'Course* it ain't the same without the horses! It's lonelier of a cold night, for one. But these mountains is sheep country. If we bring horses too much farther upcountry hereabouts, the land's so steep and rocky and the paths is so narrer that we'd spend more'n half our time walkin' the poor beasts 'stead of ridin' 'em like civilized men. And even so, every time we'd turn 'round there'd be another sorry nag with his leg broke and no hope but a quick death at sword's point. So what's the use of draggin' horses along?"

"Wull . . . we'd eat better, cap'n."

The Gorgorian officer let fly with the business portion of the cat, deftly removing half the outspoken gourmet's beard with one flick of the wrist. "My salty rump we would!" he shouted. "You ever *tasted* the ruination what these Hydrangean fibbity-fobs does to a good, honest slab of horsemeat? 'Senough to make a grown man cry."

While this discussion was going on, Ludmilla pulled herself creakily to her feet, smoothed down her skirt, and picked up the basket with the babies. "Excuse me, young man," she said, pushing past the Gorgorian soldier who had been so summarily shaved. "This has all been quite charming, but I have business to attend to. However, if you should ever find yourselves in the capital, do stop by the Duck and Crusty Things Inn. I have strong reason to believe that the cook there knows just what to do with a good slab of horsemeat. He calls it beef and sells it at veal prices, that's what. Good day."

"Now wait just a minute!" The Gorgorian captain lunged after Ludmilla and seized her by the elbow, making the basket swing wildly. "You ain't goin' nowhere, Granny."

Ludmilla regarded him coldly. "Obviously not. You are a very rude person and I shall complain about you to King Gudge as soon as practicable."

"Haw! You complain 'bout me to His Majesty? There's a laugh! Why, an old bit o' leatherwork like you wouldn't get into the city gates, let alone the palace. 'Course—" his eyes got smaller and nastier, "—there's good chance as you might get into the palace after all, on my say-so. The palace *dungeons*!"

His threats cut no ice with Ludmilla. She merely sniffed once, delicately: a mannerism intended to express her disdain for him and all his ilk. Unfortunately it was likewise a mannerism that compelled her to *smell* him and all his ilk.

The aged handmaid turned pale and sat down with a thud. The sudden jolt woke both the babies, who began to cry.

"Hoi! What've we got here?" the Gorgorian captain inquired jovially. He grabbed the basket away from Ludmilla and peered inside. The infants bawled lustily, squirming in their swaddlings.

"Cheeses," said Ludmilla shortly, and yanked the basket back.

The captain did not let go of his grip on the handle. Ludmilla was old, but she was wiry, and her unexpected recovery came so strongly that when she jerked the basket handle down to her level, she brought the captain down with it. He hit the ground on his stomach, driving the full weight of his thick leather belt and ponderous ornate gilded buckle sharply into his solar plexus.

"Gar!" exclaimed one of the patrol, observing his captain's subsequent bout of roadside retching. "Woss brought that on?"

"Think as it must've been that brunch what we ate," opined the second.

The third man disagreed. "Naaah. Onliest time it's dangerous to eat a brunch is when they hasn't been proper cleaned and cooked. 'Sonly the subcutaneous membrane what's poison, and once that's removed . . ."

His fourth comrade looked at him suspiciously. "Subcu*what*? Here! What kind of language is that for a soldiering man? Got too pissing many syllabubble . . . sillybib . . . sullabull . . . 'Sgot words what's too damn *long*, 'swhat! You been having it on with that Old Hydrangean hedge-trollop up to Stinkberry village again?"

The patrolman so accused blushed. "She's the onliest one as gives a military discount hereabouts. And it's part o' the Old Hydrie tradition for the jolly-girls to have a little, y'know, mutually enriching conversation and instruction with their esteemed clientele as a, what-d'you-call-'em, intellectual prelude to subsequent physical interaction."

The captain rose from his knees just in time to deal his glib underling a sound buffet to the skull just below the rear brim of his short-helm with the cat. His victim was knocked from his feet and sat rubbing the back of his head in an aggrieved manner.

"There'll be none o' that sort o' talk in *my* patrol!" the captain thundered. "And from now on you'll keep clear of the Stinkberry slut. Good fighting men catches things that way, y'know."

"Like an education," old Ludmilla put in, unasked. "You wouldn't want *that* to happen." She was on her feet again and strolling calmly away up the mountain path for a little ways before the Gorgorian patrol overtook her a second time.

"Now you hold it right there, my fine old toad!" the captain commanded, laying a hand on her shoulder. "The penalty for lying to your natural overlords is death by eatin' a badly cleaned brunch! What's all this pigflop about what you've got in that basket, hey?"

"I told you," Ludmilla said, keeping her voice unruffled. "They're cheeses."

"That explains as why our chief was took so bad, then," one patrolman whispered to his fellow. "Cheese gives him the heave-ho something desperate."

The captain reached for the basket handle, thought better of it, and settled for yanking aside the blanket covering the infants. They were still crying. "Cheeses, eh?" he sneered.

Still cool as a duck's bottom, old Ludmilla replied, "I take it, then, that for all your talk of being familiar with King Gudge's palace, you have never seen an authentic Old Hydrangean Weeping Cheese?" She said this so sweetly, with such easy confidence and condescension, that the captain was taken aback. Ludmilla had never received any formal combat training, but she was experienced enough in the ways of the world to know when to follow up an advantage on a stunned opponent.

"But of course you wouldn't," she went on. "The Weeping Cheese is a delicacy reserved for only the highest of the highborn, and then served solely on occasions of the utmost sanctity. The custom dates back to the time when child sacrifice was just beginning to be thought in rather bad taste, particularly since it was the practice for the reigning monarch to eat whatever portions of the victims the gods rejected as not lean enough. Queen Jargoon the Dyspeptic is credited with substituting a specially made cheese for the babies previously offered, although it remained for her great-grandson, King Scandium the Decorous, to perfect the rite by the inclusion of crackers and a dry white wine."

By this time the Gorgorian captain was blinking like an owl at a firefly convention. His tiny eyes went from Ludmilla to the babies and back, desperately seeking some inspiration for a counterargument. "Uh . . . if they's cheeses, what's this, eh?" He passed a horny finger over one infant's cheek and showed the glimmer of wetness.

"Whey," the old retainer replied.

"But—but they looks just like babies! Look, all them tufts of fuzz and a nose, and eyes, and—"

"Beautiful, aren't they?" Ludmilla beamed proudly at her two young charges. "A triumph of the cheesemaker's art in every detail. We haven't had a single complaint from the gods from the first day we substituted the Weeping Cheeses for the real infants." She lowered her voice and added confidentially, "Between you and me, sometimes the gods aren't too bright."

The horrified Gorgorian made the sign of the sacred oxhorns at the old woman's blasphemy. His voice cracked just a bit when he said, "Yerrrr, but . . . but . . . but they're *noisy*! What kinda cheese, never mind how pretty it's made, makes a sound like that?"

Ludmilla sighed. "If they did not make that noise, we would have called them *Quiet* Cheeses. In the cheesemaking process, a good deal of air is trapped with the curds. All you are hearing is the normal sound of that air escaping."

"Oh."

The patrolman who had lost half his beard now came forward to help his captain in what was fast becoming a tight spot for the wrong people. "Just a minute!" he declared. "If they're cheeses, how come they're wriggling about like that, hm?"

Before Ludmilla could come up with an answer, the captain stepped in and growled, "Oh, *there's* a fine question to be asking! Make us all look like a bunch of moonwits, why don't you? Or greenhorns as never saw the inside of an honest Gorgorian messtent. Tell me this, me wide-eyed virgin tifter: Ain't *you* never seen good food move?"

"Wull . . . there *was* that load o' bread we got last week. It was rough going, keeping it from getting away 'til it was proper eaten."

" 'Course it did have all them legs," one of his companions prompted. "From the weevils."

"Natural!" the captain concluded, triumphant. "And if we can have us eats what brings a little action to the table, think these high-and-mighty Old Hydries won't? Why, I'll wager they was being served chicken-neck stew what was crawling off the plate while we was still galloping over the Litchi Plateau living on oxtail soup and roast brunches!"

The half-shaved Gorgorian looked dubious, but refrained from further comment. He ventured to take a look at the cheeses under discussion. It was then that an unmistakable aroma, even more pungent than his own, reached his nostrils.

"Agh!" he exclaimed, fanning the air as he backed away. "That settles it. Cheeses is what they be all right."

"Like I told you," his captain concluded smugly. To Ludmilla he said, "Now be on your way, Granny, and get them Weeping Cheeses where they're bound. Judging from the sound they're making, I'd say they're just about ripe."

Ludmilla dropped him a pretty curtsey. "It's always such a pleasure dealing with a real man of the world," she said, and sashayed off.

She was really too old to sashay very far. It wasn't a gait that lent itself to long distances carrying a basket full of babies, especially when the babies were still bawling and definitely needed to have their diapers changed. Ludmilla reflected bitterly that she had lost a lot of time on the road with the Gorgorian patrol. The plan she and Queen Artemisia had worked out called for her to spend the first night in the home of her distant cousin Gowena, a widow whose loyalty to the Old Order was the best that money could buy. Now it didn't look as if Ludmilla would reach the prearranged safe haven. It grew dark earlier in the mountains; already the shadows along the road were fading into the general gloom.

Ludmilla clucked her tongue. "No help for it, I suppose," she said aloud. "We must make what shelter we can, my dollybits, and go on to Gowena's house in the morning. Stinkberry village is hereabouts; we'll try for that."

She continued up the road, which soon became a poorly paved path, which in turn devolved to a dirt track that grew progressively narrower the further she went from the lowlands. "How odd," Ludmilla said, panting as she trudged on. "I don't recall the way to Stinkberry village being this rough, and I ought to know! I was a girl there scarcely, oh, not a handful of years since." It did not trouble her conscience at all that she'd have to substitute the word "decades" for "years" to get within spitting distance of the truth.

The babies didn't care how badly Ludmilla lied about her age. They were hungry and wet and soiled and tired of being passed off as dairy products. Ludmilla thought to assuage them with a sugar-tit, but when she searched the bottom of the basket for that pacifier it was gone, most likely fallen out during her recent tug-o'-war match with the Gorgorian captain. The children didn't care about excuses. Both of them had excellent lungs and used them nonstop. The effect was rather wearing on their aged nursemaid.

"Oh dear, oh dear," she muttered, peering into the dusk with eyes not all that sharp in full sun. "Is that a light I see? Perhaps I was closer to Stinkberry than I thought. There, there, my poppets," she spoke softly to the wailing babes. "Soon you'll have a nice warm place to stay and all the comforts. Look, my lovies, that light's the lantern out in front of the village tavern or I'm a goose, and there's the blacksmith's shop next door, just as I recall it, and—*whoops*!"

Ludmilla tripped over a sheep.

The basket went flying, the babies' yowls for food turned to shrieks of excitement to find themselves airborne. They landed a short distance away in the tall grass of the finest grazing lands on that side of the capital. They also landed smack in the middle of a herd of plump, fluffy sheep who took to their heels with bleats of terror at this sudden invasion from on high. It was purely a miracle that the royal infants weren't trampled.

"Oh my," said Ludmilla, and then, querulously, "Children, come back here." By this time it was full dark, with no moon worth mentioning. The babies were still just as hungry and just as wet, but their recent diversion had taken their minds off every thought except hoping for another such exhilarating ride in the near future. They lay in the grass chuckling to themselves.

Poor Ludmilla looked all around her and saw nothing. The light which had lured her into believing that she saw Stinkberry village was still there. In fact, it seemed to be coming closer, which was *not* the way a decent tavern lantern ought to behave, in her opinion. There was only one explanation.

"*Black wizardry!*" she shrieked. "Oh, it's the ghosts of all the poor wizards as was slain so cruelly by King Gudge, and now they're hot for the blood of the living! Please, oh please don't take my babies!" she cried into the dark.

"Huh!" came the unwizardly snort from the approaching light. "Why'd I want to do a damfool thing like . . . Ludmilla?"

The beam of a shepherd's lantern flooded old Ludmilla's eyes. She gazed up into a face—ancient, sunbrowned, wrinkled, thatched and bearded with gray—that she hadn't seen in . . . neveryoumind how many years.

"Odo?" she breathed, hands folded over her withered bosom.

Some time later, after having located the babies with

Odo's help, Ludmilla got them cleaned up, changed, and bedded down with two makeshift bottles of sheep's milk in a corner of Odo's hut. Duty done, she returned to the rickety table where Odo was still wolfing down a simple dinner of bread, cheese, and wild onions. Lots of wild onions.

"I still don't see where you got them babes," Odo remarked between mouthfuls. "When you left Stinkberry, you wasn't even pregnant. Not by me, anyway."

"Not for your lack of trying." Ludmilla settled herself comfortably close beside him on the one bench in the place. "It *has* been a few years since then," she said coyly. "Things happen."

Odo regarded Ludmilla with just a touch of skepticism in his flat brown eyes. "So they're yours, are they?"

"You might say that," Ludmilla replied. "Or you might not. But then again, you might. And you might be right about it if you said so. Or wrong."

"Oh." Odo munched another wild onion. "So . . . you still like sheep?"

"That depends." She arched one brow. "Do you still have the biggest shepherd's crook in the Fraxinella Mountains?"

Odo looked over to where he'd left his badge of shepherdly office propped against the doorframe. "I dunno," he said, all honesty. "I could give it a measure."

Ludmilla patted Odo's hand. "You never change, do you?" she said tenderly.

"I do too!" Odo took umbrage. "I put on my new tunic on Prunella's yearly feast day, like any good shepherd, and I changes my smallclothes once every three full moons, weather permitting, and . . ."

"I only meant—" Ludmilla edged nearer so that her thigh rubbed against his, like a pair of sticks trying to get a fire started, "—that you're still the same dear Odo I knew when I was just a slip of a girl." She plucked aside the stringy curtain of his iron-gray hair and tickled his earlobe with her tongue. "Do you remember?"

Odo frowned. "When *was* you just a slip of a gir . . . gir . . . gir . . . *oh, my lambs and lanolin*!"

For all her years, and all of Odo's too, Ludmilla was still good at stirring up more than memories. With a rough, inarticulate exclamation, Odo leaped from the table with the spryness of a man of sixty, clasped Ludmilla to him in an embrace that reeked of sheepskin and wild onions, and swept her up in his arms.

Then he put her down again and clapped both hands to the small of his back, groaning. Ludmilla clicked her tongue, shook her head, and led her former swain to the fleece-covered pallet near the hearth.

The babies, warm, dry, and full of milk, slept soundly and thus missed a unique educational experience. They did not hear the muffled sounds of aged joints cracking and popping as Odo and Ludmilla sought to recapture their youthful passion. They remained undisturbed by Ludmilla's gasped instructions to Odo concerning certain complex techniques she had picked up while in the royal service. They slumbered on despite Odo's grunts, Ludmilla's moans, and the swiftly accelerating tempo of both. What was truly astonishing was that they managed to sleep through the joyful yodel that ultimately burst from Ludmilla's throat.

This was followed by a hiccup, a gurgle, and a final exhalation.

Then, after a long moment of puzzled silence, Odo murmured, "Anthrax take it—she's dead!"

At first, Odo simply lay there, too consumed by passion, grief, and confusion to have any idea what he should do. Eventually, however, he thought to pull up his pants and look the situation over more logically, as well as more warmly, while sitting on the edge of the wooly pallet.

There was no question about whether any spark of life remained in Ludmilla. Although an impartial observer might have thought she looked rather corpselike before, the difference now was quite unmistakable. Odo had seen death often enough before to have no doubts—admittedly, he usually saw it in sheep rather than women, but the effect was really very much the same.

He had never had a woman die in his arms before, but then, he had almost never had a sheep die in his arms, either.

"Her heart must've gave out," he muttered to himself. He tugged at the drawstring of his pants. "I suppose I must've improved with practice." He glanced at Ludmilla, and added, "And she warn't as young as she let on, I'd wager." That realization took a weight from his mind; he guessed that he needn't worry about younger women's hearts.

Not that he'd ever have had a chance to find out, these days. He wasn't all that young himself any more, and the girls of Stinkberry village didn't seem eager for his company.

"Don't know what they're missing," he growled, looking at the foolish grin that was Ludmilla's final expression.

She was unquestionably dead. The question now was just what he should do about it.

Well, he couldn't bring her back to life, which meant that it was merely a matter of what to do with her remains. When one of the sheep died that meant dinner for the next week or so, unless it died of something nasty, but Odo knew that wasn't done with people. Ludmilla looked pretty stringy, anyway, he noticed—when she was still moving under her own power it hadn't been quite as obvious.

So he'd have to bury her.

He sighed. All that digging was hard work for a man his age.

Maybe there was somebody he could palm it off on; did she have any relatives who might want to claim the body?

Odo scratched his head, dislodging a few of its arthropodous occupants and wedging still more black grease under his fingernails.

The truth was, he didn't know anything about Ludmilla's background. She had turned up in Stinkberry as a mere girl, or at any rate as a reasonably young—well, young*ish*—woman when he was a boy, and one night after they both got drunk at the Shearing Festival she had come back to the mountaintop with him and stayed the night—for several months.

Then she had disappeared, and he thought that was the end of it, but she'd turned up in Stinkberry village again when they were still both young—he thought he might have still been in his thirties at the time, and she couldn't have been past fifty, sixty at the outside.

She had spent another few months on the mountain with him, and then run off with that peddler, and that was it until tonight.

He tried to remember if she had ever said anything about having family or friends. Nothing came to him.

She must have known somebody, somewhere, judging by her last few words. A woman didn't think up suggestions like that on her own, did she?

Actually, Odo had no idea what women might think up; as often as not he wasn't any too sure what he was thinking himself. Still, Ludmilla hadn't conjured those two babies out of thin air . . .

Babies.

He had almost forgotten them in his excitement. What the faradiddle was he going to do with the babies?

Whose babies were they, anyway?

He got himself upright, discovering in the process that his back had suffered more damage than he had previously realized, and crossed to the corner where the infants slept.

"Young'uns," he remarked to himself.

He considered looking for notes or messages, but there wasn't any hurry; he couldn't read one if he found it, after all, and he wasn't about to go looking for a scholar in the middle of the night. They were both quite small, with a rather squashed appearance and very similar faces.

All newborn babies look pretty much alike, but Odo thought it was more than that.

"Twins, they is," he said. He sucked on his lower lip, inadvertantly drawing a curl of beard into his mouth and forcing an innocent young louse to seek new lodging. He hadn't seen a lot of babies, but he knew lambs, and he supposed the basics held for both species. "Can't be more'n a few days old," he concluded. "They'll need nursing." He looked up.

Ludmilla wasn't going to nurse them, and Odo didn't know of a wetnurse anywhere in the area, but they had seemed pleased with the sheep's milk Ludmilla had fed them. That had come from poor little Audrea, who'd lost her lamb.

Well, why couldn't Audrea nurse them, then?

Odo was not an educated man, but he remembered hearing at his mother's knee the tale of Remulo and Rommis, ancient heroes of Old Hydrangea, who had been raised by wolverines. He remembered it well—after all, he had heard it every day for fourteen years, since his mother had been a great believer in bedtime stories but only knew the one.

If those two could be raised by wolverines, then why couldn't this pair be raised by sheep?

Odo's heart swelled with pride. Maybe he would raise himself a pair of heroes! Maybe, centuries from now, people would remember the stories of this pair, raised by Odo and his sheep before setting forth upon lives of adventure!

Of course, Odo would be dead by then, but it might be nice to be remembered. And meanwhile, when they got a bit bigger, he could get some work out of them; there was plenty to do around the mountain.

And they would need names.

Remulo and Rommis were the obvious choices, and he had seen that they were both boys when Ludmilla had changed their nappies, but Odo had a ram by the name of Rommis already, and he wasn't at all sure he would be able to keep matters straight if he named a baby that, as well. He frowned, and sucked on the wisp of beard in his mouth.

It uncoiled down his throat and choked him, sending him into a prolonged coughing fit, the sound of which woke the babies. When Odo had extracted the treacherous whiskers and regained his composure, he devoted himself to trying to quiet the boys, using a moistened finger as an impromptu pacifier.

It didn't work.

In desperation, he took a lantern and set out to find Audrea, despite the utter darkness outside. The babies lay wailing in one corner of the cottage, Ludmilla lay dead in the other, and once outside Odo seriously considered not coming back.

But that, he thought, wouldn't be right; his sheep were depending on him. He squared his shoulders, lifted the lantern high, and trudged onward.

By the time he dragged Audrea into the cottage, ignoring her bleats of protest, both babies were blissfully asleep again. Odo glared down at them, then tethered Audrea to the leg of his only table and sat down on the fleecy pallet.

"Trouble," he said, "these two'll be trouble." He sighed. "Like those two uncles of mine that got hanged down in Lichenbury." He looked down at the tiny red faces and squinty closed eyes. "They even look like 'em." He poked gently at the boy on the right. "Guess I'll call you after Uncle Dunwin," he said, "and t'other after Uncle Wulfrith."

The newly named Wulfrith cooed softly.

Chapter Four

"Listen to me, you stupid earwig," said Queen Artemisia, pearly teeth clenched almost to the splintering point. "What is so precious hard about remembering one paltry message?"

"Nothin'," replied the hapless page. He stared at his shoes and tried to get his voice up above a whisper. " 'Cept the words of it, m'lady."

Artemisia uttered a sound not meant for human lips to emit nor ears to receive. In the several weeks since Ludmilla's departure with the two boys, she had learned a great deal about uncanny, unearthly, unholy, and downright nerve-shattering sounds from her infant daughter. The princess *(No, no: the* prince*! I must always think of her as the prince,* Artemisia thought furiously. *Both our lives depend upon it.)* had a healthy set of lungs and an unhealthy case of the colic.

"Very well, nit," said the queen. "I will try just once more, and if you fail to memorize my message then, I will summon my lord King Gudge and say that you tried to ravish me. You won't like what happens next. I think it will involve wolverines."

"Yes'm," the page replied miserably.

His name was Spurge, and his Old Hydrangean pedigree was impeccable. Artemisia had felt certain that she could rely on his loyalty and discretion when she chose him for this most delicate of missions.

Alack, although the lad's qualifications looked good on parchment, showing a noble bloodline almost as blue and inbred as Artemisia's own, in her case the result was fine bone structure, fiery temper, and a congenital tendency to decorate with too much lace, while in his the end product was a mind like a sieve, a nose like a spatula, and feet like a pair of roasting pans, with the rest of his bones poking out at awkward angles all over his body, like a complete set of silver utensils concealed in a pastry bag.

Spurge didn't look capable of ravishing a newt, but even he was sharp enough to know that King Gudge's idea of justice didn't hold much truck with physical evidence—not when there were wolverines to be exercised. "I'll give it another go," he said. Closing his eyes and summoning up all seven of his brain cells, Spurge began to recite: "Greetings unto the Black Weasel, brave and heroic dashing leader of . . ."

" '*Brave* and *dashing* heroic leader,' " the queen prompted.

"Oh? Oh. Orright. Um . . ." Spurge tried to recapture his daisy-chain of thought, but the petals were long since blasted from their stems. "Urrrrh—Greetings unto the Black Wolverine—no, wait, that's not . . . Greetings unto the Black *Weasel*, brave and dashing heroic wolverine of—ooohh!" Spurge writhed like one in pain and began to gibber. His bleats of agony woke the baby, who began to wail.

Murder flashed in the queen's bloodshot eyes. "*That* did it," she pronounced with awful finality. "It took me four blessed *hours* to get that child to go to sleep, and now you've gone and done it. I'm summoning the king. When I get through telling him about you, you will *pray* for wolverines!"

Poor Spurge emitted a squeal of pure terror and bolted for the tower window. Perhaps he intended to cheat Fate, and any spare wolverines, by hurling himself to his death. Perhaps he actually believed what everyone always told him, which was: "Spurge, your head's so full of air that if you jumped out a tower window, you'd float!"

Whatever the case, it would remain a mystery. The royal cradle stood between him and the window, and as if by instinct, one of Spurge's unwieldy feet jerked out with a life of its own to snag itself in the cradle skirting. Spurge fell flat on his face, the cradle toppling after, rendering the baby airborne and Queen Artemisia paralyzed with the certainty that her precious infant was going to take a headfirst landing. (King Pyron the Goosefooted was the only Old Hydrangean king for whom there was documentary evidence to confirm that he had indeed been dropped on his head as a child, and no royal mother in her right mind wished to risk a similar fate befalling her offspring. His abbreviated reign was still spoken of with cold dread as the "Hundred Days of Metal Implements and Bad Pudding.")

What the queen did not know was that clumsy Spurge had the sharpest set of reflexes in the kingdom. It was a matter of survival. As a lad at home he had broken one priceless, unique, irreplaceable art object after another, under the horrified eye of his mother, Neurissa of the White Hand. The White Hand was also the Heavy Hand, which was why Spurge had developed the automatic reaction of moving fast—no, really fast—no, even faster than *that*—just as soon as his brain got the message: *Aaaargh! We did it again!*

There was blur of livery, a flash of leaping page, and the infant was plucked from midair by Spurge's huge, occasionally capable hands. Cuddled securely to Spurge's chest, the baby gurgled with joy, eyes bright. On bended knee, Spurge proffered the contented child to his queen, saying, "Um . . . yours, m'lady."

The queen fainted.

Artemisia regained her senses to the words, "—Weasel, brave and dashing heroic leader of the Bold Bush-dwellers. The White Doe sends to learn—to learn whether the Bun Duzzard—no, perish it all, that couldn't be it—the *Dun Buzzard* has yet placed the—uh—the brace of Golden Eaglets in your care."

She sat up slowly and turned toward the sound of the

voice. It was Spurge, still holding the baby, pacing back and forth before the queen's dressing glass as he rattled off her secret message. "Yet does the White Doe mean you to know that one of the aforesaid Golden Eaglets is not the—come *on*, Spurge, you better do this right, those wolverines have got *teeth* on 'em!—not the Rosy Hind she fancied, but the matched Silver Hart of the other." He looked at the baby. "Does that make any sense to you, Your Royal Highness?" The baby gurgled. "Nah, nor to me, either. Oh well." He shrugged and plowed on. "It is well known that the Dun Buzzard has the brains of a Squashed Frog. Thus we lay this error to her charge. If the Dun Buzzard yet roost among you, we grant you the freedom to rearrange her pinfeathers; look to't."

Queen Artemisia nodded, satisfied with Spurge's progress. What was so difficult about the message, after all? These pages always made a fuss about nothing. At the mirror, Spurge forged ahead: "Therefore—uh—therefore send one Silver Hart by your swiftest messenger that the White Doe may make of a Silver Hart a Rosy Hind and . . . and . . . and . . . Oh, plague take it! How in the name of cold fried slaw can anyone turn your heart into your behind I don't know. Nor want to." Spurge sighed. "Bring on the wolverines."

"No, no, gentle Spurge, do not despair!" cried Queen Artemisia, scrambling to her feet. "You have the message perfectly. Well, as perfectly as you ever will have it. These are chancy times. We must make do. Now go, and hasten back with the Black Weasel's reply! Oh, and pass me the prince, would you?" She gathered the sleeping babe gratefully from the page's arms, only to discover that her cherished daughter was in need of changing as well as exchanging.

She thought of having Spurge take care of the nasty business—after all, with his intelligence he might not notice that the "prince" was singularly underendowed. And if he did manage to notice, he might assume that royal boy-babies sort of . . . *acquire* such things later on in life, at about the same time they win their first sword.

But with the keen instinct of males everywhere when the chance of having to change a diaper loomed, Spurge was long gone.

"Halt! Who goes there?" cried a voice from the thickest part of the old oak's crown.

"Where?" yelped Spurge, turning around in his saddle and peering into the underbrush in an access of panic.

"Nowhere, you dope." The voice from amid the leaves sounded fed up. "I mean, yes, *some*where. There. Where you are. You. Who are you?"

"Me?" Spurge made it sound like one of the Seven Great Unanswerables of Old Hydrangean Philosophy (Number Three was: *Why is it that nothing you do, unto the conquest of countless kingdoms, is ever enough to satisfy your mother?)*

"You see anyone else around?" the tree replied. It was mighty nasty for an oak. At its foot, a thicket of gorse snickered cruelly. "Well, come on, talk! Tell us who you are and what business you've got here or . . . or . . ."

"Or we toast his kidneys for our tea!" the gorse bush shouted enthusiastically.

"Yuck," said the oak. "That is so gross that no one would ever take it seriously. And what good's a threat if nobody believes you're gonna do it?"

The gorse bush was miffed. " 'Sbetter than any threat *you* ever come up with. Hunh! Best you done was tell that wandering peddler that if he didn't swear loyalty to the Black Weasel, we'd smack him."

"The . . . the Black Weasel?" Hope lit Spurge's beady eyes. "You veggers know the Black Weasel, brave and dashing heroic leader of the Bold Bush-dwellers?"

" 'Veggers'? What's 'at?" the oak demanded.

"Um . . . you know, plants. Growing things. I mean, I heard as how the Black Weasel, braveanddashingwhatsit, was the master of the jolly greenwood, but I never knew he had a bunch of vegetables on his side."

"Who you callin' a vegetable?" There was a loud rustling from the old oak's crown, then a flurry of leaves as a small, dark object plunged from on high. It landed in the gorse bush, which yelped, "Get *off* me, Mole, you idjit! Ow! Ow! That's my *eye*!" Further tussling in the prickly foliage followed until at last the thick stems parted and the gorse bush yielded up a pair of the dirtiest, scruffiest, sulkiest lads Spurge had ever seen. One was taller and more wiry than the other, dark-haired and dark-eyed; his friend was blond, under a layer of leaf mold, with blue eyes and a sturdier build. Apart from these minor differences, the boys were equally young, filthy, and sullen.

They were also heavily armed with longbows, which they handled with disturbing expertise. Arrows nocked, bowstrings taut, both weapons were aimed at Spurge's heart.

"We may be vegetables," said the blond with an evil grin, "but you're dead meat."

It was shortly thereafter that Spurge found himself relieved of his horse and conducted on foot into the presence of the Black Weasel. He had heard tales and songs about this freebooter of the forest—quite a startling number of them, considering that the Black Weasel had not been in the forest freebooting business for more than three years at the very most.

The queen's messenger looked around him, gaping at the wonders of the Bold Bush-dweller's stronghold. The tales had not lied. There stood the king-tree, an enormously aged beech which was the central rallying point of the Black Weasel's forces. At its gnarled roots stood a gilded throne, likely plunder from some luckless Gorgorian merchant's stock, and lounging crosswise upon the silken cushions reposed the Black Weasel himself.

He was dressed all in black, of course, a fact which should have surprised no one of moderate intelligence. (Spurge was astonished.) In his gloved hands he cupped a golden goblet and sipped from it with a courtier's practiced manner. Flanking the throne were a score of youths, none among them much older than Spurge's captors. Although their jerkins, tunics, and hose were of leafy green and barky brown, the patches of flaming crimson acne dappling nearly every cheek made them poor candidates for camouflage maneuvers. They all looked peeved.

"Well, well, what have we here?" the Black Weasel drawled, slinging his legs around and sitting up straight.

"Lunch," suggested Spurge's fair-haired guard, and laughed until his voice cracked.

"Please, Your Weaselship, I—*yow*!" cried Spurge, falling to his knees before the throne to discover rather sharply that a forest floor is a bit rockier than your common Old Hydrangean reception room. Holding back tears he said, "I've got a message for you. From—uh—the White Buzzard. No, wait, the White Wolver . . . no, no, there's a behind in it someplace."

"Indeed there is." The Black Weasel arched one sooty brow and waved his men away. "I would hear what this dolt has to tell me in private. Go, my hearties, get you gone."

The Black Weasel's youthful honor-guard stayed put. "Get us gone where?" one demanded.

"Oh, I don't know," the Black Weasel said impatiently. "Anywhere. It's a big forest."

"Yeah, and there's nothin' to *do* anywhere in it," a second spindly-legged Bold Bush-dwellers pointed out.

"It's *boring*," a third affirmed.

"Why don't you go out and waylay some passing merchants?" the Black Weasel suggested.

"We done that," the first lad said. "Took all their goods an' stripped 'em of their breeches besides."

"We *always* strip 'em of their breeches," said the second boy.

"It's *boring*," the third repeated.

"Well, then, why don't you go have archery practice? Shoot at the butts."

"Done that, too," said a fourth.

"While them merchants was runnin' off."

"Boooooooorrrrrrriiiiinnnnnnng!"

The Black Weasel scowled. The boys scowled back. With a snort that rippled his magnificent black beard and moustache, the Black Weasel set down his goblet, cupped his hands to his mouth, and bawled, "Tadwyl! Tadwyl, get your worthless shanks over here at once!"

"Coming, coming!" The glade resounded with the sound of a perfectly pitched, well-modulated voice which heralded the appearance of the first full-grown adult besides the Black Weasel himself that Spurge had yet seen in the forest. He was of middling height and slim, with a merry face, trailing brown locks, and the high brow of a poet (Old Hydrangean sages agree that it took more brainpower to come up with a rhyme for "orange" than to perfect the potion for curing the common cold). "You bellowed, Black Weasel?" he inquired, holding his guitar to one side as he made a graceful bow.

"Listen, Tadwyl—"

"Ah, ah, ah!" The gentleman waggled a violet-gloved finger at his leader. "That's not the name I'm known by here and now."

"Your pardon, Purple Possum," the Black Weasel replied, raising a hand in a graceful gesture of acknowledgment. "Behold the prisoner that my able scouts, the Green Mole and the Scarlet Shrew have captured." He waved at Spurge. "He says he has a message for me, but I cannot seem to make my men understand that I wish to be alone to hear it. Do you think you might possibly . . . ?"

"He always keeps all the best secrets to hisself," the first stripling complained.

" 'Snot fair!"

"I wanna hear the message!"

"Me, too."

"Aw, who cares? It's probably *boring.*"

"Everything's boring here," the expert on boring things chimed in. He was the skinniest and gangliest of the crew, with a complexion that must have glowed in the dark.

"I hate this stupid forest. I hate this stupid bow. I hate my stupid name! Everyone else got a *good* name like the Blue Badger or the Fuchsia Ferret. How come *I* got stuck being the M'genta Marmot, huh? I don't even know what's a marmot. Nor what's m'genta, neither! I bet it's somethin' *dirty,* an' that's why everyone else is always laughing at me. I hate this whole stupid game!" He wiped his nose on the back of one hand and commenced sniveling. "I wanna go *home*!"

The Purple Possum clapped the weepy boy on the back. "There, there, lad, don't fret," he said cheerfully. "Why, I've just now finished composing the latest song in the epic cycle of the Adventures of the Black Weasel, brave and dashing heroic leader of the Bold Bush-dwellers."

"So what?" the boy asked bluntly.

"So . . . it's called 'How the Magenta Marmot Rescued the Black Weasel from a Fate Worse than Death' is what."

"What?" The Black Weasel was livid, but his shout of outrage was swallowed whole by a chorus of eager cries from the Bold Bush-dwellers.

"Wow! A new one orready? Keen!"

"You gonna sing it for us, P.P.?"

"An' it's the *Marmot* who saves the Black Weasel this time? Neat!"

"Gee, I wish *I* was the Magenta Marmot."

"Aw, c'mon, Green Mole, you already got to save the Black Weasel's life in 'The Battle of the Milfeen Bridge.' "

"One limerick, big deal."

"How come *I* don't ever get to rescue the Black Weasel, huh? All I ever get to do is shoot stupid love poems through the fair Lady Indecora's window. I don't even *like* the fair Lady Indecora. She's only twelve and she's got pimples."

"So do you."

"Do not!"

"Do too!"

"Do not!"

"Do too!"

"Do not!"

The debate ended in a pummeling match which the Purple Possum broke up in short order. Then, strumming the first bars of the ever-popular "Ballad of the Black Weasel and the Crone with the Really Big Daughter," he led the boys away into the trees.

"Good old Possum," said the Black Weasel. "I don't know what I'd do without him. We were at school together, you know. He's a miracle for keeping those little hellspits in line. Now—" he rested his hands on his knees and regarded Spurge with a wolfish grin, "—the message?"

"Gork," said Spurge. He was still staring after the wake of the Purple Possum. "Is that . . . is they . . . are them . . . I mean, in the songs and all, I always got the idea that the Bold Bush-dwellers was . . . was . . . sort of *older* than that."

"Surely you don't believe that those juvenile hobbledehoys are the *whole* of my fearless forces for the Hydrangean Resistance, do you?" the Black Weasel asked, a superior half smile curling his lip.

"Well, nnnnno, I guess not."

"Because they are." The Black Weasel smiled no more. "Do you have any idea how hard it is to get a really good Resistance Movement going in this land? Especially at harvest time. Most adult males are family men. They can't spare the time to go hanging out in a forest, ever ready to strike dread and trembling into the hearts of our brutal oppressors, when they've got a wife and kiddies to feed at home. And any man who does volunteer to join us is usually a ne'er-do-well, a lout so lazy that no decent woman would have him, a shiftless beggar who'll turn tail in a fair fight but show up early on payday."

"Oh," said Spurge.

"So I make do with the young'uns," the Black Weasel continued. "Get 'em young, train 'em up the way you'd like to have 'em, and there you are with a band of picked fighters fit to strike terror into the miserable hearts of the Gorgorians. Someday. The good thing about recruiting boys of this age is that they've got a whole lot of pent-up natural viciousness and an absolute passion for fooling around with weapons. I know I wouldn't want to run into a bunch of 'em on a dark night."

"Don't their folks object?" Spurge asked.

"Not likely. Glad to get 'em out of the house, most are. And as long as good old Tadw . . . I mean, the Purple Possum comes strolling through their home villages every few weeks to sing about all the happy adventures the sprats are having in a wholesome atmosphere of simple food, fresh air, and hearty camaraderie, their mothers are content." He stretched his long limbs luxuriously and added, "Now give me that message before I let the little slime-hounds have a bit of open-hearth cookery practice on you."

Spurge took a deep breath and launched himself upon the multicolored sea of the queen's message. The Black Weasel listened carefully to his sister's sending, even when Spurge hit the occasional clunker and had to double back several lines to correct himself. When at length the page had finished, the Black Weasel stroked his moustache and said, "I see."

"Do you?" Spurge was impressed.

"I was wondering what had happened to the babies. Old Ludmilla's a dear, but she always was a little thick."

"Oh, so it's old Ludmilla who's the White Doe? Or the Silver Hart's behind?"

The Black Weasel ignored the question. Instead he reached into a beautifully carved wooden box that stood beside his throne and removed writing materials. Having dashed off a note, he took the brassbound hunting horn from his belt and blew a long blast.

His summons went unanswered. A second blast had as little effect, and a third. In the end he gave up and just hollered off into the woods, *"POSSUM!"*

The Purple Possum reappeared, the rest of the Bold Bush-dwellers in tow.

"You shrieked, O Black Weasel?" he inquired brightly.

"Who is our best archer?"

The Purple Possum considered. "That would be the Puce Mongoose."

"Well, here." The Black Weasel flicked the note at his comrade-in-arms. "Have him send this to my sister."

Spurge watched with growing dismay as the message was plucked from the forest floor and passed to a bandy-legged redhead with a bad case of adenoids. "Just a minute!" he objected. "If that's a message for the queen, well, I'm a messenger, after all."

"Correction," said the Black Weasel. "You *were* a messenger. You *are* a Bold Bush-dweller."

"Am I?" Spurge was at an utter loss.

"Sorry about that," said the Purple Possum, patting him on the back. "It can't be helped. You weren't blindfolded when they brought you here, so you know the way to our woodland hideout. If you went back, you might reveal it."

"Toldja to blindfold him, Mole!" The blond half of Spurge's enforced escort gave the dark-haired half a nasty shove in the ribs.

"Ahhh, shuddup, Shrew!" The dark-haired lad responded with a shove of his own. "I'm not the one went an' blew his nose in our 'fficial Bold Bush-dwellers' regulation blindfold."

"I wouldn't say a word, honest!" Spurge protested. "Look, ask anyone who knows me, they'll tell you I'm lucky if I can *remember* a word!"

The Black Weasel shook his head. "It's remarkable how much more *dependable* one's memory becomes with the application of a little basic Gorgorian torture. I think it involves wolverines." He shrugged. "Welcome to the Resistance, noble patriot."

Queen Artemisia had just gotten the baby down for another nap when the arrow came zipping in through the window and lodged itself with a resounding *thwang!* in the headboard of the royal cradle. Cursing fluently, the queen yanked the missile free with one hand, using the other to jiggle the cradle in a fruitless attempt to lull the baby back to sleep.

It was not until two earsplitting hours later that Artemisia was at last free to read the missive which had been lashed to the arrow's shaft:

> "Unto the White Doe does the Black Weasel, brave and dashing heroic leader of the Bold Bush-dwellers, send greetings and regrets. The Dun Buzzard never got here. As to the fate of the Golden Eaglets, your guess is as good as mine. And *what* in the name of Prunella's Humiliation was all that side-blather you were dishing out about Silver Harts and Rosy Hinds? Look, I've got my own problems, running this open-air madhouse. Next time you have to get in touch, keep it simple and use a messenger capable of outthinking cheese, all right? Now I'm stuck with him. Give my nephew a kiss, burn this message, and try to slip a knife between Gudge's ribs if you've got a minute. The Purple Possum says hello and remember all the fun we had that last summer in the haymow. I don't remember any haymow, but never mind. Keep smiling, and death to your husband."

It was signed with a badly drawn impression of a weasel's paw that looked more like a splatted spider.

Artemisia reread the letter, hoping against hope to find it telling her a different tale. It was no use: The fatal words remained. Ludmilla had never reached the Black Weasel's camp. The princes were gone, none knew where.

The baby snuffled and began to cry again. This time Artemisia did not curse the racket. She gathered up the wailing infant in her arms and held her close. "Oh, my poor daughter," she murmured as her tears ran down to mingle with the infant's own. "Oh, my poor, darling little girl."

Chapter Five

The ancient hayrack tottered, swayed, and then slowly, with the magnificent grace of a plump dowager crossing a ballroom, it fell forward, leaving a trail of chaff floating on the gentle spring air and making a stately descent toward a black and loathsome mud puddle. Atop the wooden frame Wulfrith, age two, howled in terror and delight, flailing his arms as if he thought he could somehow propel the structure upright again, thereby sending showers of hay in all directions.

Leaping at the last minute, the boy landed atop a ewe that, until that moment, had been concerned with nothing more pressing than deciding whether or not to swallow the well-chewed grass she was currently masticating. The stuff had very little flavor left, and she had just about settled on swallowing at least part of it, when Wulfrith, with an earsplitting shriek, fell across her back and clutched great double handfuls of wool.

Her eyes flew open, and she found herself suddenly surrounded by a billowing cloud of hay and grit.

An instant later the rack splashed into the puddle, showering thin muck over sheep and passenger both, and the beast's astonishment turned to fright. With the screaming child clinging to her back, the ewe charged across the meadow, bleating hysterically.

Odo's cat, Fang, watched nonchalantly from a nearby gatepost as the terrified ovine ran headfirst into the fence, bringing herself to an abrupt stop and catapulting Wulfrith over the rail and into the open cesspool beyond.

The boy's wail of dismay ended in an abrupt splash, shortly followed by a call of, "Ooh, *stinky!*"

Fang decided that the spectacle was over, and settled down atop the post, planning to take a nap. His attempt to find the optimum comfortable position involved swinging his tail around, however, and the motion caught the eye of Wulfrith's brother, who had paid no attention whatsoever to the recent string of disasters his brother had caused.

The tail was irresistible, and in any case, Dunwin had not yet acquired the concept of resisting temptation; he grabbed for the waving line of gray fur, little fingers clamping on with roughly the same force as a pit bull's jaws.

Fang abruptly found his nap interrupted by a strong pressure and downward pull on his tail. Visions of crocodilians and canines shattered his feline composure, and eighteen razor-sharp claws dug into the weathered wood of his perch. He yowled.

Dunwin, drawing no connection between his own actions and the cat's outraged racket, tugged innocently at Fang's tail, enjoying the feel of the fur; the cat let out a renewed wail, several degrees more impressive than the one Daddy Odo had produced the night before upon finding that the boys had made up his bed for him, using the only cloth that they could handle easily, which was their own soiled diapers.

Dunwin and the trapped Wulfrith both admired this amazing new sound; suddenly noticing that it seemed to come from the cat that was attached to what he held, and eager to hear it again, Dunwin gave Fang's tail a jerk powerful enough that the cat came sailing off the fencepost, splinters spraying in every direction as claws pulled loose from weathered locustwood.

Three sheep, struck by flying debris, panicked and ran, one of them colliding with the remains of the hayrack, snapping that construction's remaining joints.

Fang gave a shriek that was heard not just in Stinkberry, but in three other villages as well.

And Odo finally woke up.

He staggered to the door of his hut and looked out at the world, expecting to find all the demons of the forty-six hells of Old Hydrangean mythology rampaging through his fields.

Instead, he found Dunwin swinging Fang by the tail in a desperate and successful effort to keep the animal's claws away from his face, while the cat continued to produce new and horribly inventive noises; he found the recently filled hayrack and its erstwhile contents scattered across half an acre; and he found his sheep running back and forth, bleating in panic.

Latoya, his finest ewe, had two patches of bare skin showing where handfuls of wool had been ripped out.

The bellow that emerged was so impressive that Fang forgot his own problems and, as best he could while swinging from Dunwin's fist, stared at Odo in admiration. The sound Odo emitted managed to penetrate Dunwin's sublime self-centeredness sufficiently to worry him. And it gave all the sheep a single direction in which to run—away from their master.

Odo marched out of the hut, breathing heavily; Dunwin thoughtfully lowered Fang to the ground and released the deathgrip on his tail, whereupon Fang decided it would be a good idea to be somewhere else for the next day or two, and, with the aid of his mystical feline abilities, vanished.

Odo stamped across the field and stood over Dunwin, glowering at the child.

"Hello, Daddy Odo," Dunwin said. He smiled endearingly.

"What in the name of all the bleeding gods is going on here?" Odo demanded.

Dunwin looked around, blinking innocently.

"Where?" he asked, genuinely puzzled.

For a moment, the boy's adoptive father stared at him, unable to speak; then, perhaps a trifle belatedly, it registered on the shepherd's consciousness that he was only addressing *one* child. "Where's your brother?" Odo asked, suddenly worried.

"Down well," Dunwin said, pointing in the wrong direction.

Odo, ignoring the pointing finger, turned in the direction of the well. "Again?" he asked wearily.

"*Stinky* well," Dunwin amended.

Odo blinked.

"Hello, Daddy Odo," Wulfrith's voice called cheerfully from the cesspool.

Slowly, Odo turned back around to face the pit. A whiff of ordure reached him—Wulfrith was stirring up the normally quiescent contents of the cesspool. Odo winced.

Lowering a rope for the boy wouldn't work; he had tried that several times when one or the other of the boys tumbled down the well. A two-year-old boy did not hold on to a rope well enough to be hauled up, and certainly couldn't climb out by himself.

Odo would have to climb down into the cesspool and carry Wulfrith out.

The idea did not appeal to him.

It wasn't the smell, so much, he told himself. Then he stopped and reconsidered.

Well, yes, it *was* the smell, he had to admit. He wasn't a sissy like those Old Hydrangean noblemen, he didn't have any objection to honest lice or a little healthy dirt, but he took a bath every year whether he needed it or not, usually on Prunella's feast day just so he'd remember and not skip a year, and he just wasn't used to dealing with what you might call a really *serious* stench. If the milk went a little sour, or the eggs were bad, that wasn't much of anything; if a sheep puked on his boot he didn't hurry to wipe it off, and he had changed the boys' nappies without complaint—but those were just *little* stinks.

The concentrated reek in the cesspool was an entirely different matter.

It was, after all, where he dumped the sour milk and

the rotten eggs and the sheep puke and the contents of all those diapers—*all* of it.

The smell down there was a whole new class of stink. He *really* didn't want to climb down there.

He could hear Wulfrith splashing about happily.

He whacked Dunwin, on general principles, and went to fetch a rope—but after a moment's thought and another glance at Dunwin, he decided to make it *two* ropes.

The amazing thing, Odo thought sourly an hour later, was that Wulfrith had only managed to fall back twice on the way up. That, and that Dunwin hadn't untied himself yet by the time Odo and Wulfrith were safely back on solid and relatively clean ground.

He scrubbed vigorously at Wulfrith's ears.

"Hurts, Daddy Odo!" Wulfrith complained.

"Well, it's your own bloody doin'," Odo growled. "I'll be moving my own bath up more'n a month, too, thanks to you."

"I didn't do nuthin'!" Wulfrith protested.

Dunwin giggled, and Odo kicked at him—sideways, so it wouldn't have hurt much even if it had connected.

When all three of them had been thoroughly bathed—Dunwin was included in the interests of fairness—Odo discovered that the hut had acquired a sort of echo of the mind-boggling, hair-curling, nose-ravaging stink that had accompanied Wulfrith and himself up from the cesspool. The clothes the two had worn, which had already showed evidence of having survived several generations of constant use, were clearly beyond any hope of redemption.

Odo had never learned to sew. Since he had had two sets of perfectly good clothes handed down from his father, he had never seen any reason to; he had always just worn them in alternate years, and had always got by. If a tunic got a little stiff, he'd just stay out next time it rained and let the water soften it up a bit.

Until now. Now he was down to one set of clothes, the fresh ones he had put on after his bath.

It was time, Odo decided, to make a trip into town and

buy new clothes—and incidentally spend a night somewhere else while the hut aired out. It was a market day, and he could order a shirt or two.

And, he thought, looking down at his ruined tunic, just maybe . . .

Well, he was really not as young as he once was, and maybe he was a little old to be looking after *two* active young boys, all by himself.

He looked around his little home, at the pile of smashed crockery by the door of the hut, the lines of drying diapers, the shattered hayrack, the broken fences, the scattered hay and wool that was strewn everywhere. There was no sign of the cat or the sheep.

Maybe, Odo thought, keeping *both* of the boys was just the slightest little bit overambitious.

Wulfrith let out a shriek, and something fell with a crash. Dunwin giggled.

Odo nodded. Overambitious, definitely.

Wulfrith and Dunwin thought that the trek down the mountain to Stinkberry was a great adventure—until they had gone about two hundred yards, whereupon they took turns announcing, "I'm tired," and "When will we be there?" and "My feet hurt," and "I'm hungry!" and "I'm thirsty!" and "Are we there yet?"

Odo ignored them and trudged on.

Complaining and giggling, they followed until they didn't. When Odo no longer heard squeals and grumbling, he turned and found them both curled up asleep by the trail.

He paused, looking down at them. They looked so sweet lying there; Wulfrith's shirt had gotten bunched up, exposing his belly, and his diaper was loose, but he was blissfully unaware of it.

Odo almost felt guilty about what he planned.

Then Wulfrith pissed on Odo's foot, without waking, and Odo's incipient guilt was washed away. Grumbling, he stooped and hoisted the boys up, one on each shoulder, making sure their little nappies were back in place. Then he stumbled on down the mountain.

Chapter Six

It was midafternoon, and the bustle of business was beginning to slow, by the time Odo staggered into Stinkberry market. It was really amazing just how heavy two two-year-old boys could be when carried a couple of miles down a mountainside.

The weary shepherd made his way to the front of the village inn, and sank slowly onto the bench out front, moving very carefully so as not to wake the boys, now that his weight was off his tired feet.

Naturally, the minute Odo's backside touched wood, Wulfrith woke up and looked around.

"Ooooh!" he squealed, "I wanna pastie, Daddy Odo!"

Odo sighed, whereupon Dunwin awoke and added his voice to the demands for pastry, honeyclots, and other sweets. The old man released both boys, who promptly went scampering out into the market square, tripping several villagers.

Exhausted by his journey, Odo leaned back and closed his eyes.

Maybe, he thought, if he stayed very quiet, and if he was *very* lucky, if the gods did not merely smile upon him but grinned broadly, the twins wouldn't come back.

It was a lovely thought, and he fell asleep there on the bench, dreaming of his farm, of sheep and furniture that stayed where they were put, of entire nights of uninterrupted sleep, of meals that did not wind up spread all over the table and the surrounding floor—all things that he had had, less than three years before, and had given up for Ludmilla's sake.

He was awakened by a very deep voice that rumbled, "Are these yours?"

Startled, Odo opened rheumy eyes and looked up.

No one was there. He lowered his gaze, and found the source of the voice.

The speaker was scarcely five feet in height, but clearly had all the weight of a much taller man. He had a curiously uneven beard, long black hair, and a squirming bundle of arms, legs, fingers, and ears in each hand.

When the right-hand burden paused for a moment to shriek, "Daddy Odo!" Odo recognized it as Dunwin. And when the left-hand burden began crying, Odo recognized Wulfrith's distinctive wail.

"Are they yours?" the stranger repeated. His voice was really quite amazing, Odo thought.

"Well," he replied cautiously, "What if they are? I suppose I might could perhaps have seen one of them before."

The stranger was clearly not satisfied with this, but before he could object Odo added, "Have they broken anything?"

"Not of mine," the stranger said.

"Daddy Odo!" Dunwin screamed.

Odo sighed. "Hand him here, then," he said.

The stranger passed the squirming child over, and Odo dropped him on the bench; the abrupt impact knocked the breath out of him, and Dunwin sat still for a moment, perhaps the first time in six months he had managed that without being asleep.

"You should warn them," the stranger rumbled, "not to interfere in the affairs of wizards."

Odo blinked, then leaned forward and looked around.

There was Goody Blackerd with her pies, and old Punkler with his silly carvings that all looked like half-melted candles regardless of what they were intended to be, and all the usual Stinkberry folks—Odo knew only the very oldest by name, but most over the age of forty were at least vaguely familiar. He didn't see any wizards.

"Why, yes," he said, puzzled, "I do suppose that'll be good advice, someday."

"It's good advice *now,*" the stranger roared. His lack of height had obviously not affected the power of his voice.

Odo blinked again, idly picked a scavenging insect from his ear and flung it aside, and mulled this statement over for several seconds.

"Well," he agreed, "I'd suppose they might be encountering a wizard at any time, mightn't they, same as if one should always be on the lookout for lightning bolts when it's cloudy."

"They have *met* a wizard, shepherd!" the fat little man bellowed. He sounded rather like thunder himself, Odo noticed. Baffled, the shepherd looked around the square again, peering down the village's only street in case a wizard might be in sight somewhere.

"Where?" he asked.

The stranger huffed mightily, then proclaimed, in a voice that shook the shutters on the wall of the inn, "*I* am a wizard, you simpleton!"

Odo took immediate offense. "I'm not from Simpleton," he said, raising his nose. "I was born and raised right here in Stinkberry, or 'tleast only a mile or three yonder on the mountains." That defense of his origins made, he let the rest of the stranger's words sink in, and his jaw dropped.

Then it snapped shut, crushing an unusually ambitious flea.

"You're not a wizard," Odo said.

Wulfrith stopped squirming and stared at his adoptive father; Dunwin looked up in surprise.

"Yes, I am," the stranger said, taken aback.

"No, you aren't," Odo insisted.

"What do *you* know about it?" the stranger demanded.

"I know a bit 'bout them wizards," Odo said craftily. "And you ain't one."

"Oh, no?"

"No."

"Well, it just so happens that I *am* a wizard!"

Odo shook his head. "Nope. Can't be. If you're a wizard, what's your name, then?"

The stranger drew himself up to his full height. "Clootie," he said proudly.

"Now, see, that proves it," Odo said, waving a finger about. "Wizards don't any of them have good, sensible names like Clootie, they have silly show-offish names like Mandragoras the Haughty, or it might be Pendorigan the Fraudulent, or Tinwhistle the Morally Challenged." He sat back and smiled, certain that he had just won the argument.

"Not all of us," Clootie retorted. "*Some* of us don't care to advertise like that, especially not since the Gorgorians moved in and declared wizardry illegal."

Odo frowned. This stranger should have just agreed, and said, yes of course, ha ha, all a joke, I'm not a wizard, and here he was talking about the Gorgorians. "What's that got to do with your *name*?" he asked, puzzled. "I mean, you can't just go about changing your name same as it was an old shirt, or something; your name's your *name,* that you're born with."

"No, it isn't," Clootie said. "Clootie isn't my *real* name. Wizards *never* use their real names."

"They don't?" Odo blinked.

"No! A real name has power!"

"But that'd mean you'd have two names."

Clootie smiled. "That's right," he said.

Odo's mouth opened slightly, allowing an odor akin to rancid cheese to escape; Clootie's smile dimmed as the scent reached him.

"But that would mean," the shepherd said, picking a louse from his beard, "that you'd be havin' *two names.*"

"That's right," Clootie agreed, nodding.

"But how would you keep them *straight*?" Odo asked.

Clootie blinked, and lowered Wulfrith to the ground, whereupon the boy dashed over and threw both arms around Clootie's leg. Whether this was intended as an expression of affection or an assault was not clear, and Clootie did not worry about it; he was too busy fathoming the depths of Odo's ignorance and stupidity.

When he struck bottom, he leaned over and said quietly, "Magic."

Odo's eyes widened.

"Well, we're *wizards,* you see," Clootie said.

Odo's eyes narrowed again. "You're just trying to trick me somehow," he said. "You're not any wizard."

"Yes, I am."

"No, you'ren't. You're too short. And you don't have fancy robes or a pointy hat or a wand—no, that's fairies, innit? You don't have a stuff!"

"Staff," Clootie corrected.

"Right, you don't. No staff."

"I left it at home," Clootie said. "I'm in disguise."

Odo squinted at him. "What about the rest of it, then? The hat and the robes?"

"I'm wearing them," Clootie said.

Odo looked at the man's bare head and green woolen tunic.

"They're disguised, too," Clootie explained. "By magic."

"What about you're so short?" Odo demanded. "You can't disguise *that* by magic!"

Clootie was about to ask, "Why not?" when he caught himself. He doubted that any attempt at logic or reason would do any good; he needed something else. If this ancient shepherd didn't think magic could disguise a man's height . . .

"You're right," Clootie said, leaning over to whisper in Odo's ear. "You're very clever, noticing that. It's not magic at all. I'm wearing special shoes."

"Oh," Odo said. It all came clear. He nodded. "You're a wizard, all right, then."

"Right. And now that we've got that settled, will you

tell your boys to stay out of my cart? They could have caused some serious trouble."

Odo nodded. "Hear that, lads?" he said, glaring at Wulfrith. Dunwin was hiding under the bench, out of sight. Odo started to lean farther over, looking for Dunwin, and then changed his mind as an idea struck him. He straightened up.

Clootie was starting to turn away, and Odo called after him, "Wait a minute, there." The ancient shepherd started the task of getting to his feet.

Clootie turned back. "Yes?" he asked.

"You're a wizard, then?" Odo asked, as he achieved a reasonable degree of verticality, his feet under him and his back slowly straightening.

Clootie sighed. "We just . . . yes. I'm a wizard."

"Well, it's . . ." Odo hesitated, trying to think of the best way to begin. "Listen, I don't need both of these boys, in fact they're a little bit wearing, as you might say, for someone who's not as young as me, and tomorrow I won't be as young as I am now, d'you see."

The plump little wizard didn't bother to answer; he just continued to look Odo in the eye.

"So I'd been thinking," Odo said, "that maybe, seeing as how this is a market day and all, that maybe I could sell the one as that I'm not able to handle anymore, which would be Wulfrith, there." He pointed.

"What would *I* want with him?" Clootie asked, looking down at the child clutching his leg.

"Oh, well," Odo said, "everyone knows as you wizards like children, not perhaps so much as children themselves, you know, but as like, maybe, for other uses, which would not necessarily be anything unpleasant, of course, I mean you wouldn't want them for sacrifices and ingredients and furniture and suchlike, after they're enchanted, and so forth, nor either to cut open to see how they work and such, necessarily. Not for anything like that. Necessarily." He tried to look casual.

"Wizards don't do any of that," Clootie snapped.

"O' course they don't," Odo agreed.

"We don't sacrifice children."

"I'm sure you don't."

"We don't cut them up."

"No, no."

"We don't enchant them."

"I'm certain."

"I've never hurt a child in my life."

"Just what I'd have thought."

The two men stood face-to-face, Clootie glaring, Odo trying to look innocent and managing only to look even stupider than usual.

In point of fact, something resembling a moral struggle was going on in Odo's head. It had occurred to him, a little belatedly, that if he were Wulfrith, he would not particularly want to be sold to a wizard who might cut him apart, or might turn him into a newt or a bit of bric-a-brac, or might sacrifice him to some nasty old god those overeducated Old Hydrangean aristocrats had dug up somewhere—not the regular sort like Prunella or Korridge, that a man could understand, but one of the others that didn't bear a lot of thinking about for most folks. Odo had heard about a few of those fancy ones, such as Spug Pagganethaneth, the hermaphroditic deity of silver-plated utensils used in inappropriate ways.

Clootie looked like the sort of wizard who might well use silver-plated utensils in inappropriate ways.

But then, that was what wizards did, after all, it was in the job description as you might say, same as being a shepherd meant butchering a lamb sometimes, and wizards had to get their little boys somewhere, and if it wasn't Wulfrith it would be someone else, and Odo would still have Dunwin to keep him company, it wasn't like Wulfrith was the last one.

And really, sacrificing the boy to Spug Pagganethaneth was at least a worthwhile thing to do, wasn't it? It wasn't like this Clootie fellow was going to eat Wulfrith.

At least, Odo didn't think he was, though you could never be sure, with wizards.

And even if he was, was that so terrible? After all, Odo ate his own sheep, sometimes, and he had had them around longer than he had had Wulfrith, and the sheep were better behaved, too. That was just what shepherds did.

Among other things. And thinking about it, some of what he did with his sheep wasn't much nicer than what this wizard would probably do to Wulfrith.

It was just a rotten old world.

As he glared at the shepherd, Clootie, too, was thinking.

The old lies about wizards, originally spread by the wizards themselves to keep people from bothering them, were a constant nuisance in his life ever since that dreadful day, years before, when he had fled the royal palace mere hours before the Gorgorians rode in.

There were those who claimed that the wizards who had fled were cowards, but Clootie preferred to think of himself as a sentimentalist; he had a long-standing attachment to his head, was, in fact, thoroughly fond of it, and he much preferred to keep it where it was, right there on his shoulders. The Gorgorians, even at that early stage of the invasion and occupation, were widely known to be much given to the rearrangement of wizardly anatomy, in particular the removing of heads.

And it wasn't as if any of the wizards' spells could have done any good against the Gorgorians. The wizards of Old Hydrangea had raised magic from a mere tool to a fine art, an esoteric study worthy of the finest scholars in a highly refined nation. That the result was of absolutely no conceivable use to anyone had been considered a great achievement—wizardry was all the purer for having no possible application to mundane existence.

The Gorgorians apparently hadn't cared for it, all the same.

"Critics," Clootie sniffed to himself. "They never appreciate true artistry."

The wizards of Old Hydrangea could show a Gorgorian a dozen colors that had never existed in nature, or cause airy spirits to debate the purpose of moonlight; their magic could not harm a single flea on the Gorgorians' heads, however, nor turn away a single Gorgorian blade.

The Gorgorians had taken great pleasure in demonstrating this latter inability.

So Clootie had fled, and had taken up residence in a convenient cave not far from Stinkberry village, where he had continued his study of magic, but with rather a different slant on it.

"If they want practical spells," he had muttered to himself many a time, "I'll *give* them practical spells."

So he had been studying and practicing, trying to re-create the cruder, less artistic, but more effective magic of a bygone day, and he had, in fact, met with some success. He was rediscovering old spells every day—well, almost every day . . .

All right, every month or two he came up with another one. If he was lucky.

He intended to put these spells to work on behalf of the Old Hydrangeans, just as soon as the people rose up against their Gorgorian overlords. Everyone knew that the rebellion would come soon, led by exiled aristocrats and patriotic bandits and all the other traditional heroic types, and one name in particular always came up; accordingly, Clootie waited eagerly for word of the Black Weasel's promised ride down from the mountains, to rally the populace and march on the Palace of Divinely Tranquil Thoughts, where they would depose and slay the despised King Gudge.

The Black Weasel, however, seemed to be taking an unconscionably long time about it.

And in the meantime, Clootie found himself living in a cave, hardly a suitable environment for a civilized person, and buying his food and other necessities from the ill-educated and ill-smelling inhabitants of the aptly named Stinkberry village, all of whom were convinced that the old wizardly lies about turning people into hedgehogs or feeding them to demons were the literal truth.

It did get rather lonely at times, and a boy might be useful about the place, fetching this or that, holding the light, that sort of thing.

"So," Odo asked at last, "d'ye want him?"

Clootie looked down at Wulfrith, who was trying to stuff a wiggling spider down Odo's boot top.

"How much are you asking?" the wizard said.

Half an hour later, Odo and Dunwin were on their way back up the mountain; Wulfrith, on the other hand, was accompanying Clootie back to his cave, somewhere on the other side of Stinkberry village.

Dunwin was rather upset by this sudden separation from his brother, but a few polite little kicks got him to quiet down about it, and he and Odo trudged up the slope together.

"Daddy Odo?" Dunwin asked, taking a final look back at the quiet hamlet below.

"Whut?" Odo answered.

"Want Wulfie."

Odo stopped and glared down at the boy. "Now, you stop that," he said. "We sold your brother fair and square. It's not like the wizard is about to eat him."

Dunwin pouted briefly, then thought better of it—he found it harder to dodge a descending fist while maintaining a good pout. He ran on ahead, up the path.

"At least," Odo muttered to himself, "I don't *think* he'll eat him."

Chapter Seven

The popular image of a wizard's cave in Hydrangea was not a pleasant one. It generally involved dripping stalactites and skeletons chained to the wall and spiders and bats and assorted less recognizable things, things that would bubble and squeak and slither. Neither a typical Hydrangean peasant nor the Gorgorian conquerers would be at all surprised to find a few odd body parts scattered about, in various states not merely of decomposition, but of animation. The Old Hydrangean aristocracy, which had had rather more contact with wizards than the other groups, tended to dismiss the idea of random corpses and extensive use of blood as a decorating motif; still, they, too, would expect bones, cobwebs, musty books, fancy ironmongery, and other mysterious objects.

Any of them—peasant, patrician, or plunderer—would have had trouble accepting Clootie's residence as typical.

Oh, the bones and books were there, all right—neatly put away in cabinets and bookcases of polished oak and beveled glass. The stalactites were there, too, but perfectly dry, and neatly broken off an even seven feet from the smooth stone floor. A few had then been pressed into service supporting chandeliers.

The walls and floor were also dry; Clootie had had his fill of noisome drips and general dankness within weeks of his arrival, and had made a waterproof sealing spell one of his highest priorities.

And because Clootie did not care to share his limited food supplies with uninvited guests, there were no spiders, snakes, or other cold-blooded inhabitants that were not safely dead and stored in alcohol.

At first, little Wulfrith found this lack of wildlife rather boring, and a clear contrast to his previous home in Odo's vermin-infested cottage, surrounded by Odo's livestock. Climbing on the overstuffed armchair was a poor substitute for harassing innocent sheep, as the armchair rarely protested and never ran away bleating; kicking the footstool with the elaborate needlepoint was much less satisfying than kicking poor Fang, as the footstool never made a sound, but simply ran and hid.

On the other hand, Clootie's furniture was less prone to break than Odo's, which meant it could be abused more extensively and more imaginatively. And the footstool didn't have claws or teeth.

Dunwin was not around, but Wulfrith, like any two-year-old, had not yet really learned to play *with* his brother, so the loss of his playmate was not all that devastating. And Clootie paid much more attention to him than Odo ever had.

What's more, there was Clootie's magic for entertainment. Once Clootie decided that Wulfrith had settled in sufficiently, he went back to his work, which the boy found endlessly fascinating. He would watch silently, hour after hour, as Clootie went about his elaborate conjurations, trying to find ways to shorten and simplify spells, or to turn them from esthetic exercises or demonstrations of philosophical concepts into practical tools.

Fairly quickly, Wulfrith began imitating his new master—for Clootie did not allow the boy to call him "Daddy," but instead treated him as an unusually young apprentice. Clootie encouraged this aping of spells, and even gave a few lectures on basic sorcery, quite sure that so young a child could not possibly understand a word of it. The wizard found it highly amusing to watch as this tiny creature, who could barely run across the room without falling, waved a stick about and babbled rough approximations of incantations. Clootie would sit in his armchair, smiling into his beard, as Wulfrith earnestly went through the motions of spell after spell.

It was on a day some six months after Wulfrith's arrival, as an early snow swirled outside the cave's mouth, that Clootie's smile abruptly vanished. He sat up straight.

His smile was not all that had vanished; so had an endtable.

"How did you do that?" Clootie demanded.

Wulfrith turned, startled. "Like you," he said. He held up a large flopping carp.

"You turned the table into a fish?"

Wulfrith blinked. "Yes, master," he said.

"Turn it back," Clootie snapped. "At once." He watched intently as the boy dropped the fish, hunched his shoulders, gathered himself together, and began a new chant. The wizard frowned. He hunched slightly himself.

He didn't know how to turn an endtable into a big goldfish, he thought worriedly; how in the name of the Seven Lesser Amorous Demons had Wulfrith done it? Not only had the boy worked *real magic* at the age of three, he had apparently gotten the result he wanted! Clootie had known master wizards with centuries of practice who couldn't always get the result they wanted twice running.

Those same masters had been decapitated and burnt for lack of reliable and useful spells. If they had been able to turn the Gorgorians, or even just their horses or weapons, into carp, the kingdom would have been a very different place these past few years. Clootie leaned forward and watched closely.

Half an hour later Wulfrith burst into tears and flung his stick away. "It won't turn back!" he wailed, holding up the fish, which was now very dead indeed. No one had thought to put it in water.

Clootie hurried to his side and threw a comforting arm around the child. "There, there, Wulfie," he said, "it's all right. That's a very hard spell, almost a grown-up spell, and you're still young. You'll learn it eventually, I'm sure."

Wulfrith sniffled loudly. "*You* fix it," he said, handing Clootie the fish.

"Later," Clootie said, putting the dead carp aside. "Right now it's time for your nap."

"Okay," Wulfrith said, still miserable, but no longer actually weeping.

"You know, even if you couldn't turn it back, you did a good job turning it into a fish at all," Clootie said comfortingly. "Why, that's at *least* a spell for five-year-olds, and you're not even four yet! Not even three and a half!"

"It *is?*" The tears stopped, and the uneasy frown turned into a gape of surprise.

"Yes," Clootie said, nodding, "really!"

"Wow," Wulfrith said quietly, impressed with himself.

The boy went happily off to bed, under Clootie's watchful eye; the minute he was certain that the child was really asleep, the wizard turned and dashed back to the shelf where he had placed the fish. He pulled it out and looked at it.

"He turned it into a *fish,*" he said wonderingly.

A three-year-old who could turn furniture into an aquatic life-form was a rare and precious resource. True, there wasn't all that much demand for seafood here in the mountains, and a good piece of carpentry generally cost more than a carp, but if the boy could do that, what else might he be able to do?

No one had ever before tried teaching sorcery to so young a child, and it suddenly occurred to Clootie that perhaps this was a mistake. Perhaps the talent for magic was *stronger* in the very young, like the talent for learning languages. It might just be because of his age that Wulfrith was able to learn how to work such a miracle.

But then, how many children that age would be able to concentrate on one thing that long at all?

Wulfrith was clearly exceptional. If he had grown up and been apprenticed in the normal way, he might not have been anything out of the ordinary, and he would hardly have discovered magic on his own; still, here he was.

That was absolutely wonderful.

It was also rather terrifying. Three- and four-year-old children can throw tantrums, and the idea of a magical tantrum was not one Clootie cared to consider. And that was not even mentioning what might happen around age twelve or thirteen.

And if the boy realized he was gifted and became a spoiled brat, the inevitable tantrums would be far worse.

Clootie decided that he would have to be very careful never to let the boy know just how special he was.

And that meant he would have to hide this dead fish and get a replacement endtable, so that Wulfrith would never know that Clootie couldn't turn it back, either.

The boy's ability would be kept secret, but at the same time, such a talent wasn't to be wasted. Clootie would start teaching Wulfrith some spells, and . . .

A grin spread across the wizard's face.

. . . And he would suggest that the boy invent a few of his own. After all, wasn't that the best way to learn?

And Wulfrith would probably never realize that Clootie would be learning those spells from *him*. He would never know how good he was.

That was perfect.

When Wulfrith woke up the fish was gone; three days later the endtable was back.

And three days after that, Clootie began to teach Wulfrith magic.

"Nothing very serious," he said. "We'll start with the easy stuff."

Clootie had intended, when he bought Wulfrith, to have the boy do various chores around the cave when he was old enough. He never did get much manual labor out of the child, however. By the time Wulfrith could hold the broom upright and sweep, he could also animate the broom to do its own sweeping—though it had a distressing tendency to sweep things under the rug, rather than out the mouth of the cave where they belonged. At age seven, when Clootie had intended to have the boy take over washing the dishes, Wulfrith chained a water elemental to the sink and taught *that* to wash dishes.

It took him four days and cost half a dozen pieces of Clootie's best china, however, in addition to the six hours he had needed to conjure the thing up in the first place.

"That's all right," Clootie said, when he saw Wulfrith's distress. "Water elementals are tricky things." He did not mention that no one else had ever kept one confined for more than three or four hours, or taught it to do anything more complex than drowning a wizard's mother-in-law.

Clootie watched the elemental as it scrubbed vigorously at a platter, spattering fat drops in all directions. The boy intended to keep it in the cistern above the sink, and the idea of having an angry water elemental so close at hand made Clootie slightly uneasy—but he could hardly admit *that* to the child, not if he wanted to keep the boy's respect.

A water elemental could probably be very useful against the Gorgorians—if anybody ever got around to fighting them again. Stories of the Black Weasel and his Bold Bush-dwellers still circulated in the valleys and villages as much as they ever had, but nobody ever seemed to mention any plans for doing more than waylaying and murdering any Gorgorians stupid enough to venture into the eastern mountains.

In fact, it rather seemed to Clootie that people were becoming accustomed to the Gorgorians.

Besides, he couldn't very well ask a seven-year-old boy to go out there and fight for the rightful ruler of Hydrangea; the boy hadn't even been born when the Gorgorians came, and nobody seemed entirely sure anymore just who the rightful ruler *was*. Prince Mimulus seemed to have vanished and might be dead, Princess Artemisia was the Gorgorians' queen . . .

It would clearly be simpler to stick to washing the dishes, and let Hydrangea take care of itself.

Chapter Eight

Queen Artemisia sat before her mirror and considered the tale it told. In the fourteen years since Prince Arbol's birth she had not acquired so much as a wrinkle or a gray hair.

As a happenstance, that would be wonderful enough in and of itself for any mother, but taking into account the constant, unremitting, merciless stress under which she lived each day, it was a miracle.

"I just don't know how I do it, Mungli," she told her lady-in-waiting. "It's not the easiest task in the world raising a child, let alone a royal one *and* the heir to the Gorgorian Empire to boot, but if you only knew the real story about Prince Arbol, it would take your breath away."

"Gkkh," said Mungli, running an ivory-backed brush through the queen's blond hair.

That was about as much of an answer as Artemisia was going to get from Mungli, now or ever, on this subject or any other. The queen's chosen lady-in-waiting was a Gorgorian wench who had gotten into a slight disagreement with her lover's senior wife; Mungli had always been one to speak her mind, and it was a very creative mind, particularly when it came to dreaming up synonyms for *old, ugly,* and *possessing the sexual attraction of silt.* The wife was one of those Gorgorian women who cultivated the magical arts, one, in fact, who had developed them to an exceptional level, and who thought it appropriate to teach the upstart trollop a lesson about keeping a civil tongue in one's head. She did this by magically removing Mungli's tongue almost entirely.

This was rather more magic than Gorgorian women were supposed to have, certainly more than they commonly used, but these were not common circumstances; most comely young Gorgorians knew better than to argue with their magically-gifted elders.

Still, while it wasn't a very nice spell, it *was* reversible—sort of a sorcerous warning shot across the bows, intended more to instruct than to punish.

Or rather, it *would* have been reversible if the Gorgorian lord over whom the ladies tussled had not come in just then, noted his senior wife's use of excessive and potentially dangerous magic, decided that if he did not do something to indicate his displeasure she might next use her powers on him, and very prudently lopped her head off.

There was general rejoicing in the harem tent and a flurry of in-house promotions all around, but poor Mungli was left out of the fun, high and dry, permanently silenced—if any of the other Gorgorian women had the ability to restore her tongue, they weren't admitting it. And although most men joked about the advantages of having a silent wife, no one seemed eager to acquire one who lacked a tongue.

It was a fortunate day for Mungli when news of her predicament reached the queen's ears and she was summoned into the royal service. With Ludmilla gone, Artemisia longed desperately for someone in whom to confide. Not confide *everything,* you understand, just bits and pieces that might casually drop into the conversation. It was such a relief finally to have someone about the queen's apartments before whom she could speak freely, without weighing every word! And, like most Gorgorians, Mungli was illiterate, so the danger of the girl writing down anything she might learn was nil.

"All those years, all those years . . . ," Artemisia mused, tilting her head to one side in a fetching manner. "I don't know how I could have managed if not for you."

"Hnng," Mungli agreed.

"Speaking of which, do be a dear and bring me my tea, won't you?" the queen requested.

Dutifully Mungli trotted off to the sideboard where a silver teapot was bubbling over a spirit-flame. To the boiling water she added three pinches of a dried herb mixture which she carried in a tiny, carefully sealed casket around her neck. When the brew had steeped to her satisfaction, she poured off two cups and brought them to the queen. Together the ladies sipped their tea.

Artemisia smacked her lips. "Hmmm, tastes delightful," she remarked. "But I'd drink it even if it tasted like stewed mule's hocks, just to be sure I never again have to bear Gudge another child! Three—I mean *he* is quite enough. He being Prince Arbol. Of course. Ah, ha, ha, ha."

"Anh, anh, anh," Mungli laughed. She patted her own flat belly smugly, a testimony to the powers of the contraceptive tea.

The queen set aside her empty cup. "Are you sure, dear Mungli, that there is no similar tisane known to the women of your tribe that is capable of, uhhh, preventing a young girl from, mmmm, ever embarking upon that stage of life where *this* tea is necessary?"

Mungli stared at the queen, then made the Gorgorian sign meaning someone did not have all his oxen in the corral.

"No, of course not." Artemisia was downcast. "It's quite natural for a woman to want to save herself from too many childbirths, but why would any sane person want to keep a girl from becoming a woman? Well, never mind."

Mungli cocked her head at the queen and made soft, inquiring noises in her throat. She was more than fond of her royal mistress, for if not for Artemisia she would have either starved in the streets or been shipped to one of the most distant Gorgorian outposts, where the men were men and the mares were skittish. She would do anything she could to relieve the queen's distress, but Artemisia waved her off.

"There's nothing for it but to trust to luck. And we have

been pretty lucky so far. Blood will tell. I recall one of my governesses telling another that I was an especially late bloomer, and the other replying that it was because I was such a hoyden, running and riding and sneaking off to take exercise with my brother Mimulus and his companion, dear Lord Tadwyl. 'If she keeps up such antics,' Lady Dromedri said, 'she'll never get Vimple's Blessing.' " The queen made a wry face. "Well, I finally *did* get blessed by good old Vimple, Goddess of Alarums, Diversions, and Minor Shocks to the System, so all those athletics couldn't keep it away forever. Oh, how I wish they could!"

Mungli was about to utter a fresh string of questioning noises when there came a tremendous clash and clatter from the stairway without the queen's apartments. Artemisia heard one of her Gorgorian guards bawl, "Halt! Who goes . . . ? Aiiieee!" and a punctuating crash at the end followed by the second guard's sheepish, "Oh, it's you, Prince Arbol. Go right on in, Your Highness."

"You bet I will!" came the gaily shouted response. The door to the queen's apartments boomed as a booted foot assaulted the delicate woodwork. Three hearty stomps and the portal flew wide. Hands on hips, resplendent in the full barbaric glory of Royal Gorgorian battle dress, Prince Arbol did not so much enter the queen's chamber as conquer it.

"Hello, Mom!" the prince said, grinning broadly. "Sorry I had to throw another of your guards down the stairs, but he was stupid."

"Dear heart, they're Gorgorians; stupid is what they do best," the queen chided gently. "It's not the guards I mind so much as the doors. Doors cost money. Hasn't your Deportment tutor been able to teach you anything about knocking?"

"He tried, but it sounded stupid, so I threw him down the stairs, too. It's all right, Mom; he landed on a guard."

"Oh, you naughty boy." Artemisia could not quite hide a proud smile. She stretched out her hands to the prince. "Now come here and let me look at you."

Prince Arbol did as bidden. From head to foot, the

young royal was all any Gorgorian monarch could desire in an heir. Well grown in height, broad in the chest, legs powerfully muscled and slightly bowed by long hours in the saddle, arms able to wield a handy assortment of small- to medium-sized weapons with grace, skill, and bloodlust, the prince was one of a kind.

Indeed.

Queen Artemisia attempted to remove Arbol's helmet and ruffle her child's curly black hair, but the prince was having none of it. "Aw, Mommmm! Come on, don't do that. If any of my Companions found out, they'd tease the breeches off me and then I'd have to kill them and half of the bastards owe me money!"

"Arbol, *really*!" The queen was shocked. "Such language. Have I taught you nothing? When you leave my chambers do you revert to being a . . . a . . . *Gorgorian*?"

The prince was nonplussed. "But I *am* a Gorgorian."

"And an Old Hydrangean, too! Never forget that."

Arbol looked down and scuffed a battered riding boot over the queen's best carpet. " 'Kay," came the sullen mutter.

"I suppose you came here to do more than sulk," the queen said drily.

The prince's head came up, all mopes burned away in the glory of a brilliant smile. "Oh, yes! I almost forgot, and it's the best news I ever heard in my entire life!"

"Your father's dead?" the queen asked eagerly.

Arbol made the your-oxen-have-escaped sign at her, then said, "No, I finally managed to wound my Dirty Combat tutor. Not mortally or anything, just your basic hamstringing and some superficial abdominal slashes, but I did him good enough for Dad to say it was about time I moved out of the schoolroom and into the world."

The queen felt her fingers knotting in on themselves. "What?" she rasped.

"He's taking me with him on campaign, Mom!" the prince exclaimed, nearly bouncing out of her riding boots.

"We leave tomorrow to ravage the western flank of the Hypoglycemian Republic. Isn't that *swell*?"

"Mungli," said the queen, "leave us."

No sooner had Artemisia's mute lady-in-waiting departed than the queen seized Prince Arbol by the wrist and dragged her disguised daughter over to the windowseat. There was a special significance attached to all conversations that took place in this stony niche whose lack of cushions guaranteed the undivided attention of the participants. It was in this niche that Queen Artemisia had told Prince Arbol about the debt of honor and blood they both owed to dear, departed, decapitated da/grandda, King Fumitory the Twenty-Second. It was here that she had instructed the prince in the holy obligation of all high-born Old Hydrangean children to never, ever, under any circumstances allow themselves to be seen naked by anyone save their mothers, lest a plague of newts occur.

It was here, now, that she said, "Darling, you can't go."

"Aw, Mommmmm!" The prince drummed her heels petulantly against the stonework. "Why not? Everybody else is going! All my Companions are going! If I don't go they're gonna tease me and then I'll have to . . ."

"Young man, if you kill anyone without my express permission, you're going to be spanked."

The prince said nothing to this, but Artemisia noticed a cold, hard gleam in her eye that as much as said *You and whose army?* The queen cleared her throat and decided to use reason.

"My love, a military campaign is not . . . is not the most *refined* of milieus. The soldiers must perforce share all things among them. There is little or no privacy, even for men of the highest rank. And of course, the higher the rank, the greater the obligation upon us to keep ourselves splendidly isolated, lest the full glory of our inborn nobility dazzle and blind less exalted folk."

"Dad says that's a load of horseflop," said the prince.

The queen kept her thoughts on the Gudge/horseflop

equations to herself. "It is royal Hydrangean *tradition,*" she gritted. "Don't you recall the happy days of your infancy when you and I remained gorgeously secluded from a vulgar and obstreperous world?"

"Yeah," said the prince. "It was boring."

Queen Artemisia counted to ten and tried another tack. "Precious, unless you are eager to find newts in your pudding, you can*not* place your modesty at risk. Surely you must recall the sacred obligation you have to keep your nakedness from all eyes save my own?"

"I guess so," the prince replied. "But—but that's just for *children*! You said so yourself. You told me that someday I wouldn't have to bother with that any more. Well, I'm not a child now. When a Gorgorian boy goes out to his first battle, they count him as a man."

The queen laced her slim fingers together and took a deep breath. "Arbol, my son, you speak the truth. By the degenerate laws and customs of your spittle-flecked father's people, you are truly a man. Yet by the infinitely superior traditions and immemorial usages of the Old Hydrangeans, know that with this manhood come further sacred obligations."

Arbol groaned. "I don't have to take a *bath* again, do I?" Arbol was not at all fond of baths, a sentiment perhaps the result of repeated childhood memories of the queen whisking her out of the tub and into a smothering towel with startling violence every time there was the slightest sound outside the royal door.

"My son, ask rather when you will next be privileged enough to have a bath," the queen intoned. "You see, the chief obligation of a Hydrangean prince is to be kind, courteous, considerate, thoughtful, and above all things to spare his subjects any embarrassment, humiliation, or chagrin."

"What's that got to do with . . . ?"

The queen held up a silencing hand. "Some years since, noble son, while you were still too young to be aware of the tragedy, a fearsome plague swept through our realm."

"Newts?"

"No, not newts. Newts would have been all right, but this . . . ! This terrible pestilence afflicted only males, and those so stricken were . . . were . . . Oh, can I bear to say it? They were most hideously—*deformed*!"

"Wow!" Prince Arbol was all ears, though she did not look properly aghast. "How deformed were they? Capsilac, my shieldbearer, showed me a two-headed hedgehog last week, but if this is better and I can tell him about it so he throws up . . ."

"Growths," Artemisia pronounced. "They got growths."

"Huh?"

"Right there." She pointed at the place where Arbol wore a specially molded piece of armor whose usefulness the young prince had often questioned to herself. The queen went on to describe the hideous growths which were the shame of so many of her male subjects.

Arbol shuddered. "That sounds . . . ugh. But Mom, is . . . is *Dad* afflicted, too?"

The queen nodded. "Why do you think I spend so much time avoiding him? Oh, it's not a pretty sight, and I want to do my best to spare him the shame of having his deformity exposed to ridicule. My boy, you are truly blessed to be one of the few men left in all Hydrangea whose generative organs are . . . normal. Think, now! If you go on campaign and heedlessly answer the call of nature in company with some soldier who was not so lucky, how do you think he will feel, beholding your good fortune and comparing it to . . . to . . . ?" She conjured up a convincing sob and threw her arms around Prince Arbol's neck.

"Swear to me, my boy!" she cried. "Promise me on the honor of Hydrangea that if you go on campaign with your father, you will do everything in your power and more to keep your body from the sight of other men. Swear this, lest you cause pain to the innocent and shame to the blameless!"

Half-smothered against her mother's shoulder, Prince Arbol said, "I mfwear."

"I accept your word, my dearest." The queen released her with a motherly kiss on the cheek. "Now go have a nice time at the war." Prince Arbol started from the room, had a second thought, dashed back to give her mother a hearty hug, and bounded off.

The queen sank back against the windowseat, exhausted. "Mungli! Mungli, come here!" The mute Gorgorian was there before her mistress had pronounced her name twice. "Mungli, writing paper!"

Mungli watched with interest as her mistress scribbled a message. From time to time the queen muttered as she wrote, or read it over aloud. Those were the moments Mungli lived for. The mute had a theory which related the queen's words to the queen's marks on paper. She was not yet certain about the details of the connection, but she was positive that here was something very, very important and deserving of further study.

When Artemisia was through with her letter, she sent Mungli to fetch a messenger. Fourteen years' practice had taught her how to build up a small, efficient, elite group of couriers whom she could trust to carry correspondence to and from her brother's forest lair. It was quite simple, really: She invited them to her apartments for tea, slipped a Gorgorian aphrodisiac into their cups, made Mungli . . . *available* to them, then told them they could have some more every time they completed a successful mission to the Black Weasel's headquarters.

The missions were growing more and more frequent, of late. The nearer Prince Arbol crept up on womanhood, the better a life in the merry greenwood was beginning to sound to Artemisia.

"If only there were another way," the queen mused as she gazed down from her window and watched her latest courier spur his steed from the palace courtyard. "It's not so much that I mind the thought of living in a forest, but it's just so—so—*arboreal*!"

With a fastidious little shiver, she rose and called for her cloak. There were one hundred seventy-two shrines and temples of gods and goddesses, Hydrangean and Gorgorian, within walking distance of the palace. Lately it had become Queen Artemisia's daily obsession to patronize every single one.

Better to hedge your bets, she reasoned, *than to spend the rest of your days bedding in hedges.*

Chapter Nine

The skies were gray, the grasses brown, the trail rocky beneath his feet, and Dunwin whistled merrily as he walked down the mountain. It was such a beautiful day—but then, *every* day was beautiful here.

Beside him, Bernice frolicked along—or at any rate, she accompanied him as far as the pasture gate, and if she was not precisely frolicking, she at least came along willingly. Dunwin told himself that his dearly beloved pet and constant companion would have come with him even if he had not been holding out a handful of sugar, and, he assured himself, he was so confident of this that he did not bother to test his assumption.

And maybe *frolicking* wasn't the right word—after all, Bernice was no spring lamb any more—but there seemed to be a little bounce to her stride, as if she, too, were feeling good about life.

Old Odo would probably have said she was just hurrying to catch up and get the sugar, and might have made some remarks about how Bernice walked strangely because she was limping after Dunwin had played a little too roughly with her, but Dunwin was not troubled by any such cynicism.

At the fence he stepped up on the rail, and his beloved ewe bleated in dismay.

"I'm sorry, Bernice," he said, "but you can't come with me. Stinkberry village isn't *safe* for a girl like you!"

She bleated again, more loudly.

"No, really," he said. "But here, maybe this will cheer you up until I get back." He held out the sugar.

She quickly licked it from his palm, her tongue moving so rapidly that some of the brown powder spilled onto the grass.

Dunwin's heart swelled with joy at the sight of his beloved Bernice licking his hand so enthusiastically. "Some might say it's the sugar," he said, "but I know it's because you love me, Bernice!"

Bernice bleated and began nosing in the grass for the spilled sweetening.

"Well, I'll be back for supper," Dunwin said, as he clambered over the fence. "You just wait for me, okay?"

Bernice didn't bother to look up, but Dunwin didn't let that trouble him. He waved a cheerful farewell and continued down the slope. A dozen paces from the fence he was whistling again.

Life was good.

The day was cool, but it wasn't raining at the moment. The path was smooth enough that he could hardly feel any rocks through his worn boots. He was on his way to Stinkberry village to buy another dozen candles, and three whole coppers were clinking in his pocket.

And at home he had the sheep to keep his company, and Daddy Odo was getting too old to beat him more than once or twice a day—what more could a lad ask?

There was no doubt at all in Dunwin's mind—he had the best life in the world. Prince Arbol himself couldn't have a better time, living in the Palace of the Ox—as the Gorgorians called it; the old fogies of Stinkberry village still called it the Palace of Divinely Tranquil Thoughts, but Dunwin preferred the Gorgorian version—because it was shorter, and because he knew exactly what an ox was, while the word "tranquil" still puzzled him.

Odo didn't have much use for Gorgorians—but then, Odo didn't have much use for anybody except the sheep. Dunwin tried to keep an open mind on political subjects, and so far, he had generally succeeded in keeping it so open that no political opinion lingered more than a few seconds before falling out. He thought it might be nice to see a real palace sometime, even though he wasn't terribly clear on just what one was, and that was about as far as his opinions went.

He had a vague idea that a palace had something to do with fancy embroidery, but he didn't quite see how anyone could live in a piece of embroidery unless it was a sort of tent.

Whatever a palace might be, Dunwin was sure it couldn't be as pleasant to live in as Odo's hut, where the roof hardly ever leaked, and the floor didn't have any rocks in it, and the cesspool was downwind.

He was pretty sure there weren't any sheep in the palace, and as far as he was concerned that made it an inferior sort of dwelling. No one like his Bernice?

He was still trying to imagine why anyone would choose to live somewhere with no sheep when he reached the village.

"Hello, mister, would you . . . oh, it's you," someone said. Dunwin blinked, and for the first time noticed Hildie leaning against the wall of the baker's shop.

"Hello, Hildie," he said. Her blouse had an awfully low neckline, he noticed; he supposed it saved fabric, but he wondered whether she got cold.

"Hello, Dunwin," she replied, tilting her head and fluttering her eyelashes at him. Her skirt had got hitched up on one leg somehow.

"What're you doing?" Dunwin asked.

"Oh, nothing much, just waiting for some nice young fella to happen along who'd be interested in a good time."

Dunwin looked around. There were four old men sitting on the bench in front of the inn, arguing about something, and Greta the butcher's wife was hanging out laundry, but no one else was in sight.

"I'll let you know if I see one," Dunwin said. "Right now I gotta buy some candles."

Hildie sighed. "Aren't you *ever* going to grow up, Dunwin?" she asked.

"I'm pretty grown up," he said, a bit hurt. "Odo trusts me to come down here by myself, doesn't he? And I'm bigger than half the men in the village!"

"Well, you're taller and broader, anyway," Hildie admitted, "but I don't know about *bigger.*"

Dunwin squinted, trying to puzzle out what she was talking about, but she waved him away. "Forget it," she said. "Go buy your candles."

"All right." He walked on down the village's only street, wondering what Hildie had been talking about. If he was taller than the other men, and broader in the shoulders, then in what way wasn't he bigger?

Sometimes he wondered about Hildie. She didn't seem to work in any of the shops, she didn't keep any livestock, whenever he saw her she was just hanging around the village, but she always had a little money. Not enough for warm clothes, to all appearances, but she never seemed to go hungry.

She was a pretty girl, he thought; sometimes, especially in the past month or so, he'd thought she was even as pretty as a sheep. He had had a few odd dreams about her, too.

He wondered what she had meant about growing up.

He could hear the men in front of the inn arguing.

". . . Wasn't like that," old Fernand was saying. "Not like that 'tall!"

"Was, too," Taddeus snapped. "They tortured old King Fumitory for six full months before he died, and he laughed in their faces the whole time!"

"Couldn't have laughed for six months," Arminter objected. "His voice'd have give out."

"Well, it did," Taddeus said, "so he just laughed in whispers, like!"

Dunwin stopped to listen. He had learned most of what he knew of history, geography, and politics by listening to these four, who were regulars here.

"King Gudge just whacked off his head," Fernand insisted. "He didn't torture him for any six months!"

"Yes, he did," Taddeus asserted. "An' old Fumitory laughed."

"Six months? Laughing?" Berisarius inquired doubtfully.

"Well, maybe not laughing *all* the time," Taddeus admitted. "A man's got to sleep, after all, and I don't suppose even old Fumitory would laugh *all* the time."

" 'Specially not with the wolverines," Arminter said.

"Right, not at the wolverines," Taddeus admitted. "You don't laugh at wolverines because it just makes 'em mad. Wouldn't be no *point* to it, like."

"Took 'is head off with a sword, is all," Fernand declared. "There weren't any bloody wolverines involved."

"Tortured for six months and laughed at 'em," Taddeus retorted. " 'Cept during the part with the wolverines."

"Whacked his head off and made himself king, then bedded the old king's daughter, is what Gudge did," Fernand insisted. "He didn't torture them any."

"Well," Berisarius suggested, "you might could say that we don't rightly know what he's done to poor Queen Artemisia. Could be he did torture her a little."

"That'd be natural enough," Arminter agreed, "a man torturing his own wife."

"I 'spect it happens all the time," Taddeus agreed, "among them what can afford that sort of thing and not have to worry about whether the house is goin' to be cleaned and the supper cooked."

"Ha," Fernand said. "And I suppose you lot would all torture your wives if you had the chance?"

" 'Course not," Berisarius said, offended. "We're not a bunch of Gorgorian barbarians!" He looked to the others for support.

There was a moment of sheepish silence.

"Well, I wouldn't go whacking off her father's head," Taddeus said.

"But Gudge didn't," Arminter protested. "You said he tortured the old king for six months!"

"Right, he did," Taddeus said. "You've got me all mixed up. He tortured Fumitory for six months, and *then* he whacked off his head!"

"What, someone whacked off Gudge's head?"

"No, no, Gudge whacked off Fumitory's head!"

"That isn't what you said before."

"Yes, it is."

Dunwin was beginning to lose the thread of the conversation.

"He whacked off Gudge's head and married Artemisia, then?"

"So he could torture his wife."

"Who'd Fumitory marry, a lady torturer?"

"Well, he didn't marry Artemisia—she's his daughter!"

"She is?"

"Right, that's why Gudge whacked Fumitory's head off, so he could marry Artemisia."

"Is that what you said before?"

"When?"

"About your wife?"

"But what about the torture?"

"What torture? I'm not even married!"

Dunwin, now totally lost, decided he had heard enough for today, and went past the four and into the inn's diminutive taproom. Stinkberry village was too small for a separate candlemaker's shop; Armetta, the innkeeper's wife, made candles in her husband's stewpot when no stew was cooking, and sold them out of the kitchen.

A man, a stranger, was seated at one of the three big tables; Dunwin nodded a polite, wordless greeting and looked for Armetta.

At that moment she emerged from the kitchen carrying a pitcher of ale in one hand, a mug in the other. She set both down in front of the stranger and wiped her hands on her apron. "It's our best," she said. "My husband's the finest brewer in the mountains!" She smiled broadly.

Of course, Armetta did *everything* broadly.

Dunwin waved to her. "Hello," he said. "Odo sent me down for candles."

Armetta looked up, startled; the stranger paused in the midst of pouring ale from pitcher to mug, and he, too, turned to look at Dunwin.

He blinked, and stared, almost spilling the pitcher.

"Candles?" Armetta frowned.

"Right, a dozen candles," Dunwin said.

"That'll be two coppers."

"I'll pay three," Dunwin replied, dimly aware that dickering was expected.

Armetta snorted. "Done," she said. She held out a hand, and Dunwin dropped the coins into her palm.

"I'll get them," she said, and turned away.

As Armetta waddled toward the kitchen the stranger stared up at Dunwin, who nervously pretended not to notice this unexpected and unwanted attention. When the woman vanished through the door, the man said, "Sit down, lad."

Startled, Dunwin hesitated.

"Sit," the man repeated, pointing to the chair opposite him.

Slowly, Dunwin sat.

"What's your name, boy?"

"Dunwin."

The stranger frowned. "Is that a Hydrangean name, or a Gorgorian one?"

"I don't know," Dunwin admitted. "It's mine, that's all I know." As the stranger continued to stare, Dunwin asked, "What's *your* name?"

"Oh, they call me Phrenk," the man said.

"Is that a Hydrangean name?"

"Yes," the stranger replied sharply.

Dunwin realized from the other's manner that he had said something wrong, had somehow given offense, and needed to recover somehow. An apology would be excessive, he knew, but he had to say something.

"Oh," he said.

The stranger was staring at him again, and it was beginning to make Dunwin uncomfortable.

"So," he said desperately, "are you from around here?"

"No," the man called Phrenk said. "Are you?"

"From around here?" Dunwin said. "Well, yeah, I am."

"I wondered," the stranger said. "You look just like someone I know."

"I do?"

Phrenk nodded, slowly, once.

"Is that good or bad?" Dunwin asked.

"That depends," Phrenk said. "I was just wondering if you might be related."

"I doubt it," Dunwin said with a shrug.

"Oh? Who's your family, then?"

"Well, I don't have much of one."

"Oh? Who are your parents?"

"Well, my father's Odo, he's a shepherd. And my mother's name was Audrea. She was a ewe."

"A me?"

"No, a ewe. A sheep."

Startled, Phrenk asked, "Your mother's a sheep?"

"Well, she was. She's dead now."

"You don't look like a sheep."

Dunwin shrugged. "I guess I take after my father."

"Um." Phrenk hesitated. "I don't think men and sheep can, um . . . procreate."

"Can what?"

"I mean, I don't think a sheep could have a human baby."

"Oh." Dunwin considered that, then admitted, "Well, Dad Odo never really said that Audrea was actually my *mother* mother, I guess. But she's the only one I ever knew."

Phrenk nodded. "And you're sure this Odo is your real father?"

"Well, yes—why *else* would he keep me around?"

Phrenk had no answer to that. "It must just be coincidence, then," he said. "It's amazing, though—you look just like him. I could have sworn that you must have the same father . . . and I'm sure that there were plenty of women . . . or maybe the Black Weasel . . ."

"Huh?" Dunwin blinked. "Weasels are too small to futter sheep. And Odo wouldn't . . . well, I mean, why a weasel when he's got sheep?"

"No, no, not a real weasel."

"Well, who, then? Who is it you think I look like?"

"I don't just *think* so, boy—the two of you are as like as two books on the same shelf."

"The two of who?"

"You and Prince Arbol, lad."

For a moment Dunwin stared. His brows drew closer together, first in puzzlement, and then in anger. He frowned deeply.

"Are you making fun of me?" he demanded.

"No, not at all!" Phrenk protested.

"D'you expect me to believe that a runty little wether like you knows Prince Arbol, or that I look like someone who lives in a piece of lacework?"

Phrenk's mouth opened, but no words came out. Dunwin's fists clenched.

Just then Armetta emerged, holding a dozen tapers tied to a stick by their uncut wicks. "Here we go, Dunwin," she said.

Dunwin turned, snatched the stick, and stormed out without another word.

Prince Arbol, indeed! When everyone said that the prince was a fine, handsome youth who took after his Old Hydrangean mother. As if Dunwin, the son of Odo and Audrea, could ever look like *that*!

The stranger had been teasing him, just because he was an ignorant shepherd boy and not some dressed-up city-dweller.

Phrenk, utterly baffled, watched the youth stamp angrily out. He was not at all sure why the boy had taken offense.

And the resemblance was utterly uncanny. Either Gudge or Prince Mimulus surely *must* have sired the lad, somehow!

Not that that mattered; both men undoubtedly had children scattered far and wide.

Still, it would make an interesting anecdote to tell the queen.

Chapter Ten

"All done, Mungli?" Queen Artemisia asked as she rapped on her lady-in-waiting's bedroom door. The door was almost immediately flung open and the rather tousled Gorgorian stuck out her head. Nodding briskly, a wistful smile playing about the edges of her ever-silenced lips, Mungli let her royal mistress know that she had seen her duty and she had done it. And it had been rather fun, too.

Behind her, Phrenk the messenger stood making the final, fussy adjustments to his palace livery. The plainer garb he had worn while in the queen's service off in the wilds of the Fraxinella Mountains lay in a heap at the side of Mungli's bed. When he was at last restored to the full glory of a proper junior-sub-head-under-footman, he stepped fastidiously around Mungli and, using the Swan Settling Upon a Lily Pond at Midnight with Variable Winds from the Northwest and the Flower Star Ascendant style of bowing, made his obeisance to the queen.

It was very prettily done, and spoke well for the young man's future in service at the palace.

"Radiant Lady," Phrenk said, keeping his eyes lowered. "Your Exalted Glory and Inestimable Beauty have done me a great honor."

Artemisia basked in the warm glow of full Old Hydrangean courtly speech. It had been so long, so very long! Since Gudge's rule, a general slackness appeared to be taking over. Even the most refined and inbred of the aristocratic stock seemed to have let themselves go shamelessly when it came to the niceties. They called it being realistic and practical. Artemisia called it one too many sessions at Gudge's nightly beer bashes.

"It is you who have done me this honor, Golden Underling," she replied. "I wish that I could send you on all of my errands to the Black Weasel. Alas, your frequent absences would be noted and your life forfeit."

"Well forfeited mote it be, O Splendor of the Sunrise," said Phrenk. "Nay, gladly wold I lay mine unworthy head a-doon upon the cruel block and kiss the hem of Death's own kirtle if such sacrifice might purchase me but a single hyaline drop of compassion's own sweet dew from the matchless lights of your regal eyn." He paused for breath. Speaking fluent Old Hydrangean courtly speech was a draining experience, and Phrenk had already gone through one of those with Mungli.

"Yes, well, that's fine," said the queen. She had not been expecting her favorite messenger to go on in the same overwrought vein, and to tell the truth, large doses of Old Hydrangean courtly speech lacked the fillip of isolated compliments. It was like the difference between munching a tasty sweetmeat and drowning in a vat of marzipan. "I wouldn't want you to get killed, that's all. You have the very best memory of any messenger I have ever sent to my brother. When you're on the job, I feel secure. I know that nothing important will be overlooked."

"Your Unrelenting Splendiferousness shows me too much favor," said Phrenk, still addressing the silk carpet. "Were it in my power, I should slice the top of my skull away with a golden sword and lay the full scroll of my humble brains at your dainty feet, the better to ensure that no detail, however small, might be lost to your ken, lest it prove vital to Your Entrancing Grace's . . ."

"Would you like to get off your knees, have a cool drink, and talk normally?" Artemisia offered.

Phrenk looked up and smiled. "I'd love it, Your Majesty."

Shortly thereafter, Mungli served them both thin goblets of Dovetongue, an unpretentious little white wine with flinty underpinnings, a pert, freckled nose, and real staying power.

"Ahhh!" Phrenk set down his empty goblet and smiled when Mungli refilled it. "What a relief this is from that awful upcountry ale I've had to drink this past week."

"Bad, was it, dear?" Artemisia inquired by way of making conversation.

"Your Majesty's pardon, but it was like drinking ox piss. No offense, darling," he added for Mungli's benefit. "I know your folk are more than a little fond of oxen."

Mungli gave a soundless laugh and made an eloquent gesture that simultaneously indicated just how fond her folk were of oxen and what they could all go and do about it.

"My, how you have suffered." The queen shook her head. "Well, when next you go, I'll see to it that you have something decent to drink on your travels."

"Your Majesty is too kind. If it's all the same to you, I'll stick with our present working arrangement: A week or so of agony on the road and an hour or so of ecstasy on my return." He leered at Mungli, who true to her upbringing did the courteous thing and unlaced the front of her gown to give the gentleman a nice, long view of matters. Phrenk sighed with longing. "It's knowing that I've got such payment awaiting me that gives me speed. I cheat many a tedious hour in those squalid mountain taverns by thinking of how, when I get safely back here, I'm going to . . ."

"Dear Phrenk, we are *so* glad you have a good imagination," Artemisia said hastily. It wasn't that she was a prude—the Old Hydrangean erotic classic, *The Mink and the Otter,* was an astonishingly complete exploration of love's more practical side, as well as being required reading for every well-bred young lady—but marriage to Gudge had brought her to the point where even hearing about someone else's amorous exploits gave her a three-day migraine.

Phrenk chuckled. "Forgive me, Majesty, I forget myself. At times, perhaps my imagination is almost *too* good.

For example, I doubt you would believe the fantastic notion that came to me on this trip. I was in one of those village taverns I spoke of—one so verminous, vulgar, and beggarly as to make *squalid* sound like a step up—when I met the most extraordinary boy."

"I really don't think I want to hear about what you and he . . . ," Artemisia began.

"Really a strange lad, no more than fourteen summers old, I'm sure, though large for his age," Phrenk said. "A little dense—he claimed his mother was a sheep!—but quite handsome. *Really* handsome, I mean. In those mountains they rate a man good-looking when he's got two-thirds of his teeth and no visible growths. So handsome, in fact, that I was willing to wager all my life and a damp cracker that he was the spirit and image of our own beloved Prince Arbol! At first I thought he must be a by-blow of either Prince Mimulus or King Gudge, though to speak truly, he had almost matching measures of both Gorgorian and Hydrangean looks about him, just like our dear prince, so there went *that* theory. It was likely just a coincidence; more likely too much of that slug-piddle the mountain folk call ale. Still, it was amusing, doesn't Your Majesty agree-*eeeegh*!"

Mungli gave a guttural cry of distress that fairly mimicked Phrenk's suddenly strangled speech. Who could blame either one of them? The Gorgorian waitingwoman was not used to seeing her gentle mistress, Queen Artemisia, grab a full-grown man by the neck, using both hands, and squeeze. For his part, Phrenk was no more used to having his windpipe be the unheralded recipient of such peculiar royal attention.

"Where was this?" the queen demanded, tightening her hold. "What was the name of the village? Tell me! Tell me at once!"

"Gggllr," Phrenk said, doing his best to please. The queen took the hint and let her grip unclench a notch.

"Stinkberry," the messenger managed to say.

The queen's hold loosened entirely. Pale hands folded

demurely in her lap, as if nothing had ever happened, she said, "My dear, dear Phrenk, you are my most valued and trusted servant. As such I am now going to charge you with a mission of even greater delicacy than any you have thus far undertaken in my service. Please wait here a moment. Amuse yourself." She nodded toward Mungli, and swept from the room.

In the inmost chamber of her apartments, Artemisia stood over an open chest and selected one item of clothing after another. All were Prince Arbol's castoffs, kept both out of a mother's doting attachment and because Old Hydrangean lore forbade that raiment that had once graced royal backs ever cover less-exalted nakedness.

Queen Artemisia had only the greatest respect for Old Hydrangean lore, following it to the letter in all cases and at all times, unless it was inconvenient. This time, she was sure she was not going to be violating a single penstroke of it. Not after what Phrenk had said. Not with his unimpeachable memory. Not when she knew that Stinkberry village was so close to her brother's forest lair. Not when she recalled that night of conspiracy just over fourteen years ago when old Ludmilla had mentioned Stinkberry as a good stopping place for her when she would have to convey the extra baby to the Black Weasel's keeping.

Something had happened to old Ludmilla en route to the Black Weasel, that much was sure, but as for the twins, . . . A tear welled up in Artemisia's eye. Phrenk spoke of only one lad bearing that uncanny resemblance to Prince Arbol. Well, perhaps it was too much to expect that both of her baby boys had survived. News of this one was miracle enough, especially when you realized that life among the peasantry was nasty, brutish, short, and filthier than Gudge's armpit. She would have to be grateful for what the gods had sent her. This boy could be the saving of her, and of Prince Arbol too!

Dashing the tear away, Artemisia made her selections. When she had packed a suitable bundle of the prince's latest hand-me-downs, she fetched her sewing box, then took her silver scissors to one of Arbol's old play tunics and set to work.

Phrenk and Mungli had amused themselves in a variety of ways by the time the queen returned. In fact, messenger and lady both had so exhausted themselves that Artemisia found Phrenk telling the Gorgorian maidservant a tedious series of the-dragon-the-knight-and-the-virgin jokes while Mungli cleaned away the broken glassware and readjusted the chandelier.

"Mungli, Phrenk, come here," she said, setting her bundle on top of the only table left standing. "This concerns you both. You are to take this package and go to Stinkberry village. There you are to find the boy of whom Phrenk spoke and bring him back here. Before you do so, you are to make him try on the clothing you will find in this bundle and alter it to fit if need be, but see to it that he does *not* travel in it. However, in this same package you will also find a mask, a hooded mask that covers the whole head. Make sure he puts it on and under no circumstances removes it until you have brought him before me. If you succeed, I shall reward you both beyond your wildest dreams." She glanced around the devastated room and with a wry smile added, "I would guess they can be pretty wild. But fail me, and I will prove to you that when it comes to punishment, the Gorgorians are strictly wolverines out of water when compared to what a real Old Hydrangean can devise."

Phrenk digested this information.

It gave him heartburn.

Swallowing hard, he said, "I'm sure Your Majesty has your reasons for these . . . these exceptional arrangements. But perhaps I am not the best choice for this mission. As you yourself said, if I am too often absent from the palace, people will talk; my life would be forfeit."

"Well forfeited mote it be, O Golden Underling," said the queen smoothly. "And don't think you can agree to this assignment and then run away. My brother will be notified if you try that. His memory for faces is as good as yours, and he's finally got the Bold Bush-dwellers brought up to the point where they're *some* earthly use to him. They are all expert trackers, and even more creative than I am when it comes to paying back traitors. Well forfeited, indeed."

Phrenk blanched to hear his own flowery offer of suicide tossed back so easily in his face, but he was no quitter—not when it came to getting out of a bad deal. Bravely he set to trying to dissuade the queen.

"The gods forbid that we should ever betray Your Majesty!" he cried. "Mungli and I will do our best to leave the palace discreetly, in disguise, but how shall we explain ourselves if we are caught? What shall we do if the boy refuses to accompany us? What if he resists, and his fellow villagers come to his aid? What shall we say if one of King Gudge's patrols intercepts us before we can slip into the palace with the masked youth? What if he screams? What if he struggles? Wherever shall we turn for aid? Whatever shall we do?"

Queen Artemisia gave the trembling messenger a hard, cold, tight, beautiful smile. "Phrenk, my dear," she said, "I don't give a damn."

Chapter Eleven

Clootie was really quite thoroughly pleased with himself as he looked over the assortment of wildlife that roared, scampered, and shrieked on the hillside. For once, it had been his very own magic, rather than Wulfrith's, that was responsible for the chaos he now watched.

That eagle, just moments before, had been a mouse; it was now screaming in confusion as it tried to run on talons and wings, rather than its four familiar feet. The rather puzzled lion had begun life as a spider; the rabbit in its jaws had been an earthworm, while the frantic cow, trying unsuccessfully to burrow under a rock, had been a rabbit. A pigeon had become a chipmunk, an ant had become a garter snake.

And Clootie had done it all, all by himself, in a matter of minutes!

His old master would have been utterly appalled. Clootie could almost hear the old fart now, muttering, "No grace, no style at all! So hasty! So *messy*!"

And that was all quite true; in the good old days, under good old King Fumitory, no self-respecting wizard would ever have done such a thing.

But under King Gudge, style and grace were not exactly at a premium. Whatever worked, worked, and no one gave points for finesse or flair.

And this spell *worked.*

Which was, Clootie thought, rather amazing. Even

with Wulfrith's help, it had been quite a job coming up with this little stunt. If it hadn't been for Corinalla's birthday party, all those years ago . . .

His thoughts flew back to that long-ago morning, when his master had received the letter at breakfast and slit it open with the handle of his grapefruit spoon—Clootie still remembered the muttered prayer to Spug Pagganethaneth that had accompanied that inappropriate use of the implement. The old man had read through the brief note, and had let out a groan.

"Revered and Honored Master, Font of Wisdom and Glory of the Ages, Beneficent Lord and Source of All Blessings," Clootie had remarked, making the sign of A Snowflake That May Be Brushed Away Unheeded Or Cherished For Its Unique Beauty, Whichever Seems Appropriate, "what failing of your miserable apprentice evokes this sound, for surely nothing else but my misbegotten self is so worthless as to trouble you?"

At the memory he glanced at Wulfrith, who was on the verge of hysterical laughter watching the spider-lion try to figure out what to do with the earthworm-rabbit, giving no thought at all to showing his master proper respect. That boy had never learned a tenth of the Old Hydrangean forms and procedures; in the old days he'd have been sent packing long ago, talented or not.

Nowadays, of course, a wizard couldn't afford to be so particular.

But back then, Clootie had observed the rules—he'd asked his question in the formal style, then bowed his head to await a reply.

"Useless toad of an apprentice," his master had answered, "it's that damned fool Horin. His spoiled brat daughter Corinalla is having a birthday celebration, and he wants me to show up and bless it, maybe do a few tricks."

"A few tricks?" Clootie had been aghast at this disrespect accorded his master.

"Oh, he puts it in flowery words, but that's what it comes down to," old Master Quankle had said—Quannikilius, really, but Clootie had always thought of him as Quankle.

And old Master Quankle didn't want to go, but he owed Horin a debt—a little matter of some six thousand florins and a trained pelican, something to do with a gorf match; Clootie had never learned the details. Under the circumstances, Master Quankle couldn't very well refuse the invitation outright.

Instead, he decided to send his apprentice. And when Clootie had protested that he didn't know any good tricks suitable for use at a ten-year-old's birthday party, Quankle had quickly taught him one, a very old-fashioned and out-of-date spell that had been abandoned decades before as insufficiently elegant for modern sorcery.

It was really quite a clever spell, much simpler and more effective than any of the others Clootie was ever taught—it had to be, if a mere apprentice was to learn it in time for the party. With a mere ten minutes of ritual, and only half a dozen arcane tools, the spell transformed white mice into doves—any number of white mice would, neat as you please, grow wings and feathers and, transformed to doves, flutter about in dazed confusion, trying to figure out what had befallen them.

Corinalla had almost been impressed, and Clootie had managed to survive the fete without any major disasters.

Of course, the spell wasn't much use anywhere else—certainly not against Gorgorians, who bore very little resemblance to white mice (beyond a certain cheesy odor in some cases). It didn't even serve to rid the kitchen of vermin, since the mice helping themselves to the odd crumb were usually not white. It was, like many of the fine old Hydrangean sorceries, a highly specific enchantment.

It was when he found mouse footprints in the butter, even before the Gorgorians came, that the idea of somehow generalizing the spell had first occurred to Clootie, but it was not until he had set up cavekeeping in the hills outside Stinkberry village that he actually worked on the problem.

And it wasn't until he watched Wulfrith at work, and

began noticing the patterns in the various transformation spells the boy came up with, that he got the first clues as to just how the spell's effects might be broadened. That very first day, when little Wulfie had turned an endtable into a fish, had been the beginning.

Now, at last, more than a decade later, Clootie finally had the spell perfected, generalized and streamlined into a magical weapon the likes of which Hydrangea had never seen. He stood, hands on his hips, and admired its effects.

The spider-lion finally stopped trying to either tie the earthworm-rabbit up or suck out its innards, and more or less by accident bit down. Wulfrith let out a loud, "Awww!" as the rabbit thrashed once and died.

The mouse-eagle, still not having caught on that it could fly, had managed an odd stumbling run down the hillside and into the forest; Clootie did not expect it to last long in there. The other creatures had all scattered.

The spell had worked on every bird, beast, or bug he had tried it on; he was confident that he could now, in less than a minute, transform any living creature he could see into something else. That would presumably include Gorgorians, though he had not had any handy as test subjects.

It was rather a shame, he thought, that he had no way of knowing exactly *what* any given creature would turn into. In some cases, such as the spider that had become a lion, the new creatures were more dangerous than the old.

It was rather difficult to imagine a Gorgorian turning into anything more dangerous, but Clootie supposed it might be possible. Even so, he thought the spell had obvious military applications; no matter how dangerous they were individually, turning all the Gorgorians into random wildlife would seriously disrupt their command structure. Even Gorgorian officers relied on speech sometimes, and unless they all became parrots or dragons . . .

No, he was making assumptions there. He couldn't be sure that a transformed Gorgorian wouldn't be able to talk.

But still, the spell was a success, and disposing of the

Gorgorians was now just a matter of logistics. Clootie smiled broadly.

The spider-lion chewed noisily, and Wulfrith backed away.

"What do we do now, Master?" he asked.

"We celebrate, my boy," Clootie said, "we celebrate!"

Together they retreated into the cave, Clootie slapping Wulfrith on the back. Giddy with success, the wizard grinned and held a finger to his lips as he hauled a case of dusty black bottles from a concealed niche that Wulfrith had somehow, in all his years of exploring their shared abode, never discovered. "A little secret of mine," Clootie explained. "When I first fled my home in the city, the vintner down the street begged me to hide these treasures from the Gorgorians—or at least, I'm sure he *would* have begged me, but he wasn't around at the time, so I decided to take the risk on his behalf without being asked. Just trying to be a good neighbor, of course."

"What are they?" Wulfrith asked.

"Ah!" Clootie grinned again as he twisted at a complicated wire device that adorned the neck of the first bottle. "A real treasure, all right, my lad! These are Elsinium Palace's Finest Western Slope Special Reserve Sparkling Divine Nectar, Demi-Sec. The '23 vintage, a *very* good year!"

"Huh?"

"*Wine*, you booby, sparkling wine! The very best!" The wire cage came free.

"Oh."

The cork popped, and wine frothed up; Wulfrith snatched up glasses and caught the spilling white foam.

"Oh, good lad!" Clootie said, filling the two receptacles. "*Do* join me!"

Wulfrith eyed the stuff in his goblet warily. It was clear and golden, which was encouraging, but it bubbled and foamed in a way that reminded him of the water elemental he kept in the sink, or perhaps of the thing that had oozed out of the kettle and eaten the footstool when one of Master Clootie's transformation spells had gone wrong the year before. Prior to this, Wulfrith's only experience with wine had been drinking dark red stuff that just sat there in the glass and that tasted like charred cabbage. That sort might develop an oily film on top sometimes, but it didn't shoot out tiny explosive bubbles or make crackling noises.

"Drink up, boy!" Clootie said, tossing down the contents of his own glass.

Wulfrith attempted a cautious sip.

Clootie smiled, poured another glass, and drank it.

Wulfrith took another sip, as Clootie refilled his own glass again.

"You know, lad," Clootie said, staring off into space and smiling crookedly, "it's been a long time, a *very* long time. I might even miss this place, once I'm back in my old house on the Street of Roses the Color of the Edges of Clouds At Sunset."

Wulfrith made a polite little noise. He was still trying to decide whether he liked the taste of the stuff they were drinking. It certainly didn't burn his throat the way the red wine did, but the flavor was very peculiar.

Clootie poured himself another glass, then settled onto a divan.

"Or maybe I won't go back to the Street of Roses at all," the wizard mused. "Maybe I'll have a place at the Palace of Divinely Tranquil Thoughts—after all, if my spell, *our* spell, saves all of Hydrangea from the yoke of the hated Gorgorians, I'll be a hero, won't I? And all the court mages who served under King Fumitory are dead, dispersed, and decapitated."

Wulfrith nodded warily. The wine was interesting, he thought, but he didn't think he would care to drink very much of it. He was about halfway through his first glass and his head already felt a trifle unsteady.

Clootie filled his glass again.

"Who knows what a grateful populace might not do?" Clootie asked a white-streaked stalactite. "Wine, women, and song, Wulfrith—I expect we'll be given anything we ask for." He drained the glass.

Wulfrith felt as if he ought to say something, to hold up his end of the conversation. As Clootie poured more wine, Wulfrith said, "I wouldn't really know what to ask for, Master Clootie."

Clootie grinned. This was not a phenomenon that Wulfrith was familiar with, and he found it more than a little disconcerting.

"Wine, women, and song," Clootie repeated. "Those *are* the traditch . . . trazish . . . tra . . . *traditional* pleasures."

Wulfrith looked dubiously at his glass. He saw no particular reason to ask for wine as any part of his reward. As for women, he had seen a few on his rare trips accompanying Master Clootie to Stinkberry village, and while he had some vague theoretical knowledge of what women were for, he wasn't clear on why he, personally, might want one or more of the creatures—though in recent weeks he was beginning to think he'd like to experiment a little.

Still, he admitted to himself, if someone were to give him a woman, at present, he wouldn't know what to do with her.

Song might be nice, if the master was right and they were to be rewarded, of which he was by no means convinced. He was not at all clear on just who was going to do what to whom that would make Clootie and himself heroes. After all, Clootie had always assured him that the magic they used around the cave was nothing very extraordinary; why was this transformation spell, which didn't seem all that special to him, so important? If these Gorgorians were the monstrous brutes that his master had always said they were, why hadn't someone turned the lot of them into newts years ago?

There was so very much he didn't understand about the outside world.

"I wouldn't know, Master," he said.

" 'Course not, you're just a boy!" Clootie gulped wine. "Don't know much of anything yet, you don't, stuck up here in this cave instead of carousing in the fleshpots of

Bentmuro. When I was your age . . . when I was . . . how old are you, boy?"

"Fourteen, sir."

"Fourteen years old," Clootie marveled, "and stuck here in a cave in the middle of nowhere, with nobody but me, all because those damned Gorgorians don't have a proper respess . . . repesk . . . respect for magic!"

"Um," Wulfrith said.

"Tell you what, lad," Clootie said. "The Gorgorians are not long for thish . . . this world, or at least, not for human form, if you can call a Gorgorian human to begin with, which I suppose you have to because you can't very well put them anywhere else taxonomically and they do interbreed naturally with humans, which means they must *be* humans, unless there's some question about whether it's natural, which I suppose there might be except that if you start saying that rape isn't natural you're going to get into all kinds of trouble, and then . . . what was I saying?" His free hand, which had begun to wave about wildly, fell into the wizard's lap; he looked down at it as if startled to find it there, and put it to use draining the last of the wine bottle into his glass.

"I don't know, sir," Wulfrith replied.

"Don't know," Clootie said. "Of *course* you don't, because you've been stuck in this cave! Well, enough of that, Wulfrith, my boy! We're celebrating, and a lad your age should get out more, so you just take the day off and go down to the village and have fun—take your time, and a dozen coppers from the box by the stove, and you go have a good time!"

Wulfrith blinked in surprise. "Are you sure, Master Clootie?" he asked.

"Of course I'm sure!"

"I've never had a day off before."

"Then it's overdue, isn't it?"

Wulfrith couldn't argue with that, and knew he probably shouldn't argue at all, but the whole idea of time off was so new he needed time to absorb it. "But who'll look after the cave?" he asked.

"*I* will, of course! You go have your fun."

"But what'll *you* do? Don't you want to celebrate, too?"

"I'll celebrate right here, lad; I've got eleven more bottles and a spell for succubi that I want to try."

"What's succubi?"

"Never you mind, you just get on down to the village!"

"Yessir." Wulfrith turned and scampered off, as Clootie struggled with the wire cage on the second bottle.

Chapter Twelve

Phrenk settled disconsolately at the table nearest the door—or rather, nearer the door, there being only two tables. He was fairly sure there had been three, or maybe even four, at the time of his previous visit, but only two remained at present. A pile of kindling by the hearth gave a clue as to the fate of the others.

Mungli settled beside him, looking around with interest. It was the first time she had ever been inside a Hydrangean building that was almost as dirty as a Gorgorian tent, and it made her oddly homesick—not that she had any desire at all to ever see the inside of a tent again; what it made her homesick for was the tidy interior of the Palace of the Ox, and specifically the queen's quarters. She felt that she would be quite happy to never see another smelly oxhide tent for as long as she lived. After all, a woman who couldn't speak would be unable to join the women's councils and learn traditional Gorgorian sorcery. Without that, the only thing of any possible interest in the Gorgorian tents would be the Gorgorian men. She could do without those; the queen's messengers might sometimes be less enthusiastic, but they were also cleaner and less hazardous to one's health.

A large woman emerged from the kitchen, spotted the two of them, and smiled immensely.

"Good to see you again, sir!" Armetta called. "And is this your esteemed lady?"

Mungli snorted; Phrenk frowned at her, then answered, "Alas, merely a friend."

"A pity for you both, then. How can I serve you?"

"Ale," Phrenk said.

Mungli glared at him and kicked him under the table.

"Ale to start with," Phrenk said, glaring back. "We've a favor to ask, once our thirst is quenched."

"Oh?" Armetta smiled and winked broadly. "I'll fetch the ale, then." She turned back toward the kitchen.

A moment later, when Phrenk and Mungli had each had time to down an ale, Armetta stood by the table, arms crossed on her breast, and asked, "Now, what was this favor?"

"We're looking for someone," Phrenk explained. "A half-witted shepherd boy, good-sized, with black hair and a handsome face."

Armetta frowned. "There's plenty around here that fit that description," she said. "Addle-Pated Kristo, for one, or Black Hender, or Bikkel of the Runny Nose."

"No, it wasn't any of those. He told me his name . . ."

Just then he was interrupted by the sound of the inn door opening. Phrenk glanced over, and didn't bother to finish his sentence.

"Never mind," he said, "that's him now."

Armetta shrugged and wandered away.

Mungli turned, and the instant she caught sight of the new arrival her mouth fell open and she stared like an idiot. The boy in the doorway certainly *did* look like Prince Arbol—in fact, if she hadn't known better, she would have sworn (had she been able to speak) that it *was* the prince.

The prince, however, had no business in Stinkberry village, and should be back at the Palace of the Ox. Furthermore, wild as the prince was said to be, surely he would never wear anything as cheap and filthy as the stained and worn dark gray apprentice's robe that covered this lad.

And Prince Arbol wouldn't look around at a dirty little village inn with that wide-eyed gawp.

"Dunwin!" Phrenk called, "Fancy seeing you again!"

The boy in the doorway stepped in, but didn't answer. In fact, he headed for the other table, nodding politely in the direction of Phrenk and Mungli.

"Dunwin!" Phrenk called again, "Remember me? We met here last month."

The lad turned and looked around the room, puzzled.

"I mean you, Dunwin!"

The boy frowned. "Are you talking to me, sir?" he asked.

"Of course I am," Phrenk said. "You're Dunwin, aren't you?"

The boy considered this carefully, chewing his lower lip, and then shook his head. "No," he said. "I don't know what a Dunwin *is*, but I'm pretty sure I'm not one."

"Your name isn't Dunwin?"

"No," the lad said. "My name is Wulfrith."

"Last time I was here you told me it was Dunwin."

Wulfrith blinked and looked about, wishing Clootie were there to advise him. "I don't remember ever meeting you before," he said, "let alone telling you that my name was Dunwin."

Mungli threw a worried glance at Phrenk; he patted her hand reassuringly, then leaned across the table and whispered, "Remember, this is the fellow who thought his mother was a sheep; he probably doesn't remember much of *anything*, and for all I know he changes his name every fortnight."

Mungli didn't look entirely convinced.

"Besides," Phrenk added, "*look* at him! Doesn't he look just like the prince?"

The Gorgorian could scarcely argue with that.

"Well, then," Phrenk said aloud, "if you don't remember meeting me, join us, and we'll introduce ourselves."

"I don't want to intrude . . ."

"Not at all! Come, sit down, we'll buy you a pint of the best."

Wulfrith, acutely aware of just how limited his funds were, couldn't resist. He took a seat at the table, where

Phrenk and Mungli stared at him. Phrenk waved a signal to Armetta, and a moment later a full mug appeared before the wizard's apprentice.

"So," Phrenk said, by way of casual conversation, "how's the sheep-herding business?"

Wulfrith blinked over his mug, puzzled. He lowered the tankard and said, "*I* don't know. How is it?"

"I don't know, if you don't," Phrenk said, caught off-guard. "I'm not a shepherd."

"Who are you, then?" Wulfrith asked suspiciously.

"My name is Phrenk; I'm just a traveler, passing through." He gestured. "This is my companion, Mungli."

"I'm . . ." Wulfrith paused. He suddenly recalled that true names have power. He had already given his, but this peculiar traveling shepherd might not remember that. "I'm pleased to meet you," he said. He nodded politely at Mungli.

It was only when Phrenk spoke again that Wulfrith realized he was staring at the young woman. He wasn't entirely sure why.

He was beginning to think, though, that maybe wine, women, and song would be worthy entertainment on two out of three.

"I'm sorry," he said, "what did you say?"

"I said, what brings you here?"

"Oh, well, we were celebrating . . ."

"We?"

"Um." Suddenly cautious, Wulfrith looked the two strangers over a bit more carefully. The man looked harmless enough, really—but the woman's dress was in the Gorgorian style, with a square-cut neckline and heavy, coarse fabric, rather than the scalloping and lace of traditional Hydrangean fashion.

And Clootie was, technically, a fugitive, or so he had always claimed. The Gorgorians had outlawed the practice of men's magic and high wizardry, allowing only the nasty hedge magics and sorceries of their own womenfolk. It hardly seemed likely that these two would be hunting down escaped wizards after all these years, but that was no reason to go blabbing everything.

"Me, I mean," he said. "I was celebrating, all alone, by myself."

"Oh? Celebrating what?"

"Oh, nothing. My birthday," Wulfrith improvised.

"Congratulations, then," Phrenk said. "How old are you?"

Wulfrith decided he didn't want to answer this, and tried to change the subject. "I'm pleased to meet you, Mungli," he said. "Are you from around here?"

"She can't speak," Phrenk said hastily. "A little accident."

Mungli shot Phrenk an unhappy glance. Accident, indeed!

Eager to get back on track, Phrenk asked, "What did you say your name was?"

"I didn't," Wulfrith lied.

"Oh. I thought you said you were Dunwin, Odo's son?"

Vague memories stirred at the mention of that name, but Wulfrith shook his head. "Nope," he said.

Phrenk frowned. "You're not a shepherd?"

"Nope."

"What *do* you do, then?"

Wulfrith hesitated. Wizardry was illegal.

"Nothing," he said.

"You know," Phrenk said, in his best attempt at casualness, "I could swear I met you here once before, and you told me that your father was a shepherd named Odo."

Wulfrith considered this, then said, "Nope. I don't think so."

"And you said your mother was a ewe," Phrenk continued desperately.

"Never met my mother," Wulfrith admitted.

"Oh. Well, where . . ." Phrenk stopped.

What did it matter who the boy thought he was, and what he had or hadn't said? Whoever and whatever he was, he looked just like Prince Arbol, and he was unquestionably the one the queen had sent them after.

He was obviously even stupider and more confused than Phrenk had originally assumed, but that wasn't necessarily a problem, and it almost certainly, Phrenk thought, wasn't *his* problem.

"Listen," Phrenk said, "how would you like to come with us to meet a friend of ours? She lives in the Palace of Divinely Tranquil Thoughts, down in the city."

Wulfrith drank the rest of his ale before answering.

This was a seriously weird request. Here were these two people he had never met before, one of whom had apparently made up a name and history for him, and ten minutes after they first laid eyes on him they were inviting him to a *palace*? And not just *any* palace, at that, but the royal palace, whatever its present name was.

That was just crazy. That made less sense than the silliest incantation he had ever heard.

It had to be a trick. These two had to be trying to trick him somehow. Maybe they were working for the Gorgorians, hunting wizards, or just out to make trouble for whatever Old Hydrangeans they could find.

If these two really *were* agents of the Gorgorian overlords, perhaps all this nonsense about Dunwins was part of the deception, and they really knew who he was and were trying to lure him into a trap. Certainly, the Palace of Divinely Tranquil Thoughts was full of Gorgorians these days; perhaps they meant to imprison him there. Perhaps he would then be bait to lure in Clootie.

But they didn't know how much magic he knew; if they didn't use wizardry themselves, they *couldn't* know. He could escape at any time, he was sure—he knew a few good spells, even if he wasn't yet half the wizard Master Clootie was.

And it would be very interesting to see the capital, and to meet some real Gorgorians, and everything.

He couldn't quite see where all this stuff about sheep fit

into the Gorgorian agent theory, though. Maybe it was meant to lull his suspicions.

Or maybe this man with the curly hair was just a lunatic. Maybe he was keeping the girl captive, and Wulfrith would be able to rescue her, and she would be so grateful she would . . . she would . . . well, she'd be grateful.

"Sure," he said. "Sounds like fun."

Chapter Thirteen

On what was surely at least the third attempt, Clootie finally managed to count the empty black bottles without losing his place. He wound up with a total of twelve, and sighed.

The succubus had been right; all the good wine was gone. And for that matter, so was the succubus; she had given up on him several hours ago and vanished in a cloud of foul-smelling purple smoke. A trace of the scent still lingered. Clootie grimaced; wasn't the traditional odor supposed to be brimstone? The cloying reek of this particular succubus, at any rate, didn't resemble brimstone in the slightest.

He leaned back against the armchair and stretched out his legs, contemplating his subterranean residence. His joints ached—one joint in particular felt as if he had scraped it raw, which he probably had. His knees and elbows showed some wear and he had several minor scratches on his back. There were a few on his chest, as well, and half a dozen hairs had been plucked out by the roots. The toothmarks were fading, but still discernable.

Well, no one had ever said that succubi were gentle.

At least he didn't have a headache. The one basic, useful spell that the most effete and erudite Old Hydrangean wizards had never been foolish enough to forsake, not even at the very height of their refinement of the arcane arts, was the Fine and Ancient Ceremony for the Peaceful and Unresentful Contemplation of the Lark Which Rises Joyfully

Singing with the dawn Regardless of the Weather, more commonly known as "the hangover cure."

The celebration, he decided, was over—just now he had no interest at all in wine, women, or song.

That meant that it was time to clean up, get everything squared away, and then set about transforming Gorgorians into miscellaneous wildlife. The question of whether to tackle the job on his own, or to contact the Black Weasel and his Bold Bush-dwellers and use them as his staff, was not yet settled. As his head cleared, though, the possibility that the Black Weasel might not immediately agree to yield command had occurred to him. There might be more to this liberating-the-kingdom stuff than he had initially thought.

First things first, though. The cave had to be straightened up, the empty bottles disposed of, the bedding replaced. Clootie gathered his strength and called, "Wulfrith!"

The cry echoed in the stony depths, but no other answer came. The wizard frowned. With a supreme effort he got to his feet and called again.

Still, no one answered.

Clootie's frown deepened. He tried to think over the entire celebration.

He had given the lad the day off, of course—partly so Wulfrith could celebrate on his own, but mostly to get him out of the cave so that he wouldn't be corrupted by the succubus, or drink an unreasonable share of the wine. That had been on the afternoon of the feast day of Himpi-Himpi, God of Small Furry Animals with Excessive Numbers of Sharp Teeth. Clootie had worked the summoning that evening, and the succubus had arrived around midnight, and then . . .

Well, there was no need to go into detail, but Clootie was fairly certain that at least three days had passed since he had last seen Wulfrith.

That was worrisome. Wulfrith was a good lad, and entirely trustworthy, in Clootie's experience. He should have returned long ago.

Something must have happened to him. Hildie, perhaps, or that ale Armetta sold.

Or, of course, it might have been something bad. The boy didn't know all that much about the outside world; Clootie had told him a few things, but that wasn't the same as living them. Wulfrith might have run into serious trouble of some sort. If the boy had let slip that he was a wizard's apprentice . . .

Well, of course, everyone in Stinkberry village who had ever met Wulfrith knew that he was a wizard's apprentice, but if word had somehow reached King Gudge and his simian subordinates that there was an Old Hydrangean wizard who was not only still alive, but who had the audacity to be training an apprentice . . .

Clootie did not care for that line of thought.

Maybe, he told himself, the boy *had* come back, but he was sleeping, or out at the privy. He set about searching the cave, just to be sure.

Half an hour later he no longer doubted; Wulfrith was missing, and he would have to be found. Clootie began gathering clothing, including his cloak and boots.

He was rather surprised to discover that it was market day in the village. He tried to tell himself that this was good, that maybe Wulfrith had just stayed to see the market, but he didn't convince anyone. More people just meant more to look at, and more trouble the boy could be in.

It was with a sudden burst of relief that Clootie spotted a familiar face, standing by the inn door and listening to the old codgers arguing on the bench out front.

"Wulfrith!" he called.

The boy didn't turn.

Clootie's relief was suddenly laced with anger. The lad *must* have heard.

"Wulfrith!" he bellowed.

Several people turned to look, but the boy at the inn was not one of them. Furious, Clootie marched down the street and thrust himself in front of the lad.

"Wulfrith," he said, "what the hell are you doing here?"

The boy blinked. "I'm not doing anything. What does 'wulfrith' mean?"

"It's your *name,* you little idiot!"

Since the lad was four or five inches taller than Clootie and at least as broad, "little" was not, perhaps, the best possible choice of words. The boy just looked more confused than ever.

"No, it isn't," he said. "At least, I never heard it before."

"Yes, you did."

"No, I didn't."

"Did."

"Didn't."

Clootie frowned. Something was not right here. "All right, then," he asked, "what *is* your name?"

The boy hesitated. "I'm not sure I should tell you," he said.

"But it's not Wulfrith? And I suppose you aren't my apprentice?" Clootie glared menacingly at the youth.

"Um," the boy said.

"What's *that* mean?"

"I dunno."

"You don't *know* that you're my apprentice?"

"I don't know what I meant. But I don't *think* I'm your apprentice." He blinked, and added belatedly, "Sir."

Clootie glared more balefully.

"I don't remember ever being *anyone's* apprentice," the lad said.

An angry mutter distracted Clootie from whatever he had intended to say next; startled, he looked around, and discovered that his argument with this person who denied being Wulfrith had attracted a small crowd.

"Let him alone, why don't you?" someone called. "If he's your apprentice, can't you see he's half-witted? What's the use of shouting at him?"

Several people murmured agreement. Clootie blinked.

Wulfrith, half-witted?

Wulfrith could be reckless, thoughtless, and clumsy, but he was certainly not half-witted, nor had he ever before denied his name or his apprenticeship.

"Um," Clootie said, his anger vanishing.

Something was *very* wrong here. Wulfrith was a straightforward, honest boy. If he had wanted to quit his apprenticeship, he would have just said so, he wouldn't have claimed to be someone else or denied remembering Clootie.

So in that case, Clootie decided, it seemed that Wulfrith genuinely *didn't* remember his name, or who he was.

"Boy," Clootie asked, "have you been hit on the head recently?"

The lad shrugged. "No more than usual," he replied.

That was not quite the clear and definite answer Clootie might have hoped for. He tried to think what else could make a man forget everything.

"Have you been keeping company with a woman, then?"

A puzzled look settled on the lad's face. "Which one?"

That response seemed to rule out a normal infatuation, Clootie thought; the identity of his love was the one thing an ardent young swain did *not* forget.

But there was another possibility. For years, Clootie had heard the stories about the Gorgorians—why they thought wizards were unmanly, why they kept their women locked away. Gorgorian warriors used no sorcery of any kind, but their women had a sort of hedge magic, female magic, crude and simple ensorcelments that they used to assist their natural feminine wiles.

Poor Wulfrith must have run afoul of woman's magic, weak and treacherous and incomprehensible. Proper wizardry might be able to cure the effects, but alas, Clootie had no idea how to go about it.

The witch who had cast the spell, though, would surely know how to reverse it, or at the very least could give Clootie some pointers.

"Have you been bothering any Gorgorian women?" Clootie asked.

The lad frowned. "Not that I know of," he said.

Clootie turned to the villagers gathered around. "Have any of you seen my apprentice with a Gorgorian woman lately?"

"Why?" one belligerent fellow demanded.

"I think he's been enchanted, that's why."

"I haven't been enchanted!" the youth protested.

"You wouldn't know it if you had," Clootie told him in his most reassuring tone.

"But I haven't!"

Clootie ignored the protest. "Anyone seen any Gorgorian women around here?"

The observers looked at one another.

"I might've maybe seen one," a man admitted. "Young and pretty, too. In the inn, there."

"And that young man was with her," a woman agreed.

"So was another fellow."

The pieces were falling into place. Clootie could imagine what must have happened; some Gorgorian wench had flirted with poor, innocent Wulfrith, her boyfriend had taken umbrage, and to prove her loyalty she had thrown a spell on Wulfrith. Clear as anything, it was.

"Anyone know who she was?" Clootie asked.

"Wasn't any such person!" the lad protested, but he was ignored as the little crowd babbled about the Gorgorian woman—what she wore, what she looked like, her anatomy and probable sexual habits, the beady-eyed, untrustworthy, curly-haired city man who had been with her.

Eventually, Clootie came to the conclusion that nobody actually knew anything about her beyond what they had glimpsed as she walked past on the street. She had been served at the inn, however.

"I'll ask Armetta," Clootie said. "Wulfrith, you wait here."

He didn't wait for an answer, but ducked quickly through the door of the inn.

Dunwin looked after him, then muttered, "My name's not Wulfrith, and I'll be damned if I'll wait here." No lunatic was going to make him be an apprentice. No Gorgorian woman had done anything to him.

Head held high, he marched off home, to see Bernice. *She* was sensible and reliable, not like these crazy villagers.

Ten minutes later, Clootie emerged from the inn; Armetta had admitted that a Gorgorian girl had been there, three days before, but would say no more than that. Clootie was unsure whether she *knew* any more than that. He stepped out the door into an empty street; the crowd had dispersed.

And Wulfrith had vanished.

The only person anywhere near was an old man seated on the bench, doing nothing, his head leaned back comfortably.

"Where did he go?" Clootie demanded.

The old man lifted his head. "You mean the boy?"

Clootie nodded.

"That way," the old man said, pointing. "Up the mountain."

Clootie followed the pointing finger.

The boy had, indeed, headed up the mountain, probably trying, in his dazed and confused way, to get home to the cave. He had, however, picked the wrong mountain.

Cursing, Clootie trotted after him.

Chapter Fourteen

Dunwin was climbing the fence, and could see Bernice grazing quietly a dozen yards higher up the slope, when he heard the voice.

"Wulfrith!" someone was calling. "Wulfrith! Wait!"

Dunwin sighed. That fat little lunatic from the village was following him.

Well, there wasn't any point in putting it off; sooner or later, if he wanted to be rid of this nuisance, Dunwin knew he would have to confront the maniac and somehow convince him that there was no such person as Wulfrith.

Might as well get it over with. He sat down on the top rail of the fence and waited.

A moment later Clootie came puffing up the trail, still calling occasionally for Wulfrith to wait. Dunwin resisted the temptation to shout back either, "I *am* waiting," or "My name isn't Wulfrith!"

Instead, he sat silently as Clootie staggered up. He watched without a word as the older man struggled to catch his breath.

"You walk fast," Clootie gasped out at last.

"Helps keep up with the sheep," Dunwin said.

Clootie ignored this remark, and continued, "Listen, Wulfrith, I know you don't remember, but you really *are* my apprentice. That Gorgorian witch must have put a spell on you, made you forget it all—maybe she was frightened by the idea of *real* magic."

Dunwin frowned. "What are you talking about?" he asked. "What witch?"

"That Gorgorian girl, at the inn down in Stinkberry village. Armetta—you remember Armetta?"

"Of course I remember Armetta, and she's no Gorgorian!" Dunwin protested. "Not much of a girl anymore, either," he added thoughtfully. He was beginning to notice the ages of women lately, though he wasn't all that sure why, as yet—only that the ones between puberty and parenthood looked like the best company.

"No, no," Clootie said, "of course not, she's an innkeeper, and a loyal Hydrangean, I'm sure."

"Then why did you say she was a Gorgorian witch?"

"I didn't, I . . . let me start over."

"Go ahead." Dunwin was determined to give this lunatic every chance. Maybe the poor man would realize how foolish he was being, if Dunwin let him ramble on about his fantasies.

Clootie took a deep breath.

"I talked to Armetta," he said, "and she told me that she saw you talking to a Gorgorian woman, three days ago—a girl who was traveling with a male companion. That was the day I let you take a day off and go into town, and you were supposed to come home that night. So today, I came looking for you, to see why you hadn't come home, and I found you like this, with no memory of your true identity, wandering up the wrong mountain. So the Gorgorian must have been a witch, and she's put a spell on you."

Dunwin scratched his head, dislodging minor vermin.

"I wasn't in town three days ago," he said. "And I never met any Gorgorian girl, and nobody put a spell on me, and this isn't the wrong mountain. See? There's Bernice, waiting for me."

Clootie looked. He saw no woman or girl who might have been the Bernice the boy referred to, only a rather fat sheep and some rocky hillside. He sighed.

"Listen, Wulfrith," Clootie said, "I don't know what

she's done to you, exactly, but if you'll come home with me, I'm sure we can fix it."

"I'm *going* home, and my name isn't Wulfrith."

"Of course it is. Your name is Wulfrith, and you're my apprentice, and we live in a cave over that way." He pointed.

"What sort of apprentice lives in a cave?" Dunwin asked curiously.

"An apprentice wizard, of course," Clootie answered.

Dunwin snorted. "There aren't any wizards anymore," he said. "And even if there were, *you* couldn't be one!"

"Why not?" Clootie demanded angrily.

"Because you're too short," Dunwin said. "And too fat. And your beard's crooked; who ever heard of a wizard with a crooked beard? And your hair isn't white."

"Well, it just so happens that I *am* a wizard!" Clootie replied, hands on hips. "If I *looked* like a wizard, the Gorgorians might have decapitated me with the rest of 'em!"

"I'm not sure there ever really were wizards at all," Dunwin said. "I think it might've all been a bunch of tricks; how else could the Gorgorians have caught and killed them all so easily? I mean, if there were real wizards, couldn't they have just blasted all the Gorgorians into little tiny bits?"

"No," Clootie explained, "because they'd gotten out of practice and forgotten all the big, showy spells like that." That was the short and inaccurate version, of course; he didn't see any point in taking the time just now to lecture his poor deranged apprentice about the hazards of overrefinement.

"Well, maybe," Dunwin said, "but *you* still aren't a wizard, you're just a fat little lunatic. My name isn't Wulfrith, it's Dunwin, and I never saw you before in my life, and I don't live in a cave, I live up on the mountain here with my Dad Odo."

"I *am* a wizard, damn it to the forty-six exquisite hells of the ancients!"

"No, you aren't," Dunwin insisted.

"Yes, I am!"

"Then do some magic, show me a spell!"

"You think I can't?" Clootie began. He raised his hand, then stopped.

The boy might be right, in a way—maybe he couldn't. He hadn't brought his staff, or his orb, or any of the tools of the arcane trade.

But there was the transformation spell—*that* didn't need any gadgets!

"Not a wizard, eh?" He laughed. "Watch this!" Clootie raised both hands, gestured, and spoke the appropriate Word of Power, thrusting out his fingers.

Dunwin watched with tolerant amusement until the brief incantation was complete. Before he could say anything about the performance, however, Bernice bleated; Dunwin whirled.

As the lad watched, the ewe's wool turned iridescent green and seemed to shrink down around her. Her neck and tail began lengthening rapidly. Crooked little growths sprang from her back and expanded swiftly. Her cloven hooves grew longer and curved, and split further, until she had four claws on each foot. Her legs were thickening, her body growing. Her eyes turned to golden slits, her snout stretched; gleaming white fangs appeared.

"Bernice!" Dunwin shrieked. He tried to jump down from the fence, but his tunic snagged on a splinter and held him, the laces almost strangling him as he struggled.

Bernice cried out again, and this time it was no bleat, but a choking roar, accompanied by a thin jet of smoke. Her serpentine tail lashed; the growths on her back spread wide, and Dunwin and Clootie could see that they were gigantic bat wings. Her wool had become shining scales, her hooves were razored talons; head to tail she was now easily thirty feet long.

Dunwin finally managed to detach himself from the fence and promptly tripped over his own feet, landing face down on dried mud.

By the time he untangled himself and got upright once again, the transformation was complete; Bernice had become a dragon. This was completely obvious to both Dunwin and Clootie, though neither of them had ever actually seen a dragon before.

It was not, however, obvious to Bernice. Bernice had never heard of dragons; as a sheep, she had never had much of an education in folklore, or for that matter in anything else. Dunwin had told her a few things, but he had never mentioned dragons, and her understanding of the Hydrangean tongue had been very limited, in any case. Sheep are not noted for linguistic talent.

Sheep, if the truth be known, are not noted for *any* sort of intellectual accomplishment. They are, in fact, generally believed to be quite stupid.

This belief has a sound basis in fact.

However, even to a sheep, it was quite obvious that something out of the ordinary had happened. Bernice could see her claws, great nasty-looking things; her head was much too far off the ground, and there were these odd things on her back that were fanning her. She felt oddly light on her feet, despite her new size. Her tail, which had heretofore generally hung there uselessly but had not gotten in the way, was dragging on the ground and whacking uncomfortably against various rocks and stones.

And her brain was beginning to work in oddly unsheeplike ways, for while there is good reason to think that sheep are stupid, this has never been a safe assumption to make about dragons.

Even so, while she might be green and scaly, and her head might be fifteen feet off the ground, she was still a sheep at heart, and when confronted with the unknown, a sheep reacts in one of three ways: ignore it, try to eat it, or run away in terror.

Bernice could scarcely try to eat her own scales, and she could not bring herself to ignore the changes, which left only one course of action for a proper ewe.

She fled in terror, bounding up the mountainside in an awkward ovine gait, unsuited to her draconic body. She flapped her wings instinctively, trying to keep her balance, and within moments she was airborne.

Far down the slope, Dunwin and Clootie stared after her as she soared upward and out of sight.

"Bernice!" Dunwin called hopelessly.

"Bernice was a sheep?" Clootie asked, in sudden comprehension.

"I always thought so," Dunwin answered, still staring after his vanished companion.

"When you talked about Bernice, I thought you meant a person."

Dunwin blinked, and turned to look at Clootie. "There aren't any people around here except you and me."

"Well, *I* know that," Clootie said, "but I thought you were imagining things because of that witch's spell."

"There wasn't any . . ." Abruptly, Dunwin stopped. "You really *are* a wizard," he said accusingly.

"Yup." Clootie nodded proudly.

"You turned Bernice into a dragon."

"Yup."

"Can you turn her back?"

"Um . . ." Clootie hesitated. He looked at the lad, noticing the broad shoulders and solid mass of muscle, truly remarkable for one so young. He also observed the dismayed and rather hostile expression on the youth's face. "Uh . . . yup," he said at last.

"Do it, then," Dunwin said. "Bring her back, please—she's my best friend."

"A sheep is your best friend?"

"Hey, a day spent herding sheep is not exactly a great opportunity for socializing," Dunwin replied defensively.

"You're a shepherd?"

"Of course I'm a shepherd, and you're a wizard. Now, bring her back—please!"

"I can't," Clootie admitted. "I can only change her back if she's right in front of me; I can't make her come back, and she's too far away now." This was not the exact and complete truth; the truth was that Clootie had no idea whether he could turn the dragon back into a ewe under *any* circumstances. Making his great new spell reversible had not been high on his list of priorities; who would ever want to turn a Gorgorian back?

Just at the moment, he wasn't really even thinking about it, but was instead lying automatically while he considered something else. Old memories were stirring in the back of his brain. A shepherd. Dunwin. Daddy Odo.

"Oh," he said, as Dunwin wailed.

"Bernice!"

"Oh," Clootie repeated. "You really *aren't* Wulfrith, are you?"

"I've got to go after her," Dunwin said. "Maybe I can bring her back."

Clootie nodded. "I get it, now—you're Wulfie's *brother*. I'd almost forgotten there were two of you. And it never occurred to me that you'd still be around, and that you'd look so much like your twin." He eyed the youth. "It's really quite an amazing resemblance, you know."

"She's never flown before," Dunwin said. "Do you think she might hurt herself?"

"Oh, I don't think so," Clootie said, offhandedly. "I don't suppose you've seen your brother anywhere lately?"

"I don't *have* a brother."

"Of course you do," the wizard told him. "Your Daddy Odo sold him to me when you were just babies. His name's Wulfrith, and he's missing."

"I don't care about that," Dunwin said. "*Bernice* is missing! I've got to go after her."

"Good luck," Clootie said. "*I've* still got to find Wulfrith." He waved cheerily, then turned and started back down the mountain.

Dunwin, on the other hand, ran *up* the mountain, and headed eastward, on the track of his lost Bernice.

Chapter Fifteen

"Here," Phrenk said to Wulfrith. "Put this on and don't ask questions."

Wulfrith took the strange object from Phrenk's hand and studied it. For almost the entire length of their journey from Stinkberry village down into the rich lowlands, Wulfrith had found his companions to be fairly sane. They let him eat when he got hungry, rest when he got tired, and answer any other calls of nature when he was so moved. Mungli wasn't much by way of a conversationalist, but there was something . . . *expressive* about the way she moved and the way she occasionally looked at him that made Wulfrith feel as if there were a lot of questions he had that only she could answer, and she wouldn't need to say a word to do it.

Still, there was the way the man called Phrenk kept insisting on calling him Dunwin. Every so often, sometimes several times in an hour, Phrenk would sidle up to Wulfrith and ask him if he was *sure* he didn't remember Daddy Odo and Mommy Ewe and a parcel of other nonsense besides. All Wulfrith had to do was shake his head and Phrenk would go away, muttering.

Until the next time.

It was all very tiresome, and Wulfrith had been tempted many times to chuck the whole sorry puzzle and go home to the cave. But then there was the lure of the palace. He had never seen a palace. He had read about them in some of Clootie's more worm-eaten texts, to be sure. As a rule, palaces appeared to be populated exclusively by damsels of extraordinary beauty.

Wulfrith wasn't entirely sure what a damsel was. When he asked Clootie, his master had gotten that puff-cheeked, hem-hawing look that meant *I am going to tell you a whopper of a lie now,* and replied, "Damsels are a rare and especially delicious breed of plum."

Somehow Wulfrith could not see all of those armed and mounted Hydrangean warriors risking their lives for a pretty fruit. And how did you put a plum in distress? Threaten to make it into jam?

If nothing else, he had to get to the palace just to find out what a damsel really was, and that meant putting up with Phrenk's little oddities.

But this last one took the cake.

"What is it?" Wulfrith asked, dangling the object from his fingertips at arm's length.

"Never mind what it is, put it *on,*" Phrenk commanded.

"If I don't know what it is, how can I put it on?" Wulfrith asked quite reasonably. "I won't know *what* to put it on if I don't know what it is." He helped himself to another sandwich from Mungli's basket.

Phrenk sighed and leaned back against the tree. Any passerby on the road would see their little group as merely a trio of merrymakers enjoying a picnic. It was a ruse the queen's messenger had used many times in their descent from the mountains, as the traffic on the roads grew thicker and the need to hide Dunwin's face more urgent. Phrenk felt anything but merry, though. Two days on the road with this loony shepherd had sapped a good deal of his ordinarily easygoing nature and all of his patience. Could anyone really be even half as stupid as Dunwin pretended to be? If so, Phrenk would pay a year's salary for the privilege of never meeting them.

"It's a mask," he said. "It's to hide your identity. Now where do you *think* you should put it?"

"Oh," said Wulfrith, nodding. He set aside his sandwich, stood up, and tried to shove his foot through one of the eyeholes.

"What are you *doing?*" Phrenk screamed. Luckily for him, the few travelers on the nearby road mistook his distress for the cry of a helpless victim of cutthroat robbers and hurried on about their own business.

Phrenk snatched the mask from Wulfrith's hands before the lad could tear the rich old cloth. "It covers your *face,* idiot!" he snapped, and jerked it over Wulfrith's head before the boy could protest.

Wulfrith pulled the mask off almost at once. It was one of those hooded affairs, the kind nine out of ten fashion-conscious executioners and tax collectors preferred, but the wizard's apprentice knew little about fashion. All he knew was that the mask was hot, tickly, and smelly, and that Phrenk was weird.

"Put it back on," Phrenk said, gritting his teeth.

"I don't think so," Wulfrith replied. He was quite calm. If Phrenk was about to lose the last few marbles in his mental pouch, Wulfie was entirely prepared to toss a spell at him right here and now, out in the open. It wouldn't be a very showy spell—during their frequent picnics he'd spied one or two Gorgorian patrols on the highroad and he didn't want one of them to catch him working sorcery—just something domestic and unpretentious, like giving Phrenk the sudden, irresistable urge to take a nap, and Mungli . . .

Funny, every time he looked at Mungli his mind started thinking of other sudden, irresistable urges. Unfortunately, he had no idea at all of what to call them or what to do about them. It was even more uncomfortable than the mask.

Which he was *not* going to put on again, and that was that.

Phrenk must have read Wulfrith's decision in his eyes, for he dropped the bullying approach at once. "Look here, Dunwin, my boy," he said, casually tossing the mask aside. "You don't have to wear the mask if you don't want to. We can still have a lovely time at the palace if you refuse to wear it." He sighed. "It will be a great disappointment to Mungli, though."

Mungli gave Phrenk a startled look that as much as said *It will?* For the first time since they had undertaken this mission, he had the supreme satisfaction of being able to stretch out his legs and surreptitiously give her a vicious kick in the ankle, just the sort she'd doled out to him under the table at the village tavern. She took the hint and put on a wide-eyed, moist gaze of bitter disappointment.

That look pierced Wulfrith's heart. "Will it?" he asked, bewildered. "But—why?"

"Ah, the innocence of you young upcountry lads." Phrenk patted Wulfrith's shoulder. "How refreshing it is to meet a youth who has absolutely no idea of civilized manners. You see, my boy, a palace is not at all like your smoke-stained, reeking, rushes-and-dog-droppings-on-the-floor village tavern."

(Here he closed his eyes and said a silent prayer to Belchops, God of Fishermen, asking forgiveness for having told such a barrel-thumping whopper without a rod and line in his hands. The truth of things was that ever since King Gudge's ascension, most of the ceremonial public rooms in the royal Hydrangean palace would have to improve to meet minimal rushes-and-dog-droppings-on-the-floor standards.)

"No, no," he went on. "There are certain customs, laws and usages proper to palace life. You can respect them and enjoy the many delights a palace has to offer, or you can be a fierce free spirit who does whatever he likes—*outside* the palace walls."

"What's that got to do with Mungli?" Wulfrith asked.

"Mungli has become rather . . . *fond* of you, lad," Phrenk said, putting a full load of insinuation on the word "fond."

"You have?" Wulfrith asked Mungli. The Gorgorian bobbed her head so enthusiastically that the fledgling wizard feared for a moment that it might snap off.

"Mungli is not a lady to bestow her . . . *fondness* upon

just any man," said Phrenk. He made a strange noise in his throat which anyone with a keen enough ear would recognize as the sound of hysterical, scornful laughter being pummeled into the shape of a cough. Mungli gave him a cold glare.

"Really?" Wulfie gazed at the lady in question warmly. "I'm honored."

"As well you might be, my boy," Phrenk assured him. "However, much as she is . . . *fond* of you, she is forbidden by law to show you just how . . . *fondly* she feels until she has introduced you to her royal mistress. You see, lad, Mungli is no less a person than chief handmaid to her Serene and Gloriously Flowering Highness, Queen Artemisia." Out of sheer reflex, Phrenk made the gesture of Milky-White Chrysanthemum Blossoms At Dawn Of A Frosty Morning Being Not Half So Entrancing And Worthy Of Poetic Adoration As The Noble Person Whose August Name These Unworthy Lips Have Just Mentioned.

Wulfrith was sure Phrenk was having a fit. That would be perfectly in keeping with his other behavior, after all.

"As Queen Artemisia's chief handmaid, Mungli must reside only in the queen's own apartments," Phrenk lied. "It is a sacred custom that no man outside of the royal family or the palace service may enter these apartments unless his face be completely masked. Am I going too fast for you?" he asked, noticing the odd look that had come over Wulfie's face.

"No," Wulfrith admitted. "I understand what you're saying, I just don't see the sense in it, that's all."

"Oh, well, *sense!*" Phrenk made a shorter, less exotic gesture, waving away the very idea. "If it's *sense* you want, you might as well have stayed at home."

Wulfrith thought back to the last thing he had seen at home. The spectacle of all those transformed animals blundering about might be called many things, but *sensible?*

Then he thought about all the things a simple word like *fond* might mean.

Without another peep of objection, Wulfrith got up, retrieved the mask, and put it on.

"The eyeholes go around to the front," said Phrenk.

Queen Artemisia sat stiff as a carved image of Vimple, her fingernails gouging slivers from the armrests of her chair. Mungli had just burst in upon her, waving her hands madly and leering so broadly that only an idiot or a Gorgorian could fail to understand that the mission had been a successful one.

A furious series of yes-or-no questions on Artemisia's part quickly revealed that the faithful Phrenk had managed to slip the young man into the palace and was presently awaiting word from his queen that the coast was clear before attempting to bring him up into the royal apartments. Artemisia made a few arrangements, then sent Mungli off to fetch the men. Now she could do nothing more than wait.

A footstep sounded in the hall outside—several footsteps, in fact. The Gorgorian guards did not challenge the queen's guests—Artemisia had merely mentioned that she was expecting a visit from her dear son, Prince Arbol, and for some reason all the guardsmen at the same time discovered that they had very urgent business elsewhere. It was a remarkable coincidence, but better a coincidence than an unscheduled trip headfirst down a flight of stairs.

The door opened and Phrenk and Mungli came into the queen's presence. Between them they dragged a weakly struggling young man in a hooded mask. He was wearing the very clothes Artemisia had sent along with her messenger, and at first glance his build did indeed resemble the lithe, selectively muscular body of the prince.

So did the bodies of about three-quarters of Prince Arbol's chosen Companions.

"Leave us," said Artemisia. Her voice was hoarse and tense. Phrenk and Mungli bowed, then cast inquiring eyes at the queen's bedchamber door. "Oh, yes, yes, go ahead if you must," she replied impatiently. The pair sprinted off, slamming the gilded door behind them hard enough to send glittering flakes to the floor.

"Where did Mungli go?" Wulfrith asked wistfully.

"Never mind," the queen snapped. "Sit." She pointed stiffly at a stool which she had set nearby on purpose.

Wulfrith did as he was told. The same texts from which he had learned so tantalizingly little about damsels had been remarkably clear when they spoke of kings and queens. Even the highest of high-ranking wizards obeyed when a king or queen gave them an order. Not one of the wizards in the old books ever stopped to ask why he—presumably capable of turning the royal personage into something small, green, and hoppy on a moment's notice—was taking the orders instead of giving them.

Of course, Wulfrith reasoned, the books all took place in palaces, and hadn't Phrenk said that common sense always got left on the palace doorstep with the extra kittens?

Sensible or not, Wulfrith now knew one thing with all the certainty of his heart: He wanted to stay in the palace. It had nothing to do with Mungli. His body had been sending him so many confusing and upsetting signals lately that he was fed up with all twinges, throbs, shivers, and tingles of unknown origin.

Ah, but his mind was another story! His mind knew what it liked and what it wanted and, more importantly, how to get it.

What his mind wanted was the Royal Library. All of it. Now.

When they had first entered the palace, Phrenk had whisked him straight into the Royal Library because it was the one place no self-respecting Gorgorian would ever go. Wulfrith took one look at the racks and stacks and shelves and piles of wonderful books and fell in love. That was why, when Mungli came scampering back to fetch him into Artemisia's presence, he had dragged his feet and struggled. He didn't want to go.

He would do anything it took to stay.

"What is your name?" Artemisia asked.

"Wulfrith, ma'am," he replied. "Only Phrenk calls me Dunwin all the time. I know he works for you and all, but if you don't mind my saying so, he's a few vermin short of a plague, if you know what I mean."

"To be sure, to be sure," said the queen. She was only half-listening to the lad. His voice! It was not the exact duplicate of Prince Arbol's—that would be too much to ask—but training might overcome that. The tone was close, and it was only slightly deeper.

"Can you keep a secret, Wulfrith, dear?" she asked.

"Yes, ma'am." Wulfrith restrained an impulse to snort derisively. What sort of wizard's apprentice would he be if he *couldn't* keep a secret?

"You have been brought here on my orders. I hope you don't mind." Artemisia batted her eyelashes at him in her most fetching manner. She felt rather awkward about flirting with someone who might well turn out to be her own son, but she was desperate.

"Oh, I don't mind, ma'am. I like it here," Wulfrith said sincerely.

He looked like a man bewitched. *I've still got it,* the queen thought with some satisfaction. Artemisia had no way of knowing that all of Wulfrith's tender yearning was not for her, not for Mungli, but for, among others, a first folio copy of *The Elements of Elementals* which he had glimpsed in the Royal Library.

"I'm so glad," she cooed. "Well, since that's settled and we're such good friends, why don't you take off that mask of yours?" She tried to sound offhanded about it.

"May I?" Wulfrith jumped at the suggestion. "I was told that unless I work here at the palace, I have to stay masked while I'm in your apartments."

"Well, then we'll just have to find a job for you, won't we?"

"I'd make a good librarian," Wulfrith suggested.

"How sweet." Artemisia's laugh was brittle. "I'm afraid we have no use for a librarian in these sorry times.

Take off the mask, dear. I can often tell which job a person is best suited for by examining his face."

"But if I got the library into better shape, more people would use it and then . . ."

"Take it off!" the queen shrieked, as the suspense finally got the better of even her iron self-control. Poor Wulfrith almost wrenched his wrist yanking the mask off so quickly.

Then for a long moment he sat, blinking at the queen, wondering just what was really going on.

Artemisia stared. There could be no doubt: Here was one of her long-lost babies come home again. It was a miracle. Her lips were parted, but it was an effort to breathe. She thought she was going to burst into tears and knew that she must not. Years of training and centuries of breeding came to her rescue. She took a deep breath and smiled.

"Oh, how charming!" she remarked lightly. "What a funny coincidence. You look ever so much like my own darling son, Prince Arbol. *Such* a surprise! Well, that certainly settles the matter."

"Yes, ma'am," Wulfrith replied, a little dubiously. "I'm glad it does. What matter?"

"Your job, dearest." Try as she did, the queen could not help allowing a tinge of real feeling to seep into her words as she gazed hungrily at Wulfrith. "You shall be Prince Arbol's official food taster. Oh, don't fret—it's purely a ceremonial appointment. Hardly anyone tries to poison the heir to the throne these days. But your real job will be to serve as the prince's companion. If I know Arbol, the prince will be just as enchanted as I am by the *truly amazing coincidence that has no other connection with reality* which makes the two of you look so similar."

"Oh," said Wulfrith. He had heard of food tasters. He had also heard of Prince Arbol. "Yes, ma'am. Um, this job of mine—does it mean I get to live in the palace?"

"Certainly."

"And I can go anywhere I want?"

"Within limits, you naughty boy. And only when you aren't serving the prince."

Wulfrith's eyes shone.

"There's only one thing," said the queen. Wulfrith looked worried. "You have to wear the mask. It's traditional for Royal Hydrangean Food Tasters. If their identity is hidden, traitors can't seek them out with bribes and foul conspiracies. There is also the advantage that, should one food taster suffer an—ahem—occupational setback, he may be replaced without anyone being the wiser."

"Occupational . . . setback?" Wulfrith echoed, a trifle shaky.

To his utter amazement, the queen threw her arms around his neck and exclaimed, "Oh, but that will never happen to you! It mustn't! I won't allow it! Oh, please say you'll accept the job, dearest Wulfrith. Please, please, please!"

Wulfrith was thoroughly confused now. Nothing he had ever read prepared him for Artemisia's outburst. Did queens always conduct job interviews like this? To use one of Clootie's favorite sayings, she didn't seem to have her cauldron on the fire.

Then he thought of the library.

He pulled the mask back over his head and announced, "What do I taste first?"

Chapter Sixteen

As Clootie watched Dunwin recede in the east, in hot pursuit of his vanished Bernice, it occurred to the wizard fairly quickly that perhaps, if he had himself mistaken Dunwin for Wulfrith, old Odo had mistaken Wulfrith for Dunwin, and had dragged the wrong boy home to do his chores.

In that case, Wulfrith might be in Odo's cottage at this very moment. Accordingly, the sorcerer marched up the mountainside.

Odo's cottage was chiefly distinguished from the surrounding mud by virtue of having windows; the rocks and mounds of earth around it were not equipped with shutters, and the holes in them were generally dark and lifeless, while the faint glow and rancid stench of a sheep-fat lamp emerged from the openings in the cottage wall.

Clootie stepped up, and, seeing nothing he immediately recognized as a door, called through one of these openings, "Hello in there! Odo!"

"Go 'way," someone called back.

Thus encouraged, Clootie located a piece of wood that he assumed to be a door and knocked loudly thereupon. He continued to do so until at last the exasperated Odo flung the portal wide and stared out.

"What do *you* want?" he demanded.

"I'm looking for Wulfrith," Clootie explained.

Odo spat. "Not my name," he said. "My uncle Wulfrith was hanged years ago." He started to step back inside, but Clootie held up a restraining hand.

"I know that," the sorcerer said. "Your name's Odo, right?"

Odo glared suspiciously. "It might be," he admitted.

"Yes, well, Odo, I was wondering if you'd seen Wulfrith."

"My uncle Wulfrith was hanged years ago," Odo repeated. "Tole you that a'ready."

"Not your uncle, the other Wulfrith."

Odo considered this for a long moment. "What Wulfrith would that be?" he asked at last.

"Dunwin's brother."

"That was my uncle that . . ."

"No, the *other* Dunwin. The young one. I mean the Wulfrith that's *his* brother."

Odo puzzled at that for a moment, and finally worked it out. "Oh, *that* Wulfrith!" he said.

"Yes, that Wulfrith," Clootie agreed.

"I sold him," Odo said. "Years ago." He squinted at the wizard. "Come to that, war'n't you the one that bought him?"

"Yes, I was," Clootie said, "but I've lost him—mislaid him, anyway—and I was wondering if he'd come back here."

Odo shrugged. "Not so I've noticed."

"He looks almost exactly like Dunwin," Clootie explained. "I wondered if maybe you'd thought he was Dunwin and brought him back here with you."

Odo eyed him suspiciously. "Are you asking for your money back?" he asked. "Because you'll not be gettin' it. You bought Wulfrith fair and square, and you're stuck with 'im, and besides, it's spent long since."

"No, no—I want *Wulfrith* back!"

"I ain't got 'im."

"Well, that's what I wanted to ask—are you *sure* you don't have him?"

"Of course I'm sure!"

"You don't have someone here you think is Dunwin?"

Odo scratched his head, dislodging assorted arthropods. "If I did have someone here I thought was Dunwin, it'd bloody well *be* Dunwin!" he said. "Wouldn't it?"

Clootie coughed. "Well, no, it wouldn't, I'm afraid."

"And why not?"

"Because Dunwin's run off after Bernice."

"That's naught new," Odo said. "He's run after her plenty of times. He'll catch her soon enough."

Clootie explained, "But this time Bernice was turned into a dragon, and she flew over the fence and got away."

Odo glowered wordlessly at him.

"Really," Clootie said, weakly.

"Bernice *what?*"

"She turned into a dragon. Or rather, *I* turned her into a dragon."

Odo spat a gob of something green off to the side. "You what?"

"I turned her into a dragon."

"How'd you do that?"

"By magic—I'm a wizard, remember?"

"You're no wizard," Odo said. "You're too short."

Clootie sighed. "I'm in disguise," he said.

"No, you're on my mountain."

Clootie was determined not to argue his wizardhood again, and furthermore, he had no idea what Odo was talking about. He attempted to drag the conversation back on course. "Look," he said, "is there *anyone* here besides you? Dunwin, or Wulfrith, or anybody?"

"Not just at this minute," Odo admitted. "I sent Dunwin into town, and he should be back any minute now."

"Well, that's what I was *telling* you," Clootie explained. "He was on his way up here when I turned Bernice into a dragon, and now he's run off after her. So he won't be home."

"Then why'd you ask if he was here?"

"Because if he was here, he'd be Wulfrith."

Odo stared silently at the wizard, and Clootie ran his last statement over again in his mind.

It didn't really make much sense, did it?

"Oh, never mind," Clootie said. "It's been a pl . . . I've enjoyed . . . it's been a challenge talking to you, Odo."

"Same to you, I'm sure." Odo turned and stamped back into his cottage, slamming the door behind him.

Clootie turned away in disgust. That was *one* place Wulfrith wasn't.

Unfortunately, there were plenty of other places to look.

Over the next few days, the magician searched the environs of Stinkberry village quite thoroughly, all without finding any trace of Wulfrith; toward the end, when word of what he was doing had leaked out, he endured the taunts of the villagers as they watched from a safe distance.

"Some wizard! Can't find his own apprentice!"

"Couldn't find his own backside if it wasn't attached."

"Probably turned the boy into a newt while he was drunk, and forgot all about it!"

"I never saw a newt drunk," old Berisarius, somewhat confused, replied to this sally.

"No, when the wizard was drunk, numbwit!" Fernand retorted. "He got good and drunk, and the lad sassed him, and the wizard turned his own apprentice into a newt—*that's* what I'll wager happened!"

"I'll take that wager if you give me three to two . . ."

Clootie tried very hard to pay no attention to any of this, but he couldn't help hearing it, and it added considerably to his growing annoyance.

Even in the convoluted and refined arts of Old Hydrangean sorcery, Clootie thought, there was probably some relatively simple, easy spell for locating lost apprentices; it was, after all, a common enough occurance, an apprentice being mislaid, and such a spell would be private—there would be no public display of functionality, with the consequent loss of face.

Unfortunately, Clootie had no idea at all what the

spell might be. He had never expected to need it. The boy had no call to disappear like this. If he'd gotten himself kidnapped . . .

Well, the boy was a wizard—if the truth be known, Clootie admitted to himself, the boy was probably a better wizard than his master. He could take care of himself.

He would *have* to take care of himself, since Clootie couldn't find him.

It had been rather odd, running into Wulfrith's brother Dunwin like that, the little wizard thought; how had they managed to avoid meeting, all these years? Clootie supposed the fact that he hardly ever left his cave might have had something to do with it.

Maybe Wulfrith *had* met Dunwin, and had gone off with him, and the whole encounter with Dunwin and Bernice, and the argument with Odo, had been an act. That didn't really fit the facts or make very much sense, but as a theory it had a certain perverse appeal.

In *that* case, Wulfrith had left of his own free will, and to one of the more baroque hells with him.

In fact, whatever had become of him, Clootie thought, to one hell or another with him. To hell with everybody. He was a wizard, possibly the last surviving true Old Hydrangean wizard, and he didn't need to put up with a lot of half-witted teasing from a bunch of smelly villagers. He didn't need to spend hours climbing mountains to argue with imbecilic shepherds. He didn't need an inconsiderate, oversized apprentice making his life difficult. He didn't need anything from the outside world at all. He would just go home to his cave and be a hermit henceforth.

And Wulfrith could go live with Odo and Dunwin, if he wanted, if that was what he was doing.

Clootie rather hoped that was where the lad had gone. At least the boy would be out of harm's way.

And he hoped that Wulfrith's brother, that Dunwin, hadn't gotten himself hurt chasing after the dragon. He supposed that the boy would have given up and gone home after a few hours.

* * *

Odo, too, hoped that Dunwin hadn't gotten himself hurt. He didn't know whether the boy had given up his hunt for Bernice; he did know, though, that he hadn't come home.

Some days after Dunwin's departure in pursuit of Bernice, Odo looked unhappily around his home and sighed loudly.

He had tried to clutter the cottage up, to make a nice, comfortable mess of the place, but he just couldn't do it. He didn't have that natural flair for untidiness and sloth that teenage boys have. Ever since Dunwin had left, no matter what he did, the place didn't have that same familiar a-tornado-came-through-here-probably-several-times look to it that it had always had when Dunwin lived there.

It didn't really make very much sense, Odo told himself. He had gotten along just fine for years, living by himself, before Ludmilla had come and died on him. He had been eager to get rid of one of the boys. Why should it bother him that the other one had left?

And it wasn't as if Dunwin had simply disappeared; that funny little man who wasn't really a wizard but who could do magic anyway had explained all that. The boy had gone off looking for Bernice, who had been turned into a dragon.

Right at the moment, Odo wasn't really very clear on what a dragon was. He had forgotten, though he had known once—wasn't a dragon a sort of soldier, or something like that? Of course, the funny little man had said something about Bernice learning to fly, and soldiers didn't usually fly, except if you meant "run away," which soldiers did a lot, and which some people called flying. But it wouldn't get you over fences, would it?

Well, maybe if you were scared enough, it would.

Still, how a ewe could be a soldier he wasn't sure; he didn't see how she could hold a sword, and besides, girls weren't supposed to be soldiers.

So maybe a dragon was something else besides a soldier, and his memory was playing tricks on him again; he wasn't as young as he once was.

Or maybe they'd changed the rules.

"Changing everything these days," he muttered, looking at a malodorous heap of dirty clothing that sprawled in the center of the cottage floor.

The boy hadn't wanted to let Bernice get away and leave him alone, so he had gone after her. That stirred a faint spark of admiration somewhere in Odo.

The boy hadn't wanted to be left alone.

Well, demme, Odo thought, *I* don't want to be left alone, either! With sudden determination he stood up and began rummaging through the debris in search of his boots.

"You find Bernice, boy," he muttered, "and then I'll find *you*!"

Half an hour later, he stood atop the mountain, three of his most trusted sheep at his side, and gazed out over the broad landscape. Off to the east were the forested hills, a maze of leafy trails and hidden byways where the Black Weasel and his Bold Bush-dwellers still fought against the Gorgorians; to the west lay the open plain, and the capital city that was now the Gorgorian stronghold.

If Bernice was a soldier now, he knew where to find her—probably better than that fool boy of his did. Fighting and glory in the east, or a rich, peaceful city in the west, full of cheap wine and cheaper women—it was obvious where all the soldiers would be.

He turned west, and marched down the mountain toward the city.

Chapter Seventeen

"I need a food taster?" Prince Arbol asked doubtfully.

Queen Artemisia nodded emphatically. "Yes," she said, "you do. You need *this* food taster."

Arbol eyed the hooded figure. "Dad doesn't have a food taster anymore," the prince pointed out. "He threw the last one out the window because he didn't hand over the pasties fast enough. Why do *I* need one?"

"Because *you,*" the prince's royal mother informed her offspring, "are a true Hydrangean prince, not just a Gorgorian usurper."

"I am, *too,* a Gorgorian!" Arbol shouted, offended.

"Yes, you are," the queen agreed hastily, "worse luck. But you are *also* my child, and therefore a true scion of the Royal House of Old Hydrangea. And you will have to learn to behave accordingly. Really, dear, must we have this argument every time I see you?"

The prince did not answer that, but said instead, "I'll throw him down the stairs if he annoys me."

Wulfrith, who had listened thus far in silent befuddlement, snorted. If this gawky idiot tried to throw him anywhere, Wulfrith might just forget about the ban on sorcery and turn Arbol into a newt, or a carp, or something.

Or maybe he wouldn't; he didn't have his staff with him, or any of the other trappings of a wizard, and if he tried using Clootie's new spell he might wind up with a rhinoceros, or some other inconvenient creature.

But the prince didn't look any bigger than he was himself, so maybe, Wulfrith thought, he just wouldn't *let* himself be thrown down any stairs.

The queen had mentioned that Wulfrith bore a resemblance to the prince, and Arbol did have a certain odd familiarity, Wulfrith had to admit. There was a resemblance to the queen, of course, but it was more than that.

"Can I see him with that silly mask off, so I know who I'm talking to?" Arbol asked.

Queen Artemisia hesitated.

This was an awkward moment. Sooner or later, her daughter would have to find out what was going on, but surely, she didn't need to know yet . . .

"I mean, for all I know, Mom, you could have a *girl* under there!" Arbol said.

Artemisia, who had been drawing a deep breath in preparation for making a speech, choked suddenly and bent over, coughing. Prince Arbol and Wulfrith watched her nervously, not knowing what they should do, but the fit passed quickly, and with it, some of her caution.

"All right," she said, "you can see him without his mask. Arbol, my child, this is your new food taster. He says his name is Wulfrith."

Wulfrith was unsure whether to bow first, or to take off the mask, so he attempted to do both simultaneously and managed to tangle the mask in his hair and poke himself in the eye with a thumb, but a moment later he had the silly thing off and was able to stand upright and look the prince in the eye.

Those eyes *did* look familiar, and quite a bit like the ones he saw in the mirror.

"Mom," Prince Arbol said, startled, "he looks like *you*!"

Wulfrith blinked.

"Actually," the queen said, as she stared at her two children, "Wulfrith looks like *you*, dear."

He really did. The resemblance was uncanny, even for the children of a single birth. The scholars who had tutored her as a child had taught Artemisia about identical twins, but these two *couldn't* be identical, she told herself. They weren't the same sex, and her teachers had insisted that identicals were identical in that, too.

But there could be no doubt at all that they were siblings. And seeing two of her children together for the first time in more than fourteen years produced a very strange mix of emotions in the queen, leaving her unable to say any more for a moment.

"He does?" Arbol studied Wulfrith, who returned this scrutiny. "I guess he does, a little."

Wulfrith snorted again. He had seen himself in mirrors any number of times, during various magical exercises, and he could see that he and Arbol looked a *lot* alike. What had made it less than immediately obvious was that the prince was a real person, not just an image—and of course, even with a mirror, Wulfrith had never seen himself from the side before.

"Is that why I have to be a masked food taster?" Wulfrith asked. "So people won't get me confused with Prince Arbol?"

The prince's face suddenly lit up. "Oh, Mom," Arbol said, "I know! You wanted him here to take my place, so I could go off hunting, and nobody would know I was gone! He can sit through all the boring stuff here in the palace!"

Caught off-guard, Artemisia said, "Uh . . ."

Sometimes, she reminded herself, she forgot that her daughter was not stupid. The child didn't bother to think if she didn't have to, but she was not stupid.

And it appeared that her brother wasn't, either.

"Is that it?" Wulfrith asked doubtfully. "I don't know about that. I don't know anything about being a prince."

"Of course not," Queen Artemisia acknowledged. "You've been a shepherd all your life, haven't you?"

"Well . . . ," Wulfrith began uncertainly. It was really very inconvenient, this whole business about wizardry being illegal. "Not exactly a *shepherd* . . ."

"Whatever." The queen waved away the unimportant

details of rural job classifications. "In any case, my dear Wulfrith, my dear, *dear* Wulfrith, of course you'll need to learn a great deal about palace life—but yes, I had hoped that you might be willing to fill in for my darling Prince Arbol at certain . . . functions." Artemisia hesitated, then added, "Not right *away,* of course."

"I guess," Wulfrith said, unenthusiastically.

"I think," Artemisia said, "that you two should get to know each other a little better. If Wulfrith will be filling in for you, Arbol, he'll need to know more about *you,* as well as about being a prince."

"Okay, Mom," Arbol said, "we can go practice with swords together! Dad says that's the best way to get to know a man—try to hack his head open, and you'll either see his brains or you'll get an idea how he thinks."

"No!" Artemisia shouted.

"We'll use the wooden ones, Mom—honest! I won't kill him!"

Wulfrith threw the queen an alarmed glance.

"*No,* Arbol! No swords, at least, not yet! A food taster isn't supposed to fight, he's supposed . . . supposed to eat. And Wulfrith would have to keep his mask on, we don't want anyone to know we have a substitute for you, and that wouldn't be fair, would it?"

"Maybe if we enlarged the eyeholes?"

"*No,* I said. Wulfrith doesn't know how to fight—do you, Wulfie?"

"No, ma'am. Uh . . . shepherds don't use swords much." And wizards, he thought, have better weapons—at least, the smart ones.

"Oh, all right." Arbol looked at the new food taster. "What *do* you want to do then, Wulfrith?"

Wulfrith lit up. "We could study together, in the library," he suggested.

Arbol frowned. "The library?"

"The big room with all the books," Wulfrith explained.

"Oh." Arbol was puzzled. "What do you do, throw them at each other?"

"No, silly, you *read* them!"

"Hey, don't call me silly! I'm the prince!"

"I'm sorry," Wulfrith muttered, glancing at the queen, uncomfortably aware that he had made an error in etiquette, and that he was bound to make many more. The stories all said that palace etiquette was very important and very complicated.

"Well, that's okay," Arbol said. "So you like reading?"

"Oh, yes!"

"Wulfrith will be staying in the library, for now, when he's not with you or up here visiting me," the queen interjected. "He won't be bothered there."

"That's for sure!" the prince agreed.

"Maybe I can learn about being a prince by reading some of the books," Wulfrith suggested.

Artemisia sighed. "I'm afraid you'll find them out-of-date," she said. "But it can't hurt to try."

"Well, come on," Arbol said, heading for the door. "I'll walk down there with you, and maybe you can show me a good book to read. One with lots of pictures of swords and horses."

"Put your mask on, dear," the queen said, as Wulfrith followed the prince.

The lad obeyed, and then had to scamper to catch up; the prince's idea of "walking" was what Wulfrith would have considered a fast trot. He wondered what Arbol would call a "run."

Even more dismaying was the fact that Arbol kept up a steady stream of chatter the entire way. "It'll be great having you around here," the prince said. "Sometimes it seems like people avoid me, because I'm the crown prince, you know, and I'll be king when Dad dies, which I hope he never does of course, I like him a lot, even if he is kind of a slob, and of course he killed my grandfather, the old king, did you know about that? His name was Fumitory the Twenty-Second, which is one of those fancy old-fashioned Old Hydrangean names, and I think I'm supposed to have one of those too, except I don't, I mean, Arbol's a good old Hydrangean name but it isn't so prissy, except maybe I really do have a fancy name, I mean another one, because someone told me once that my name was supposed to be Helenium, which I think is a really stupid name, don't you? This is the library, isn't it?"

Wulfrith, a trifle out of breath, nodded. Without thinking he waved his hand in a simple opening spell, and the heavy gilt-and-enamel doors swung wide.

"Hey!" Arbol demanded. "Who did that?"

"Um . . . I did," Wulfrith admitted.

"But you didn't touch the door, I was looking!"

"No," Wulfrith said, shamefaced, "I used magic." He hastened to add, "I'm not a wizard or anything, nobody needs to cut my head off, it's just a trick I learned."

"Hunh." The prince looked at this odd masked companion, then at the door. "Maybe you *are* a girl, after all. I mean, real men don't do magic—that's women's stuff."

"I'm not a girl," Wulfrith replied, a bit hurt.

" 'Course not," Arbol agreed, stepping into the library. "I was teasing a bit. You can't be a girl—you look too much like me!"

"That's right," Wulfrith agreed, following.

The library was equipped with several tall, narrow windows squeezed in between towering bookshelves, but all of them faced southeast, and the afternoon was winding down toward evening. Combined with the fact that nobody had washed the glass in fourteen years, that left the room dim and shadowed.

Seeing how gloomy the library had become, Wulfrith once again acted without thinking, and lit the half-dozen nearest candles.

(That was a very simple spell; it involved using three-finger sign language to sweet-talk a fire elemental through an invisible window from the nether realm. Clootie had never gotten the hang of it, which still mystified Wulfrith.)

Arbol stopped dead.

"Was that more magic?" the prince demanded.

"Oops. Yes, sir," Wulfrith admitted.

"Well, *stop* it! I'm a prince, I can't be seen with some limp-wristed sissy who uses magic! Act like a man!"

"Sorry."

In the candlelight, Arbol looked around at the endless shelves and stacks of dusty, sometimes mildewed volumes, and remarked, "A lot of books."

Wulfrith nodded.

"Are any of them any good?"

Wulfrith blinked in surprise. "Um," he said. "Um." The concept of books not being "any good" was entirely unfamiliar. Some books were better than others, of course, but these were all *books*, which meant learning and wisdom and wonderful words, stories and spells and ancient lore.

Arbol ignored the other's discomfiture and pulled a thick folio off the nearest table. The prince squinted at the faded title, and then, unable to puzzle it out, opened the book at random and read a few lines.

Wulfrith watched, and saw Arbol's lips moving. Whatever positive traits the prince might possess, scholarship did not appear to be among them.

Well, reading was one of those things that one could do just as well alone, Wulfrith reminded himself.

"This is all about somebody named Pollestius, who offended a woman by wearing a ruby ring on the wrong finger," Arbol said, slamming the book shut. "Who cares about that?"

Wulfrith, although he wondered why a lady would care where someone wore a ring, had to admit that it didn't sound terribly exciting.

"What about this one?" he suggested, pointing to a volume he had noticed before, *A Compendium of Mystic Rituals.* He hauled it down from the shelf and opened it.

Arbol took one look at it, then sneered, "It's more magic!"

Wulfrith had somehow failed to realize that people who didn't approve of *practicing* sorcery would not care to *read* about it, either. After all, he liked reading about adventures and battles, but he wouldn't care to be involved in any.

"Oh," he said.

"Listen," Arbol said, "I have other things to do—I think it's almost time for my riding lesson, and we're going to do peasant-trampling today. You go ahead and look around here all you want, and maybe you can find some good stuff for me, for when I come back."

"All right," Wulfrith agreed, looking hungrily at the vast expanse of leather and cloth bindings. "It's been good meeting you, Prince Arbol."

"Yeah. See you later!"

With that, Arbol departed, closing the door carefully.

Wulfrith snatched off the ridiculous hood he wore, and began prowling the stacks.

The books on magic were very tempting, but magic was not what was wanted, here at the palace. The prince apparently wanted adventure stories, or maybe books on combat or horsemanship; for himself, Wulfrith remembered that he was supposed to try to learn something about the business of being a prince.

He wasn't sure just where to start looking. There was so *much* here!

It was then that he noticed a small alcove at the back, one that was dimmer and more shaded than the rest of the room, half-hidden behind a particularly complex tangle of shelving. Curious, he picked up a candle and went to investigate.

At first glance the alcove was ordinary enough—three walls were lined with books, while a dusty table and threadbare upholstered chair stood in the center. Rather fewer of the spines had visible titles than the average, perhaps, but otherwise, Wulfrith saw nothing special about them.

Still, it was a bit cozier and less daunting than the remainder of the Royal Library, so Wulfrith decided to check out a few of the books. He put the candle on the table and studied the nearest shelf.

One title immediately caught his eye. Fortune was with him, he decided, as he pulled *The Prince and the Pretty*

Peasant from its place. He blew off the worst of the dust, then opened it carefully.

There was a finely etched frontispiece. Wulfrith's eyes widened. He sat down suddenly on the chair, ignoring the cloud of dust and mildew that sprayed up on impact, and began turning pages. Choosing a paragraph at random, Wulfrith read:

> "Oh, my Lord, the Wench gasped, I grow faint, for ne'er before have I glimpsed One so Large! Certes, I fear that such as That could make me great Harm, but by the Blessed Goddess Concupiscia, I swear, 'twould perchance be Well Worth It." And with those words, she laid her back upon the Couch, her Skirts flung up to her Thighs.

Wulfrith looked at the illustration on the facing page.

This was a long way from spells or stories of heroic virtue, but there was certainly a fascination to it. Wulfrith saw readily that this might not teach him much about being a prince, but still, he thought it would be very educational indeed. Quickly, he flipped back to the beginning and settled down for a long read.

Chapter Eighteen

Prince Arbol leaped from the saddle and swaggered over to the fifth newly fallen foe of the afternoon. "Had enough, Pentstemon?"

"I had enough about three hours ago," came the cranky reply. "What's gotten into you, my lord?"

Arbol just laughed and offered the fallen Companion a hand up. "You know I've always liked a friendly contest."

"Friendly!" Pentstemon spat out two teeth and part of his horse's tail, which had somehow found its way into his mouth when Arbol's sideways blow with the practice lance sent him tumbling heels over head off the animal's rump. "If that was friendly, I'd hate to have you for an enemy."

The prince leered. "Exactly. That's what Dad says is the whole idea behind kingship: Scare your allies into loyalty and your enemies into line."

Pentstemon shook his head. Then he thought maybe he'd better not. Too many things besides his teeth felt loose and ready to give way. He was one of the Prince's favorite Companions—a corps of likely young men, all of the purest Old Hydrangean blood, all specially selected by Queen Artemisia herself.

(King Gudge didn't meddle much with the prince's upbringing. He had been heard to say during many a royal "council meeting" that he didn't much care what his queen did about bringing up Arbol so long as the prince picked up a proper measure of the traditional Gorgorian Three Bs:

Beer-guzzling, Bashing-in-of-selected-skulls, and Bastard-begetting. "Otherwise I'll have to kill him.")

Later on, after Arbol had dished out enough "friendly" wallopings for all of his Companions to have decided *en masse* that they had to leave him and go do their math homework (math homework was always done in the palace kitchens, where there were plenty of school supplies), Pentstemon held forth on the subject of the prince's new friskiness.

"I don't know what it is," he told the other Companions, "but there's something odd about him lately."

His friends were too busy studying the mysteries of Addition by seeing who could convince the harried kitchen wenches to bring them another keg of beer. ("We've only had two, darling, and if we have just one more that'll just make four. No one'll notice.")

Only young Salix felt like discussing the matter. (He'd had a bit too much to drink and had just demonstrated a Subtraction exercise all over the kitchen floor by taking away one lunch from one stomach.) Looking very pale and fragile he asked, "How d'you mean, odd? 'Shalf Gorgorian. Can' get mushodder'n *that.*"

"No, no, that's not it." By this time Pentstemon's head felt secure enough for him to risk a dubious shake. "I can't put my finger on it."

"Be'er no' try." Salix giggled. "Cut'm ri' off, Arbol would." He made a vicious slicing motion with his hand. "Kaplowie!" He stared at his hand then, surprised that it had made such an inappropriate sound effect. "No. No' kaplowie. I mean *skoosh!* Uh. Maybe I don'. Anyway." He shrugged and toppled over backward.

"What's the matter with *him?*" asked Prince Arbol, joining the keg crowd.

"The usual," Pentstemon replied, a little puzzled by the question. *Everyone* knew about Salix. His drinking was as regular as clockwork—more regular, since the night King Gudge got it into his head to dissect every clock in the palace. Busy councilors had been known to tell the time by whether or not the lad was still standing, and if he was down by measuring the length of the shadow cast by his nose.

"Is he drunk?" asked the prince, kneeling beside the fallen Companion.

Pentstemon frowned. He wondered whether he'd gotten more than his teeth knocked loose in that last bout with Arbol. "You don't *know*, my lord?"

The prince seemed to rouse from some sort of waking dream, and blustered, "Well, of course I *know* he's drunk!" Arbol leaped up and strode back and forth beside the gently snoring body. "I just meant shouldn't we *do* something for him is all!"

Pentstemon smiled. This was more like it! Last time the prince had found Salix in this state, a truly inspirational tableau had been arranged. On waking from his stupor, the victim found himself wearing a chamberpot on his head, hollowed-out pumpkins on his feet, and a frilly lady's undergarment just barely covering his body. There was also a prize Hydrangean hog sharing his bed. Only Prince Arbol's inability to find a voice-throwing mountebank in time for Salix's awakening prevented the beast from asking, "Was it good for you, too?"

"By all means, Highness," Pentstemon said, offering Arbol free access to poor, unwitting Salix. "You get started, I'll bring the hog."

"Hog?" the prince repeated, somewhat distracted. "Hogs are for swamp cough. This won't take but a moment." Arbol knelt beside Salix and passed one hand over the lad's body, as fingers twitched and wiggled strangely.

Salix's eyelids fluttered, then lifted sharply. With a loud war whoop, he sprang to his feet, thumped his chest, took several deep breaths and leapfrogged his way over every kitchen servant until he vanished up the stairs.

Two of the remaining Companions ran after him. They returned shortly to report: "He's galloped out the postern gate and out of the city into the fields. Last we saw of him, he was catching rabbits."

"Well, a little hunting's good for clearing the head," Pentstemon said.

"He wasn't on a horse," said one.

"He was catching them in his teeth," said the second.

Pentstemon and all the other Companions stared hard at their prince. "What did *I* do?" Arbol demanded.

"That's what we'd like to know," Pentstemon replied.

Before Arbol could reply, a soft, sweet voice came purring out of the shadows. "Now, now, boys, we can't have you fighting down here. It upsets the cooks. When they're upset, they make mistakes—untasty mistakes. You *do* know how our beloved king hates untasty mistakes. And you know what he does to the cooks who make them. Good help is so hard to keep, these days, especially when it's been minced into very small pieces."

A dark, voluptuous woman in Gorgorian ceremonial dress emerged from the archway leading to the banquet-hall stairs. Around her neck she wore the heavy gold seal of the King's Foreteller, the only office of high responsibility that the Gorgorians allowed a woman to hold. (Gorgorian men might disdain magic as a weak and silly woman's plaything, but it was handy to have one of the ladies around who could accurately tell the king what he'd be getting for his dinner a few days in advance, so he knew what to kill—the wild game or the cook.)

Pentstemon felt his mouth go dry. Out of the corner of his eye he saw that this woman had affected all of the other Companions in the same way. Even Prince Arbol was licking slightly parted lips in a nervous manner. Those Companions who were older than the prince knew just why the lady's presence was making them sweat. Those of an age with the prince, or younger, didn't know why, but they surely did think it would be fun to find out.

The Gorgorian woman drifted across the kitchen floor like a cloud of musky smoke. Her eye lit upon the prince and she smiled. "Ah, there you are, Your Highness," she breathed. "I've been hoping to find you alone."

"But I'm not . . ." The prince swallowed words of

protest as she leaned forward just enough to tilt her low-cut neckline to an attractive angle. "Oo," said the prince.

The lady's smile widened for a moment, then snapped into a bud of annoyance. "I *said* I was hoping to find him *alone.*" Her cool gaze swept the circle of lip-licking Companions. It was a very meaningful gaze. All of a sudden, Pentstemon seemed to recall wild rumors about how some Gorgorian women were supposed to be able to perform magic—not just fortune-telling. He was too young to remember the Old Hydrangean wizards and their showy, useless spells; all he knew about magic was what he'd read in talebooks, and in these the magic was always used to turn people into things. Green things. Slimy things. Things that went "Kneedeep! Kneedeep!" in bogs.

"We were just going, Lady Ubri," he said hastily.

Apparently his fellow Companions had read the same books as Pentstemon, because they all fled the kitchen at once.

Lady Ubri's smile returned as she watched them scamper. It was amusing to toy with these pathetic Hydrangean puppies. Unfortunately it was almost too easy to do. Ubri always enjoyed a challenge—but she was a very poor loser. When she looked back down to where Prince Arbol still sat on the kitchen floor, where in fact the prince had remained ever since Salix's remarkable recovery, she was painfully reminded of her biggest—and only—loss. She had been little more than a girl, just fifteen, but it still rankled—as well such a loss might.

Damn! How could Gudge have been such a fool as to marry that prissy, petal-soft Hydrangean princess when he could have had *her*? Ubri did not understand much about politics and dynastic marriages, but she knew what she didn't like.

She didn't like Artemisia.

She did like power.

It was a bitter memory indeed, learning that Gudge preferred the pale, golden doll-queen. More bitter, because he'd told her all about it by yanking the sheet out from under her and saying, "You'd better get out of here, uh, what'syourname, Uki? I'm getting married in the morning. Come back day after tomorrow."

Well, she *hadn't* come back, not in *that* capacity. She remained in the palace, hoping Gudge would come to his senses. After awhile she understood that Gudge had no senses to come to. By this time, Artemisia had given birth to the royal heir, Prince Arbol. As day followed day and Ubri jealously watched her rival's child grow up, Ubri's rage grew too.

Then one day, it stopped. For the first time in years, the Gorgorian noblewoman smiled.

The prince was growing up! And a grown-up prince will some day be a king. And a king needs . . .

"A queen," she whispered to her self. "Arbol's queen, if not Gudge's." She glanced at her reflection in one of the palace mirrors. She might be old enough to be Arbol's mother, but you couldn't guess it by looking at her. The years had been very good to Ubri. Stay-at-home Hydrangean customs were so much kinder to the skin than the old Gorgorian way of tramping across mountains, rivers, steppes and such, all with the merciless sun beating down and ruining a girl's complexion. Ubri's face was dark, but not leathery, her black hair still silky, her generous curves enhanced by the healthier diet available to her since the conquest and settlement of Hydrangea.

"I really owe a lot to these people," she mused. "When I am their queen, I shall try not to slaughter too many of them right away."

Now that she was a woman with a plan, Ubri was happy. "The way to a prince's heart is through his stomach . . . and points south," she said. She set out to put that plan into action right away, by cozying up to the prince every chance she got.

It wasn't easy. He wasn't often alone, and when he was, he just didn't seem interested. Arbol was always charging around the palace, scattering guardsmen left and right, or else romping through his military lessons. Ubri knew you can't seduce what you can't catch.

There was the time he'd gone off to war with his royal father and no one had seen him for months. Ubri figured on taking advantage of that trip. She'd disguised herself as a man, hoping to snag the prince on the march. He'd be alone, homesick, maybe a little frightened. She'd be the only woman for miles around—the minor army of camp-followers didn't count, as far as she was concerned. She would reveal herself to him and let Nature take care of the rest. If Arbol had a single drop of Gudge's blood in him, he'd do her job for her.

It was a lovely plan and Ubri was sure it would've worked, except for some reason the prince had his very own tent and allowed no one else to enter, not even his page. Something to do with royal Hydrangean modesty, rumor claimed. When Arbol did emerge, Ubri managed to sidle up and whisper, "Your Highness, I am in truth a woman in man's disguise. I have done this dangerous thing—following you into the teeth of battle—for love of you."

"You're a *girl?*" the prince responded, eyeing her from top to toes. He laughed. "A girl disguised as a man! That's funny. What a great game, dressing up like the opposite sex. I'm going to have to tell the Companions all about it. We've got to try it ourselves, some day, and see if we can get away with it. Will you lend me a dress when we get home?" He tipped her three silver Gorgorian *gexos* and went off to kill some more enemies.

Ubri was fit to be tied.

Which was why she was so pleasantly surprised now. Arbol was staring at her. She knew that breed of stare; she'd gotten it many times over the years, from many men. It was better than central heating. (The Gorgorians might be barbarians, but they understood central heating. You conquered a city and set fire to the biggest building in the center of it.)

Ubri sank down to the floor beside Arbol. "It's such a nice change to find you by yourself, Your Highness," she murmured in his ear. The kitchen servants milling about were just as invisible to her as the camp-followers had been. "If you're not loitering with those silly Companions, you're dawdling around that fusty old bookroom with your new food taster. Why do you waste so much time with him? He's only a servant."

"Oh, he's all right," the prince said rather uneasily.

"You know, if he becomes too great a pest, I could always prepare him a little . . . *snack,* Gorgorian style." Her smile was as bright as a beartrap.

"I wish you wouldn't," the prince replied. "We're . . . we're rather attached to him."

"Well, if that's what you want, my liege. I'll be only too happy to do anything you want. *Anything.*" She edged closer, her gown hissing over the kitchen slabs. "Now, where were we?"

"The library!" cried the prince, for no earthly reason Ubri could see. He sprang to his feet. "I forgot about the library! I was supposed to be there to meet . . . I have to go. Good-bye. See you later." He sprinted off, leaving Ubri on the floor, growling native Gorgorian curses.

He didn't stop running until he reached the library. Once inside, he shot the bolt and leaned back, panting.

"Well, did it work?" came the question. Queen Artemisia looked up from her place at one of the tables.

He just nodded. "No one saw anything different."

"Good." She reached into her sleeve and drew out the food taster's mask. "Then put this back on. We'll play again tomorrow, and this time we'll let Arbol wear the mask and see if people think he's you at the same time you're pretending to be him."

As Wulfrith tugged the mask back on, he wondered whether he ought to tell the queen about the very friendly Gorgorian lady he'd met down in the kitchens.

He decided he wouldn't. This game Queen Artemisia had devised was lots more fun than anything he'd ever done with old Clootie. He didn't want to spoil it for anyone.

Especially not if that nice Gorgorian lady wanted to play.

Chapter Nineteen

"What ho, lad!"

Dunwin looked up, mildly startled, as a large young man in leafy-green forester's garb (with clashing sky-blue lapels) plunged out of a tree onto the roadway in front of him.

"Hello," Dunwin said, as the other landed on the path and fell to his knees, only keeping himself from flattening out completely by throwing out a hand at the last moment.

The fellow in green got quickly to his feet, brushing dirt from his hose with one hand, and shaking the other to restore circulation; Dunwin could see that the palm was bright red from the force of the impact.

"Ho, lad! Stand where you are!" the man called, squinting down at his knees and deciding that they would do.

"I *am* standing where I am," Dunwin pointed out. "How could I stand anywhere else?"

The young man looked up. "Here, now, none of that! We don't take kindly to those tricksy wordgames around *here*! We're simple, straightforward men of the greenwood, we are!"

"Jumping out of trees doesn't seem like a very simple, straightforward thing to do," Dunwin pointed out.

"Ah, but that was to get the drop on you, so that you'd have no time to call your men or draw your sword!"

Dunwin blinked. He turned and looked back down the highway, then peered down at his empty belt.

"I don't have a sword," he said. "Nor any men."

"I can *see* that," the other said, a bit rattled. "But if you *had*, I mean. We couldn't tell from up there whether you had any men with you. Or swords."

"Oh." Dunwin looked up, and saw two other men in brown and green tunics sitting in the same giant oak that the one had jumped from. He waved a polite greeting; the two waved back.

"Terrible view from up there," the leaper explained, "with the leaves in the way and everything, but it's got such nice branches for dropping out of, and it's sort of traditional."

"I see," Dunwin said politely.

For a moment the two of them stood there, facing each other; then Dunwin said, "Well, if that's all, I'll be going on, then. I've got a lost ewe to find. A sheep." He took a step forward.

"Not so fast!" The man in green held up a hand. "Don't you know where you are, and who we are?"

Dunwin scratched an ear, dislodging three or four fleas. "I'm in the eastern hills," he said, "and you're some stranger dressed in a silly costume who's just fallen out of a tree for no very good reason that I can see. I don't see how either of these has anything to do with me or Bernice."

"Ha ha!" The man did not laugh, he simply said, very loudly, "Ha ha!" Dunwin thought this a very odd thing to do. "You are in the domain of the dashing and heroic Black Weasel, and we before you are his Bold Bush-dwellers, come to exact his toll!"

"I don't have any money," Dunwin said. "Can I go on now?" He took another step.

"Not so fast!" the other said. "You're a likely-looking young fellow; if you've no coin, then you'll pay with a year's service!"

Dunwin shook his head. "Look, I'm very sorry, but I

don't have time for that. I've got to find Bernice." He took another step.

The Bold Bush-dweller braced his feet apart and thrust out a hand, catching Dunwin's chest. "You shall not pass!" he proclaimed.

Dunwin reached up and removed the hand from his chest. The Bold Bush-dweller tried to prevent this, and Dunwin was forced to use pressure.

The man in green managed not to scream as his wrist was squeezed and pushed aside. It felt as if the bones were scraping against each other, squashing the flesh out from between them like soft cheese.

When Dunwin let go, the Bold Bush-dweller stared at his hand for a moment, watching the color gradually return to normal, and glorying in the pain he felt; he had been very much afraid that that hand might never feel anything again. The shepherd was stronger than he looked, and he didn't exactly look like any nine-stone weakling to begin with.

The sensible thing to do would obviously be to let him go on looking for his sheep. Unfortunately, the Black Weasel's orders were very definite and very emphatic, and as every Bush-dweller knew, the Black Weasel was not a sensible man. *Every* traveler had to be stopped.

By the time he could work all his fingers again, the shepherd had walked on past; the Bush-dweller turned and ran after him, grabbing the back of his tunic with both hands.

"Not so fast there . . . ," he began.

He did not finish the sentence, as he was distracted by the novel sensation of traveling through the air horizontally. It felt surprisingly different from the familiar vertical drop out of the tree.

Then he abruptly stopped traveling at all, having arrived in a large thornbush. Any concerns about the Black Weasel's orders were put aside until he had dealt with the rather more immediate problems posed by several hundred inch-long, needle-sharp thorns and the accompanying leaves and woodwork.

He did hear the sound of two large objects thudding onto the road, and assumed that his companions were following instructions and had dropped from the tree to subdue the reluctant shepherd boy. He supposed they would have no trouble. The lad had to be a bit winded after heaving a fifteen-stone man into a thornbush that stood a good five yards from the roadway, and the other two Bush-dwellers knew that their target was not the harmless oaf he had first appeared.

He concentrated on disentangling himself while retaining a maximum amount of unpunctured skin.

He did not really pay attention to the voices exchanging words, or the thumps as they exchanged something a little heavier than words, or the clatter as the Bush-dwellers took up their staves and the shepherd boy snatched up a fallen treelimb to defend himself.

Eventually, though, he was able to stand upright on his own two feet without any direct contact with sharp objects. He brushed himself off, lightly touched the innumerable scratches on his cheeks, shuddered at the discovery of how close some had come to his eyes, and then turned to look at the others.

He was astonished to find the battle still raging. Ochovar—his official nickname of Off-White Chipmunk had failed to stick, as had many of the later coinages—was swinging his staff wildly, warding off the shepherd boy's attack; the other Bush-dweller, Wennedel, sat on the ground nearby, clearly dazed, his staff in pieces beside him.

"Hey!" the former resident of the thornbush called. "You can't do that!"

"Why not?" Dunwin asked, startled. He turned an inquiring glance toward the speaker, and promptly received a solid whack across the back of his head from Ochovar's weapon. He staggered.

"Because there are three of us, all highly trained in every form of combat, and only one of you, and you're just a poor ignorant shepherd boy," the Bush-dweller explained, as Ochovar drew back for another swing.

"Oh," Dunwin said. Ochovar hesitated, staff held ready. His companion nodded; humanity was all very well, but there was no point in taking stupid chances.

Ochovar put everything he had into it, coming up from the knees, his whole weight in the swing; even so, Dunwin managed to roll with it somewhat.

He still went down, facefirst. Ochovar promptly sat on him, staff held ready for another whack.

Wennedel, moving stiffly, joined Ochovar. The third Bush-dweller approached cautiously, then sat down cross-legged in front of Dunwin's face. He waited, picking thorns from his hose, and studied the shepherd's face.

There was something rather familiar about it.

When the boy's eyes showed signs of focusing, the Bush-dweller said, "As I was saying, lad, you show promise, but you clearly don't stand a chance against the likes of us. I like you, though, so I tell you what we'll do. We'll take you to meet our leader, the mighty Black Weasel himself, and we'll let him decide what to do with you. You tell him about your lost sheep, and maybe he'll even help you find her."

Dunwin blinked. "Well, why didn't you say so in the first place?" he asked. He got to his feet, sending Ochovar and Wennedel tumbling, and picked up his fallen tree branch. "Let's go," he said.

Ochovar looked at the spokesman; Wennedel looked at Ochovar. "How hard did you hit him?" Wennedel whispered.

"As hard as I bloody well could, of course!" Ochovar hissed back. "What do you *think*?"

"I think maybe you knocked the brains right out of him, only he hasn't noticed yet," Wennedel replied.

The spokesman shook his head. "No, I think he was *always* like that," he said quietly. "I mean, who'd be chasing a lost sheep here in the forest?" Aloud, he asked, "What's your name, lad?"

"Dunwin," Dunwin said. "After my uncle that got himself hanged."

"That figures," the spokesman muttered. Aloud, he

said, "Good to meet you, Dunwin. I'm called the Blue Badger." He held out a hand to shake, but Dunwin didn't notice it, and after a moment it was withdrawn. The Badger frowned slightly.

"We better blindfold him," Ochovar said. "I don't know if the boss will want to keep this one."

"An excellent point," the Badger agreed. "Who's got the cloth?"

After a moment of embarrassed silent exploration, the Badger let out a sigh. "Well, this tunic was ruined anyway," he said, tearing a strip of thorn-pierced fabric from his own garment.

Dunwin made no protest as the blindfold was tied in place; he had no reason to, since the multiple thornholes left him well able to see. He saw no need to mention this.

Thus prepared, the three Bush-dwellers led the lad through the forest by secret paths—Dunwin knew they were secret paths, because the letters carved on the trees marking the route clearly said SECRET PATH, DO NOT ENTER. BOLD BUSH-DWELLERS ONLY—until they arrived in a small clearing, at the center of which stood an ancient beech tree. Beneath the beech stood a large, badly weathered chair that had apparently been gilded once; lounging comfortably in the chair was a rather tired-looking man dressed entirely in black, holding a golden goblet.

"Yes, Badger?" the man in the chair said wearily.

"Oh, Black Weasel, brave and dashing heroic leader of the Bold Bush-dwellers in their valiant struggle against the abominable Gorgorian oppressors who have plundered our fair kingdom," the Blue Badger said, "we captured this fellow on our way back from town."

"Did you get the salt? And the nails?"

"Yes, Black Weasel. Wennedel—I mean, the Crimson Slug has them."

The Black Weasel nodded. "Good. Now, about this lad you caught—is this one signing up for a year's service, or is he a recruit? Or are you being playful again?"

"This one's not decided, Black Weasel," the Badger

said. "He shows a real talent for brawling, but he's only interested in finding a lost sheep."

The Black Weasel sighed. "Is he even an Old Hydrangean? All the best brawlers these days seem to be runaway Gorgorians."

"Of course I'm Old Hydrangean," Dunwin said, offended.

"I think he is, Black Weasel," the Badger interjected. "His face has the look; I'd say there's even a faint resemblance to yourself."

As he spoke, the Blue Badger took a closer look. There certainly *was* a resemblance, he saw. Dunwin was bigger across the chest and his skin perhaps a shade darker, but his features definitely echoed the Black Weasel's, and the hair was the same lustrous black.

Mere coincidence, of course, the Badger told himself.

"Well, that's a good start, anyway," the Black Weasel said. "You're a shepherd, boy?"

"That's right, sir."

"Well, *I* am the Black Weasel, brave and dashing heroic leader of the Bold Bush-dwellers in their valiant struggle against the abominable Gorgorian oppressors who have plundered our fair kingdom."

"Pleased to meet you, I'm sure." Dunwin was unsure whether he should bow, and decided not to bother. "My name's Dunwin. I'm looking for Bernice."

"Bernice is your lost sheep?"

"Yes, sir."

"Well, we don't see very many sheep around here; what does she look like?"

Dunwin hesitated.

"Well," he said, "she's very big, for a sheep. She's green, and sort of shiny, and all over scales, sort of like a lizard, or maybe a water snake."

The Black Weasel's attention had wandered somewhat: he had been staring off across the clearing, but now he sat up straight and stared directly at Dunwin.

"Your *sheep* is green and scaly?" he asked.

Dunwin nodded unhappily.

Ochovar smothered a snicker. The Blue Badger shrugged expressively. Wennedel tapped his head significantly.

The Black Weasel pondered this for a long moment, then turned to the Blue Badger. "*How* good a brawler?" he demanded.

The Blue Badger said, "Pretty good. He threw me in a thorn bush, then took on both my men, their quarterstaves against a tree branch, and had Wennedel down before Ochovar caught him a sound buffet."

The Black Weasel drummed his fingers on one arm of his chair, thinking; then he announced, "Dunwin, my lad, we're here to aid all good Old Hydrangeans. We'll find your sheep for you! But first, we ask that in exchange, you join our merry band. We'll train you in fighting, we'll give you a fine sword, and when the time is ripe, you'll join us in the battle against the foul Gorgorians! What do you say?"

Dunwin looked around. He noticed that in addition to the three who had captured him, and the Black Weasel himself, there were at least a dozen other green- and brown-clad men watching from among the surrounding trees.

"You'll help me find Bernice?" he asked.

"My word on it," the Black Weasel said. "If any of us ever see a green, scaly sheep, or hear word of one, we'll let you know at once."

Dunwin glanced around at the watching warriors again, then shrugged. "All right," he said, "I'll do it."

Chapter Twenty

"You know," said King Gudge to the freshly severed head before him, "it's all right if *I* say stuff like that about Prince Arbol—the unnatural brat's my son, after all—but that doesn't mean it's all right for just anyone to go around making personal remarks about the spunkless little worm." He belched eloquently and tossed the head backward over his right shoulder.

Lady Ubri caught it in midflight and brought it back. "The *left* shoulder, my liege," she murmured. "Left for luck."

"Stupid woman's nonsense," the king snarled, glowering at the head.

"If you don't believe me, you can look it up yourself, Your Majesty; the facts are documented. Toss it over the right shoulder and we get rain."

"Damned girlie mumbo-jumbo." Gudge gave Ubri a dirty look, but he did toss the head over the rainless shoulder. Rain was nasty stuff; gave a man a bath whether he wanted one or not.

The remainder of Gudge's royal council sat in pale-lipped silence through the whole of this Gorgorian ritual. They had been shocked into utter stillness, to a man, when the late Lord Kaber had made his last, unfortunate remark, namely: "Boys will be boys, as you say, Your Majesty, and even though the brothel which our beloved Prince Arbol's Companions raided was one of my properties I am less distressed by the fact that I lost so much income last night as by the fact that your own dear son was not a member of the raiding party, and I do wonder—in light of how much time the young man seems to spend in the company of his food taster—if perhaps his, ah, inclinations ought to be looked into, with an eye to the future and the ultimate continuation of your own royal line which will *not* be continued, as you well know, if the prince does not show at least some casual interest in the female of the species."

It was a very long last remark, one which Gudge edited curtly with his sword.

"There is nothing wrong with my son!" the king roared, slamming his fist onto the council table top.

"Of course not, Your Majesty," came the instant reply from Lord Viridis. He was seated next to Lord Kaber's headless corpse and had suddenly developed a nasty nervous tic in his right cheek. "Not a thing. Perfectly normal young man."

The king shook his head. "Why he's got to spend all that time with that masked-up food taster fellow, though—I can't say I like it."

"You could kill the food taster, if you want." The suggestion came from a councilor who always chose a seat well out of sword's reach. He was therefore one of Gudge's bolder advisors.

"Think I don't know that?" the king bellowed. He chucked his empty goblet at the upstart.

The goblet was made of solid gold set with heavy jewels and large enough to hold a full bottle of wine. It made a lovely, ringing *p-toinnnng!* as it struck the outspoken councilor right in the middle of his forehead. He managed a shaky, "I th-thank Your Ma-Majesty for noticing this unwo-unworthy servant," before he slid under the board.

"The trouble with having royal advisors," the king muttered half to himself, "is that they're always trying to give a man *advice*!" He was still grumbling and grousing when Lady Ubri slipped unnoticed from the hall.

Lady Ubri knew that it was a normal part of living for

human beings to sometimes wish they were someone or something other than what they'd been born. Some men wished they could become women, some women yearned to be men, many hard-working peasants envied the easy life of the cat by the fire while the starving stray desired nothing more than to be a peasant with a roof over his head and a belly that was filled at least some of the time.

At the moment, Lady Ubri wished the unthinkable: She wished she were King Gudge.

It wasn't about power, for once. No, what Ubri envied her royal lord was his brain. It didn't make sense, at first glance. Indeed, when the wish initially showed itself, her own fine mind had shrieked, "*What* brain?" But Ubri knew that Gudge had one; it was just very, very small. There was no room in it for doubts. He knew what was what, and acted accordingly. If he didn't like the way matters stood, he killed people until things got better. And he was never confused about his son, Prince Arbol.

Lady Ubri wished she could say the same. Her plot—her wonderful, shiny, simple plot to seduce the prince and rule the kingdom through him—had gone splat. If she didn't know any better, she would swear that Prince Arbol had a plot of his own, a plot called: Let's See How Fast I Can Drive Lady Ubri Crazy.

The Gorgorian noblewoman ground her pretty teeth as she recalled, in painful detail, every single encounter she had had with the prince. She had been very lucky, managing to get the boy alone a score of times. Unfortunately, her luck only went as far as giving her the opportunity to seduce him. Half the time, he had been either cold to her advances or just not aware of them. The other half she imagined he was warming up nicely, but what good did it do her? Despite his obvious interest in her charms, the prince kept fidgeting around as if he had somewhere else to be and a lot of important people waiting for him to be there.

"He toys with me," Ubri murmured darkly. "It is like *skizbrax*, the happy game of my childhood, where you hang an enemy naked from a tree in a pit, using a noose too slack to strangle him immediately. Then you release a starving wolverine, only you keep yanking the rope every time the beast leaps." She could not help but smile over the innocent pastimes of her youth.

A hard glint came into the Gorgorian lady's eye. Hers was a stubborn race. If they hadn't been so stubborn, they would still have been sitting around dung fires in the middle of the Gorgor Plateau, waiting to see what happened next. Stubbornness had gotten them where they were, off that damned plateau and into a palace, and stubbornness was going to get Lady Ubri onto the palace throne or she'd know the reason why.

"Quitters never wear crowns," she told herself, and set out once more to locate the vacillating prince.

"Well?" said Prince Arbol as Wulfrith stole back into the royal heir's private rooms. "Did you fool them?"

Wulfrith threw himself heavily down in a chair by the fireside and wiped cold sweat from his brow. "Let's just say I tried."

Arbol dragged a stool nearer Wulfrith's chair and assumed an eager, listening pose. "Tell!"

"Well, your Companions aren't as stupid as they look."

"Who could be *that* stupid?" Arbol commented pleasantly.

"When I told them I wasn't going to take part in the fighting practice today because I had the case of the Gorgorian Sliders, most of them just grunted and nodded. A few of them—the ones with no teeth?—even fell to their knees and said a thanksgiving prayer." Wulfrith pondered, then asked, "I wonder why such young fellows don't have any teeth left?"

Arbol just grinned.

"Anyway, I said I only wanted to watch. Then up comes this big bastard, Pentstemon by name, and he says to me, 'So it *is* true; you heard I bought this new sword and you're afraid of it!' "

"What new sword?" Arbol's brows knotted.

"Oh, a silly thing, not worth much, really. It seems he bought it off a Gorgorian woman who claimed it was magic." As he spoke, Wulfrith felt a throb of professional curiosity as to the Gorgorian method for enchanting cold steel, but in his present circumstances he was unable to pursue that course of inquiry. Clootie had always been more inclined to study the effects of magic on living beings, and Wulfrith followed suit. Privately he resolved to check out the royal library as soon as possible. Perhaps there were some books down there that covered the subject.

And if not, there were always those . . . *other* books that did quite well at *un*covering a number of far more interesting subjects.

"Well, go on!" Prince Arbol demanded. "So Pentstemon said I was afraid to face this so-called magic sword of his. Then what?"

"Then . . ." Wulfrith took a deep breath. It wasn't a comfortable memory. "Then I had to prove he was wrong, of course. I mean, that's what you would've done, isn't it?"

"You bet I would!" Arbol leaned closer. "So you fought him, Wulfie?"

"It *is* what you'd have done. I challenged him to a match on foot, swords only, with just a couple of the Companions present to act as field marshals. Neither one of us wanted more witnesses."

Arbol nodded. "Magic swords are contraband. If Pentstemon's blade did anything spectacular, the other Companions wouldn't want to be hauled up before Dad as witnesses." A wistful, childlike expression came into the prince's eyes. "*Did* the sword do anything spectacular?"

"No." Wulfrith closed his eyes and once again saw himself standing in the little courtyard, facing off against Pentstemon. The courtyard adjoined the palace dungheaps and there was a good supply of blowflies buzzing about. It had taken the work of a moment for Wulfrith's magic to attract one of them to perch unnoticed on the tip of Pentstemon's sword. Then, a swift transformation spell uttered just as the burly youth raised his weapon, and *whoops!*, over backwards Pentstemon tumbled with a fat, startled albatross clutching the edge of his blade with wings and flippered feet. The bird flew off, bewildered, and Wulfrith grabbed his chance. He had his own sword pointed at Pentstemon's throat before the other lad could rally.

All he told Arbol, though, was, "I cheated, so I won. It was no honorable victory."

"Who cares?" the prince said. "It's the winning that counts. Dad says that all the time. Isn't this a *fun* game Mom invented for us, Wulfie?"

Wulfrith thought about it. "No."

"Oh, all right, you don't have to pretend you're me for fighting practice any more; just for those stupid court ceremonies and sometimes with my math teacher. Besides, I like fighting practice myself too much to give it away. Good thing, too. If you *did* like to fight, and since we're getting so slick at swapping places, one day you just might get it into your head that you could take my place for keeps." Arbol sighed. "Then I'd have to kill you."

"Don't bother." Wulfrith stretched his feet to the fire. "You can keep your crown. I'm happy being who I am, doing what I do, and liking what I like." He reached into his belt pouch and pulled out the hooded mask. Settling it over his face as he rose, he said, "And one thing I do like is going to the library. May I, Your Highness?"

" 'May I, Your Highness?' " Arbol taunted. The prince leaped up and gave his friend a Hydrangean hotknuckle on the upper arm. "I thought we were pals, Wulfie! What's all this 'Your Highness' dung?"

"Well, you were getting so all-fired protective about being the prince, I just thought—" Wulfrith rubbed his sore arm. "All right, if that's how you want it, I'm going to the library whether you want me to or not . . . Stinky!"

"That's my pal!" The prince laughed and sent Wulfrith on his way.

Accelerating rapidly as he left Arbol's rooms, Wulfrith almost raced to the royal library. As much as he had come to enjoy Prince Arbol's friendship, his first love would always be books.

Especially *those* books. The ones in the alcove. The books whose text and helpful illustrations were a source of never-ending fascination to Wulfrith's young eyes.

"I am a wizard; nothing human disgusts me," Wulfrith remarked self-righteously as he closed the library doors behind him, removed and stowed his mask, and made a beeline for the alcove. He did not have the plain honesty to admit to himself that disgust was hardly the sentiment *those* books stirred in him. And they stirred plenty.

He was deep into Chapter Twenty of *The Pomegranate Chamber: An Instructive Inquiry into the Flexibility of the Nubile Youth or Maiden,* and had just reached the part about winning the confidence of the Untried Partner, when he became aware of a heavy, musky presence in his immediate vicinity. Discretely he gave his underarms a cursory sniff, then realized that he was not alone.

"Ooooh, Your Majesty, how happy I am to find you."

She stepped from between two bookcases, her eyes smoldering. With an undulating walk that would leave most snakes perishing of envy, she smoothly approached him and draped herself over one arm of his chair. Leaning forward so that poor Wulfrith was left breathing bosom, she said, "I've heard how much of a scholar you've become, my lord. I, too, am most interested in ancient knowledge."

"Ungh," said Wulfrith as the full impact of her scent got him where he lived.

Snuggling partway into his lap, the lady went on: "Now isn't this a marvelous coincidence! You're reading the very same book I've been studying in my spare time. Alas, I am only a simple woman. I'm afraid I lack Your Highness's wisdom. There is *so* much of what I've read that I don't understand." Ubri slowly licked her forefinger and turned a few pages in the book until she found an illustration that she thought would do. She could not read to save her life, but one look at the open book in the prince's lap told her all she needed to know. If she tossed away this gods-given opportunity, she deserved to let Queen Artemisia rule in peace forever.

"Ah! There it is." Ubri slipped fully into her prey's lap when she pointed to the illustration of her choice. A sly smile curved her lips as she sensed the young man's growing interest. "I really don't know anything about such matters." She brought her lips so close to his ear that her tongue gently brushed it. "Would you explain?"

Four hours later, while Wulfrith was explaining Chapter Forty-Nine to Ubri all over the alcove carpet, the doors opened and King Gudge walked into the library. The Gorgorian monarch was still mumbling to himself—something about "Right shoulder, rain; left shoulder, luck. I still say it's a load of ox apples!" He scanned the imposing rows of books and spat. "Look it up *myself,* the wench says. The facts are *documented,* she says. Documented my hairy bum. Documented *where,* I want to know? Damn. Should've brought one of those Old Hydries with me. I bet you've got to know how to read to find out where this right-shoulder-left-shoulder swill's written up!"

A dim spark of thought, solitary and forlorn inside Gudge's skull, flickered with a memory: *Libraries are where you look for documented facts*—"I know that!" Gudge snapped. "Why else would I be wasting my time here?"—*and librarians are who you get to do all the scutwork for you.*

"Oh." That was an idea Gudge could use. He looked around the dusty shelves but didn't see any librarians there. He gazed upward, but none were hanging from the rafters. Then he heard some interesting sounds coming from an alcove. "Sounds like a librarian," he decided, and went to fetch it.

It wasn't a librarian, but it was a sight to bring joy to a simple barbarian king's fatherly heart.

"That's my boy, Arbol!" shouted Gudge, frightening poor Wulfrith, who had been too busy to hear the king's approach, all the way into Chapter Fifty-Two.

Chapter Twenty-One

"But . . . ," Wulfrith said, as he tried to tie the drawstring of his breeches. Being pounded on the back by the king added considerably to the difficulty of the task; so did his confusion and fright at having been discovered under such circumstances.

"But nothing, Arbol," Gudge told him. "If you think there's any 'but' then you've been listening to that damned mother of yours too much."

"But . . ."

"It's about bloody time you became a man," Gudge continued. "Why, you're what, almost fifteen? I was . . . well . . . I was . . ." Gudge had never been good with numbers, but the memory did eventually surface. "I was scarcely fourteen! That's two years I've been waiting for you, boy!"

"But . . ." Wulfrith was too concerned with questions of mistaken identity to pay any attention to the royal grasp of mathematics.

"Your mother probably hasn't told you what comes next," Gudge said, heading for the door and herding Wulfrith ahead of him. "Ox's blood, she probably doesn't even *know*, being a Hydrie, and a woman."

"Next?" Wulfrith had been desperately trying to find some way to tell the king that he was not Arbol that would not result in decapitation, or evisceration, or other impediments to further vitality, but King Gudge's latest words had entirely distracted him.

Next?

None of the books mentioned anything *after* Chapter Fifty-Two, not unless you wanted to count washing up, or getting married, or disemboweling unfaithful wives, or any of that sort of thing.

Well . . . some *did* mention a few things, but Wulfrith hadn't really taken those seriously. And they didn't agree with each other, anyway.

Gudge clapped Wulfrith on the shoulder, staggering him, and announced, "Now, my boy . . . now we get *drunk*!"

"Oh, Your Majesty," Ubri said from behind them. She had finally managed to get her skirt back to the general vicinity of her waist, and to get herself upright. "Your Majesty, I'm so pleased . . ."

"Good! Just a beginner, and he's already pleasing his women!" Gudge exclaimed, not looking back.

"No, I mean I'm happy that your son . . ."

"Me, too," Gudge said, interrupting her, "but I won't be if you don't shut up. This is *man* talk." His hand fell convincingly to Obliterator's hilt, and Ubri stopped dead in her tracks and watched the two males depart.

She sighed. It was progress, at any rate, very good progress indeed, where the prince was concerned. And Gudge had certainly been feeling mellow; he'd given a warning first. She supposed she should feel lucky.

Wulfrith was unsure, as he left the library and Lady Ubri behind, whether he should consider himself lucky or cursed. Being mistaken for the prince even by Arbol's own father, when he wasn't even trying, was quite an accomplishment for an impostor—but he wished he could get away from the king long enough to find the *real* Prince Arbol. The idea of getting drunk with King Gudge was rather terrifying; everyone knew the attrition rate among the king's drinking companions ran very high, and besides, if this "getting drunk" Gudge talked about was a *special occasion,* what were all those rowdy, bellowing, blood-stained evenings that used up so many drinking companions?

And just what would be involved in this "getting drunk" that was *not* part of those evenings?

He wished he could find some excuse to get away, but he couldn't think of anything. His brain seemed to have shut down in panic, and his body was mostly interested in lying down somewhere and relaxing a little, not in slipping away.

Not that the king was offering any obvious opportunities for escape.

The first stop in "getting drunk," Wulfrith discovered, was the kitchen, where the king happily swatted various serving wenches on their respective bottoms and sent a steward down to the cellars for wine—"A little something to hold us until we get there," Gudge explained, as the steward handed him an immense earthenware jug. Wulfrith nodded unhappily.

Gudge pulled the cork with his teeth and gulped down approximately half a gallon, then handed the jug to Wulfrith. "Take a swig, boy," the king commanded.

Obediently, Wulfrith took a sip. He gagged, but kept the stuff down.

It tasted . . . well, once, when one of the real prince's Companions had taken a good whacking in fighting practice, he had soiled his pants, bled all over them, and fallen sitting into a mud puddle. Wulfrith happened to have seen the lad's breeches on their way to the palace laundry; more to the point, he had smelled them as they were carried past.

That smell was what the stuff in the jug tasted like. Only worse.

Wulfrith was not stupid enough to say anything about the taste; besides, he was unable to say anything at all for several seconds.

The second stop in "getting drunk" was the palace stable, where the grooms hurried to obey the king's bellowed orders, fetching and saddling Gudge's and Arbol's favored mounts.

Wulfrith had never played Arbol outside the palace before; this whole ordeal was growing steadily more terrifying.

At the third stop, however, some of the fear subsided; Wulfrith finally discovered what sort of a celebration "getting drunk" was, in this context.

"Getting drunk" consisted of marching into a tavern, loudly announcing one's presence, and then proclaiming, "My boy's a man today! Drinks for everyone!" Any arguments from tavern proprietors were cut short with Obliterator.

Then the king would down a gallon or so of whatever the place served, while everyone else (including Wulfrith) drank a pint apiece. After that, Gudge held forth in lurid and increasingly fictional detail about his son's amorous feats, gulping liquor between sentences.

When the need to piss exceeded his thirst, Gudge would march out, splatter the tavern's front wall, then jump on his horse and ride off to the next tavern, while Wulfrith, who was by no means an experienced rider, struggled to keep up.

When the taverns directly adjoined each other, as a few did, the riding hardly seemed necessary, but Gudge apparently considered it part of the ritual.

With each tavern, the descriptions of the supposed Arbol's amatory prowess grew more obscene and less coherent, but the king's temper grew ever better. By the fourteenth stop, objections to the royal progress were no longer necessarily fatal; Gudge was too drunk to handle Obliterator with any skill, and instead simply punched anyone who did not immediately oblige his whims, usually aiming at the annoyance's face, but not always hitting it.

Wulfrith, harried and embarrassed, watched all this with growing amazement. He was convinced that he had seen the king imbibe several times his own volume in alcoholic beverage, and he did not quite understand how that was possible, even allowing for the amount that had then been distributed against various tavern walls. Gudge's face had turned a truly amazing shade of purplish red.

It had never occurred to Wulfrith how many taverns a city the size of the Hydrangean capital could hold; the number was well over a score, apparently.

It was at the conclusion of their visit to number twenty-two or twenty-three, a peculiar and nameless little place far up on the hill in the Old Hydrangean section that appeared to serve only peppermint liqueur, that Wulfrith, fairly intoxicated himself at this point, got up the nerve to ask, "Are we going to visit every tavern in the city?"

Gudge, cheerfully pissing in the general direction of the tavern wall, turned a bleary grin on his son. "Tha's gen'rul idea, yeah. 'Less we fall down firs'."

"Oh. After we've visited them all, what do we do then?"

Gudge blinked. "An' we haven't fallen over yet? We start over again!" His grin grew impossibly wide, and he belched loudly.

"How . . . how many . . ."

Wulfrith had intended to ask how many taverns there were, in all, and maybe how the king came to know every single one of them, but Gudge was no longer listening; he was, instead, climbing onto his horse.

Wulfrith provided a steadying hand before clambering onto his own mount.

"Thanks, Arbol," Gudge managed, as he wavered in the saddle. He shook the reins, dug in his heels, and his tired horse set out at a fast trot.

Wulfrith hurried after, his head swimming with every step his horse took. He had drunk far more liquor than ever before in his life, even if it was only a tiny fraction of the king's consumption, and the effects were definitely making themselves felt. He was beginning to lose touch with the world around him, and with details of who and where he was and what he was doing.

"Y' a goo' boy, Arbol," Gudge called, grinning.

"My name's not Arbol, is it?" Wulfrith said, more to himself than anyone else. " 'Snot Dunwin, either. It's Wulfrith. I'm sure it is."

"'*Swhat?*" King Gudge, somehow forgetting that he was on horseback, turned to face his son. He was now sitting sidesaddle on a large horse trotting down a steep hill, over cobblestones.

Wulfrith giggled. The king looked so *silly*, swaying like that. He vaguely recalled that he hadn't meant to tell Gudge who he really was right away because the king might be angry, but so what if he got angry? How could Wulfrith be scared of anyone who rode that way?

"I'm not Prince Arbol," he said between giggles, "I'm his food taster!"

"No!" Gudge bellowed, and, still sidesaddle, tried to draw his sword.

That was too much; the god who looks after fools and drunkards threw up His intangible hands in disgust, and Gudge toppled backward from the saddle. He landed head-first on the cobbles, heavily as a sack of grain; he rolled several yards down the steep slope, then stopped and lay very still indeed.

Wulfrith's drunken amusement turned abruptly to horror; the pleasant alcoholic haze dissipated rapidly, as he struggled to rein in his own mount. When he managed it, he dismounted quickly and hurried to the fallen Gorgorian. He felt for a heartbeat, for a pulse, for breath, for any sign that the king still lived.

There was none.

He looked around for help, and spotted three of the King's Own Guards, as his old Gorgorian raiders were now called, walking by at the foot of the hill.

"Hey," Wulfrith called from where he sat beside the late King Gudge. "Help!"

Despite his lingering drunkenness, he then realized this was probably not the cleverest thing he had ever done. Wouldn't it have been better to get back to the palace and put his mask back on, and leave the king to be found by someone else? What if they thought he, Wulfrith, had murdered King Gudge? What did Gorgorians do to regicides?

"Who's there?" one of the guards called, and Wulfrith knew he'd wasted his chance.

He wasn't sure who he should claim to be just now, so rather than identifying himself, as the soldier probably expected him to do, Wulfrith called, "It's the king! He's fallen from his horse!"

He saw the soldiers glance at one another; then all three of them came charging up the hill. A moment later they stood around, looking down at the dead king and the live boy.

"That's old Gudge, all right."

"Dead as a rock, ain't he?"

"Looks it. I s'pose we should take him back and let one of them Hydrie doctors make it official."

"And yer the prince, ain't you?" One of the guards squinted at Wulfrith's face. "Hard to see in this light."

"Um . . ." Wulfrith wasn't quite ready to claim to be Arbol; admitting he wasn't, however, seemed like a very bad idea just now.

" 'Course it's Prince Arbol," one of the others said. "Ain't you got eyes? Moon's up, innit?"

"Yeah, but . . . stand up, boy, let's get a look at you."

Wulfrith got unsteadily to his feet.

"Tha's the prince, all right." The three soldiers nodded. "Assuming the old king's dead," the tallest one remarked, "there's no use in wasting time. I wanna be first to say it."

"Say what?" The other two looked at the speaker doubtfully.

"Oh, come on, you know."

"So say it, then."

Wulfrith looked at their faces with no idea what the three were talking about. Then the tall one grabbed the boy's hand, raised it over his head, and shouted, "The king is dead! Long live King Arbol!"

Chapter Twenty-Two

"Just to the library?" Wulfrith pleaded with the guard. "I'll come right back, I promise."

The guard, a Gorgorian from the roots of his lice-infested hair to the tips of his grime-imbedded toenails, snorted with laughter—or perhaps he simply snorted. At any rate, the resulting gob that splatted to the floor of the tower chamber was impressive. "Yer Majesty's got a good sense o' humor, I'll give you that. The libr'y! What for? It's all books down there."

"Yes, well, um, I—" Wulfrith bit his lip. "I like books," he finished rather feebly.

The guard gave him the fish-eye. "Here! You sure it wasn't you as plunked down on yer head on them cobbles?"

"No, I'm sure—I mean, I'm pretty sure, but—"

"Nice bit o' business, that," the guard added. "Gettin' the old bastard drunk an' then givin' him a little push off the saddle, spong onto the stones."

Wulfrith was flabbergasted. "I did no such thing!"

The guard just shook his head, smiling fondly. "Oh, don't worry about it. If you ain't the sort to brag, I'll keep mum. 'Course it's a fine old Gorgorian tradition, kings' sons skrinking their dads. Not one you'd've been like to hear on. Some reason, the kings allus try t' keep that branch o' learnin' from their boys."

"I'm telling you, I didn't kill anyone! The king got drunk and he fell off his horse when I told him that I—"

The guard wasn't in a listening mood. He leaned on his spear and stared dreamily off into space. "Aye, now yer t' be crowned king, you'll be a right change fer us, an' no mistake. Got a good bit o' Gudge in you, but there's that Hydrie strain as well." He was one of the more thoughtful Gorgorian warriors. Had he but known, he was a rarity. In the days before the Hydrangean Conquest, most Gorgorian men were so busy looting, raping, and burning things that they didn't have the time for pondering the future. Nor was there much use for such a talent; given the nature of their chosen profession, very few of them lived long enough to have a future.

Wulfrith sighed and gave up, leaving the guard to his meditations. Back in the inmost room of his tower suite, he reviewed his own situation and found it ghastly.

Ever since that ill-fated "celebration of manhood," he had been kept confined to this suite of rooms in the Tower of Smug Reflection. The royal council, for once relieved of the danger of unexpected decapitations while in session, took over the instant that news of King Gudge's death reached the palace. They were waiting for him in the courtyard when Wulfrith returned, accompanied by the patrol and Gudge's corpse. Before the boy could escape to inform the real Prince Arbol of what had happened, they threw a heavy white velvet cloak over his head and bundled him away.

It was decreed before a solemn assemblage of the Gorgorian chiefs that Prince Arbol would remain in isolation until all the proper coronation rites had been performed, in the correct Old Hydrangean style. The chiefs saw no harm in this, as long as one of Gudge's bloodline wound up on the throne. They named one of their number—a Gorgorian worthy called Bulmuk—to be their representative and oversee the whole process.

"Don't wanna," Bulmuk said. "I wanna go to Gudge's funeral."

His colleagues told him that he had to stay with the Old Hydries, to look out for Gorgorian interests and make sure none of their fussy customs did anything to hurt Gudge's only son and heir.

"Who cares?" Bulmuk replied. "He dies, one of us gets the crown. Lotta blood, more funerals. I wanna go to Gudge's funeral."

The other chiefs assured him that while they didn't mind a little civil war now and then, they'd rather not have one just at the present. They also told him that if he refused, the first funeral would be his.

Bulmuk drew his sword and moodily hacked an under-butler to pieces. "I'll stay," he said, pouting. It was very affecting to see the tears of disappointment in his eyes.

His friends promised that when the funeral was over, they would tell him exactly what everyone there was wearing and who killed whom using what and how many warriors drank themselves to death and if there were any grave treasures buried with Gudge that might be worth stealing later. They also swore on the Sacred Gorgorian Ox that they'd bring him back a couple of leftover kegs and some fruit.

Pacified, Bulmuk took his place among the Hydrangean nobles. From time to time he would come up to Wulfrith's room to demand whether the lad knew anything at all about the upcoming coronation rituals.

"Anything to drink there?" he asked.

"I don't know," Wulfrith had to admit.

"Stupid Hydries," Bulmuk grumbled and went away until the next time.

In spite of his recent bad experience with strong drink, every passing day made poor captive Wulfrith long for a snootful, if only to help him forget his situation. They hadn't even let him out to attend the late king's funeral, and they refused to let him communicate with anyone.

Wulfrith sat in a sumptuous chair and stared at his hands. He was fairly sure that his magic could have unlocked the door, and he could have transformed the guards—though he couldn't be sure what he'd get—but then what? He had no idea where to go, or what to do, if he got out of the tower room, and there would be guards and Gorgorians all over the palace, probably. He couldn't transform them *all* before someone stuck a sword through him or did something equally drastic.

And if he did get away, what sort of trouble would that make for the *real* Prince Arbol?

Bitterly, he wished that his wizardry included the knowledge of how to send messages over great distances. He desperately wanted to contact Arbol and the queen.

What must they think of him? He didn't want to know. Palace rumors traveled faster than palace roaches. By now Queen Artemisia must have concluded that Wulfrith was a treacherous schemer who had waited his chance, then murdered her beloved husband before snatching the crown from her true son and heir. He had to get word to her and explain that it was all an accident. He hoped she'd believe him.

He hoped even more than Prince Arbol would believe him about not wanting the crown. He and the prince were friends, but he knew Arbol's attitude about the kingdom: *Mine! Mine! Mine!* summed it up nicely. Too, Arbol had inherited his father's temper, and he was better with a sword than Wulfrith was with a spell.

Wulfrith put his hands protectively around his neck. If the prince found a way to get to him before he got to explain things to the prince, it was going to be ugly.

There was a knock on the door, followed by a fanfare of trumpets and a peal of silvery bells. A strong tenor voice bleated, "Hail in all humbleness the royal sun where he awaits below the dawn's horizon! May entry be vouchsafed the servants of his magnificence who loyally attend his pleasure?"

"Huh?" Wulfrith shouted back.

The door opened a crack and young Lord Alsike's needle-sharp nose poked in. "May we come in?" he whispered.

"I guess so." Wulfrith waited. No one moved. "What's the matter? I thought you wanted to come in."

"You have to say something like, 'Enter and be welcome to partake of my grace for howsoever long it please my regal condescension,' " Alsike informed him.

Wulfrith smiled for the first time in days. "You're kidding."

"No, we are not." Lord Alsike sounded peeved. "Look, we've got to get the coronation rites under way. The sooner you're crowned king, the sooner we don't have to eat lunch with Lord Bulmuk any more. So how about it?"

"I'll do my best." Wulfrith took a deep breath and declaimed, "Enter and be welcome to, uh, enter and—"

"Good enough!" Alsike brightened, then called over his shoulder, "His Majesty in his infinite grace and wisdom has bid us enter. Stop shoving!"

Before long, Wulfrith found himself surrounded by the entire royal council, several musicians, a host of richly dressed servants he'd never seen before, and Bulmuk, who looked like he could surround a whole city all by himself. There weren't anywhere near enough chairs for everyone.

Lord Alsike began by introducing Wulfrith to the silk-and-satin–clad servants. "These are the Official Royal Hydrangean Keepers of the Coronation Ritual. It is a hereditary post, passed down from father to son." The Keepers all bowed beautifully.

Wulfrith noticed that each Keeper was attended by one to three young men, not so nicely dressed. "Who are they?" he asked.

Lord Alsike explained: "Some of them are the Keepers' sons, if the man has more than one. If he's only got one male child, the others attending him are apprentices. The job pays very well, even if the Keeper never has to perform his ceremonial functions even once in his lifetime. However, part of his duties entail passing on the ritual knowledge. The apprentices are kept on in case the Keeper's son dies or turns out to be too stupid to remember the rites."

"What's so hard about a coronation?" Wulfrith asked.

He was soon very, very sorry he had.

The first Keeper, a tall man wearing too much green

satin, hurried forward, sank to his knees before Wulfrith, and pressed the boy's hands to his lips. It was like having two shucked oysters crawl over your skin.

"Your Pending Majesty, I am Olk, Principal Keeper of the Coronation Ritual, and this is my son, Oswego." He made a lovely flourishing gesture of introduction at the empty air to his left.

"Why is he invisible?" asked Wulfrith.

Keeper Olk did a double take that ended when his eyes lit upon his son way over on the other side of the room. The boy was engaged in animated conversation with Bulmuk. He was just saying, "Wow, all the way *through* a human skull on the downswing?" when his father grabbed him by the collar and yanked him away.

"The idea! Consorting with barbarous Gorgorians!" Olk fumed. Then he recalled one little detail about His Pending Majesty, the prince, and a sickly smile oozed over his face. "That is—I mean—*some* barbarous Gorgorians. The rest are perfectly delightful to consort with."

Oswego stuck out his lower lip, and it was a doozy. His father gave him a healthy clout in the back of the head. "Now be a good boy and tell His Pending Majesty all that I've taught you about the first three days' schedule."

Wulfrith and Oswego hollered *"The first three days?"* in such perfect unison that any listener would assume they had been practicing for some time.

"The *first* three days, did you say?" Wulfrith added.

"Preliminary rituals of valor and chivalrous address," Olk replied. "Simple things, really, but the peasants find them entertaining. Go on, Oswego, recite the way Daddy taught you."

"I don't remember," Oswego said. The lip was out again.

"But it's so *simple*! You remembered all right this morning."

"Didn't wanna be a barbarian this morning," Oswego informed his father. "Talk about simple; there's the life! Don't like how someone's treating you, *whack*!" He cut a mighty swath with swordless hands. "There goes his head, bouncing down the breakfast table." He gave his father a disturbing smile.

Lord Alsike tapped his foot. "Olk, if your son is unable to recount the rites to His Majesty—"

"His *Pending* Majesty," Olk corrected, letting Oswego have a clandestine thunk in the noggin.

"—then either do it yourself or let your apprentice handle it."

"Can I, sir? Can I? Can I?" Olk's apprentice was named Clerestory, a bright, eager lad with more get-up-and-go than a nest of insane fox terrier puppies. Without waiting for the go-ahead from Olk, the boy began rattling off, "Day One, dawn: Ritual of the Nine Cups and a Lemon. The king-to-be must inspect nine golden cups and find out which one has the lemon in it. Originally done with three wooden cups upside down and a dried pea hidden beneath one, this rite has evolved to nine cups rightside up and a pretty large fruit. Day One, before breakfast: Ritual of the Three Virgin Kitchen Wenches and the Tavern Slut. The king-to-be must use the virtue of his own spirit to find the one impure woman. Tavern slut is encouraged to dress the part. Day One, breakfast: Ritual of the Ox."

"We put that one in," said Bulmuk, smiling. No one else was. "You gotta kill an ox with your bare hands. Great tradition of the Gorgorian kings. *Only* tradition of the Gorgorian kings."

"At *breakfast*?" Wulfrith yipped.

"Whaddaya think you get to eat *for* breakfast?" Bulmuk countered.

"It's all right, Your Pending Majesty," Alsike whispered. "We'll drug the beast first, and maybe line up a couple of brawny guardsmen to be the official carvers. Who's going to notice if they start carving a little before you're quite done killing the ox bare-handed?"

Olk's apprentice leaped in and resumed his recitation of the many small and annoying rituals that would dog Wulfrith through the first three days of the coronation. Some of them involved dogs.

As young Clerestory went on and on about holy swords and enchanted doorknobs, Wulfrith began to feel calm for the first time since that awful night. So much time, so many things to do between the beginning of the coronation rites and the actual moment when the crown was placed on his head! Surely in all that time he *must* be able to get word to the queen!

Clerestory ran out of wind and passed the torch to the next Keeper, who informed Wulfrith about the rites awaiting him for the *next* three days. All in all, what with quests and vigils and receiving homage from almost everyone in the kingdom, the whole business wouldn't be done with for about three weeks.

So it was that when the seventh Keeper said, "And then the only rite left before the coronation ceremony itself is the public bath," Wulfrith did not flinch. This seemed to surprise the Keeper. He cleared his throat and repeated, "The public bath. In public. With people there to see. The king-to-be is entirely naked to the gaze of the populace, that all may know there is no defect of person about their ruler." In an undertone he added, "You have to take all your clothes off."

"Very hard to be naked with them on," Wulfrith replied cheerfully.

The Keeper let out a long breath. In the long intervals between coronations, he and his fellows often found themselves with little to do but listen to palace gossip, and he had, in recent years, heard from various sources about Prince Arbol's surprising modesty—*and* about the Prince's ill temper, presumably inherited from his father. It was a great relief to find that for once, the rumors were apparently false.

Of course, it meant he should find better sources, but for now, sticking to the matter at hand, he simply said, "I am pleased to hear Your Pending Majesty say so. There have been times in our history—notably during the so-called Short Dynasty—when the king-to-be balked at this ritual."

Wulfrith clapped the Keeper on the back. "A king's gotta do what a king's gotta do," he said.

"*Whack!*" Oswego yelled, only this time Bulmuk had loaned the boy his sword. Something bounced across the chamber floor.

There was a field promotion for Clerestory on the spot, and drinks ordered in afterward. All in all, by the time the delegation left him in peace, Wulfrith was feeling rather optimistic about what awaited him.

His wizardry, which had failed to provide any way to make contact with Arbol and Artemisia, didn't include a means to read the future, either.

Chapter Twenty-Three

"So tell us again about your green sheep," Ochovar called through the twilight gloom.

Dunwin let out a sigh; he was sitting with his back to a tree and his feet to a campfire, letting his supper settle. He didn't really want to answer any more silly questions.

But if he didn't, the others would hound him all night.

"Her name's Bernice," he said wearily. "She's about fifteen feet tall and thirty or forty feet long, I guess, with great big claws, and shiny green scales, and a long pointy tail."

"How do you get wool off her, if she's scaly?" someone asked; Dunwin didn't see who spoke.

"If she gives green wool, it'd save some dyeing, anyway," the Purple Possum remarked from across the fire, where he was repairing a lute.

"She doesn't have wool anymore," Dunwin explained. "She *used* to, when she was really a sheep."

The Possum looked up from the tuning peg he was whittling. "How's that?" he asked. "Isn't she a sheep any more?"

Dunwin stared at him in angry astonishment. "Of *course* not," he said. "Whoever heard of a green sheep?"

The Possum smiled wryly. "Up until the Blue Badger brought you to us," he said, "not a one of us here ever had."

"Well, of course not," Dunwin said. "There's no such

thing as a green sheep, not that *I* ever heard of. Bernice was white, when she was a sheep."

The Possum put down the peg and whittling knife. "Then what is she now?" he asked.

"Well, what *else* is scaly and green and forty feet long?" Dunwin asked, amazed. "She's a dragon, of course. That wizard turned her into a dragon."

"Wizard?" several voices said.

"Dragon?" several others said simultaneously.

The Purple Possum leaned forward and said, "Dunwin, my lad, I don't think you've ever told us the whole story. Would you care to explain what you're talking about?"

"It's simple enough," Dunwin said, puzzled by this sudden interest. He had been trying to tell the Bold Bush-dwellers all about it ever since he had arrived at the camp, but up until now all they had wanted to hear were descriptions of the dragon Bernice had become—descriptions that usually produced great merriment and much giggling.

The merriment had never, after the first day, taken the form of attacks on his person, however; a few broken bones had settled that, and once he started his sword lessons . . .

But he had never managed to tell the entire story before.

"I got into an argument with a wizard," he said. "I don't remember all of it, but it had something to do with his apprentice. And he got mad at me, and turned my favorite sheep, Bernice, into a dragon. And she flew away, and I followed after, looking for her. And that's what I was doing when you people found me."

"You were chasing a *dragon*?" Ochovar asked.

Dunwin nodded.

"What would you have done if you *found* her?" the Blue Badger asked curiously.

"Talked to her," Dunwin said. "She's still *Bernice,* after all—she's still my best friend, that I brought up from a lamb. I'd ask her to come home with me."

"You think she'd have come?" the Purple Possum

asked, intensely interested, and unaware, as yet, of the figure standing in the shadows behind him.

"Of course!" Dunwin said, startled that anyone would even think to ask. "She's *Bernice*!"

"What would you do with a dragon, once you got her home?" Ochovar asked.

Dunwin shrugged.

"The question is, my Bold Bush-dwellers," the Black Weasel said suddenly, stepping from the shadows, "what could *we* do with a tame dragon? Dunwin, my lad, do you love your country?"

Dunwin blinked. "It's okay," he said.

"Would you put yourself and your beloved pet at the service of your people, the true lords of Old Hydrangea?"

Dunwin thought for a moment, then answered, "I dunno."

"This dragon, this Bernice—does she breathe fire?"

Dunwin considered, and said, "I dunno."

"She can fly?"

"Yeah, I saw her do that." He was relieved to have an answer other than "I dunno" for once.

"She has claws?" the Black Weasel asked.

"Great big ones," Dunwin affirmed.

"And teeth?"

"Big as my fingers." He held up a hand in illustration.

The Possum cast an involuntary glance at Dunwin's huge fingers and shuddered.

"Dunwin," the Black Weasel said, "this beast of yours might be just what we need to strike utter terror into the craven hearts of the barbaric Gorgorians! In their simple, primitive minds, a dragon must surely look like a demon incarnate, wouldn't you say?"

Dunwin scratched under one ear, considering the question. He was fairly certain the answer would be "I dunno," but he wanted to explore all the other possibilities first.

"And what about the wizard?" the Possum asked. "If there's a wizard out there who can turn a sheep into a dragon, maybe he can do other useful things as well."

"A good thought, Tadwyl, an *excellent* thought," the Weasel agreed. "Hard to believe a wizard could ever be of any use, though."

"So if we had this dragon and that wizard," someone said, "could we *please* attack the capital and get it over with?"

"Maybe," the Weasel replied, "maybe. All in good time. Wouldn't do to rush anything."

"My lord," the same voice said, "I've been out here in the merry and festering, musty, damp greenwood with you for fourteen years now. I don't think we're rushing."

"Is that you, Spurge?" the Possum called. "Can't see a thing in the dark."

"Yes, it's me," Spurge replied.

"Well, then, Spurge," the Black Weasel said, "if you're so eager as all that, then on the morrow, you and a few men of your choice will see if you can't find this poor boy's little lost sheep. You can start looking in those old dragon-caves in the South Cliffs. Would that suit you?"

"Not really," Spurge said, "but I'll do it." He sneezed. "Anything to get out of this damp." He hesitated, then added, "At least, anything that hasn't got wolverines in it."

"About the wizard . . . ," the Purple Possum began.

"Ah, yes, the wizard," the Black Weasel said. "We'll send someone after this wizard, too—Dunwin can give directions, I'm sure. You, Pelwyn—I mean, Green Mole—you take care of it. Take along a couple of the others if you like."

"Yes, sir," said a voice from a nearby tree. "In the morning?"

"Right."

"Shall we get some sleep, then?" the Possum suggested.

Despite a consensus in favor of retirement, the conversation dragged on for some time before finally fading out. Dunwin lay on his blanket, smiling and staring up at the stars that peeked through the leaves above.

They were finally seriously going to try to find Bernice!

It was very late when he finally dozed off; consequently,

he slept much later than he had intended, and was awakened by a great commotion. Voices were shouting, equipment banging about; Dunwin sat up and looked wildly about, trying to figure out what was happening.

Everyone seemed to be gathering at the King–Tree, the big beech; Dunwin picked up his blanket, drapped it across his shoulders to keep out the morning chill, and headed in that direction.

He stepped into the little clearing from one side just as the Black Weasel himself, looking rather the worse for wear and none too pleased to be awake, entered from the other. In between, most of the Bold Bush-dwellers were milling about.

And in their midst stood a rather exhausted-looking fellow in very fancy, if somewhat tattered, clothing.

"All right, all right," the Black Weasel bellowed, "what's going on here?"

"It's a messenger!"

"From the capital!"

"It's the king!"

"It's our chance! Now's the time to strike!"

"Shut up, all of you!" the Black Weasel shouted. He shoved his way through the crowd and took his place in the battered throne.

"Now," he said, "I see we have a messenger, despite the earliness of the hour."

"Yes, oh, brave and dashing Black Weasel, leader of the Bold Bush-dwellers in the fight for freedom from the foul invader!" the messenger proclaimed.

"That's not quite right, is it?" The Black Weasel frowned, then waved it away. "Never mind. I can see you're new at this; I suppose Phrenk and the others weren't available. It doesn't matter. What's the message?"

"I have come here from the Palace of Divinely Tranquil Thoughts at the express urgings of Her Majesty Artemisia, Queen of Hydrangea!" the messenger announced.

"Yes, of course," the Black Weasel agreed. "Get on with it."

"Without stopping, I have made my way across the mountains to come here, traveling day and night . . ."

"Get *on* with it!"

"I bring momentous news! Such is the news I bring that your hearts will sing with . . ."

The Black Weasel stood up and drew his rapier; moving slowly and gracefully, he placed the tip of the sword on the messenger's Adam's apple and growled, "Shut up and tell me what you're doing here."

The messenger blinked.

"That's rather a contradiction, sir," he said. "If I were, as you put it, to 'shut up,' then how . . ."

The tip of the sword drew blood. The Black Weasel adjusted his stance to prepare for a thrust. "You're new at this," he said. "If you ever want to be *old* . . ."

He let the threat hang unfinished.

"All right all right all right!" the messenger shrieked. "King Gudge is dead!"

The Black Weasel froze. Utter silence descended; for a moment nothing moved, no one spoke.

"There, are you happy now?" the messenger said. "You've ruined the whole thing, and I had this great speech all set to go, but now you've spoiled the ending for everyone."

The Black Weasel withdrew his sword and wiped the tip carefully with his pocket handkerchief.

"The usurper is dead?" he asked.

"That's right," the messenger said. "Fell off his horse while he was drunk and broke his neck. Or maybe he was pushed; Prince Arbol was with him at the time, and there's been some talk."

"Is the prince safe?"

"Safe?" The messenger stared. "Of course he's safe! He's the new king, isn't he?"

"Is he?"

"Of course he is! The Gorgorians don't care whether Gudge was pushed or not."

"What about the queen?"

"Her Majesty Queen Artemisia is in mourning, of course," the messenger said, his expression appropriately somber. "She sent me because she could not bear to be parted from her trusted companions in her hour of grief." He hesitated, then added, "But she seems to be bearing up well. The funeral was held according to the rites of the king's own ancestors, but even so, Her Majesty only threw up twice at the ceremony. The bruises are reportedly only superficial. Her laughter is being attributed to mere womanish hysteria, and her dancing down the street singing is being called an attempt to deal with overwhelming grief."

"A Gorgorian funeral, hey?" The Black Weasel considered. "I wonder what their funerals are like, then?"

The messenger shuddered delicately. "You don't want to know," he said. "The Grand Hall for State Occasions Involving Death or Other Unpleasantness has been closed, and the architects aren't sure if they can repair it or whether it will have to be torn down."

"So I suppose they'll be putting Prince Arbol on the throne, then? With some barbaric ceremony of their own?"

"No, O brave defender of the people," the messenger said, "a compromise was arranged—a Gorgorian funeral, but the coronation will follow all the traditional rites and procedures of Old Hydrangea, to ensure that no one will ever accuse Prince Arbol of being a mere usurper, as his father was."

"That takes three weeks, though."

The messenger nodded. "They started about four days ago. It took me a while to come here and find you."

"So he hasn't been crowned yet," the Black Weasel muttered thoughtfully.

"No, of course not."

"Besides, he's still a usurper," the Black Weasel said. "The throne rightfully belongs to *me*—I mean, to Prince Mimulus, the queen's brother."

"Not according to the Gorgorians," the messenger pointed out.

"Well, *damn* the Gorgorians!"

This elicited a loud cheer from the gathered Bush-dwellers.

"Let's go throw them out!" Spurge shouted from the crowd.

"No need to be hasty . . . ," the Purple Possum began.

"Hasty, nothing!" Spurge replied. "Listen, with Gudge dead, the Gorgorians don't have a real leader—their new king is just a boy, and besides, isn't he going to be all locked away until the whole coronation ceremony is over? And with that wizard Dunwin told us about, and maybe Dunwin's dragon, or even a *couple* of dragons—this is the best chance we're ever going to have! If we don't go now, we might as well admit we're *never* going to drive out the Gorgorians!"

Several people applauded. Dunwin was one of them, though he wasn't entirely sure why.

The Black Weasel looked out over the cheering throng; he stroked his beard thoughtfully. The Purple Possum, who had intended to make further protests, also looked over the crowd and decided to keep his mouth shut.

"Yes!" the Black Weasel said at last. He stood up on his throne, narrowly avoiding an overhanging branch, and called, "Yes! At long last, my faithful friends and followers, the time has come! I know the coronation rituals, and when the grand climax comes, when the new king emerges from his holy bath in the Hallowed Hall of Sacred and Ever-Flowing Royal Enthronement, and makes the march from the Palace of Divinely Tranquil Thoughts out to greet his people in the Square of Munificent Blessings from Those Gods Worthy of Our Attention, every eye will be upon him. And when all the attention of the capital is on the ceremony, we will strike! With our patriotic Hydrangean dragons and our heroic wizards, and with the strength and courage of our own hearts, we will drive the dreaded Gorgorian from this land forever! Are you with me, lads?"

Dunwin and the rest cheered more loudly than ever.

"Good, then! We'll find that dragon—Spurge, I want you to organize . . ." The Black Weasel saw the expression on Spurge's face just then, and thought it was perhaps a shade too eager. "No, on second thought," he said, "you come with me. Badger, *you* organize search parties to explore the South Cliffs. And Pelwyn—I mean, Green Mole—you go find that wizard. The rest of us will see about finding disguises, so we can enter the city unobserved. And we'll rendezvous in the Square of Munificent Blessings seventeen days from now!"

There were more cheers.

"And when we do, Hydrangea will be free!"

There were more, louder, cheers. People were waving swords and spoons and other such things in the air.

Dunwin cheered as loudly as anybody; it wasn't until much later that he realized he really didn't care whether Hydrangea was ruled by Old Hydrangean aristocrats, or by Gorgorians.

All he wanted was Bernice.

Chapter Twenty-Four

"Stop sulking, dear," Queen Artemisia told Prince Arbol. "You'll get wrinkles."

In a corner of the inmost chamber of the queen's apartments, Prince Arbol slouched back against the wall and drummed her bootheels against the stones. "Who cares if I do?" she snarled. "Wrinkles make kings look fierce and solemn and wise."

"Yes, but—" The queen stopped herself. She had been about to say, *But wrinkles make royal princesses damned hard to unload on the interkingdom marriage market,* until she thought better of it. Arbol still did not know the truth of her own sex. It was hardly the sort of thing a mother could break to her child all of a sudden.

The queen smiled a secret smile. There would be plenty of time for bringing Arbol around to see that the life of a princess was not so bad. Things were going beautifully. Gudge was dead, which was perhaps the most beautiful thing of all, and if rumor had it right, Artemisia's own darling son had had a hand in his father's death.

I always knew my children were special, the queen thought fondly. Aloud, however, she said, "I don't see why you're making such a silly fuss, Arbol, dear."

"Silly?" The outraged prince leaped to her feet and started kicking the wall for a change. "My rightful place as king of this realm has been usurped by a perfect stranger and you say it's *silly* to be upset about it?"

"Precious, Wulfrith's not a *stranger;* he's been working here for, oh, ever so long. Why, he's practically family." Artemisia patted her child's cheek. "I'm sure everything will work out for the best," she said. "You'll see. The coronation rites have been going on for weeks now, and we certainly can't interrupt them at this point."

"Why not?" Arbol demanded. She fidgeted with the hilt of her dagger. "It wouldn't take me long to kill the traitor."

The queen put on her sternest face. "There will be none of that talk, young la—man! Really, sometimes I think you're pure Gorgorian—as if there could be anything pure about those hairy beasts. I work and I slave over the hot funeral pyre, trying to get your father properly out of our hair for good, and this is the thanks I get! I don't know why I ever had any children."

"Dad forced you to," Arbol said, very matter-of-factly. One look at the queen's cold eye snapped the prince back into a more docile frame of mind. "All right, Mother, I promise I won't do anything to mess up the stupid old coronation," Arbol said glumly.

"There's a dear," Artemisia said, mollified. "I know what's bothering you: You're bored, being cooped up like this with just your mother for company. I've got an idea! Why don't we try to think of something that's lots and lots of fun to do, just to keep you busy and happy?"

"Like what?" the prince grumped.

"Like kill Lady Ubri," the queen suggested.

"Huh?" This suggestion was sufficiently unheralded to startle Arbol out of her foul mood and into simple befuddlement.

"Darling, surely you've heard?" Artemisia asked, a hand to her breast. "Lady Ubri's been going around telling anyone fool enough to listen that she is the betrothed of the new king. The nerve!"

"I remember Lady Ubri," Arbol said, still puzzled. "She's that Gorgorian woman who kept following me around making all these stupid remarks about bulls and towers and lances and swordfish when there wasn't a bull, tower, lance or swordfish in sight. And then she was always trying to tell me these dumb jokes about the traveling barbarian horde and the sheepfarmer's daughter—" The prince stopped. "Why should I kill her?"

"Because it will be neat," Artemisia said simply. "You see, my love, once the coronation rites are finished and my so—Wulfrith is king, Ubri will almost certainly be his queen. If we show up and announce that they've crowned the wrong person, Wulfrith can be set aside with no problem." *Except we will* not *do that,* Artemisia thought. "However, if he has a queen—even though he rule but for a minute—and the queen be found to be with child, by Old Hydrangean law that child has as good a claim to the throne as you. You wouldn't want to have to kill the poor little thing then, would you? Historians tend to make such a to-do about kings who murder their child-rivals."

"Nnnnno," Arbol said slowly. "I guess not. But it's all right if I kill Lady Ubri now? If she's pregnant, I'll still be killing my child-rival."

"But we don't *know* she's pregnant, love," Artemisia wheedled.

"If she's not pregnant, I shouldn't have to kill her to prevent her child from ever trying to take my crown because there is no child," the prince argued.

"But we don't *know* there is no child," the queen countered.

Prince Arbol sat back down in the corner, holding her head. "I hurt," she announced.

"That's because you need some exercise." The queen seized hold of Arbol's arm and hauled her to her feet. "Swinging a sword is very good exercise, especially when there's such a big target. Run along, now, dear. Oh, and don't forget to put on your mask! It wouldn't do to have anyone recognize you in the halls and upset—"

"—the coronation ritual; yeah, yeah, yeah."

Prince Arbol did as instructed. Her head was still spinning as she left the queen's apartments by one of the many secret passageways with which the Palace of the Ox's Tranquil Thoughts was honeycombed. Ever since the arrival of Wulfrith, life had gotten much too complicated for the prince's taste. Then Dad had to go and get himself killed and complicate things even more.

Arbol did not miss her father, exactly. All she remembered of old Gudge was something large and furry that always smelled of stale beer. Or maybe that was her pet dog, Vexmor. No; Vexmor never threw up on people's shoes. Also, Vexmor couldn't swing a sword the way Gudge did during that military campaign on the border. Arbol remembered that all right. Gudge kept barging into Arbol's private tent making loud, nasty remarks about stupid Old Hydrie customs that kept a lad all closeted up like a linen towel when he should be out at the ditch pissing side by side with his men. Then he kept pushing all these women in front of the prince.

Some of the women were ugly, some of them were old, some young, some pretty, some pretty old and pretty ugly, but all of them were smiling all the time. As soon as each one smiled, Gudge would always bawl, "Look! She *likes* you! Go for it, boy!"

"Go for what?" Arbol always asked. For some reason this made the women smile more, then laugh, then make a grab for Arbol's trousers which the prince easily sidestepped. Arbol couldn't understand why they'd want to do something so silly. It was all very confusing and Prince Arbol became convinced that she would never understand women.

Understanding men was a different matter altogether. Arbol understood men just fine. From her father she learned that there was just a single one-word thought behind anything a man ever did: MINE! This applied equally to land, gold, livestock, women, beer, and kingdoms. It was all quite simple. Gudge liked things simple.

Arbol liked things simple, too. This business about killing Lady Ubri was *not* simple. Arbol decided not to do it.

On the other hand, her decision to kill Wulfrith *was*

simple. If the traitor died before the coronation ritual was done, he would never be king. Therefore, Lady Ubri would never be queen. *Therefore,* it wouldn't matter whether she was pregnant or not. All very nice and simple.

Prince Arbol had been raised in the Palace of the Ox, once called the Palace of Divinely Tranquil Thoughts, now widely referred to as the Palace of the Ox's Tranquil Thoughts for some reason beyond the prince's understanding. She just called it "home." If there was one thing the prince knew, it was how to get from here to there inside her own home, even if *there* was the super-secret apartments of isolation where they were keeping Wulfrith.

The Palace of the Ox's Tranquil Thoughts was a maze of corridors, but it was also a web of secret passageways that had the official corridors outnumbered three to one. If Prince Arbol had ever bothered to stay awake during her history lessons, she might have learned that the secret passageways owed their existence to generations of her Old Hydrangean royal ancestors playing an unending game of "Tag, You're a Corpse" with their blood relatives.

Arbol didn't give a fig for history (in fact, Arbol hated figs). It was enough that the passageways existed and that she knew them like the back of her swordhand.

So it happened that Wulfrith was seated alone in his tower apartments, catching his breath between waves of coronation rituals, when a very fine tapestry illustrating the Old Hydrangean Wolverine Dance was flung aside and a masked figure leaped into the room, dagger drawn.

"Prepare to die, vile traitor!" Arbol shouted, tearing off her mask.

"Oh, it's *you*!" Wulfrith exclaimed, face and voice a study in pure joy. "You've got no idea how happy I am to see you!"

Arbol could not have been more dumbstruck if Wulfrith had used his magic to drop a catapult on the prince's head. Her dagger fell to her side. She gave Wulfrith the sort of stare usually reserved for three-eyed, eight-legged calves. "You're *happy* to see me?"

"Ecstatic!" Wulfie rolled his eyes heavenward.

"But—but you stole my crown!" Arbol stammered. "You usurped my throne!"

"They're saying I killed your father, too," Wulfrith added, looking very embarrassed. "It's not true."

"What isn't? The part about my father?"

"Right. Oh, and the rest, too. I mean, it all happened so suddenly. One minute there I was, riding along with the king, trying not to throw up, and the next there he was, dead on the cobbles. Then there were these guards and—"

Briefly, Wulfrith told Arbol the whole story. By the time he was done, the two young people were seated side by side in a padded window niche, enjoying a good chuckle over the whole affair.

"And to think I nearly stuck a foot of steel into your throat!" Arbol roared with laughter.

"And to think I would've killed you if you'd tried!" Wulfrith got the giggles.

"What! You kill me? Haw! Like to see you try." Arbol swung her legs up and rested her boots on Wulfrith's lap. "You're not half the man I am!"

"There's other things than men to be," Wulfrith retorted, putting on that smug, knowing expression Clootie used to wear whenever he spoke of the advantages of the life sorcerous. "Better things."

Arbol spat casually out the window. "In a pig's eye. There's only one thing better to be than a man."

"What's that?"

"King."

Wulfrith suddenly looked very weary. "You wouldn't say that if you'd've had to go through what I've been going through. Powers preserve us, how did your Old Hydrie ancestors manage to get any use out of their kings? By the time all those coronation rites are done, the poor bastard's a hundred seventy-three years old."

"They're not all done yet, are they?" Arbol asked, tensing. "You haven't been crowned yet, have you?"

"No, but almost. There's just one more bit of flashy

foolishness left for them to do before the actual crowning, and I'm happy to say I won't be there for *that.*"

Arbol grinned. "And I'm happy to know I won't have to go through all the stupid rituals that go before because *you've* taken care of them for me."

"Right. You owe me."

"I paid you. Let you live, didn't I?"

Wulfrith shoved Arbol's legs out of his lap and retrieved the hooded mask. "I only hope the last ritual's nastier than all the rest put together, just to teach you." He yanked the mask on.

"You don't know what it is?" the prince asked. She looked a little worried.

"I'm sure someone must've told me *all* about it before," Wulfrith replied. "That's part of the torture: They *tell* you all about the great big fat historical significance of every single lousy detail of each miserably boring coronation ritual they're going to inflict on you, then they go on and do 'em to you! If I were king, my first act would be to declare that the Official Royal Hydrangean Keepers of the Coronation Ritual can either *tell* the new king about the rites or *do* 'em to him, but not both. That's cruel."

"My first act as king will be even better," Arbol declared. "I'm going to gather all the Official Royal Hydrangean Keepers of the Coronation Ritual into one room, I'm going to *tell* 'em how they're going to die, and then I'll *do* it to 'em. Personally."

"It's all the same to me," said Wulfrith with a shrug. "I'm out of all this, and I'm happy to be out." He started for the door.

"Whoa! You can't go out that way!" Arbol shouted. "The guards will stop you."

Under the mask, Wulfrith's face twisted into a wicked smile. "I'll take care of the guards," he said, flexing his fingers. Now that he knew the crown would be going to the right person, he felt no qualms about merely walking out of the tower room. There was a spell he'd come across in one of the old library books—a spell written on a parchment being used to mark some long-dead reader's place in the *Garden of Exhausting Pleasures*—and he wanted to try it out. He was fairly certain it would add an interesting variation to his own shape-changing spell which had so impressed Clootie: The change in the victim's shape would reverse itself at intervals, without warning, leading the hapless subject to believe that he was off the hook only to discover he was on again, off again, on again, until he went quite satisfactorily mad.

"Suit yourself." It was Arbol's turn to shrug. "But listen: I want you to go back to my mother's apartments and tell her that everything's all right now. Don't go running away or anything."

"Run away?" Wulfrith's grin got wickeder. "And miss being a witness when they make you suffer through that last rite? Not for the world!"

Arbol grew thoughtful. "You know, maybe you shouldn't say anything to Mom. She just makes things more complicated than they are. She might even insist that I have to repeat all the rites they did to you or they don't count."

Wulfrith clucked his tongue and said, "Awwwwwwww," like he really didn't mean it at all.

"Oh, come on!" the prince wheedled. "Make believe you're me, all right? You'll get good seats for the last rite, and when it's over and I'm crowned you can rip off that mask and we can both jump up and yell *Surprise!* Then we'll turn the coronation into a big wedding and—"

"*Whose* wedding?" Wulfrith asked, startled.

"Yours, of course," Arbol answered. "You're marrying Lady Ubri, aren't you?"

"No, I'm not." Wulfrith had never sounded surer of anything in his life. "That's just what she's been telling everyone, and I've been stuck up here or too busy with the rituals to say anything about it. She thinks I'm you. *You* marry her."

"Me? I don't even like her. She can't tell any good jokes."

"Well, I don't like her either, any more. She's a lot of

fun, but—" Wulfrith couldn't quite put his second thoughts about the lady into words. He was certainly grateful to her for everything she'd taught him, but he felt the same student/teacher gratitude toward Clootie and he had absolutely no desire to marry the old wizard either.

"Never mind, we'll find someone who'll take her," Arbol said. "Someone who likes swordfish. Now go back to Mom."

"See you on the throne," Wulfrith called over his shoulder as he slipped out the door.

Arbol heard the guards raising the challenge, then heard Wulfrith utter a number of strange words that made no sense. The prince next caught a sharp whiff of something acrid wafting under the door. The guards' voices ended in terrified squeaks that trailed off as the pit-a-pat of little rodent paws scampered down the stairs, followed at leisure by Wulfrith's own footfalls, skipping away.

"How did he do that?" the prince wondered aloud.

Then, true to her Gorgorian heritage, she yawned once and forgot all about it.

Chapter Twenty-Five

The Black Weasel was not in a good mood. Having spent the better part of a day divvying up his men into four parties—two to search for Dunwin's gods-blasted sheep-turned-dragon, one to hunt up Dunwin's friend the wizard, and one to accompany the Weasel himself back to the palace—he was, in fact, at his tether's end. Most of the Bold Bush-dwellers might have grown from boys to men during their years with him, but he couldn't truthfully say that any of them had grown *up*.

"All that miserable bickering," he complained to the Purple Possum as they lightly slipped from tree to tree along the road, in accordance with the best tradition of Applied Woodsy Lore for Righteous Rebels. "Sniveling and fighting over who got to go look for dragons and wizards and who got the honor of coming along with me."

"Don't take it so bad, Black Weasel," the Possum said. "We finally convinced *some* of them to come with you."

The Black Weasel snorted. " 'Some'? Since when is two 'some'?"

"Three if you count me," the Possum prompted.

"A fine thing!" the Black Weasel exclaimed bitterly. "A leader of my stature, and the best I've got for an escort is the dregs of the forest from a forest famous for its dregs."

A loud crash echoed through the roadside woodland as if to affirm the Weasel's words. Spurge picked himself up off the dirt track and looked sheepish. "Sorry."

"Idiot." The Black Weasel's hand darted out of the trees, seized Spurge by the collar, and hauled him back through the branches. Up close to the hapless former messenger's face he snarled, "How many times must I tell you? Bold Bush-dwellers do *not* just saunter down the road while en route to reconquering the enemy stronghold. It could cause us all manner of inconvenience, particularly if we should happen to run into a Gorgorian patrol."

"Well, I told you years ago that I wasn't any good at this," Spurge said by way of excuse.

The Black Weasel shook him so hard that it took the Purple Possum a minute or two before he could make his leader let go. By that time poor Spurge's tongue was hanging all the way down to his chin, and his eyes were rotating in opposite directions.

"Wonderful!" the Weasel declaimed. "*This* was all that saw fit to attach its worthless self to my train!"

"It's not like he had a choice," the Possum murmured. "The other parties wouldn't take him." He jerked his head backward. "Or him."

"What *about* me?" Dunwin demanded.

"Oh, nothing."

"It was so too *something.*" If the Black Weasel was in a foul mood, Dunwin was in a fouler one. When the Bold Bush-dwellers split up into their various search parties, naturally he had wanted to join one of the two sheep-seeking groups on the sensible premise that he would know Bernice when he saw her.

Unfortunately, his wishes had been ruthlessly and unanimously squashed. In the short span of time Dunwin had spent among the Black Weasel's men he had managed to acquit himself so skillfully in all forms of armed and unarmed combat that there wasn't a Bold Bush-dweller alive who didn't hate his guts. It was pure envy, seasoned with a healthy dollop of fear, that ostracized Dunwin. He had tried to bull his way into the search party of his choice, only to have the Purple Possum in person intervene.

"Now, now, Dunwin," the Possum said. "Think this

through. What if the dragon-searching party you're with isn't the one that finds Bernice? You could still be wandering aimlessly around the hills looking for her while the successful search party rejoins us in the capital. *But!* If you come with us, you'll be right there to greet your sheep the instant they bring her in. Besides, unless I can convince one more warrior to accompany the Black Weasel, he'll have a fit of the sulks, call off the whole search party idea, and who knows when you'll see Bernice again! So come with us. It makes more sense, doesn't it?"

Dunwin allowed that it did, but it still didn't sit right in his craw. He expressed his frustrations by refusing to flit lightly from tree to tree, the way he'd been taught. Instead he just clomped along slashing the roadside underbrush and branches into splinters with his sword and making enough racket to attract every Gorgorian patrol in the hills.

For some reason, though, there did not seem to *be* any Gorgorian patrols in the hills. The four travelers commented on this phenomenon freely that night as they made camp.

"Maybe they're all still in mourning for the king," the Possum suggested.

"The vile, lawless, accursed usurper, you mean." The Black Weasel was swift to correct him. "Well, if they are, it's all to our advantage. From what I hear, these Gorgorian swine use any excuse to get rip-roaring drunk." An ironic smile curled his upper lip. "What better way to send off their louse-ridden leader than in floods of strong drink? And what better time for us to strike than while the invaders are helplessly stewed to the eyeballs?"

"Daddy Odo used to serve me stewed sheep's eyeballs on my birthday," Dunwin remarked dully. He poked the fire with a dry branch.

"Euw," said Spurge, turning pale green.

"Didn't use any of your Bernice's relatives for the purpose, I hope?" the Possum inquired politely.

"Speaking of stew, is dinner ready yet?" the Weasel asked, peering into the depths of the little cookpot merrily bubbling over the flames. "Which of you men's in charge of it tonight, eh?"

"Me." Spurge raised his hand. "I did my best. Don't blame me if it's no good. We passed a perfectly decent-looking farmhouse a ways back today. Would've been the simplest thing in the world for me to slip 'round to the front door and offer to chop up some firewood in trade for a chicken and some veggers, but oh no! Live off the woodland, you said. So I tried. I'm not much good at that, either, so don't blame me for how it tastes. It's not much of a stew, 'thout any meat except some of that dried stuff the Possum carries in his pouch, but I managed to scare up enough trimmings besides to—"

"Are you *done*?" the Weasel snarled.

Spurge nodded.

"Then so is the stew," the Weasel decreed. "Dish it out now. I want us to eat, sleep, and get an early start in the morning."

There wasn't much stew, but that didn't matter since there weren't very many takers. Spurge refused to sample his own concoction because the Black Weasel had hurt his feelings. Dunwin was too upset about Bernice to do more than stare at his portion, announce that there were mushrooms in it (he hated mushrooms), and dump it back into the pot untasted. The Black Weasel and the Purple Possum shrugged and fell to.

Shortly after dinner, they fell over.

It was several days later when the Black Weasel opened one eye and saw that there was a plain whitewashed ceiling over him instead of the leafy forest canopy he'd expected. He turned his head and pain shot from the base of his spine all the way up his backbone to the top of his skull. Clean sheets wrapped him, but they were soaked with sweat, and the smell of a sickroom overwhelmed the feeble scent of the wildflower bouquet on the table beside him. He groaned.

"Oh, good. You're alive." A plump, pretty woman leaned over the Black Weasel's bed to wipe his clammy brow. "That means the worst is over. You'll be on your feet by tomorrow, and on your way the day after."

"Who—who are you?" the Black Weasel asked. "Where am I? Where are my men?"

The lady chuckled, a sound warm and comforting as fresh-baked bread. "I'm the Widow Giligip and you're in my farmhouse. Your sick friend's dossed out in the main room, in front of the fireplace—he's fine too, never fear—and as for the other two . . ." She hesitated, a look of concern darkening her rosy face.

"Yes? Yes? Tell me!"

"Well, the big one's been a tremendous help to me these past two days, looking after my livestock so kind the way he does, especially the sheep, but the other one—he's run off. Just bolted for the hills hollering that no one was to blame *him* for anything. Did that soon after they brought you here and I recognized what was wrong with you."

A nasty suspicion accompanied by nastier stomach cramps clutched at the Black Weasel's soul. "Which was—?"

"Mushroom poisoning."

Chapter Twenty-Six

Still holding tight to the short straw, Wennedel edged his way down the hillside toward the gigantic green beast. The nearer he got, the bigger it seemed, the stronger it stank, and the more he wanted his mother. His comrades' assurances that they would keep their loaded bows trained on the beast's heart the whole time were cold comfort. *They* were all holed up safely behind a fall of boulders, and how could he be sure any of them knew where a dragon kept its heart?

They did know where a man's heart lay, though, and had offered to show Wennedel his own, all nice and red and out in the open, if he refused to accept the mission which Fate and the short straw had awarded him.

"Uh . . . Dragon?" Wennedel's voice came out like a mouse's squeak. He was facing the monster's rump and got no reply. "Your—Your Dragonness?" he tried.

Still no response. He inched a little closer to the front end of the beast. The dragon was sitting very still. It had been thus motionless from the instant the search party spotted it, down in this small dip between the mountain peaks. There was a stream running past the dragon's front end and plenty of rich grass all around, liberally sprinkled with bright yellow, white, and red flowers—all in all a very pleasant spot, if not for having a monster plunked down in the center of it.

"Um, yoo-hoo?" Wennedel tried again to rouse the dragon's attention. To no avail. The beast remained unmoved, its beady eyes fixed upon a particularly thick clump of flowers. "Draggie? Thou Dragon? O Ineffable Dragonhood?"

"Shut up, twit," said the dragon, and with one short sweep of its tail batted Wennedel all the way back up the hillside and over the boulders. Then it dipped its head and tore up the whole clump of flowers with its teeth. It munched on these very awkwardly—dragons' teeth being all wrong for the task—then made a face and spat out the mangled blossoms.

Meanwhile, the Bold Bush-dwellers had checked Wennedel for vital signs and, relieved to find him still breathing, got him restored to consciousness, back on his feet, and shoved downslope once more. The poor lad staggered badly, but he managed to reach the dragon.

"You again?" the monster remarked, raising the draconian equivalent of an eyebrow. "Can't I be miserable in peace?"

"*You're* miserable?" Wennedel could not keep the wonder out of his voice. "You're a dragon! You can't be miserable."

The dragon took this information coldly. "Why not? I was minding my own business, getting on with my life—not that my future was anything to frisk and gambol about, but I suppose we're all meant to end as mutton someday, one way or another—when suddenly I'm fleeced, flayed, and fixed up in *this* absurd coat of clinky-clanks!" At this point, the beast reared up onto its haunches, the better to use its forepaws to indicate its own scaly belly.

As the dragon rose, Wennedel followed it with his eyes. The creature was imposing enough crouched on all fours, but when it sat up to its full height it was astounding. The Bold Bush-dweller was not feeling very bold at all, now, and there was a suspiciously damp feeling to his breeches.

"Mu—mu—mutton?" he cheeped. It was a foolish remark, as he well knew, but he was desperate for something to say to fill the dragon-heavy silence. "You *did* mention mutton?"

Down came the dragon with a crash that knocked Wennedel from his feet. Its tone was icy when it spoke. "Yes, I mentioned the m-word. So what? I was raised to be a decent ewe from the moment I was lambed, but I've been under a lot of stress lately. Victimized, torn from my home, separated from my one and only darling, precious, beloved—um—well, actually we're just good friends, but—"

"Bernice!" Wennedel cried out with joy, and did a little jig of triumph.

"Twit," said the dragon, and lobbed him back over the boulders. "Calling me by name when we haven't even been properly introduced," she grumbled. "Of all the nerve!"

It was some time and several formal introductions later that Bernice stopped her grousing. The rest of the Bold Bush-dwellers of the Search Party of the First Part came out of hiding, encouraged by the knowledge that this was the right dragon—a dragon so new to dragonhood that she was still trying to eat sheep fodder. They made haste to ingratiate themselves with her, informing Bernice of sundry helpful facts. Some of these concerned dragons—their powers and privileges—while others dealt with the current political situation in the capital.

"Ah!" said Bernice when they were done. "Now ask me if I care."

"But you must care!" the Puce Mongoose insisted. "We're giving you the opportunity to fight for the liberation of Old Hydrangea."

"And I'm giving you the opportunity to leave my valley with your head still attached to your shoulders," Bernice countered. "Hydrangeans! Gorgorians! What difference does it make to me what they call themselves before they chow down on my chops? I say it's all mint sauce and I say to hell with 'em!"

"They can't, you know. Eat you, I mean." It was the Blue Badger who spoke. He weighed his words carefully, sensing that Bernice was not the sort of beast—sheep or dragon—to do anything for anyone unless there was plenty in it for her. "Not us Hydrangeans, anyhow."

"Really? Then who was it devoured my Granddam Selma if not Hydrangeans? And her granddam before that! Don't tell me it was Gorgorians because there wasn't even a *whiff* of Gorgorians anywhere around here in those days!"

The Badger raised his hands in surrender. "I admit that we Hydrangeans have been known to eat the odd bit of—the *m*-word. However, that's not your lookout any longer."

"Isn't it?"

"Not when you've become the *d*-word."

A look of profound revelation washed over Bernice's face. "By golly, that's right!" She gave the tender valley flowers a wistful glance. "No wonder they don't taste the same." An appalling rumble came from her stomach. "No wonder I'm sooooo hungry," she concluded, sounding miserable enough to convince Wennedel, had he been awake to hear her.

The Blue Badger nibbled his lip, considering his next move. What he had to say must be put just so, for the unlucky turn of a word could mean the difference between a future as the Blue Badger, Hero of Restored Hydrangea or as the Blue Badger, Passing Gas-bubble in a Dragon's Gut.

"You wouldn't be hungry for long if you came to the capital with us," he said.

"Oh?"

"Your problem, you see, is that you're all confused by your new body. You don't know what's good for it and what's bad. What we've already told you about dragons—able to talk, incredibly strong, insufferably wise—is just the tip of the dagger. You deserve *better*. You deserve *more.*"

"You're right!" The hard glint of determination shone in the dragon's eyes. "I do!"

"You deserve an official, genuine, royally appointed *dragonherd*!" the Badger concluded, triumphant.

Bernice brought her huge head inches from the Badger's left ear and nearly deafened him when she whispered, "Say what?"

The Blue Badger shook his head to stop the ringing, opened his mouth as wide as it could go a couple of times to make his ears pop, and when sufficiently recovered he replied, "Look, when you were a sheep, didn't you need a shepherd? An expert on the care and feeding of sheep? Someone to keep watch over you and look out for your best interests and stick up for you?"

Bernice's slit-pupiled eyes filled with pints of tears. "Dunwin," she rasped. "My Dunwin always stuck up for me."

"Well, that's what a dragonherd does for his dragons!" The Badger smiled. "He knows all about what's best for dragons the same way a shepherd knows sheep from the ground up. Only thing is, you can't find a good dragonherd outside of the capital. If you come with us and give us a wee smidgen of assistance now and then—just in the course of destroying the Gorgorians and restoring the true Hydrangean king to the throne—I personally guarantee we'll find you the best dragonherd in the kingdom and as the gods are my witnesses, you'll never be hungry again!"

"No," said Bernice.

"*'No'?*" The Blue Badger was mortified.

"No one could ever replace my Dunwin." She sniffled and cloudy wads of dirty smoke puffed from her nostrils.

"No one will," said the Badger. "Your Dunwin is in the capital as we speak."

There followed a flurry of *What's he doing there?* and *How is he?* and *Why didn't you say so in the first place?* and *Does he miss me?* It all ended on a rousing note of *What are we waiting for!* and the Bold Bush-dwellers set out for the capital, dragon in tow.

Wennedel came to his senses just in time to be told that they had accomplished their mission. He managed a muzzy smile. "Bet the Black Weasel'll be pleased."

"He ought to be," the Blue Badger agreed. "It isn't every day you find a dragon."

Several miles away, Ochovar peered into the gloomy interior of the cave, then turned and slid quickly back down the slope.

"I don't see anything," he said. "I mean, except for a bunch of bones."

"All right, then, let's go on to the next," the Silver Squirrel said.

"Not so fast!" another Bold Bush-dweller protested. "Where'd all those bones come from, if there's no dragon?"

"Oh, there's any number of ways they could've got here, I'm sure," Ochovar replied with a shrug.

"Name one."

"Well, it could've been trolls, or bears, or ogres, or maybe a kraken that left them."

"Ocho," the Squirrel pointed out, "we're in the mountains, and krakens live in the deepest part of the ocean; how would a kraken get up here?"

"I never said there were krakens up here," Ochovar replied defensively. "I said maybe that's where the *bones* came from!"

"But if we're in the mountains, and krakens live in the ocean . . ."

"Maybe they got *washed up* here, years ago!"

The rest of the party stared at him silently for a moment.

"All *right,* forget the kraken, then," Ochovar shouted. "It still could've been trolls or something. And even if it *was* a dragon, how do we know how old those bones are? They could've been there for years! The dragon might have died ages ago, been slain by one of those heroes that goes about slaying innocent dragons, you know . . ."

"And it might just be out getting a snack," Red said—he had had an official Bush-dweller animal name once, but he hadn't liked it much, and after a few judicious thrashings, the others had conveniently forgotten everything but the color.

"Well, yes, I suppose it might, *if* it's a dragon at all, but really, I don't think . . ."

"Take a closer look at the bones, why don't you?" the Squirrel suggested. "You can see if they're fresh, or old and dry."

Ochovar cast the Squirrel a look that would have curdled skim milk. "I don't see the point," he said, "when it might just as well be trolls. There's no good in my getting eaten by trolls when we're looking for a dragon, is there?"

"Can't you outrun a troll, then, if you have to?"

"I don't know," Ochovar admitted, "and I'd just as soon not find out!"

"Trolls don't come out in the daylight," Red pointed out.

"Bears do."

Red pulled an arrow from his quiver. "If it's a bear, I'll shoot it before it can eat you. Honest."

Ochovar was not entirely convinced, having seen Red's performance at the last archery match—he had placed eleventh in a field of twelve, after Dunci had caught an elbow in the eye and missed three shots running. However, Ochovar saw that he wasn't going to get out of this without a lot of argument, and that it would be much quicker to just get it over with.

And the quicker, the better, in case the dragon came back from getting a snack.

"All right," he said, "I'll go check the bones."

The others made encouraging noises. Moving rapidly but without enthusiasm, Ochovar clambered back up the slope to the mouth of the cave, climbed inside, and made his way down the broad passage, moving as quietly as he could, so as not to disturb anything that might be sleeping in the darkness below.

There were really quite a *lot* of bones, he realized—the cave was larger than it had looked from the outside. It widened out into a big round chamber, almost circular, the sides curiously smooth and even save for an immense boulder that stood against the back wall, details such as color and texture lost in the gloom.

Fortunately, there was no sign of ogres or bears or trolls.

Ochovar snatched up a bone—and then dropped it again; it rattled on the heap. He had been expecting something old and dried out, and the one he had picked was not dry at all. It was wet.

And it still had meat on it.

And when he had lifted it up into the sunlight, he could see that the meat was still red.

"Help yourself," a deep voice said. "I've had all I want."

Ochovar spun around, expecting to see a great green dragon's head in the mouth of the cave, but all he saw was blue sky and sunshine.

"Over here," the voice said.

Ochovar whirled again, back toward the interior of the cave, but all he saw was the heap of bones, the big rock on the far side . . .

The big rock with its two golden eyes, staring at him.

"Hello," Ochovar said, in a weak gasp.

"Hello," the boulder rumbled. It uncoiled somewhat, and Ochovar realized that it was, indeed, a dragon—a very large dragon. "What brings you here? If you're looking for a fight, I'd really rather not, and you're welcome to back down now—I don't much like fighting on a full stomach. And if you came to commit suicide, or to sacrifice yourself to me for the good of your village, wherever it might be, I'm afraid your timing is all wrong; I've just eaten, and I'm really quite full. Perhaps you could come back tomorrow, or next week—I'd be glad to make an appointment."

The dragon stretched its forelegs, each considerably larger than Ochovar, displaying claws the size of cats.

"That's quite all right," Ochovar said, "I don't mind if you don't eat me." The dragon's speech had relieved a good part of his anxiety, and he was now merely terrified, instead of utterly panic-stricken.

"Good," the dragon said. "Would you go away, then, and let me finish my postprandial nap?" It closed its eyes and lowered its head to a comfortable position on its fore-claws.

"Uh . . . I'd be glad to, but . . ."

"But what?" One golden eye opened, and Ochovar didn't care for the expression in it.

"Well, I hope you'll excuse me . . ."

"But what?!" A curl of yellow flame flicked from the monster's jaws, and the blast of sound and warm air sent Ochovar reeling. When he recovered, the dragon's eyes were wide open, its neck was extended, and it was glowering down at him from several feet up.

For a few seconds Ochovar stared, frozen, up at the beast; then, when it occurred to him that it was getting even *more* annoyed, he quickly asked, "Is your name Bernice?"

The dragon blinked.

"Is my name what?"

"Bernice," Ochovar said.

"What kind of a name is *Bernice* for any self-respecting dragon?" the dragon rumbled.

"Well, it's . . . it's not," Ochovar stammered. "It's a name for a sheep."

"A name for . . ."

The dragon stopped in midsentence, and fixed one eye on Ochovar. It glanced at the mouth of the cave, where Ochovar's companions were conspicuously absent, then back at the terrified young man.

"All right," the monster said. "Ordinarily, at this point, I would fry you to a crisp and eat you as an after-dinner snack, but I just know that if I did that, I'd regret it afterward. I'd get a stomachache, I'm sure, and I'd also never find out what in the forty-six green and purple hells of the ancients you're doing here. So I'm going to keep my temper, interrupted nap or no, and I'm going to sit here and listen while you explain to me just *what in the bloody world you're talking about,* and if I'm not satisfied by the explanation, *then* I'll toast you. Now, would you mind telling me what *I* might have to do with sheep, or with anyone named Bernice?"

Ochovar gulped, and then explained. Not just that they were searching for a dragon named Bernice who had once been a ewe; one thing led to another, and he found himself telling the dragon about the Gorgorian invasion of Hydrangea, and the Black Weasel's brave and determined and ineffectual resistance movement, and King Gudge's reported demise, and the wizard who seemed to be doing thoroughly unwizardlike things such as working *useful* magic, and all the rest of it.

His voice gave out eventually, and he stood there, looking woefully up at the beast.

The dragon looked back, then sighed—fortunately, not including any flame, though Ochovar cringed before the blast of hot, fetid air.

"An amazing tale," the dragon said, "simply amazing. And no, I'm not this Bernice you're looking for—I am Antirrhinum the Inquisitive, and I'm a true dragon, born and raised a dragon, the scion of at least a dozen generations of respectable purebred dragons."

"Ah. Well, in that case, I'm very sorry to have disturbed you, Lord Antirrhinum, sir." Ochovar bowed, and then began inching toward the cave entrance.

"You should be," Antirrhinum remarked, in a rather distracted fashion.

It was at that moment that the Silver Squirrel abruptly tumbled into the cave and came rolling down the passageway, to stop a few feet away.

He lay dazed for a few seconds, then caught sight of Ochovar's worried face.

"Oh, there you are!" he said. "Ocho, we were getting worried. What took you so long?"

"The dragon," Ochovar said, and for the first time the Squirrel noticed the creature watching, with mild interest, over Ochovar's shoulder.

"Oh," the Squirrel said, in a voice roughly the size of a nit.

"Lord Antirrhinum, this is my companion, called the Silver Squirrel. Squirrel, this is Antirrhinum the Inquisitive. This is his cave we're in." Ochovar glanced up at his host, and added unnecessarily, "He's a dragon."

"Oh," the Squirrel said again, in a slightly larger voice.

He swallowed, and said, "He's not Dunwin's Bernice, then? He's a real dragon?"

"Quite real," Antirrhinum said drily.

"Um . . . would you like to help us conquer the kingdom anyway, maybe?" the Squirrel asked.

"I'm afraid not," Antirrhinum said. "I had other plans. Thank you for asking, though."

"Oh," the Squirrel said again.

"And now, if you don't mind, I really *would* like to finish my nap," the dragon said.

"Of course," Ochovar said, hastily snatching the Squirrel's hand and yanking him to his feet. "We'll be going, then, and thank you very much."

"Yes, thank you," the Squirrel said, as Ochovar dragged him backward up the passageway. "Thank you ever so much."

It was only when they were both safely out of the cave that the Squirrel turned to his compatriot and asked, "Thank him for what?"

"For not eating us, you idiot!" Ochovar said, whacking the Squirrel on the ear. Then, together, they slid down the slope to their waiting fellows.

Antirrhinum watched their departure from the comfortable depths of his cave, then settled back down, curling himself once more into the shape of a boulder, and tried to sleep.

Sleep did not come. Instead he found himself thinking about everything Ochovar had told him.

Gorgorians in Hydrangea? Antirrhinum had eaten a Gorgorian once, decades ago—tasty, once you got the dirt off. And wizards turning sheep into dragons? That was entirely unheard of, in all his long experience—ordinarily, the only process that turned mutton into dragonflesh was draconic digestion. There was something rather perverse, Antirrhinum thought, in making a dragon from a live sheep. That wizard might want some talking to. While the world could perhaps use a few more dragons—things had gotten rather lonely of late, especially after that last fad for heroism and knighthood a century back—it wouldn't do to have a lot of Draco-come-latelies cluttering up the landscape and eating the livestock, stealing the food from the mouths of deserving members of the old established families.

And this impending civil war might be amusing to watch. Humans always took these things so seriously.

He would have to look into this. Really, life had gotten a little stale of late, and an excursion to the Hydrangean capital might be just the thing to liven up the situation.

He *would* go take a look—as soon as he was done with his nap.

With that resolved, he yawned a great gout of crimson flame and fell asleep.

Chapter Twenty-Seven

"I don't see a cave," Pelwyn—also known as the Green Mole, when he wasn't traveling incognito—said distrustfully, as he stared at the rocky hillside.

"Well, of course you don't," his native guide, Armetta by name, replied. "It's a wizard's cave, innit? So it's whatchacallit, invincible."

Pelwyn turned to stare at her, rather than the hill. "It's what?"

"Indivisible?" Armetta frowned. "Oh, you know the word I mean—you can't bloody *see* it."

"Invisible?" the Mole suggested.

"*That's* the one." Armetta's customary smile reappeared.

"Then how do you know it's there, if you can't see it?" Pelwyn demanded.

"Oh, that's simple enough—because it's where the wizard lives."

"How do you know?"

"Because it's where he goes when he goes home, o'-course."

"You've seen him go into this invisible cave?"

Armetta considered that. "No," she admitted, "I can't say as I have."

"Well, then," Pelwyn said, "how do you know he *does*?"

"Well, he has to go *somewhere*, doesn't he?"

"Yes, but how do you know it's *here*?"

"Because 'tis."

"But . . . oh, never mind." He kicked at a rock, only discovering upon impact that it was not, in fact, a *loose* rock, but rather, one that was still solidly attached to the outcropping on which it sat.

"Can I go, then?" Armetta asked. "I've an inn to see to."

"Go on," Pelwyn said, resisting the temptation to hold his injured foot in his hand while hopping up and down and howling. It had never before occurred to him that it was possible to be seriously tempted to do something like that, but the urge was really very strong indeed, and distracted him from any reason he might have had to keep Armetta around. The pain in his foot, as much as anything else, convinced him that he was never going to get any sense out of her.

That there was no logical connection between his stubbed toe and the innkeeper's mental processes didn't trouble him; he was too busy keeping both feet on the ground.

Armetta stumped off down the hillside, leaving Pelwyn and the other two Bold Bush-dwellers in his party to their own devices.

"I don't see a cave," the Vermilion Sparrow said.

"*I* don't see a *wizard,*" the Fuchsia Ferret added.

Pelwyn glared at them.

"The wizard's probably bloody invisible, too, just like his cave," he announced.

"Then how do we know there *is* a wizard?" the Ferret asked.

"We don't," Pelwyn said, "and for all I care, the damned wizard can rot in his invisible cave."

"The Black Weasel won't like that," the Sparrow pointed out.

"I know, Dunci—I mean, Sparrow," Pelwyn sighed. He looked the hillside over once again, but saw nothing resembling the mouth of a cave. They had searched the area for days before hiring Armetta, and found nothing; it was rather disappointing that after hiring her, they *still* found nothing.

Armetta was so certain, though; the cave had to be here *somewhere.*

"All right, listen," he said, "if we can't go to the wizard, we'll just have to make the wizard come to *us,* won't we, lads? Like that old proverb, you can lead a horse to the mountain, but you can't make him out of a molehill."

The Ferret and the Sparrow looked at one another, confused.

"What?" the Sparrow said.

" 'Snot how I heard that one," the Ferret said.

"Oh?" Pelwyn sneered at his longtime companion. "And how did *you,* O great scholar, hear it?"

" 'Twas something like, you can't break a horse without him stepping in molehills, or thereabouts."

"But wasn't there one with mountains in it somewhere?" the Sparrow asked.

"Oh, that one," the Ferret said. "That was, if you can't climb a nice mountain, don't climb any mountain at all."

"No, that's, if you can't climb a mountain, sit right here by me, isn't it?"

"Shut up!" Pelwyn shouted. "Forget the proverbs! What we have to do is get the wizard to come out where we can see him!"

"Oh, like the wolverine on Wolverine's Day?" the Sparrow asked. "And if he sees his shadow, he'll eat your foot off?"

"No, if he sees *your* shadow, he'll eat your foot off," the Ferret corrected.

"Isn't it his *own* foot?"

"No, that one's got traps in it somewhere . . ."

"Shut up!" Pelwyn's scream carried a warning hint of hysteria. The pair shut up, and watched their leader in wary silence.

After a moment of quiet, in which the loudest sounds were rustling leaves and the call of a distant bird, the Green

Mole had sufficiently collected himself to say, "Now, we need to get this wizard out of his cave. Has either of you got any idea how we can do that?"

The Ferret and the Sparrow looked at one another, then shrugged in unison.

"Nope," the Ferret said.

"Um," the Sparrow said.

Pelwyn eyed the Vermilion Sparrow. "Um?" he said.

"Well, I was sort of thinking . . . ," the Sparrow said.

" 'Sort of' is probably as close as you'll ever get," Pelwyn muttered to himself.

". . . I was thinking, wizards do stuff with magic, sort of, don't they? I mean, sometimes?"

"I would have to agree with that," the Green Mole said. "Invisible caves might be considered a form of magic, I'd say. What of it?"

"Well, then, shouldn't we do some magic to make this wizard appear? I mean, demons do magic, and to get a demon to appear, our granddad always said, you had to do just all *kinds* of magic, and even then he said there was a good chance the demon would eat your head, which is why he always advised us against raising demons."

"I don't think it's quite the same," Pelwyn said, "but you might have a point." He stroked his beard, considering, then asked, "Does either of you know any magic? Anything you picked up from your grandfather, maybe?"

Both his companions shook their heads vigorously.

"We could fake it, I suppose," Pelwyn said, more to himself than anyone else.

"Once when I was a boy," the Ferret said, "I had a ferret—that was how I got my name, see, when I joined up—anyway, my ferret had gone down a rathole and wouldn't come out, and we got 'er out by putting a dead mouse nearby and waiting until she got hungry."

"Bait, to lure it out," Pelwyn said, nodding. "That's a good idea, too."

The Ferret smiled proudly.

"But what sort of bait do you use for a wizard?" Pelwyn asked.

The Ferret's smile vanished.

"Magic?" the Sparrow suggested timidly.

"We don't have any," Pelwyn pointed out. He frowned. "But when my Uncle Binch used to go fishing, he used bugs made out of feathers and sticks and wire for bait, and they worked just as well as real bugs. So maybe we could fake it."

The other two nodded enthusiastically.

"So how do we fake magic?" the Sparrow asked.

"Talk funny, and wave your hands around," the Ferret said. "I saw an actor do that once in a show, pretending to be a magician."

"And they use wands, and stuff, don't they?" the Sparrow asked.

The Ferret nodded. "And they brew stuff in kettles."

"We can make wands out of some of those sticks," the Mole said, pointing.

"Come on!" the Ferret shrieked, suddenly overcome with enthusiasm.

Five minutes later the three of them were dancing about the hillside, waving sticks around and chanting nonsense at the tops of their lungs, all of them smiling and laughing, Pelwyn's damaged toes forgotten.

Forty-five minutes after that, they had switched to taking turns resting, and the chants had gotten less enthusiastic and more repetitive—Pelwyn's had settled down to, "Ka *mon* ya *sa* na va *bich*, ka *mon* ya *sa* na va *bich!*"

An hour later, the Sparrow stood alone on the slope, drearily waving a stick and reciting, "Wizard *appear*, wizard come *forth*, wizard *show* yourself, wizard get your arse *out* here, wizard *appear*, wizard come *forth*, wizard *show* yourself, wizard get your arse *out* here . . ."

And shortly thereafter, he flung down the stick and said, "To hell with it! Mole, there isn't any wizard here!"

Pelwyn awoke, startled. "Whu . . . ?" he said.

"There isn't any wizard here," the Sparrow repeated.

"Or if there is, he's not coming out," the Ferret said.

"If we stay here much longer, we'll miss the coronation!" the Sparrow pointed out. "What good will *that* do anyone? If the Black Weasel wants to overthrow the Gorgorians at the coronation, he's going to need every man he's got—even us!"

"That's why he wants the wizard," the Mole said.

"But we can't *find* the wizard," the Sparrow insisted. "And even if we could, he probably wouldn't do any good. Maybe all he knows how to do is turn sheep into dragons—what good would that be against the Gorgorians? They don't keep sheep in the capital, from what I've heard—just oxen and horses. So even if we *could* find this wizard, it wouldn't help!"

"Besides," said the Ferret, "if the others found Bernice, she might not like having the wizard around. She'd probably just eat him."

Pelwyn didn't think that was very likely, but on the other hand, he was just as bored as his companions.

"All right," he said, "forget about the wizard. On to the capital!"

The Ferret and the Sparrow cheered loudly.

"And we'll start with a good meal at the inn in Stinkberry village, to prepare for the journey!"

The cheers grew even louder. Together, the three trooped off down the slope.

Behind them, the rock outcropping shifted slightly, and Clootie peered out at the departing men.

A coronation?

The Black Weasel?

Bernice?

This all sounded very interesting. When that fool had first kicked at Clootie's doorhandle, the wizard had thought it was just another young idiot eager to buy aphrodisiacs or other love potions, and he had ignored the trio. The dancing and chanting had been funny enough to deserve a look, but that had grown boring after awhile.

It certainly wasn't any temptation to come out and talk; Clootie liked his privacy.

It was just luck that he had happened to take another look, to see if they were still there, just as the youngest one got fed up; he might easily have missed that final conversation.

But he hadn't, and a very interesting conversation it was.

Coronation?

The Black Weasel?

Bernice? *Dunwin's* Bernice, the sheep-turned-dragon?

This was too good to miss, the sorcerer decided. He turned and scurried deeper into the cave, to pack a bag.

He had a coronation to attend—and who knew, perhaps a Gorgorian dynasty to overthrow. The Black Weasel would surely have uses for the transformation spell!

Chapter Twenty-Eight

"*There* you are, dear," the queen whispered as a hooded figure sidled up to take the seat beside her in the Hallowed Hall of Sacred and Ever-Flowing Royal Enthronement. "I've been so worried. Where have you been?"

Wulfrith's head was still terribly muzzy. He recalled leaving the rightful heir to Gudge's crown in possession of the tower suite. He recalled turning the two guards into hamsters. He recalled feeling very pleased with himself as he skipped down the winding tower steps two at a time.

Most especially, he recalled how all that skipping made his hooded mask get turned around with no warning whatsoever. He was in midskip when half his vision had abruptly become obscured, ruining his depth perception and causing him to land not on the next step down but facefirst up against the tower wall.

This, in turn, had made his rate of descent go from brisk to faster-than-a-rolling-beer-keg as he barreled all the way to the bottom of the tower. He had only just awoken a few hours ago and had spent the intervening time trying to find out which hall the coronation rite was being held in—he had never bothered to learn the ornate Hydrangean names for the various chambers and halls—and whether he had missed the whole thing.

He hurt.

"Precious child, what is the matter with you?" the queen pressed, laying a hand on Wulfrith's sleeve. "And what in the name of the thirty-four hundred styles of sonnet are you wearing?''

Wulfrith looked down. He was still clad in the richly embroidered tunic proper to a king-in-the-making, neither he nor Arbol having thought to switch clothes as well as identities. ''Uh . . . I thought I should change into something appropriate for the coronation,'' he explained. The excuse sounded feeble, but so did he.

The queen's brow furrowed. ''You're not planning on making a scene, are you?''

''Who, me?''

''You must swear to me that you will do nothing to disturb the rituals until the coronation itself is finished.''

''Oh, I swear.'' Wulfrith made the arcane sign of the Wizard's Seal of Truth by using the first two fingers of his right hand to trace a large *X* over his heart.

''After all,'' Artemisia went on, ''I know how much you want to be king, and . . .''

''No, I don't,'' Wulfie replied. ''Not really. You see, I've thought it over, and I don't think I'm really cut out for the job.''

The queen's frown deepened. A look of downright skepticism etched its bitter way across her face. ''Are you all right, dear?'' she asked suspiciously. ''You didn't fall on your head or anything, did you?''

Before Wulfrith could lie, there was a flourish of trumpets, a roll of drums, and a rumble of many bronze wheels coming down the central aisle of the Hallowed Hall as five snow-white milk goats accompanied by seven fair-haired virgins clad all in blue entered, hauling the biggest, shiniest, most ornate marble bathtub in the kingdom. Virgins and goats alike wore garlands of pink and white flowers, but only the virgins were singing the Old Hydrangean hymn to the new king.

The goats would have done it better.

The bathtub reached its destination, the foot of a canopied, damask-draped platform at the head of the Hallowed Hall. Here the virgins and goats were relieved of duty by eleven strapping guardsmen, Gorgorians all, who saw to hoisting the tub onto the platform. There was much sloshing, but only a little of the foaming water slopped over the lip. The scent of orange blossoms and rose water filled the hall, overpowering the aroma of goats, virgins, and Gorgorians.

Seated beside the queen in a place of honor reserved for the Old Hydrangean nobility, Wulfrith had an excellent view of the proceedings. As soon as the tub was in place, the curtains behind it parted and three men emerged. Wulfrith immediately recognized young Lord Alsike carrying a scepter, the overenthusiastic former apprentice Clerestory carrying a sword, and a glum-looking Bulmuk the Gorgorian bearing the great royal crown of Old Hydrangea, more properly known as the Holy Royal and Ancient Crown of Volnirius the Oblique, on a cushion.

"Would you look at that!" the queen said, with a sniff of disgust. "Those beastly Gorgorians have attached a band of oxskin to the crown, and—oh, my gods, tell me that's *not* an oxtail hanging off the scepter!"

Wulfrith couldn't tell her anything of the sort. It was most definitely an oxtail. "It's only a *little* one," he temporized.

Artemisia's teeth made a harsh sound as they ground together. "If they have taken any more liberties with the regalia, I shall . . ."

She didn't complete the threat, for just then the curtains parted once more and the prince emerged, looking as splendid and purely Old Hydrangean as the queen might desire. Arbol wore a long, unbelted robe of cloth-of-gold, exquisitely brocaded in a pattern of pomegranates and peacocks. Silver slippers were on the prince's feet, and a slender diamond diadem bound the royal brow, small potatoes indeed when seen beside the ornate tangle of gems, wire, and velvet that was the Volnirian crown—and that was equally true with or without oxskin hatband attached.

The curtains parted one last time as an old man hobbled forward to the edge of the platform and almost toppled off.

Only the prince's quick reflexes saved him. "Yes, yes, that's all right, I'm fine," he said, nodding vaguely to all quarters of the assembly. "Just the thing for this time of year, a nice hot . . . oh!" He blinked as if just waking up, then looked over at Lord Alsike. "This is it, is it?" he asked him.

"Yes, it is, so get *on* with it," the young Hydrangean lord replied.

"Just so, just so." The graybeard bobbed his head, then found he couldn't stop until Arbol gave him a sharp whap on the back.

"Beloved people!" the sage cried out, and for a wonder his quavery voice carried the length and breadth of the Hallowed Hall. "Behold your king-that-shall-be! Behold that he comes to you having acquitted himself nobly of all the tasks, labors, challenges, and proofs of royalty laid before him! Behold that he is a worthy ruler! Behold that he shall here enter into the ritual bath, in sight of you all, and wash himself clean of any lingering taint or folly of his younger days! Behold that his trust in you, his people, is without flaw or imperfection, even as his royal body is without flaw or imperfection . . ."

There were several more *beholds* in the old man's speech, but Wulfrith missed them because suddenly Artemisia gave him an elbow in the side and snarled in his ear, *"I thought I told you to kill her!"* The queen's finger jabbed across the aisle to where Lady Ubri sat, watching the coronation's progress and smiling.

"Um, I meant to," Wulfrith began, "but I had to change my clothes, and . . ." He wondered why the queen would want Lady Ubri dead.

"Is that what you were trying to tell me with all that gibble-gabble about not wanting to be king any more?" Artemisia demanded, her eyes shooting sparks. "Because if that's so, let me tell you that it's not just kings who have an obligation to keep their word to their mothers. Just wait until this is over and I get you alone! *Then* you'll hear . . ."

But Wulfrith was not destined to hear another word on the subject of filial duty to commit murder. The old man on the platform had reached the end of his oration. Servants scurried up to remove the prince's silver slippers; other servants materialized behind, poised to remove the golden robe just as the gaffer proclaimed, *"Behold your king!"*

The robe came off. The people beheld. There was a very loud hush, and then . . .

"The king's a *girl*!" someone bellowed. It was Bulmuk. Arbol punched him in the stomach, kicked him where it counted, slammed both fists down hard on the back of his neck when he doubled over, and snatched the sword from his hands as he collapsed.

"Call me that again and I'll make you sorry!" she shouted.

"But—but he *is* a girl!" the old man stammered. "I mean *she* is. *You* are, Your Majesty. Don't hit me. Oh, dear. There's nothing in the rituals about this."

A wild hubbub seized the assembly. The Old Hydrangean aristocracy froze where they sat, their breath coming in strained gasps. The Gorgorians were equally divided between those who were making rude remarks while shamelessly ogling their king and those who were muttering, making strange handsigns, and mistrustfully eyeing all the Gorgorian women present.

"Oh dear," the old man said. "Oh dear, oh dear."

The queen, seizing the moment, stood up and screamed.

"Witchcraft!" Artemisia cried, wringing her hands. "Vile witchcraft! See how it has unmanned my beloved son, your rightful prince, your king! Oh, evil, loathsome, wicked machinations! Oh, desperate strategem of most atrociously infernal premeditation which has rendered my darling son effeminate, willy-nilly!"

Galvanized by the royal mother's anguish, for the first time at any public occasion Old Hydrangeans and invading Gorgorians were heard to join voices and with one accord respond, *"HUH?"*

"She did it," Artemisia explained, pointing at Lady Ubri.

The guards closed in on the shocked Gorgorian woman, the prince was disarmed and bundled off to points unknown, and the whole beautifully orchestrated coronation dissolved into amateur night at the hog-slaughtering festival. In the midst of chaos, a stunned Wulfrith slewed his eyes toward the queen to see how she was taking all this.

He could understand hysterical tears at such a time. He could understand hysterical laughter.

He had never heard of hysterical cartwheels.

Chapter Twenty-Nine

Tired and a little dizzy, Clootie dismounted in front of the Tavern of Wonderfully Digestible Foods. After a moment's thought, and seeing no hitching post or rail, he slipped his homemade harness off his horse and released the poor, terrified animal.

He felt a twinge of guilt that he couldn't turn the miserable creature back into the rabbit it had once been, but he still hadn't found a way to make his transformations reversible. He still hadn't found any way to decide what a given specimen would turn into, either; it had taken him twenty-six tries before he had gotten something he could ride, and the unsuccessful attempts had left an astonishing variety of wildlife roaming the vicinity of Stinkberry village before he produced the horse.

Of course, having once been a rabbit, the horse had a tendency to charge headlong in one direction for awhile, then abruptly make a right-angle turn and dash off in another direction entirely. The makeshift bridle hadn't done much to combat this tendency, which accounted for the wizard's dizziness. His route to the capital had been only a very vague approximation of a straight line.

The beast had, however, gotten him there very quickly indeed. And a rabbit never tried to attack anyone, not even someone who climbed on his back and kicked him, which was certainly an advantage.

There had been distractions along the way, of course—

every time the animal had scented a female rabbit, for example. If someone could redirect that enthusiasm from the old species to the new, Clootie thought, that horse could be worth a fortune in stud fees. But having now reached the capital, Clootie had no more need for rapid transportation, so he released the creature, and marched into the tavern in pursuit of food, drink, and news.

One piece of news was of particular interest: Was he in time for the coronation?

He could just ask, he supposed, but he hated to draw any attention to himself, even the minimum amount such a query would bring. Surely, if he just listened, someone would mention it—a coronation was a major event, after all, and bound to be the subject of gossip.

He found a seat at a mostly empty table; there were none that were completely unoccupied. This was a small one, with two empty chairs and one unconscious old man slumped across the table. Clootie could see little of his sleeping companion except a ragged coat, a battered, wide-brimmed hat and a pair of wrinkled hands, one of them locked in a deathgrip on an empty bottle. From the height and angle of the hat, Clootie judged that the head beneath it had the right ear to the tabletop; the sound of rather damp snoring emerged from beneath the drooping headgear, and one edge of the hat's brim vibrated erratically in response. A rather rank odor accompanied the snores.

Whoever the fellow was, he raised no objection to Clootie's presence; the wizard settled in his own chair, turned, raised a finger to the proprietor, then dug in his purse for a coin. When he found one he tapped it on the table and sat back to listen.

He could hear the murmur of voices at the surrounding tables as he waited for his ale. A lively discussion was going on; Clootie couldn't follow all of it without visibly eavesdropping, but he caught snatches.

". . . crazy Gorgorian women . . ."

"Probably didn't know about the bath—maybe they

thought if we had a girl for a king they'd be able to get away with their schemes . . ."

". . . didn't know those witches could *do* anything like that . . ."

"Pretty damn frightening, the idea that if I get some Gorgorian bitch mad at me I could wake up one morning with a draft in my pants, if you know what I mean . . ."

"*I* don't think it was those silly witches at all," one man proclaimed, very loudly. "*I* think it's some trick by our own Old Hydrangean wizards, trying to get back at Gudge for killing them all!"

"Oh, shut up, Dudbert," a companion said. "If the wizards could've done it, why'd they get Gudge's *son,* and not the old man himself?"

"Because how long did those spells of theirs always take, anyway?" Dudbert persisted. "They've probably been working this one up for the whole fifteen years since the Gorgorians got here! All our Old Hydrangean stuff's all like that; I mean, look at all that silly rigamarole everybody went through instead of just saying, Here, Arbol, here's the crown, you're king now."

"Well, if they hadn't done it all up proper, there wouldn't have been a public bath, and we wouldn't know the king's a girl, would we?" someone argued. "The old ways have got their uses, you know—if you ask me, Dudbert, someone might think you're about half Gorgorian yourself, the way you talk sometimes."

Clootie listened to all this in puzzlement.

King Arbol was a girl?

If they'd already gotten to the royal bath, then the coronation was over—but if someone had turned Arbol into a girl . . .

Just then the old man across the table made a noise like a tornado sucking up mud and stirred himself sufficiently to turn his head over onto the left ear.

"Say, friend," Clootie said, tapping a mildewy shoulder. "Do you know anything about this stuff about the king?"

"Murmph," the old man replied.

"The Disaster of the Bath, the scholars are already calling it," someone said from just behind Clootie; startled, he turned, and almost spilled the tankard of ale the proprietor was delivering.

"Oh?" Clootie said.

"That's right," the tavernkeeper said. "Someone turned the prince into a girl last night, at the coronation, right as he got ready to step into the bath—big flash of light and a sound like thunder, they tell me."

"Really? And then what happened?"

"Well, Queen Artemisia said it was the Gorgorian women as did it, and everybody went running about screaming and hitting each other, and someone knocked the crown on the floor and stepped on it, and that was the end of the coronation, and now nobody knows which way is what. There's the Gorgorians saying they'll have to have a match to pick a new king by seeing who can kill the most peasants—they used to do it by killing each other, I hear, but they've got civilized now, they say, after living here all these years. Most of 'em, anyway. And there's the Old Hydrangeans saying that they have to trace the royal family tree and find another claimant, 'cept for the ones say we could just have a queen, like as we done three hundred years ago with Queen Nilemia. And meanwhile nobody's in charge, and it's like as not that the whole stupid war might start up again and the Gorgorians start killing everybody, and not just peasants, neither."

"Amazing," Clootie said. A situation such as this would surely provide opportunities for someone; as the wizard gulped his ale he tried to think what he could get out of it for himself.

Just then the old man, scenting alcohol, lifted his head and stared at Clootie.

The wizard lowered his tankard, licked his lips, and then gave a start of recognition. He stared back.

"By all the little gods who crawl around in the dark," Clootie said. "It's old Odo!"

It was, indeed, Odo the shepherd; he stared at Clootie, recognition slowly dawning.

"You," he said, "it's *you*!"

"It's good to see you again," Clootie said. "Have you found your Dunwin, by any chance? Or seen Wulfrith anywhere?"

"*You!*" Odo screamed. He jumped to his feet, sending his chair over backward, and stood, swaying slightly, as he pointed an accusing finger at Clootie. "You're the stinking wizard who turned my boy's sheep into a dragon, and made him run off, and ruined my life!"

"It was an accident," Clootie protested.

A sudden silence fell over the room as the other patrons of the tavern all stared at the two travelers. Odo turned to face them and announced, in slurred and unsteady words, "This is the wizard who turned m'boy's sheep inna a dra . . . dragon!"

Then drink overcame him once again, and he toppled forward, sprawling on the floor.

"What'd he say?" someone asked.

"He said that fellow's a wizard," someone answered.

"Said he turned a boy into something in his sleep."

"Something about someone in drag?"

"I thought he said damsel."

"Turned a boy into a girl?"

"Did what?"

"He turned a boy into a girl."

"You mean the king?"

"What, him?"

"Is he the one?"

"He's the one turned the king into a girl?"

"He's the one turned the king into a girl!"

"He did it!"

"Get him!"

"Make him turn her back!"

"Stop him before he gets away!"

"Hang him!"

"Burn him!"

Clootie didn't even have time to phrase a coherent protest before the crowd came surging toward him.

Thinking quickly, he unleashed his transformation spell upon the first of his attackers; unfortunately, he got a gorilla, and no one even noticed the change. A second brawler became a very surprised snake, and managed to crawl away under a table; a third found himself suddenly wearing the shape of a wombat, which was to prove particularly distressing in the coming months because he would be unable to find anyone who could tell him what he had become, as wombats are unknown in Hydrangea and the surrounding lands. Matters of proper diet and behavior would be a mystery to this unfortunate ever after, and though he might make do as best he could, he would be always aware that he might be letting his adopted species down.

For the moment, though, the wombat followed the snake's example and simply tried to get out of the way, as did a new-made pigeon and an unexpected ant. The ant, alas, did not make it, and had Clootie been able to spare any attention, he might have been gratified to learn that his transforming spell was indeed permanent, and was not terminated by the death-by-squishing of the subject.

The wizard, however, had no time to worry about matters of craft; he simply wanted to create enough of a distraction to allow him to reach the door. He thought he might have a chance, until some person far too clever for his own good called, "Grab his arms! It's that waving about he's doing that's turning people into things!"

The gorilla took this suggestion, and the transformations ceased. Clootie looked into the big yellow eyes, studied the big yellow teeth, and decided against further resistance.

Someone found a rope, and a bar rag made an adequate gag; moments later, the wizard was securely trussed up, the gag in his mouth, his hands tied behind his back, legs lashed together from ankle to knee, arms strapped to his sides.

That done, the crowd stepped back and gazed admiringly down at their handiwork. Clootie stared back, regretting that he had ever heard those idiots outside his cave. If he had stayed safely at home . . .

"Now what?" someone asked.

No one had thought that far.

"Now," someone suggested, "make him turn the king back into a boy!"

"Right!"

"Yes!"

A score of voices shouted agreement. Someone knelt before Clootie's face and demanded, "Will you turn the king back?"

Clootie replied, "Mrmf."

The spokesman snatched the gag from the sorcerer's mouth and repeated, "Will you turn the king back?"

"I can't," Clootie said, regretfully. "I mean, I'd *like* to, but I don't know how."

The crowd muttered angrily, and Clootie suddenly realized he should have lied. If he'd waved his hands about and chanted something, and said, "There, all fixed," they might have let him go. But no, he'd had to go and tell the truth.

Having started off that way, though, he thought he might as well continue. "Listen," the wizard said, "I could turn her into something *else*, maybe—a frog, or a cat, or a horse, or something. Would that help?"

The mob considered that, but eventually decided against accepting the offer—the determining comment came from someone in the back who shouted, "I'm not going to take any royal decrees from a damned pussycat!"

Clootie decided it was time to abandon honesty as a policy, and was about to explain that if someone would fetch him a gill of virgin's blood and a dragon's liver he'd be *glad* to restore the king's manhood, he just hadn't had the right ingredients before, but before he could get a word out the crowd's spokesman stuffed the gag back in his mouth. As Clootie made unhappy noises and strained against his bonds, the spokesman asked, "What'll we do with him, then? He won't turn her back!"

"Kill him!"

"But then we'll *never* get the king back."

"Take him to the palace! *They'll* make him turn her back!"

"Take him to the palace!" The shout became an enthusiastic chorus.

"Who at the palace?" the spokesman asked. "The Gorgorians, or who?"

"Whoever we find," someone answered. "Let *them* sort it out."

"Sounds good to me."

"Me, too."

"Right, then," the spokesman said. "I'll get his feet, a couple of you get his arms, and let's go."

Together, the entire crowd spilled out into the street, about thirty people and a gorilla; together, they carted Clootie away, leaving the tavern occupied by a disgruntled proprietor, an unconscious shepherd, a snake, a pigeon, and a very confused wombat.

Chapter Thirty

A small but pungent group of Gorgorian women was assembled outside the palace in the cool light of morning. They had been sent as a formal delegation to greet the liberation of the lady Ubri, and as such wore their most ceremonial garb. Good Gorgorians all, they had spent most of their lives in tents, and as a result, when they decided to dress up, they chose to resemble tents as closely as possible. From head to foot they were draped in layer upon layer of richly brocaded and embroidered cloth, diaphanous veiling, and plain old headscarves until they looked like the floor of Queen Artemisia's closet when she was in one of her I-haven't-a-*thing*-to-wear moods.

"I don't think she's going to come out, Bungi," said one pile of cloth.

"Yes, she will, Jigli," another replied. "My man told me to get my arse out here to greet her. It's not every day they let a woman go free for a crime she didn't commit."

The other fabric mounds muttered agreement. When it came to women, traditional Gorgorian justice worked on the principle *Well, even if she didn't do* this, *she's probably so pissed now that she's sure to do something* worse *later on, so let's kill her anyway and play it safe.* There were very few female criminals among the Gorgorians, or at least none stupid enough to get caught. Ever since they'd received the news that Ubri was to be let go, every Gorgorian—male and female—had been most impressed.

"I'm so happy they caught that wizard!" The mound named Jigli fairly trembled with relief.

A third heap of splendid remnants scuttled over to ask, "Has he turned the prince back yet?"

"He claims he can't."

"So does this mean we're going to have us a queen?"

It was impossible for a bundle of cloth to sneer, but Gorgorian women had ages of experience pushing body language into the outer world through twenty-nine layers of clothing, so Jigli managed. "You're a married woman, Crosbi, and you ask *that*?"

"Oh. Right." Crosbi's swathed body sagged. "Still, it'd be nice. All our men being forced to take orders from a woman."

"They'd cut her head off, first."

"From what I hear, that wouldn't be so easy. Prince Arbol's a demon with a sword, and his Companions are as murderous a bunch of brats as you'd ever want to meet. Faithful, too. They all took the Oath of Blood and Spitting in Your Palm when they became the prince's Companions, and they're clean scared to death of him besides."

"That was when he was a *he,*" Bungi pointed out. "Do you think any young warrior, Hydrie or Gorgorian, would ever admit he was scared of a *girl*?" Her eyes added, *That's* their *mistake.*

"So what's been done with the prince, then?"

The cloth rose and fell as Bungi shrugged. "That's something Lady Ubri will have to tell us. At least now she's free, there's an end to all the riots these fool townies were pitching about the rest of us."

"Silly nits," Jigli remarked. "One little magical unmanning of their prince and the whole kingdom goes on a witch-catching binge! It's not like they knew what to do with a witch even could they catch one. Half wanted to burn any Gorgorian woman they found, the other half went sneaking around the back of our tents trying to hire our great magical services to unman their enemies."

"I earned almost enough to buy a reliable assassin to cut my man's throat," Crosbi said demurely.

"You lying bitch, you never did!"

"Did so." She jumped up and down in place, jingling with the coins secreted everywhere upon her person. The other women cocked expert ears to gauge the worth of the sound.

"Crosbi, love, you're being too modest," Jigli said. "For that much you can buy a fine killer. Just go 'round to the Wheelwrights' and Gravediggers' Union Hall and ask for a recommendation. You've got more than enough to cover the fee."

"Aye, but I'm a heavy tipper."

Before Jigli could reply, the door in the palace's great gate opened and Lady Ubri emerged. She was still dressed in her palace garb, which looked both scandalously indecent and chilly to her Gorgorian sisters. They immediately began pelting her with layers of cloth torn from their own costumes until she felt as if she were caught in a ring of self-stripping artichokes.

"Stop that!" she commanded, flinging aside the veils. "I'm perfectly all right."

"Just looking at you makes me shiver. Put something on!" Bungi directed.

Crosbi sidled up to Ubri and with much effort got a hand free to touch her dress. "Couldn't you make them give you back your clothes?"

"These *are* my clothes!" Ubri snapped. "What I couldn't make that cursed Artemisia do was give me back my position in the palace."

"Artemisia? The queen?"

"Artemisia the bitch on wheels. It was humiliating." Ubri's brow darkened at the recent memory. "She had me hauled out of the dungeons into the second-best throne room. The throne itself was empty, of course, but there she sat on her fat behind, handing down judgement from a comfy old chair. My jailors dumped me right at her feet. By the time I got the hair out of my eyes I saw that I wasn't the only one there."

"Where, in the second-best throne room?"

"No, stupid, at Artemisia's feet. Of course the room was packed with *men.*" She made the word sound a lot like *vermin,* only not so tasty. "Gorgorians and Hydries three-deep all around, staring like a bunch of constipated owls. And there in the center of it all along with me was the wizard."

"A genuine Old Hydrangean wizard," Bungi mused. "To think there's one still left alive!"

"Not for long," Ubri said grimly. "Artemisia told me, in that snotty voice she's got, that because the wizard refused to admit I was his accomplice, and in view of the fact that he had worked a transformation spell before witnesses, I was free to leave, and the sooner I left and the farther I went the better. So I'm off the hook but out on my ear."

"What about the prince?" Crosbi asked.

"The wizard won't turn him back—*can't* turn him back, he claims. At first he said he was willing to try, if someone would only have the kindness to fetch him a gill of virgin's blood and a dragon's liver. But then Bulmuk said that there weren't any dragons around and virgin's blood only works when the donor is older than twelve, so lots of luck there! This is the city, after all."

"We're so sorry, dear," Bungi purred. "We heard that you and the prince were, well—"

"I *had* him, damn it!" Ubri shouted. "I had him right in my hands."

"Oh, so that's where you had him," Crosbi purred.

Ubri ignored the barb. "It was all set: As soon as he was to be crowned king, I'd be named his queen, but now—" She spat.

"Engagement's off, is it?" One of the piles of cloth had a sarcastic streak.

"The prince is a *girl.*" Ubri eyed all the piles with equal scorn. "That makes our—prenuptial agreement null and void under Old Hydrie law *and* Gorgorian custom. Anyway, one of my jailors came 'round to tell me that when they asked Arbol did he—*she*—want to come down to the dungeons and say good-bye to his—*her*—ex-fiancée, Arbol just asked, 'Who?' and when my name was mentioned the miserable pup made gagging noises and said he—*she*—wasn't crazy yet."

"Well, it looks as if the wizard's spell changed the prince's mind, too," Bungi remarked.

"Or his taste," Crosbi murmured. "For the better."

"Did it ever occur to you lot of ragbags what it would've meant could I have made myself queen?" Ubri snarled. "What it would've meant for all Gorgorian women?"

"No."

"Tell."

"For one thing, there's plenty of influence a woman can bring to bear on her man, even when her man's a king," Ubri said, folding her arms across her chest.

"Until he hits you," Jigli reminded her.

"Arbol's half Hydrie. Hydries don't hit."

"They don't?" Jigli grew thoughtful, a phenomenon which could only be perceived if you listened to her pile of veiling closely enough to pick up a faint *hmmmm* sound. "You know, I've got a little coin put by. Maybe it's time I paid a visit to the Wheelwrights' and Gravediggers' Union Hall myself. These Hydrie men aren't half bad to look at, and they do smell better."

"Oh, what doors I might have opened for us all!" Ubri exclaimed. "Now it's ashes, *ashes*!" Her scowl deepened and she shook her fist at the palace towers. "Mark my words, Artemisia: If I ever get the chance to do you a mischief, it'll be the sort that ends with your subjects tossing great handfuls of your intestines up in the air and shouting *Whoopeee!*"

"Hmph!" Bungi snorted. "Not like you'll get that chance. Things've calmed down now, though for a while it looked like everything was running to chaos. Such a messy thing, chaos. Gets all over everywhere, and next thing you know, people with no taste in clothes are parading through the streets with the heads of royalty impaled on pikestaffs."

"Pikestaves," Jigli corrected.

"Sit on one, then tell me," Bungi suggested.

Ubri said a word that was dirty even in the mouth of a male Gorgorian. Then she burst into tears. The clothstacks gathered around and patted her on the back until she got the hiccups.

"There, there, dear, don't you fret," Crosbi said. "I'm sure something will turn up."

"Like what?" Ubri's voice was flinty. The hiccups vanished like dew in the desert.

"Oh, I don't know. Like something awful to upset the queen or at least you finding somewhere to lay your head tonight. I was just saying it as empty words of comfort, you know. I haven't got a dog's notion of what will cheer you up, or even if anything ever will."

"DRAGON!" bawled the horseman who galloped past the knot of Gorgorian women and almost slammed into the great gate of the palace. His steed reared and pawed the air, its ironshod hooves gouging huge splinters from the closed portal.

"Here! You watch that beast, will you?" a guardsman shouted down from a handy turret window. "We just had that gate sanded and shellacked."

"DRAGON!" the rider reiterated, still at the top of his lungs. "Over there!" He gestured wildly with his riding whip, indicating no particular direction.

"Where?" The guard shaded his eyes.

"Over where all that black, oily smoke is rising, you idiot! The city outskirts beyond the walls!"

"Not the poorer sections?"

"There *are* no poorer sections of the city outskirts, dolt! You pay that much extra for a cottage so you get the privilege of being as far from the government as possible and still having public fountains! Now open this damned gate!"

The guard's face vanished from the window. He was muttering something about dragons being not part of his job description. By the time he reached the gate, he had been joined by several other men-at-arms, a few of them Old Hydrangeans.

"You want to say all that again, slow?" the original guard asked of the rider. "Just so's the natives get a chance to hear about it?"

"I said—" the rider drew a deep breath, "—DRAG-ON!"

All the guards, Gorgorian and Hydrangean alike, agreed that there was no need to shout. The rider, very red in the face, proceeded to give the details of the story while Ubri and her escort of Gorgorian women drew near to eavesdrop, unnoticed and unmolested.

"It was off in the Exhalations of Persistent Happiness quarter, outside the city gate, where it happened," he said.

"Ah, yes," a Hydrangean commented. "Near the tanneries."

"It's quite a nice little section of town—or was, before it got charred to ashes. I run a livery stable out there and I was just seeing to the horses when what do I spy ambling down the road big as my wife and twice as ugly but a dragon."

"What, just the one?" The Hydrangean snickered. "Not accompanied by any other magical critters of myth and legend, was it? No pink elephants? No yellow-striped wolverines? No wombats?"

The rider's glare would have peeled paint. "All this dragon was accompanied by was a corps of the scruffiest, dustiest, most ragtag bunch of itinerant roadscum as I ever laid eyes on. All footsore, they were, and complaining about blisters to the high heavens."

"Why didn't they just ride the dragon, then?" a Gorgorian asked, and clasped his sides as he shook with laughter.

"I'd like to see any man ride a dragon!" the horseman spat. "It's not likely to happen in *this* world. At any rate, the dragon's companions caught sight of the trade sign over my stable and one of 'em came sauntering up, bold as you please, to demand I make him a sandwich in the name of freedom."

"A what in the name of which?"

"Well, I told him I didn't run any sort of an eating-house. He pointed to the trade sign and said when a man displayed that end of the horse, he was either advertising authentic Gorgorian cooking—which he didn't like, but he was too hungry to be fussy—or else philosophy lessons. When I set him right, he turned around and demanded I give him a *horse* in the name of freedom."

"Cheeky bastard!"

"I don't need to tell you what I *did* give him in the name of freedom," the rider said, looking very satisfied. It only lasted an instant before his face fell and he added, "Then they were all around me, all demanding horses, and meanwhile no one's minding the bloody dragon! The Exhalations of Persistent Happiness quarter isn't that heavily populated—not many people feel secure living beyond the capital walls, you know—but it's no desert either. While this rabble was swarming me, the neighborhood kids came out to have a gander at the beast."

The rest of his tale was short and bitter. One of the children, famous throughout the quarter for having inexplicably bad luck keeping a pet, tried to set off a string of firecrackers under the dragon's rump. The dragon merely glanced down at the youngster's attempt at wit, sneered, raised one huge haunch, peed liberally over the firecrackers and their patron, and then announced, "You like setting fires, do you, you horrid little mound of rabbit turds on the pasture of life? Well, so do I."

And she did.

By this time the streaks of smoke rising from the Exhalations of Persistent Happiness quarter were growing too thick for even the most mole-eyed guard to shrug off. Smoke from a hearthfire wasn't that black, burning leaves smelled better, and cityfolk never incinerated their garbage but threw it in the nearest river, like civilized people. There was also a large cloud of dust approaching. Gorgorians and

Hydrangeans alike knew that such clouds generally arose when large numbers of people were on the road in an awful hurry to get away from something nasty.

"Dragon, you say?" the first guard asked, his tongue having suddenly gone all papery.

"And headed this way," the rider affirmed.

A loud, inarticulate cry that sounded like someone putting badgers through a mangle made all the men jump out of their skins. The horse uttered a terrified whinny, bucked off his rider, and pounded away into the palace courtyard, scattering the badly shaken guards. The wailing was still going strong, up and down several scales, by the time they all regained their feet.

It was Ubri. She had her head thrown back, her eyes rolled up so that only the whites showed, and she appeared to be either suffering a conniption fit or doing a spot of folk dancing.

"Oh, the vision! The vision!" she howled. "Oh, darkest fate of complete draconian devastation! Oh, fiery fiend that falls upon our frail festivities!"

"What's the matter with her?" the well-bruised rider asked one of the shrouded women.

"It is a holy vision," the lady explained. "The women of my tribe, we have the power to see the future. Sometimes. A little. Some more than others. Nothing too fancy, you understand, no guarantees, we're not show-offs, and if it doesn't always come true it's because *you* have to believe in it, too, or else—"

"The dragon is at the gates!" Ubri declaimed, looking very striking in her dungeon-soiled finery, her hair and eyes wild. "The city, the *kingdom* cannot stand against its might. We are all doomed, condemned to have the flesh seared from our bones, our blood gouting from our headless necks as the dragon rends us limb from limb!"

"Wait a minute," the first guard said. "How can the dragon rend us limb from limb, blood gouting and all, if it's already seared the flesh from our bones?"

Another Gorgorian guard gave him a smart thwack in

the head and said, "It's a holy vision, you clod. Things don't need to make sense when they're holy visions."

"Oh, agony, agony," Ubri chanted. A crowd began to gather, though none of them looked as if they wanted to stay once they got there. With every dire prognostication that fell from Ubri's lips, they all shifted nervously from foot to foot and cast uneasy glances all around, looking to see whether anyone else was walking away. No one was bold enough to take the first step, so everyone stayed and suffered.

This went on for some time.

It was getting a little old and Ubri was running out of evil tidings to scatter when an Old Hydrangean guardsman actually found the backbone to announce, "Well, this is all very nice and picturesque and an authentic display of the Gorgorian folkloric tradition of silly woman's stuff, but the fact remains that we've got a dragon coming to pay us a visit. Has anyone done anything practical about it?"

"Practical?" The Gorgorian captain-of-the-guard was astonished. "You, a Hydrie, asking us to do something *practical*? Sure you don't just want the rest of the day off to write a poem 'bout it or something?"

"I want the rest of the day off to fireproof my house, or run away, but that's about it," the Hydrangean retorted.

"I hear as how they've locked and barred the city gates," someone from the back of Ubri's crowd piped up.

"The gates lie smashed and shattered!" Ubri cried. "The dragon's fire leaves them smoking in the dust. Oh, fools, fools to think that mere gates made by the hand of man can ever hope to stand against so great a monster! The lowest slug that beslimes the face of earth knows that there is but one hope of diverting a dragon!"

This latest pronouncement scared up a flurry of renewed interest in Lady Ubri's words. Suggestions flew hither and yon as the crowd battled to come up with the answer to dragon diverting. Most of these were shouted down as soon as they were uttered, and the unlucky soul who recommended sending out a company of street mimes was beaten senseless.

"*No,* you lackwits!" Ubri shouted, miraculously snapping out of her holy vision trance. "None of those will do. Gods, don't you ever patronize marketplace storytellers? What every dragon wants is a nice, fresh, royal virgin staked out to await its pleasure."

"A *royal* virgin, ma'am?" The captain-of-the-guard rubbed his forehead. "The way I heard it, the dragons never checked the poor girl's pedigree before . . ."

"*Royal.*" Ubri showed every tooth in her head in a grin that would send most wolverines yipping for their dens. "Else the beast will know, and its wrath will be great, and there will be weeping and wailing and gnashing of teeth, and a dreadful plague of toads with the croup will fall upon the land, and—"

"Yes, but a royal virgin—!" The captain blew his lips like a winded horse. "It's not like we're over-rich in such. Finding a royal *woman*'s scant enough pickings. Queen Artemisia was married to Gudge, after all. No way we could fix her up so's the dragon would think she's still—"

"But, my friends, don't you see?" Ubri spread her arms wide and beamed at the mob. "The gods are kind. They have foreseen this very disaster and in their mercy they sent you the solution even before the disaster fell upon you!"

"That was nice of 'em," someone commented.

"Aye, for once," another bystander replied. "Makes a pleasant change from all that smiting and cursing and so forth they're usually up to."

"So where's this solution the gods sent us, then?"

"The prince!" Ubri exclaimed, pointing at the palace. "The *princess,* I mean! Arbol's transformation, which was ascribed to witchcraft by some royal fool—I'm not mentioning any names but it starts with *A-r-t-e-m-i-s-i-a*—is in reality the work of the gods! O wise and noble people, now you may clearly see the only course open to you, the one way in which you may save your lives, and the lives of your dear ones, and your more expensive possessions."

"We may?"

"We do?"

"I don't mind the part about saving my life, but do we have to save my brother-in-law, too?"

"Most expensive possession I've got's a new rutabaga."

This time when Ubri howled at the sky, she meant it. However, not everyone there present missed the true meaning of the Gorgorian noblewoman's words. The captain and his men were right behind her, especially after the Hydrangeans among them passed on a few of the local myths about what happened to people who overlooked the gifts of the gods.

"I never heard of celestial wolverines before," remarked one Gorgorian as they marched into the palace to do what needed to be done.

Of course there was some resistance, but Queen Artemisia was easily restrained and Prince—*Princess* Arbol could not stand against so many guards, especially since she had been forced to wear a long dress and Artemisia had confiscated all her favorite weapons because swords weren't ladylike.

Thus it was that when Bernice and her contingent of Bold Bush-dwellers approached the city, they were confronted by a large banner reading WELCOME DRAGON, draped above the city gate. They entered the capital only to find the streets deserted. There were other banners hanging from balconies and windows, most saying things like WE GREET YOU WITH WILLING SACRIFICE and THIS WAY TO FEAST and SORRY YOU'VE GOT TO EAT AND RUN and MY BROTHER-IN-LAW IS A ROYAL VIRGIN TOO IF YOU'RE STILL HUNGRY AFTER.

"What a bunch of jerks," Bernice remarked after one of the literate Bold Bush-dwellers read her the signs.

"It's all that city living," the Blue Badger replied.

"But I *am* getting hungry," Bernice told him. "And the signs do say there's a feast. I think it's meant for me. How nice."

"You can't eat yet!"

Bernice's huge head turned slowly toward the Blue Badger. "Says who?"

"If you eat too much, you may get all sluggish."

"So?"

"So a sluggish dragon's no use to us in the fight for freedom."

"Ask me if I care."

"You promised you wouldn't do anything until we rejoined the Black Weasel."

"Promises are such slippery things."

"And then you'll have come all this way for nothing."

"Not if the feast is any good."

The Blue Badger got a canny look in his eye. "Sluggish dragons are pretty easy to slay, you know."

"Oh." Bernice was abruptly silent.

"Look, don't take it so hard," he coaxed. "As soon as we find the Black Weasel, we'll all have a nice snack and then we'll free the kingdom and—and then we'll probably throw a party after and you can eat all you want."

"All right," Bernice growled. "I'll wait for the Black stupid Weasel."

"Well, you did promise."

"I said I'd wait! Isn't that enough for you? Because if it's not . . ." Bernice's narrow eyes got even narrower.

"It's enough, it's enough. Let's go."

On they went, but not too much further before they came to a great public square. A crowd had gathered on the far side of the square, being held back by a troop of very skittish-looking guards.

In the center of the square was a platform and on that platform was a pole and on that pole were a set of iron shackles and locked in those iron shackles was Princess Arbol in a white satin gown. She was cursing alternately in fluent Gorgorian and Hydrangean. When she saw the dragon, she just cursed louder and started screaming for someone to bring her a sword so that she might slay it.

The big banner spanning the square above the princess's head said EAT HEARTY! THEN GO AWAY.

"No!" the Blue Badger cried, seizing Bernice by a

scale. "The Weasel's not here yet. You promised you'd wait for the Weasel."

The princess called the dragon a bad name. It was a name so bad that it made Bernice blush, no easy thing in a dragon.

"I'll wait," she said, scowling. She sat down with a sound like thunder, pitching several Bold Bush-dwellers off their feet. "But I'm not going to wait forever."

The princess called the dragon another name.

"You kiss your mother with that mouth?" Bernice roared.

The royal virgin gave her intended devourer the royal raspberry.

Chapter Thirty-One

Wulfrith really wished that Queen Artemisia would answer his question. It was such a simple question, after all.

Had Arbol been a girl all along?

Everyone else was assuming that she'd been a boy, but Wulfrith didn't see how that was possible. He might be only an apprentice, and to a mere bush-wizard who lived out in a cave in the mountains, rather than to one of the great magicians of the royal court, but he still thought he knew something about magic, and he just didn't see how Arbol could have been changed into a girl without a great deal of fuss and bother that would have been very hard to hide.

But after reading some of the more lurid romances and adventures in the palace library, he was reasonably familiar with the notions that girls might sometimes dress up as boys, and that kings preferred sons to daughters.

So had Arbol been a girl all along?

He had asked Queen Artemisia right after the Disaster of the Bath, and she had shushed him without answering. He had asked again later that evening, and she had told him not to worry about such silly things, which wasn't an answer.

Wulfrith didn't know everything that was going on, but he had the definite impression that Arbol was in trouble—*big* trouble—because she was a girl. He felt a twinge of guilt every time he thought of it; if he had bothered to remember everything the silly ritual people had told him, he might have *warned* her about the bath, and maybe all this wouldn't have happened.

Not that he had *known* she was a girl, but he had suspected she wasn't fond of bathing.

And now the queen was out bullyragging people, or some such; he hadn't seen her in hours. She had dropped him off in these same apartments, where he had been kept when they were readying him to be crowned, and had told him to stay put. It all seemed foolish; why bring him *here?* Arbol, whether male or female, was the heir to the throne.

Maybe the queen just thought this was somewhere he could stay out of trouble. And at least here he didn't have to wear that stupid mask. He sighed, and picked threads out of the red velvet upholstery on the arm of his chair.

Had Arbol been a girl all along, or was it really magic? Maybe the Gorgorian women really *did* have some strange magic that wasn't anything like the stuff he knew.

That would be interesting; he wondered if there was any way he could learn about it. That Ubri . . . but she was probably going to be beheaded, or burned, or fed to the wolverines, or something.

That might be entertaining to watch, but it seemed like something of a waste. He had only just started to learn things from Ubri. Reading the books simply couldn't convey everything the way hands-on experimentation could.

He sighed again, just as the door burst open.

"Wulfie?" Artemisia said, charging in.

He sat up and smiled at her.

"Oh, good, you're still here," she said. "Is everything all right?"

"It's fine, Your Majesty," he said. "I mean, except for Arbol being a girl and everything."

"Yes, well . . ."

"Was she *always* a girl, Your Majesty?" Wulfrith asked quickly, before he could lose his nerve.

Queen Artemisia gave a nervous little laugh as she began rummaging through a chest of drawers, not looking at the boy. "*Always* a girl, Wulfrith? Of course not, how silly you are!"

"So Ubri and those other women really changed her?"

"Well, *I* think so," Artemisia said; even with her voice muffled by the contents of the second drawer, Wulfrith didn't think she sounded completely convincing.

"Does everyone think so?"

Artemisia straightened up and turned to glare at him.

"As a matter of fact," she said, "no. This multiply damned wizard had to go and turn up at exactly the wrong time, after fifteen years in exile, and show off how he could turn people into assorted beasts, so of course *he* got himself blamed for it, now, and they're letting that harridan Ubri go, and they've thrown the wizard in the dungeons in her place. But that's not important right now."

Wulfrith blinked. "It's not?" Ubri saved, and a wizard in the dungeon in her place? How could that not be important?

A wizard . . .

"No, it's not," Artemisia told him, turning back to the drawers, "because right now they're talking about sacrificing your sis . . . I mean, Prince Arb . . . I mean, *Princess* Arbol to a dragon, and I need to find a way to prevent it. Damn!" She kicked the bottom drawer shut. "Don't they use dragonsbane in any of the ceremonies? I could have sworn they did!"

"I don't remember any," Wulfrith said.

"You wouldn't," Artemisia replied, looking angrily around the room.

"What's dragonsbane look like?" he asked.

"Oh, *I* don't know," Artemisia snapped. "Green, I suppose. Maybe I should check the herb gardens." She turned, and before Wulfrith could stop her, she stormed out.

He grabbed for the doorknob just as he heard the click of the key turning in the lock; he stopped, stared, and started swearing as the queen's footsteps faded down the hallway.

He stood for a moment, glowering at the door.

Dragonsbane. Dragonsbane was a myth, an old wives' tale, according to Clootie. *That* wasn't going to save Arbol from a dragon.

But then, there weren't any dragons anywhere near the capital anyway; hadn't been in centuries. Everyone knew that. If someone wanted to sacrifice Arbol to a dragon, he'd have to carry her all the way up to the mountains, where the nearest dragons were.

Wulfrith decided that the stress of the last few days—the king's death, the switching of the heirs, the Disaster of the Bath—had driven the queen mad. Why would anyone go to the trouble of hauling Arbol way out to the mountains and feeding her to a dragon just because she turned out to be a girl? That was crazy.

What about the rest of it, then? Was there really a wizard in the dungeon?

Well, that was almost as silly; the only real Old Hydrangean wizard left was Clootie, and Clootie . . .

Wulfrith's anger faded, and he swallowed hard.

Clootie could change people into various creatures, just as Artemisia had said. Clootie had been in safe exile for fifteen years.

And Clootie just might have come to the city to recover his missing apprentice.

And if that was what had happened, then not only was Wulfrith's dearly beloved master locked in the palace dungeons, but it was Wulfrith's own fault!

He had to get down there and check for himself, as fast as possible, before they did something terrible to poor Clootie. He rattled the doorknob, pounded desperately on the panel, to no avail. He had to get *out* of here, regardless of the Queen's instructions.

But then, he knew there was no way out; he'd spent weeks cooped up in here . . .

No, what was he thinking? He *had* gotten out! He had the unlocking spell he had found in the library.

But if anyone saw him roaming the palace without his mask, how could he explain himself? They'd think he was

Arbol, and she was supposed to be fed to a dragon. And the only way to prove he *wasn't* Arbol would be to show that he was male, and the way things went in this madhouse of a palace they might want to make him king if he did that.

He didn't want to be seen, he decided—but then, thanks to Arbol, he knew how to avoid it.

Quickly, he headed for the secret passage.

An hour later, after several wrong turns, innumerable doors and corridors and stairways, and two transformation spells that had eliminated two guards and produced a rat and a canary, Wulfrith finally found himself in a narrow and unpleasantly damp stone passageway roughly twenty feet below ground level, lit only by a foul-smelling and smoky torch.

If this wasn't the palace dungeon, then some interior decorator had entirely the wrong idea.

Wulfrith crept along carefully, moving through corridor after corridor as silently as he could manage, peering through cell doors, and always watching for guards. True, he had his transformation spell ready, and it had served him very well so far, but sooner or later he was going to get something nasty when he used it. Most of the time it produced small, harmless creatures, but that was simply because the vast majority of creatures *are* small and harmless. Anyone who paid attention could see that the world was simply full of bugs and worms and rodents of every description, while nasty predators, with fangs and claws and the size to be dangerous, were relatively scarce.

The big nasty ones were still out there, though. And the transformations didn't seem to be *completely* random, in any case; mammals came up far more often than random chance would account for. Wulfrith had no idea what *did* determine the exact result, but he was sure that if he kept transforming people, either with the original spell or the intermittent version, sooner or later he'd get something like a lion or a wolverine.

That could be a serious threat to his continued health.

It was preferable, therefore, to be as quiet as possible while sneaking around the dungeons.

And he was very much afraid that he was going to have to do quite a bit of sneaking around, as the dungeons seemed to go on and on in all directions, with narrow little side corridors in unexpected places, and quirky twists and turns, and unnecessary steps up and down. There were any number of cells to be investigated—though so far, every one he had checked was empty.

Something screamed in one of the cells; it didn't sound like Clootie, but Wulfrith hurried toward the sound. At least it was someone alive, other than a guard. Someone was clearly being tortured, and if it *was* Clootie . . .

The scream sounded again, and Wulfrith was able to identify which cell the sound came from; he peered in through the tiny barred window, expecting to see a hellish scene of inhuman cruelty.

A bearded face looked up him, startled, and said, a bit peevishly, "Move aside, would you? You're blocking my light."

"Sorry," Wulfrith said, leaning as far to one side as he could while still seeing into the cell.

It was tiny, but reasonably clean, with fresh straw on the floor and a bucket in the corner. The occupant was seated cross-legged in the center; he wore a ragged white robe, most of it hidden beneath billows of hair and beard.

"Thanks," the man in the cell said. "You might want to cover your ears; I'm going to scream again." Before Wulfrith could reply, the man let out a bloodcurdling shriek.

When the lad's ears stopped ringing, he demanded, "Why'd you do that?"

" 'S my job," the prisoner explained.

"It's what?"

"It's my job."

"What kind of a job is that?" Wulfrith demanded angrily.

"What kind of a dungeon is it that hasn't got some poor wight screaming?" the prisoner countered.

Wulfrith's mouth opened, then closed. The screamer took pity on him and explained. "The basic problem, y'see," he said, "is that the Gorgorians aren't any good at torturing people."

"They aren't?" This did not accord with what Wulfrith had previously heard.

"Not really, no. Oh, they do pretty good with the public spectacles and the short-term stuff, your burnings and wolverines and so forth, but they haven't got the patience for the really slow stuff, the stuff that keeps a dungeon busy for months on end and keeps up a good, steady supply of screams and whimpers and so on. They aren't really much on prisons at all, they'd rather just kill someone and get it over with. Anything that lasts over a week, the Gorgorians get bored and go get drunk, or just lop the victim's head off."

"I can see that," admitted Wulfrith.

"Yes, well, you can't run a self-respecting dungeon that way; a bunch of empty cells, that's what you'd have. In fact, most of the cells here *are* empty. I'm doing my best to keep up appearances, but I'll tell you, lad, it's not easy."

"So did you . . . I mean, how'd you get the job?"

"Oh, well, I was a prisoner here when the Gorgorians took over, fifteen years ago. They let a lot of prisoners go, if they were here for political reasons, and they lopped the heads off a bunch of others, but they couldn't figure out what to do with me, since nobody could remember why I was here in the first place."

"Why *were* you here?"

The prisoner shrugged. "Haven't the faintest idea," he said. "I forgot long ago. Been here since I was a boy."

"Oh."

"Anyway, so they were arguing about what to do with me, and it looked like they were going to whack my head off just to be on the safe side, and I suggested that they could just leave me here, to give the dungeon some style, as it were. Took some talking, I can tell you, but they agreed in the end." He smiled proudly.

Wulfrith smiled weakly in return.

"So I've been here ever since, as their professional screamer. They give me good fresh straw and empty the bucket regular, or I go on strike and stop screaming. It's not the best position, I suppose, but I'm satisfied."

"Oh." It occurred to Wulfrith that he was wasting time. "Well," he said, "it's been nice talking to you, but I need to see if they have a wizard I know locked up somewhere down here."

"A wizard?" The prisoner cocked his head. "You're looking for the wizard they just brought in? Oh, he's in Number Forty-Three—down that way, turn left down the steps, then it's the sixth door on the right."

Wulfrith blinked in surprise.

"Oh," he said.

"Thought I'd save you some time," the prisoner remarked.

"Thank you," Wulfrith replied.

"Now, get out of my light, please."

"Yes, sir."

Wulfrith retreated down the corridor as screams echoed from the stones behind him, and followed the directions.

The turn was half-hidden by a cluster of old chains, and he might well have missed it on his own, and never found Cell Number Forty-Three; as it was, in five minutes he was prying at the rusted lock, assuring the bound and gagged Clootie that he would be free in just a moment.

Chapter Thirty-Two

Three dusty figures slipped in through the city gate and paused, looking about in confusion.

The streets were deserted. This was not in accord with their expectations, nor with any of the plans they had discussed along the way.

This wasn't the first surprise; finding that a suburb or two had apparently been torched as part of the coronation celebrations had been a bit startling.

"I hadn't thought the Gorgorians did that anymore," the Purple Possum had remarked. "I'd been hearing that they were really quite restrained nowadays, more sensitive to the quieter tastes of the Hydrangeans."

"Oh, shut up," the Black Weasel had said. This had been a common reaction for him ever since awakening in the Widow Giligip's house; when the Possum commented that it might almost be considered rude, were the Black Weasel not deposed royalty, the Weasel had very nearly apologized, blaming his ill temper on a headache that simply wouldn't quit.

And now, as they stared at the city, his head hurt more than ever.

"Oh, look, there's the Street of Delights Not Spoken of in Polite Company," the Purple Possum said, pointing. "I feared I'd never see it again."

The Black Weasel mumbled something, but didn't tell

the Possum to shut up. He, too, was enjoying the sight of the city he had fled so long before.

"What's that banner up there for?" Dunwin asked, pointing back at the gate. "Is that always there?"

"What banner?" the Black Weasel asked.

"The one that says WELCOME DRAGON," Dunwin replied.

The Weasel and the Possum looked at one another.

"Did you see a banner?" the Weasel asked.

"No, my lord," the Possum admitted. "I was studying the suburban architecture. Did you notice how they've built houses that imitate the shape of the Gorgorian campaign tents?"

"I didn't bloody well notice *anything,*" the Weasel snarled, "because my head was pounding like a smith with a royal deadline to meet, and I kept my eyes toward the ground, where the sun's glare wouldn't make it pound any worse."

"We could go back out and take a look," the Possum suggested.

"There are more banners," Dunwin mentioned, pointing.

"So there are," the Possum agreed, startled. He looked over the hastily painted signs that were draped here and there along the main street up toward the palace. The Black Weasel, forgetting his headache for the moment, did the same.

"A feast," he said. "Maybe we didn't miss the coronation after all."

"Or maybe they left the banners up afterward," the Possum suggested. "The Gorgorians aren't much on housecleaning, after all."

"If they're for the coronation," Dunwin said, "why does the big one out there say WELCOME DRAGON?"

The Possum shrugged. "Maybe that's a symbolical reference to the new king?"

"Maybe it's Bernice," Dunwin said.

"The Gorgorians use an ox," the Weasel said thoughtfully, "and the royal house has always been represented by the sallet, not a dragon. I think the boy's right—they mean it literally, and Bernice is here before us."

"Then what are we *waiting* for?" Dunwin shouted. He turned, and began to charge up the street in the direction indicated by the arrows helpfully provided on several of the banners.

As he started to pass, the Purple Possum thrust out a foot; Dunwin tripped and fell headlong, to lie dazed upon the cobbles.

The Weasel looked at the Possum; the Possum looked at the Weasel, and shrugged. "I didn't think we should be hasty," he said.

"Oh, I agree completely," the Weasel said. "But I suppose we'll have to go see what all these banners are about."

"Yes, my prince," the Possum replied. "I suppose we had better."

"You know, though," the Weasel said, glancing about at the empty streets, "it doesn't look as if this is going to work."

"Oh?"

"I don't see any sign of my men, and those banners would seem to imply that the city's people have the dragon under control. And the coronation *must* be over by now, after we spent all that time spewing into buckets after that idiot Spurge poisoned us. I think the moment's passed."

The Possum considered that, stroking his narrow beard thoughtfully.

"Should we, perhaps, retreat to the forest once more, and await another opportunity?" he asked.

The Weasel shuddered. "Do *you* want to spend another fifteen years out in the bushes?"

"I think," the Possum said warily, keeping a careful eye on his master's expression, "that I'd rather trust to your nephew's beneficence . . ."

"So would I, damn it. And there are always the secret passages, you know—I think I might do better at palace intrigue than this hiding-in-the-hills nonsense. It's really more in my family line, you know."

"Then what should we do now?"

"We should, first of all, find out just what in the nineteen variegated hells of the forbidden gods of Dhum is going on around here."

"And how do we do that, Your Highness?"

The Black Weasel, brave and dashing leader of the Bold Bush-dwellers, sighed mightily. "We pick Dunwin up and go to the feast, I suppose," he said.

The Purple Possum suddenly found something utterly fascinating on a nearby balcony, to judge by the intensity with which he stared at it as he said, "Need we bring Dunwin? While the lad certainly has his virtues, he has peculiarities, as well. For example, he's prone to fixations, such as his obsession with his lost Bernice. If this dragon truly *is* his Bernice, I fear his behavior might be completely uncontrollable, which might be inconvenient."

The Black Weasel looked down at the prone figure before them. "You have a point," he said. "Come on, then."

Together, the two men marched up the street, following the banners, leaving Dunwin where he lay.

They were out of sight for less than a minute before Dunwin rose to his feet and shook his head to clear it. Discovering he was alone, he looked about in confusion, spotted the banners, and remembered.

"Bernice!" he said.

He didn't know where the Black Weasel and the Purple Possum had gone, and he didn't much care; he wanted Bernice. He started up the street.

Meanwhile, in the great square, the crowd was becoming bored; although at first it had seemed as if most of the population of the city was standing along the side of the plaza in eager anticipation, many had drifted away during the long wait, and those who remained had settled to the cobbles. Some now sat on blankets or cushions brought from home, while others made do with bare pavement.

Bernice, for her part, was very irritable indeed. She had been sitting there for over an hour, listening to Arbol produce a truly astonishing string of vituperation. Voices from the audience were beginning to be heard, as well.

"Go ahead and eat her!"

"Get it over with, charcoal breath!"

Bernice paid little attention; she had become fascinated, despite her anger, with Arbol's ability to spew out insult after insult without repeating. Despite having lived most of her life as old Odo's property, she had never heard anything remotely like it.

The Blue Badger sat unhappily by the dragon's foreclaw, trying to figure out what had gone wrong.

"He left before us," he said for the fifty-seventh time. "He *must* have reached the city before us. He *must* be in hiding somewhere close by. He *must* know what's going on here!"

"Unless he got lost," the Puce Mongoose said, for the thirty-third time. "Or something else went wrong."

"Why don't we just let Bernice eat her?" Wennedel asked. "Then the Gorgorian royal family would be gone and they'd have to crown a Hydrangean!"

"But we want 'em to crown the Black Weasel," the Badger pointed out, "not some silly third cousin of old Fumitory or something." He hesitated, then added, "Besides, I don't really understand all this political stuff very well, and I don't want to do anything serious until the Weasel gets here and says it's okay."

"But what if he doesn't show up? If he doesn't get here soon, Bernice is going to . . . well . . ."

"I know that!" the Blue Badger shouted. "And he'll be here! He left before us, he *must* have reached the city . . ."

The argument rolled on.

Across the square, another argument was continuing, as well.

"I say we slay the dragon and free him . . . I mean, her," Pentstemon said.

"Why?" a Gorgorian soldier asked.

"Because she's the rightful king!"

"She's a girl—saw it myself," the soldier retorted. "A girl can't be a king."

"Well, she can't help being female!" Pentstemon said, waving an arm about wildly. "I'm one of the Prince's Companions, and that means I'm supposed to defend the prince, not stand here while they feed him to . . . I mean, feed *her* to a dragon!"

"Not a prince, if it's a her," someone pointed out.

"But she used to be!" Pentstemon insisted.

"How'd we slay the dragon, always supposin' we wanted to, which I am not sure of?" a soldier asked.

"Hack its head off!" Pentstemon shouted.

The soldier shrugged. "You've got a sword," he said. "Go right ahead."

Pentstemon glared, and did not draw his blade. A thought struck him.

"Arrows!" he said. "We could put its eyes out with arrows, then . . ."

"Then it'd thrash about and mash half the city to kindling," a grizzled old Gorgorian pointed out. "My great-grandda tried something like that with a swamp dragon, or at least that's what he claimed, but he had a cliff nearby for it to fall over, which we don't happen to have here in the middle of the city, so far as I can make out."

Pentstemon glared about, and had to admit that there was no cliff in the middle of the square. He also noticed that the dragon's wings looked quite functional, and suspected a cliff wouldn't be very effective in any case.

And at that moment, the Black Weasel and the Purple Possum emerged from the street into the square, a few yards behind the dragon, where the Puce Mongoose immediately spotted them.

"Look!" he shouted. "It's the Black Weasel!"

Arbol shrieked an obscenity involving vegetables and female ancestors; Bernice cocked her head thoughtfully, repeating Arbol's phrase to herself. Then she nodded.

"Got one," she said. "About twenty minutes ago. I *knew* she couldn't keep it up forever!"

Then the Mongoose's shout registered, and she swung her head around to look at the two rather bedraggled new arrivals.

"Is that him?" she asked.

"Well, yes," the Blue Badger admitted. "That's the Black Weasel. Now, just wait a minute, and I'm sure he'll tell us what we should do . . ."

"Wait?" Bernice snorted, and the Blue Badger felt his hair singe. "*Wait?* I've been waiting for an hour, listening to that filthy little bitch insult me, and now she's finally started repeating herself, so there's nothing more to learn, and your Black Weasel's here, and *you* said, you *said* that when the Weasel got here I could eat her."

Bernice got to her feet.

"You said wait for the Weasel; well, there he is, so now I'm going to eat that nasty little thing."

In no particular hurry, she started across the square.

Dunwin was almost running by the time he reached the square; he charged past the Black Weasel and the Purple Possum without even noticing them, past the other Bold Bush-dwellers as they called uselessly after Bernice.

He had eyes only for her. At last, at long last, he had found her.

"Bernice!" he called.

No one heard him over the racket the Bold Bush-dwellers were making. He charged on into the square, which had begun to fill with Gorgorian soldiers and other citizens, all rushing about trying to do something useful with no idea at all what that might be.

A bowstring twanged; Pentstemon had finally convinced someone. An arrow tore through the air mere inches from Bernice's face, and she stopped, startled, in her advance on the platform in the center of the square.

Arbol spat at her, and Bernice growled. She took another step, and three more arrows flew; one missed cleanly, the other two ricocheted off hard green scales.

"No!" Dunwin screamed, running forward and almost

stumbling as he struggled to draw his sword without slowing. "No, don't hurt her! Wait, I'll save you!"

A sudden hush fell, as everyone—soldiers, civilians, and Bush-dwellers—watched Dunwin charging madly toward the dragon, sword waving.

"He's going to save the princess!" someone shouted.

"He'll slay the dragon!" someone else called back.

"Make way! Make way for the dragonslayer!" The cry went up from several throats.

Bernice paid no attention; alone of everyone present, she had not yet noticed Dunwin. She was concerned only with her potential dinner and the annoying little arrows that whizzed about her. She reared up before the platform and looked down at Arbol.

The princess continued to shout invective, and Bernice smiled at the thought of silencing that foul mouth once and for all.

And just then, another figure leaped up on the platform, sword in hand. Uncomfortably aware of the traditions of dragonslaying, thanks to the Blue Badger's warnings, Bernice turned her attention from Arbol to this intruder. She lowered her head for a better look, and to get within flaming range, ready to yank her head back the instant that sword came too close.

"Bernice!" Dunwin shrieked. "It's me!"

Bernice blinked; her jaw dropped in astonishment, and she ducked down for a closer look.

"It's getting ready to breathe fire!" someone shrieked from the crowd.

Dunwin, seeing Bernice's scaly green face approaching, dropped his sword and flung both his arms around her neck in an eager bear hug.

"Oh, Bernice," he said into her ear, "it's so good to see you!"

"By all the gods!" someone called. "He's trying to strangle it with his bare hands!"

"Who *is* that?" asked another voice.

"What a hero!"

"What an *idiot*!"

"What's the difference?"

And as all the city watched, Bernice the dragon raised her head upward, Dunwin still clinging to her neck, his feet waving about in empty air.

Chapter Thirty-Three

Wulfrith didn't like to be disrespectful or anything, and he knew that he should treat his master with all possible courtesy and deference, but really, he thought it was a little inconsiderate of Clootie to have passed out before he was even out the door of his cell.

The old wizard had let out a tremendous gasp of relief when his gag was removed, had moaned as his bonds were cut away and discarded, and had then fainted dead away, and Wulfrith had been utterly unable to rouse him.

At last, the lad had hoisted Clootie up onto his shoulders, and had carried him out of the cell and through the dungeon corridors, heading for the exit.

At least, he thought he was heading for the exit. After awhile, he began to realize that he didn't really know where he was going. He had not bothered to ask the screamer for directions for leaving the dungeons, nor had he noticed just where he entered in the first place.

What's more, after he had wandered through the tunnels for awhile, Wulfrith began to tire. Disgraceful as it was to concern himself with anything so mundane, he wished Clootie had lost those few pounds he always said he wanted to lose.

Still, he staggered on. What choice did he have? There was no one around he could ask for directions; he hadn't even seen a guard since he freed Clootie, but only endless gloomy gray corridors, lit here by a flickering torch, there by a trace of sunlight filtering in from somewhere overhead, and over there by nothing at all. Cobwebs adorned the walls and ceilings, and in time, they adorned Wulfrith's hair and hands as well, and covered Clootie in a thin gray lacework. Dust lay thick on the floor. Water and other liquids dripped and oozed here and there, keeping the flooring treacherously slippery.

It seemed as if he wandered for hours; after a time, he no longer seemed to see any cells, but just endless blank-walled corridors. If the passages had not remained so uniformly dank and unpleasant, Wulfrith might have thought he had left the dungeons behind.

And in truth, he thought maybe he *had* left the dungeons behind, but he still had no idea where he was. He forged on.

Eventually, he came up against a large, locked door that barred the corridor he was in. He stared at it for a moment. A few times, he had found himself in dead ends where he had had to turn around and retrace his steps. He really hoped that this was not another—but those had ended in walls, not doors.

And although he couldn't be sure, since a reasonable amount of daylight seeped into this particular corridor through a small overhead grille, he thought he could see light coming under the door.

That was not something he had seen before. He thought that just perhaps he had, at last, found a way out.

The door was locked, of course, but that wouldn't stop him. His magic could deal with most locks.

The lock-opening spell was so simple he didn't even need to put Clootie down to work it. He made the requisite gesture one-handed, and managed to speak the incantation without grunting.

The door creaked open, and blindingly bright sunlight poured in; adjusting his master's weight, Wulfrith stepped forward, blinking.

He had assumed that he would emerge from the passages into the palace cellars, or perhaps a corridor or guard-room somewhere; it appeared that that wasn't the case at all. He was in a narrow little courtyard somewhere, walled on all sides but open to the sky, and with a narrow door at the far end. He could hear voices and noises, not so very far away—the sounds of the city, he thought.

He looked around, and realized that he couldn't see the palace over any of the walls; he guessed that just like in the old stories, he had found a secret escape tunnel from the palace, one that came up somewhere else in the city.

For a moment he wondered why none of the Old Hydrangean nobility had used the tunnel on that day fifteen years before when the Gorgorians came into the city, raping and pillaging and slaying. Why hadn't old King Fumitory fled into exile through it?

Then he realized that in all probability, the old king hadn't been able to *find* the escape tunnel. It wasn't exactly well marked or easy to travel. Just like Old Hydrangeans to make things hard on themselves, he thought.

He stepped out into the courtyard and started for the small door.

As he walked, he realized that the sounds he was hearing were probably not the sounds of the city going about its everyday business; at least, he had never before noticed that the city's everyday business involved *that* much screaming and shouting. Something was clearly going on. He quickened his pace.

The narrow door was locked; annoyed, he worked the opening spell again, and stepped quickly through, without looking to see what lay beyond.

He found himself in a great square, where people were seething in various directions, yelling at each other. In the center of the square was a platform, and on the platform stood a post, and chained to the post . . .

"Arbol!" the lad shouted. "Is that you?"

Arbol paid no attention, probably didn't even hear him over all the other noise and confusion, and Wulfrith suddenly realized what Arbol was staring at. At first he had taken it for some sort of green backdrop; now he looked up, and saw that it was a dragon, a dragon with someone clinging to its throat, clearly in a hopeless life-or-death struggle with the monster.

And Arbol was quite obviously there to serve as dragon-bait.

She was not, however, taking naturally to the role. "Cut me free, somebody, and *I'll* kill it!" she shrieked; Wulfrith noticed for the first time, despite the incredibly inappropriate timing, that Arbol's voice had never really changed. Maybe she really *had* been a girl all along.

He lurched forward, Clootie's limp hands thumping against his ribs, taking in more details.

The dragon was making noises, almost as if it were talking—did dragons talk? And the lad clutching its neck was saying something, as well; Wulfrith couldn't make out a word of it.

There were Gorgorian soldiers over there, arguing about something.

There was another group of people behind the dragon, dressed in silly costumes with green tights and brown tunics and funny hats—or sometimes brown tights and green tunics, and one of them was all in black, but they all had the funny hats. They were arguing, too.

There was a group of Gorgorian women, with Lady Ubri at their head, marching up one of the streets into the square.

Queen Artemisia was off to one side, being restrained by Phrenk and Mungli and some other people Wulfrith didn't recognize, including a very large Gorgorian.

Just about the entire population of the city, in fact, seemed to be gathered in the square, watching this young stranger battle the dragon.

There was a sword lying on the platform; the warrior who was trying to strangle the dragon must have dropped it, Wulfrith decided. He looked up, and decided there was no way to get the weapon back up to the young man.

Whoever he was, Wulfrith thought, he was very brave. He didn't deserve to be devoured.

"Get me *out* of these stupid things!" Arbol shouted.

Wulfrith frowned. Arbol didn't deserve to be devoured, either. He worked the opening spell.

The iron shackles sprang open and fell from Arbol's wrists.

In an instant, the former prince had dived to the platform and come up with the sword. She stood, feet braced apart, and swung the blade over her head.

"Yo, Dragon!" she shouted, puffing out her chest. "Put that idiot down and deal with *me*!"

Chapter Thirty-Four

"Arbol, you put that sword down *this instant*!" Queen Artemisia yelled. She broke free of Phrenk and Mungli, but was intercepted by Lord Bulmuk, who had been instructed to keep an eye (and both hands) on the queen until the sacrifice could be accomplished. Angry and frustrated, Artemisia thrashed and kicked, but it was no use. She had to be satisfied with calling out imperiously to her daughter, "That's no way for a lady to behave!"

"In a minute, Mother," the princess hollered back, never taking her eyes off the dragon. "Just as soon as I kill this ugly beast."

Still clinging to Bernice's neck, Dunwin couldn't help but overhear Arbol's words. "Does she mean me?" he asked his long-lost companion.

"Don't be an idiot," Bernice replied, taking a few steps backward. "She means me, and the little bitch is right: I *am* ugly."

"You'll always be beautiful to me, Bernice," Dunwin said fondly, stroking her scales. "It is kind of weird without all that wool, though."

"Tell me about it." Bernice sidestepped as Arbol took a swing at her. "But life's full of little changes. You get used to 'em."

"I don't think I'll *ever* get used to how big you've gotten."

"Size isn't everything."

"Is it my imagination, or did you always used to talk back to m—*ulllp!*" Dunwin almost lost his grip on the dragon's neck as Bernice made another jerky sideways hop to avoid Arbol's blade. "Don't do that, please," he said.

"No, I'll just stand still and get sliced," Bernice commented drily. "Sure I will."

"Let that sorry bastard *go*, you coward!" the princess bawled, turning red in the face. "Let's settle this like men!"

Bernice didn't respond to Arbol, but the look she gave her was sarcastic enough for a whole brigade of Gorgorian drill sergeants. "Dunwin," she said quietly, "I'm going to put you down now."

"But I just found you again!" Dunwin protested.

"I know, dear," Bernice said. "But another thing about life is you don't get anywhere until you establish your priorities."

"What's 'priorities'?"

"It's like making a list of what you've got to do first, second, third, and so on. You know, first you find a nice meadow, then you crop the grass, then you chew your cud, then you turn into a dragon." Arbol lunged at her with the blade and she slithered backward so fast Dunwin almost lost his grip again. "So right now, dear, my priorities are first to put you down, second to devour that foul-mouthed wench with the sword, and *then* we can snuggle."

"You're going to *eat* her?" Dunwin was aghast. "Bernice, you never used to *eat* people."

"No, I didn't, did I." It was not a question, but a realization. A dangerous note crept into Bernice's voice as a second realization crept in to keep the first one company. "As a matter of fact, as I recall, it used to be *people* who ate *me*. Not me personally, perhaps, but there was the nasty affair of Cousin Veronica, and the unfortunate matter of Aunt Ingrid, and the tragic loss of Great-Aunt Fern, and the unspeakable shish-kebabbing of Cousin Kimberly, and—" Bernice's eyes got narrower and narrower with every name. A low growl rose in her throat that finally burst out in a roaring, *"It's payback time!"*

Before he could say "mint jelly," Dunwin was flung clean off the angry dragon's neck. He landed smack on top of the thickest part of the crowd. As he picked himself up off several flattened peasants he said, "See? She gave me a nice, soft place to land. She *does* care!"

"Looks like the only thing that monster cares about is killing our prince," muttered the peasant at the bottom of the pile. "I mean, princess."

"If that's so," said the next man up, " 'twon't be half the holiday the beast'd fancy. I never did see a girlie swing a sword like that!"

The peasant's remark was almost identical to something Lord Bulmuk the Gorgorian was saying at about the same time, which was, "She's good. You sure she don't have a man-thing under those skirts?"

"Certainly not!" one of the Hydrangean nobles huffed. "You were there for the Disaster of the Bath. What did you think then?"

Bulmuk pondered, then said, "I thought, *Nice ones!*"

Now the battle between former prince and former sheep joined in earnest. The crowd watched with a mixture of astonishment, admiration, and awe as Arbol gave a display of swordsmanship that was Hydrangean in elegance, Gorgorian in efficiency. Even Bernice was impressed.

"Not bad," she said, making another of those easy dodges of hers. "For lunch."

"Coward," Arbol repeated, breathing hard. "You'd be a pile of cutlets on my blade by now if I weren't wrapped up in this stupid dress."

"For the first time in my life, I'm sure I'll never be anybody's cutlets," the dragon responded. She spat a thin stream of fire at the princess's feet, deliberately letting it fall short. The hem of Arbol's skirt caught a spark, which the princess extinguished with some common spit of her own. Bernice whistled. "Right on target. Good shot."

"The Companions and I used to have spitting contests off the top of the Tower of Architectural Misgivings," Arbol replied, smiling grimly. "I could hawk a wet one onto the head of any of the courtyard workers you picked, better than nine out of ten."

Something odd and unsheepish stirred in Bernice's armored bosom. As she'd told Dunwin, life was full of changes, but she wasn't prepared for this one. It went beyond mere shape and size, all the way to attitude. Sheep just wanted to eat, sleep, reproduce, and avoid milkmen with cold hands and butchers with sharp knives. They wanted to get on with their lives any way they could.

Dragons were different. Dragons seemed to be born with a natural appreciation of that fine old Hydrangean concept, *style*. Too much style and you got *chivalry*, too much chivalry and you got killed for stupid reasons, but dragons never reached that point.

All Bernice knew was that for the first time it mattered to her that this fight to the death be a fair one.

"Lose the skirt before you trip, clumsy," she directed the princess. "I'll wait."

Arbol gave her a suspicious look, but managed to slash the heavy skirt off with her sword. It was a rush job, leaving her wearing a ragged tunic that fell a little above the knee. With her legs clear, she kicked off her elaborately jeweled shoes as well, then sprang back into her fighting stance. She was too preoccupied to know or care where the flying shoes landed. She had a dragon to slay.

One shoe sailed over the heads of the crowd and clonged a scruffy old drunk who was holding up a nearby tavern wall. The effect was stimulating instead of stunning. Royal Hydrangean cobblers were justly famous, their work in demand among shoe fanciers and fetishists alike. When you got hit in the head with a work of Art, it was an eye-opening experience.

"Coo," Odo breathed, rubbing his head with one hand and using the other to retrieve the sparkling shoe. "How'd this get here?" The gems seemed to dance in the sunlight. "Worth a pretty, I'd say. A man tries to trade something like *this* for a drink somewhere, he won't get throwed out, I'll be bound." He glowered at the closed tavern door. "Tell me ye don't take baubles," he growled. He dug into his pouch and pulled out a pair of old medallions decorated with miniature portraits. "Call 'em 'objects dirt' to my face, would 'ee?" He hammered on the door, but got no response. While he'd been stupefied, the tavernkeeper had locked up shop to go watch the dragon-doings. Grumbling, Odo wandered off until he tripped over a pile of peasants.

"What're you doing there, blocking honest men's way?" he shouted, wanting to take out his ill humor on someone.

"Go sit on a clam, Grampa," one of the sprawled peasants replied. "We was just landed on by a hero. It ain't something you get over in a hurry."

"A hero?" Odo echoed. "Such as takes up the righteous causes of poor, downtrodden scum o' the earth who's been unfairly thrown out of taverns?"

"Could be. Tried to kill the dragon bare-handed, he did, so a tavernkeeper wouldn't be nowt to him, I fancy. That's him over there, trying to get back at the dragon." The peasant jerked his thumb.

Odo shaded his eyes and looked in the direction the fellow pointed. There was a healthy slice of humanity standing in his way, but his quarry towered head and shoulders above most of them. Odo could hardly believe what he saw. He gave himself a few extra knocks in the head with the princess's discarded shoe to make sure, then looked again.

"*Dunwin!*" he cried. He started fighting his way through the crowd to reach his boy.

Meanwhile, Arbol's second shoe had come in for a hard landing on Clootie's head. The Old Hydrangean wizard moaned and stirred, opening his eyes slowly.

When he saw where he was and what was going on, he closed them again, fast. "By all the useless gods of my ancestors," he murmured, "did I lose my mind in that unspeakable dungeon?" He decided that he would be happier if he curled himself into a ball and stayed where he was.

He would have done so, too, if not for some inconsiderate lout who grabbed hold of his shoulders and shook him unmercifully.

"Go away or I'll turn you into a porcupine," Clootie mumbled.

"*Can* you? Oh, that's wonderful!"

Clootie had to open his eyes then, if only to see who this lunatic was who seemed so eager to spend the rest of his days as a living pincushion. "Wulfrith?"

"I didn't know you'd learned how to control the shape-changing spell," Wulfie went on. "That's great! And wait until you see what *I've* learned. There's this library and this alcove and this Gorgorian woman and—" An ear-splitting roar shook several tiles loose from the surrounding roof-tops. "—and I guess it'll all have to wait until after the dragon," Wulfrith concluded. "Excuse me, I've got to go help Arbol." He scampered away before Clootie could even stand up.

"Ungrateful whelp!" the wizard yelled after his apprentice, waving the princess's cast-off shoe.

"They're all like that," came a sweet, though weary, voice. "Children! When they're little, they step on your toes; when they're big, they step on your heart. Then they take their clothes off in public."

Clootie turned around and found himself facing the queen. For a wonder, she was unaccompanied.

"I know you!" the wizard exclaimed. "You're old Fumitory's daughter. You're the one who kept trying to talk some sense into everyone at my trial."

Artemisia gave the wizard her most charming smile. "Of course. Anyone with a grain of sense could tell you were innocent." The smile twisted slightly. "Unfortunately, that lets out the Gorgorians. I'm so pleased to see you've made a heroic escape. I expected no less from a wizard of your magnificent powers, to say nothing of your splendid good looks."

Clootie had spent enough time around the palace in the Good Old Pre-Gorgorian Days to know that Artemisia wanted something from him, which was why she was giving him this two-shovel snow job. Any stable in the realm would be happy to hire her on the spot.

Still, she was a fine figure of a woman, and just because a man had spent the best years of his life in a mountain cave didn't mean *everything* was petrified.

"You are too kind, Your Majesty," he said. "I appreciate all you tried to do for me."

"I'm so glad to hear you say that," the queen replied. She cast a nervous glance over one shoulder. "Perhaps you wouldn't mind doing me a small favor, in that case?"

Clootie bowed low, a gallant gesture which allowed him a long, slow look at Artemisia from neckline to knees. "Anything, Your Majesty. How may I serve?"

The crowd gasped as a huge gout of flame went up from the battleground. Women were shrieking and men were cheering, then men shrieked and women cheered for a change. The queen grabbed Clootie's hand, her face pale.

"I managed to break free of my captor when Arbol cut off her skirt and showed all that leg," she explained. "Bulmuk drooled on his hands and I was able to slip away. Even as we speak, the Gorgorian beast is wallowing through the crowd, looking for me. I can't just stand idly by while my child is in danger of death and indecent exposure. I must go to her! I must make her put something *on*! Use your powers to take me to her side, I implore you."

Clootie did not hesitate. "At once, Your Majesty," he announced, snapping to attention. Then he plunged into the mob, jerking Artemisia after him.

It was rough going, but they were determined. Most of the women moved aside when shoved, but the men were another story. With them, Artemisia bellowed, "Make way for your queen!"

If that didn't work, Clootie would tap the stubborn party on the shoulder and whisper, "Hello, I'm the wizard who turned your prince into a princess. How would you like to spend the rest of your life singing soprano?"

That did it. Before long they were clear of the crowd, right out in the open with an excellent view of the battle.

The fight was winding down. Even with her skirts hacked off, Arbol was starting to tire. If Bernice wanted to escape the princess's sword, all she had to do was jump. One dragon-sized jump left a lot of open territory between the combatants, territory Arbol had to sprint across if she wanted to reach her foe. Sometimes Bernice would allow the princess to get into sword range, sometimes she would spit flame, forcing Arbol to race backward. The fight went run-swing-leap-run-flame-run away-run back-swing and so on. All that roadwork took it out of a person, especially when she was hauling a heavy sword.

"Stop it!" the queen cried out in anguish, pounding Clootie's back. "Use your magic to turn that dragon into something harmless!"

Clootie tried, but the spell fell flat. The scholar in him made a mental note that here was proof that living things, once transformed, did not resume their original shapes so easily, if at all. The man in him felt his heart go out to the poor, unhappy queen and mother. "I'm sorry," he said. "I tried."

Arbol leaned against the post where she had been so recently shackled and gathered her strength for one last lunge. The cheers of her Companions filled her ears. She could hear Pentstemon yelling something about who cared if the prince was a girl, what a follow-through!

Someone else shouted, "Yep, the lady sure is a spunky little vixen!" Arbol promised herself that if she survived this fight, she would hunt that person down and kill him.

Unfortunately it didn't look as if there would be much chance of that. The dragon had backed off, not out of fear but sportsmanship; it was allowing her time to catch her breath. Sweat streamed into her eyes, blurring her vision, as she took one last look around the square. There was that dumb hero, who'd tried strangling the beast; he was pushing his way to the front, hollering, "Don't hurt her! Don't hurt her!" Arbol didn't know if he meant her or the dragon.

There was Wulfrith, too, who had magically freed her from her shackles. She wondered where he'd picked up that little trick, and whether he had any more. If so, she hoped he wouldn't use them on the dragon. This fight was a matter of honor. Judging by the expression of consternation on Wulfie's face, it didn't look as if she'd have to worry about that; just about staying alive.

Funny: Wulfrith's face looked an awful lot like that free-lance hero's face. Wulfie's face also looked an awful lot like hers. "Later," Arbol said to herself, wiping the sweat away. "I'll worry about that later."

If there was a later. Arbol hoped there would be. She had an awful lot of questions she wanted to ask people, starting with her mother.

Speaking of whom, there stood Artemisia, next to the wizard they'd charged with Illegal Transformation of a Prince. Arbol knew it was a silly accusation: She'd always been shaped the same way, from the time she was old enough to notice such things. Now she understood that *this* shape meant "female." What she didn't understand was *why* Mother had kept it a secret from her all these years.

So she was a girl. Big fat green scaly deal. She could still whip any of her Companions in a fight, she could still out-spit, out-drink, and out-cuss most Gorgorians, and she even understood how to get her own way at council sessions. You just kept chopping heads off until people saw your point of view. The only disadvantage she could see to being a girl was that some moron would always turn up and start calling you a spunky little vixen.

Arbol tried to raise her sword for the charge. It was too heavy, all of a sudden. Her muscles felt like ribbons. The dragon watched her, beginning to look impatient. There was probably just so long the beast would give her to get her strength back, then ready or not, here it would come. She braced herself against the pole and prepared for death.

A cold smile curved Bernice's lipless mouth. She only had eyes for Arbol. She didn't even notice that five other people had detached themselves from the mob and were doggedly making their way to the princess's side, nor did she notice a long and curious shadow stretching across the square.

"Soup's on," said the dragon, and took a deep breath, readying a healthy stream of flame. No one had ever asked her, but Bernice was fairly sure she preferred her meat well-done.

"I wouldn't," said a voice as chill and heartless as her own. A heavy paw fell on the draconic equivalent of Bernice's shoulder, that tricky little joint just above where the wings attached. She swiveled her neck and saw a face as green and scaly as her own.

After an instant of startlement, she hissed defiantly, "Why not?"

"Because there are rules," the other dragon replied. He lowered his head and began to whisper in her ear.

An uneasy ripple ran through the crowd. "Does this mean we're goin' t' have to scare up another royal virgin?" someone asked.

"Ha! Like we could." Someone else in the mob guffawed. "First come, first served, that's what I say. Here, you! You other dragon. Clear off."

The second dragon gave this upstart a cool glance. "My name is Antirrhinum and as soon as I have explained matters to this beguiling creature, I am going to rip your liver out. Then we can talk." He returned his attention to Bernice while the unlucky speaker scampered away.

The five people who had joined Arbol at the stake closed ranks while the two dragons conferred. On the far side of the square, a bunch of men wearing grubby tunics and tights in a variety of woodsy shades gathered together to form their own subsidiary mob. They were all gesturing, arguing, and pointing at the dragons. Pretty soon the din they made grew so loud that the original crowd dispatched a representative to complain about the noise to the Gorgorian nobles.

Before Lord Bulmuk and his cohorts could do anything to restore order, the two dragons raised their heads in a menacing manner. Dead silence fell over the square.

"Pitiful," Bernice commented. "Look at them shake! Just pitiful. I like it."

"So you see now why we must have these rules of ours, dear Bernice," said Antirrhinum. "In the first place, the majority of humans are not especially succulent morsels, but they do provide excellent sport-hunting on occasion. It wouldn't do to slaughter them at random, easy though it would be—we must practice conservation. And there *are* certain hazards, if one gets them sufficiently angry—while a lone human, even a hero, is generally harmless, they can be quite clever when they gang up. Shall I continue to explain?"

"Please do." Bernice linked forepaws with Antirrhinum and the pair waddled a short distance away.

"Hey!" Ubri called from her place among the Gorgorian nobles. "Hey, Dragon, aren't you forgetting something?"

"Like what?" Bernice asked.

"Like eating the prince!"

"Princess," Bernice corrected. "Nope. Not gonna do it. Once a princess has been rescued from the place of sacrifice by a sword-carrying hero willing to fight the dragon, she's off-limits." She turned to Antirrhinum. "Did I get that right?"

"Perfect." He nodded approvingly.

"But—but aren't you allowed to eat the hero who freed her?" Ubri demanded.

"Yeah. So?"

"So there's your sword-carrying hero." The Gorgorian jabbed a finger at Arbol. "Eat her!"

Bernice considered this option carefully, then pronounced, "Mmmmnope. Can't do it."

"*Why not?*" Ubri's face was crimson.

"Because she's the princess who was rescued from the place of sacrifice," Bernice explained, "and you don't eat a properly rescued princess."

Ubri's scream shattered every glass window for a seven-block radius.

Chapter Thirty-Five

"Clootie!"

"Dunwin!"

"Odo!"

"Wulfrith!"

"Arbol!"

"Aw, Mommmmmmmmm!"

The group at the stake didn't take long to sort out their situation or what had drawn them all there, to stand together against the world. Wulfrith and Dunwin stared at each other for a moment, then shrugged off what was a fuzzy memory and felt like nothing more than a remarkable coincidence. They wasted another few heartbeats staring at Arbol, who stared back, but none of the three had much leisure to swap any questions. Just because the dragons were taking a break didn't mean they were out of danger yet.

Danger was an ugly thing. So was Lord Bulmuk. He plowed through the crowd, the massed Gorgorian nobility trailing in his wake, and took a stand facing the place of unsuccessful sacrifice.

"*Real* nice ones," he said, indicating the princess's naked legs.

Lady Ubri thrust him aside, then turned to the remaining Gorgorian barons. "Behold!" she declaimed.

They beheld.

It was quite a striking spectacle, Wulfrith, Dunwin, and

Arbol all lined up in a row. One of the nobles rubbed his eyes. Another pulled a small bottle out of his tunic and smashed it against the cobblestones.

A third one, however, demanded, "What in the name of the sacred oxsallet is going on here?"

Queen Artemisia stepped forward. "Oh, what's the use?" she said. "Once the dragons have settled things, we may all end up as one big happy fricassee, Hydrangeans and Gorgorians both, so why go on pretending? When I think of all that I've had to give up just because of a stupid superstition—" She cast a fond, regretful glance over her children, then sighed and prepared herself to face a peril more dire than dragons and Gorgorians combined: telling the truth.

As she spoke, the square grew very quiet. The only thing heard, apart from her voice, was the sound of Antirrhinum still explaining the dragon rules to Bernice and Bernice's occasional giggle when Antirrhinum tickled her under the chin.

"—and I never knew what became of my sons until recently," Artemisia concluded. "I missed them so much! I still carry the little talisman that old twerp Ludmilla tied to my daughter's wrist by accident." She fished a gold chain out of her neckline and showed everyone the miniature portrait of Prince Helenium the Wise.

The crowd gasped.

"Arrrh, that ain't nothin'." Odo came forward. "That's just one object dirt. I got two of 'em!" Proudly he displayed the naming tokens bearing the likenesses of Lord Helianthus the Lawgiver and Queen Avena the Well-Beloved and spoke of what had happened following that last unlucky tryst with old Ludmilla all those years back. Clootie spoke up every now and then to confirm Odo's tale and make his own additions.

"Helenium?" Wulfrith repeated with some distaste after the queen announced the identities of the people portrayed in the miniatures. "You named me *Helenium*? Yuck."

"Helianthus?" Dunwin laughed. "They'd run you out of Stinkberry village on a rail if you had a prancy name like that!"

"*Avena.*" Arbol pronounced the name with supreme scorn and tightened her grip on the sword just in case anyone got any ideas about calling her something that stupid.

"You know, none of this would have happened if you Gorgorians would just take the time to *look* at twins," Artemisia said. "When two babies are born looking just like each other, how could they possibly have two different fathers? And even when they're not identical, there's still a strong family resemblance. Just look at my darlings! You can't tell one boy from the other, and they look so much like their sister that we were able to substitute Wulfrith for Arbol several times with no one any the wiser, including my late, thank the gods, husband."

Bulmuk rubbed his stubbly chin. "Got to admit, they *do* look a lot like old Gudge."

"Are you mad?" Lady Ubri cried. "Three children at a birth means three different fathers. You know that!"

"But they *all* look like Gudge," Bulmuk repeated.

Ubri snorted. "Hardly any resemblance at all. You'd have to be a fool not to be able to tell them apart."

"Oh, really?" Wulfrith and Arbol said together, giving the lady matching smiles that spoke volumes, most of them volumes from the library. Knowing whispers darted through the crowd. Details of the circumstances surrounding Ubri's abbreviated engagement to the prince were common barrackroom and marketplace gossip. The lady blushed and retreated.

"So they're all three of 'em Gudge's brats. That don't mean dog droppings," said Lord Ingruk. "What we've got to settle on is which of 'em's Gudge's rightful *heir*!" The other nobles agreed.

Wulfrith looked at Dunwin. "You want to be king?"

Dunwin looked at Wulfrith. "Nah. I'm more the outdoors type. You?"

Wulfrith shook his head. "I wouldn't have time to do the job right. There's still a lot of magic I'd like to learn, and there's all those books in the library I haven't even started to explore."

"I'll do it," Arbol said, holding her sword at an aggressive angle. "Or else."

The brothers shrugged, and spoke in unison. "Okay."

"No, it is *not* okay!" Lord Ingruk roared. "For as long as I am a Gorgorian and have the fighting men who will stand with me, I refuse to be ruled by a woman!"

"Oh, come on, Ingruk," Bulmuk wheedled. "Try it. Remember how Gudge used to be with the women? She's his daughter, so maybe she'll be the same with the men. And brother, has she got some nice ones!"

The eldest of the Gorgorian barons, Lord Vomgup, raised his own objection. "If you let a woman rule us, soon we shall become as soft and degenerate as the abominable Hydries!"

"Who's soft?" Pentstemon yelled. "*I'm* a Hydrie and I bet I can lick you, old man!"

"And can you also defeat my household troops?" Vomgup shouted back. "I swear that as long as my hand can close around the hilt of my sword, I will not allow this wench to sit on the throne! Who is with me?" He reached for his sword.

"I am, and all of *my* household troops!" Lord Ingruk cried, reaching for his.

Clootie had been feeling for some time that he ought to do something useful, and this seemed the perfect opportunity. He gestured, accompanying it with a few curious words.

Lord Vomgup turned into an armadillo.

"His hand can't close around the hilt of his sword now, can it?" the wizard said, pleased to have been of help.

"My men to me!" Lord Ingruk bellowed.

"Bernice!" Dunwin bellowed louder.

Bernice looked at Antirrhinum. "Can I, honey?"

The elder dragon looked at her indulgently. "Oh, go ahead, sweetie-scales," he said.

Lord Ingruk got the chance to make one last wild swing with his sword, striking nothing but air, before Bernice ate him.

Chapter Thirty-Six

"Your Majesty," the Minister of Protocol whined, in a final, last-ditch effort to maintain some of the traditions, "can't we at least enter you in the *archives* as Queen Avena? It isn't as if anyone ever reads them . . ."

The new monarch of Hydrangea glared at him. "My name's Arbol," she said coldly.

"But Your Majesty . . ."

The new queen glowered. "Don't you people realize that all your rituals and ceremonies and rigamarole almost got you all killed? If you'd paid more attention to reality, instead of rules, maybe my father's men wouldn't have been able to march in here and take over!"

The minister was scandalized. "Oh, but a proper respect for tradition . . . ," he began.

"To hell with tradition!" the new queen replied. "I'll go along when it makes sense, or at least doesn't get in the way or confuse anybody, but no further than that! Is that clear?" She dropped a hand to where her swordhilt would have been, if she hadn't let her mother convince her not to come armed to the coronation.

The minister trembled at the royal anger, but he persisted. "Your Majesty, *please*," he said. "We've set aside the claims of your brothers and your uncle Mimulus and even your own mother, we've eliminated the Ceremony of the Bath, we've incorporated the Gorgorian ritual breakfast, we've moved the coronation out of the palace to accommodate the . . . um . . . the dragon—isn't that practicality enough? *Must* we enter you in the official records with a masculine name? Your brothers allowed us to list them as Helenium and Helianthus . . ."

"They did?" the queen said, startled.

"Yes, Your Majesty," the minister said, nodding vigorously. "So could we . . ."

"That was stupid of them," Arbol said.

The minister's mouth came open, but nothing came out. Arbol pushed past him, and marched up the steps onto the hastily erected dais that now stood at one end of the Square of Munificent Blessings from Those Gods Worthy of Our Attention.

The crowd gathered before the platform burst into spontaneous applause—or at any rate, most of it did. A few portions had to be coaxed.

But then, there were plenty of people ready to do the coaxing. Quite aside from the anticipated benefits of a queen who was both Gorgorian *and* Old Hydrangean, who had proclaimed that she would favor neither group over the other, nobody particularly wanted to anger a monarch who had demonstrated that she had not just one, but *two* dragons on her side; not just one, but *two* powerful wizards working for her; and who was, despite her sex, probably the best swordsman in the kingdom—all this, in addition to the more usual partisans and advocates.

It must be admitted that not everyone was clear on just how Arbol had gone from being a royal sacrifice to a sword-wielding hero, and then from fighting a dragon to befriending it, but then, not everyone had yet gotten straight how the prince had turned out to be a girl, either.

"Never know where you are with these people," a peasant muttered darkly. "Half girl, half boy, half Hydrie, half ox-lover, can't make up her mind whether to kill the dragon or kiss it . . ."

"Oh, shut up and cheer," his wife said, jabbing him in the ribs. Her own applause was loud and enthusiastic.

At the back of the crowd, Bernice lounged comfortably

against a palace wall; a large area around her was understandably vacant, save for Dunwin, perched atop the battlement, who leaned over and scratched at the itchy spot behind the ears that even a dragon can't quite reach for herself. He wore an expression of utter gloom.

"I think it's going to be fun, having a sister," Dunwin said, in a voice that did not sound as if he were planning to have that fun any time soon. "Especially one who's queen. I'm glad you didn't eat her, Bernice."

"I'm glad, too," Bernice said calmly. "She'd probably taste even worse than that Ingruk character. It was partly the sword and those muddy boots, I suppose, but Antirrhinum's right, you people aren't half as tasty as crabgrass, let alone a good buttercup or a clump of clover. Only good for sport, the lot of you."

Dunwin hesitated, unsure how to bring up the subject most on his mind, then asked unhappily, "Are . . . are you sure you won't stay here? I'm sure Arbol wouldn't mind."

Bernice snorted, and the rearmost row of the coronation audience flinched in near-perfect unison. "What would I do *here*?" she said. "No, Antirrhinum's got a lovely little cave—we flew out there and he gave me a tour, while you people were getting all this set up. We'll be married next week, and the honeymoon—well, Rhiney says dragons take their time about these things; it could be a few years before you see me again."

"That's a pretty quick courtship, isn't it?" Dunwin asked hopelessly. He blinked away tears at the thought of losing his precious companion.

Bernice shrugged, which involved moving several square yards of scales. "Why wait? It's not as if there are many dragons around here; Rhiney thought he was the last one in all Hydrangea. That's why he came to find me." She added, with a bit of a simper, "I'm glad he did."

"But what about *me*?" Dunwin asked, with a bit of a snivel. "Bernice, I'll *miss* you so!"

Bernice let out a draconic sigh, and a few people decided to find other places entirely. "Dunwin," she said, as quietly as a dragon could, "there comes a time when everybody grows up. I'm not a sheep any more, and you're not a little boy. You were lonely up there on the mountain, and we were friends—but now I've found someone else, one of my own kind. And you're a prince now, here in the palace—isn't it time *you* found one of your own kind?"

"But I love *you*, Bernice . . ."

"Dunwin, I'm a dragon, you're a prince—it just wouldn't work."

"I know, but . . ." He sniffled.

"Try to be brave, Dunwin. Aren't there any human women who catch your fancy? I know they have those odd bumps, and aren't as pretty as sheep, but couldn't you perhaps find some distraction?"

"I don't know," Dunwin said—but he stopped snuffling. The thought of meeting women did have a certain appeal to it. He had noticed his long-lost brother with that Ubri person.

"Well, think about it, Dunwin. Because I *am* going away with Antirrhinum, and you don't want me to ruin my honeymoon by spending it worrying about *you*, do you?"

"No, of course not . . ."

"Then find some other friends. Meet some girls, and just try not to look at those silly bumps."

Dunwin looked down from his perch on the battlement at the crowd below—and more particularly, at some of the younger females in the crowd. The view from above had certain interesting features—appropriate wear for coronations ran to low-cut necklines.

"I hadn't really thought about it," he said slowly, considering that view. "You know, I think I kind of like those bumps, actually."

"Well, there you go," Bernice said, relieved. "Take a good look at a few after the ceremony, why don't you?"

Dunwin nodded thoughtfully, still looking over the crowd, and not only were his eyes drying quickly, but for a moment he even forgot to scratch Bernice's head.

The cheering was dying down now, and the participants were taking their places for the ceremony. Arbol was at the center, of course, with a half-ring of Hydrangean functionaries around and behind her. Artemisia, the Queen Mother, had a place of honor on the new queen's right; Prince Wulfrith, newly appointed court wizard, stood to the left.

Beside and a step behind Wulfrith, Lady Ubri whispered, "I still think you shouldn't have given up the crown so easily, Wulfie. I mean, love, a man like you *deserves* to be king . . ."

"Ubbie," Wulfrith whispered back, "I'd sooner cut my throat than try to be king, and if you ever mention it again I'll turn you into a warthog."

Ubri sniffed and flung back her head. "Warthog, indeed! If that's all you think of me . . ."

"Oh, it's not all," Wulfrith said, smiling. "Have you ever seen a book called *One Hundred and One Intriguing Amatory Alternatives* that's in the library here? It was banned by three kings in succession, and condemned by the Midwives' Guild. I think you'll like Number Seventy-One . . ."

Across the dais, Artemisia spotted Clootie in the front row of the audience.

"You're sure you won't stay?" she called. She did not entirely trust Wulfrith's magic—her son was still just a boy, after all—and she certainly didn't trust anyone's loyalty to her daughter; a backup wizard would be handy to have around.

"I'm sure," Clootie called back. "I've gotten used to the old cave, you know. It's so much *simpler* than city life ever was." He smiled. "But now that I'm not hiding, you'd be welcome to visit, Your Highness."

Beside him, Odo called, "*I'll* be stayin', Yer Gracious Goodness." He grinned toothlessly.

Artemisia shut her eyes for a moment, then opened them and concentrated her entire attention on her daughter.

Lord Bulmuk, whom Arbol had named Commander of

the Palace Guard, and Prince Mimulus, perhaps better known as the Black Weasel, were bringing out the double crown—the simple Gorgorian band of kingship had been welded onto the Holy Royal and Ancient Crown of Volnirius the Oblique, just above the band of oxhide. The spindly frame of the Volnirian crown had begun to sag rather badly out of shape a century or two back, and had finally given way completely after being kicked around at the Disaster of the Bath; this new addition served to restore its shape rather nicely, while adding considerable decorative panache to the rather plain and unconvincing Gorgorian crown.

Arbol had dispensed with the Keepers and appointed her own officials for the coronation, and two of them were now looking at each other over the conjoined crowns.

Lord Bulmuk, while holding his side of the supporting cushion, was watching Prince Mimulus closely. "You're sure you're not planning anything?" he muttered. "Haven't got a knife tucked away under all that fancy embroidery you're wearing?"

Prince Mimulus sighed. "No, my good Bulmuk," he said, "I am not planning anything. I am quite content to see my niece crowned."

"That's good. I've taken a fancy to the girl, you know; wouldn't want anything to happen to her. You're sure?"

"*Absolutely* sure," Mimulus replied. "After fifteen years in the forest, I don't think I'm up to ruling this place—particularly since it would take a miracle for me to survive assassinating Queen Avena."

"Arbol," Bulmuk corrected him.

Mimulus sighed. "Arbol," he agreed. "No, Bulmuk, when this ceremony is over, I'll be glad to settle into my natural role as my niece's advisor."

Bulmuk continued to eye him suspiciously, and the quondam Black Weasel did his best to look bored and innocent as the pair placed the pillow and crown upon the table behind Arbol. Mimulus understood the suspicion, though he doubted that the Gorgorian realized that the "natural role" for a Hydrangean prince was to skulk about the palace looking for an opportunity to shorten the line of inheritance.

Of course, Arbol was deadly with a sword. She had dangerous allies, including his own sister. She had those two brothers. She had united the Gorgorians and the Hydrangeans in supporting her; she was, in fact, already beloved by most of the people, even before she was formally crowned, for her restoration of Old Hydrangean rights and of the surviving Old Hydrangean nobility while keeping the Gorgorians placated by retaining them among the nobility as well. Her brother Wulfrith had been given a free hand to do whatever he could to restore scholarship—and wizardry—to their former levels of achievement. She had even found posts for all the Bold Bush-dwellers.

It was really rather amazing; with her mother's advice and the help of her allies, Arbol seemed to have pleased just about everybody. Removing such a monarch, and replacing her, without winding up beheaded for treason or killed by an angry mob or turned into something furry and quadrupedal, appeared quite impossible. It looked like a happy ending all around, for Arbol and her friends.

Mimulus smiled as he lifted the crown and placed it on his niece's head.

He always had loved a challenge.

About the Authors

Lawrence Watt-Evans's maternal grandfather, Jock Watt, went to sea at the age of fifteen and became, yes, a Scottish ship's engineer. Watt-Evans's maternal grandmother, Florrie Watt, once woke up in her berth in the middle of the night so certain that her train was going to crash that she got dressed, so as not to have to evacuate the wreckage in her nightgown; it *did* crash, though no one was hurt. His paternal grandfather, "Poker" Evans, scandalized Princeton's Class of 1897 by telling an evangelical group that they were welcome to hold their prayer meeting in his apartment so long as they didn't disturb the card game in the back room. His paternal grandmother, Beatrice Anne Briley, insisted that her middle name had two syllables. His great-uncle Sam was apparently murdered by claim-jumpers during the Yukon gold rush. His parents worked together on the Manhattan Project, and received a top secret ashtray as a wedding gift.

With all this, Watt-Evans had to write fantasy; nothing else could be as bizarre and cliché-ridden as his real-life background.

Unfortunately for an otherwise more picturesque biographical sketch, Esther M. Friesner's ancestors did not do much of anything colorful except raise horses in Poland, make cigars in New York City, teach in the Brooklyn public school system, and try not to get killed during the various "religious discussions" of European history. No one came over on the *Mayflower* because, in her father's words, "We were slow dressers." For about the same reason, none of her immediate ancestors fought in any United States wars. ("We didn't fight; we got along with everybody." —*Author's father*) If it's any help, one of her husband's ancestors was a spy for the American side during the Revolutionary War and several more fought in the Civil War on whichever side they fancied.

All of this was great preparation for settling down in suburban Connecticut and *not* fighting with her husband, two children, one well-aged cat, and a fluctuating population of household hamsters. The hamsters fight everyone.